AN UNOFFICIAL GRAPHIC NOVEL
FOR MINECRAFTERS

SAVING XENOS

CARA J. STEVENS
ART BY WALKER MELBY

SKY PONY PRESS
New York

This book is not authorized or sponsored by Microsoft Corporation, Mojang AB, Notch Development AB, or Scholastic Corporation, or any other person or entity owning or controlling rights in the Minecraft name, trademark, or copyrights.

Sky Pony Press books may be purchased in bulk at special discounts for sales promotion, corporate gifts, fund-raising, or educational purposes. Special editions can also be created to specifications. For details, contact the Special Sales Department, Sky Pony Press, 307 West 36th Street, 11th Floor, New York, NY 10018 or info@skyhorsepublishing.com.

Sky Pony® is a registered trademark of Skyhorse Publishing, Inc.®, a Delaware corporation.

www.skyponypress.com.

10 9 8 7 6 5 4

Manufactured in China, January 2018
This product conforms to CPSIA 2008

Library of Congress Cataloging-in-Publication Data is available on file.

Cover design by Brian Peterson
Cover illustration by Walker Melby

Many thanks to several talented Mine-imator creators for the use of their amazing rigs: Nimi, for 1.11 The Exploration Update rig pack; CraftinPark for the Book rig; EthanForeverAlone for the Mirror rig; SharkleSparkle for the Phone rig; and Josh the Stupad for the Welcome to California sign rig.

Print ISBN: 978-1-5107-2719-9
Ebook ISBN: 978-1-5107-2724-3

Printed in China

Designer and Production Manager: Joshua Barnaby
Interior layout: Nick Grant

INTRODUCTION

If you have played Minecraft, then you know all about Minecraft worlds. They're made of blocks you can mine: coal, dirt, and sand. In the game, you'll find many different creatures, lands, and villages inhabited by strange villagers with bald heads. The villagers who live there have their own special, magical worlds that are protected by a string of border worlds to stop outsiders from finding them.

Our story takes place on the small border world of Xenos. It is home to an assortment of villagers and miners who are learning to live peacefully with each other, as well as a family of pollinators who are entrusted with building new worlds, and a monastery filled with monks who ensure their safety.

When the leaders of Xenos's main village turned Phoenix away for being a troublemaker, Phoenix, her family, and many of their friends settled outside the village walls. The nickname of their settlement, Phoenixtown, stuck, making Phoenix's family proud, but it made poor Phoenix uncomfortable every time she heard it.

We last left off as the evil Defender was exiled to a seed world, and life once again promised to be peaceful. Little did they know that the Defender left behind one last surprise: a glitch that could destroy all of Xenos and everyone in it forever.

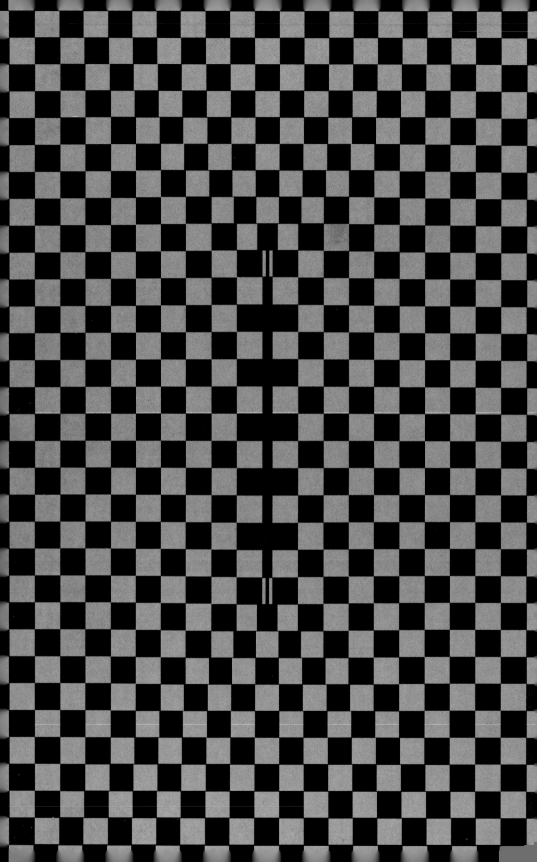

CHAPTER 1

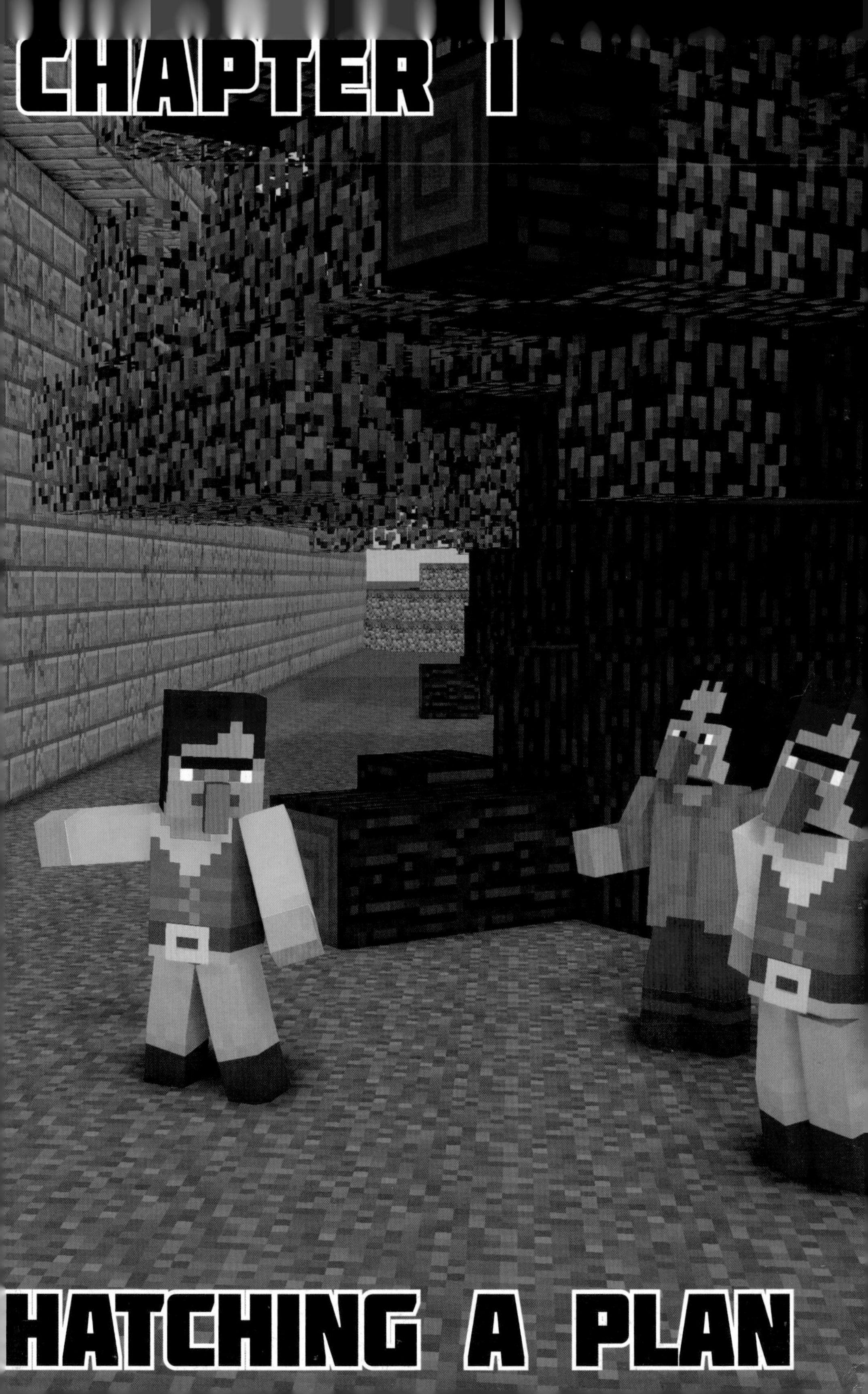

HATCHING A PLAN

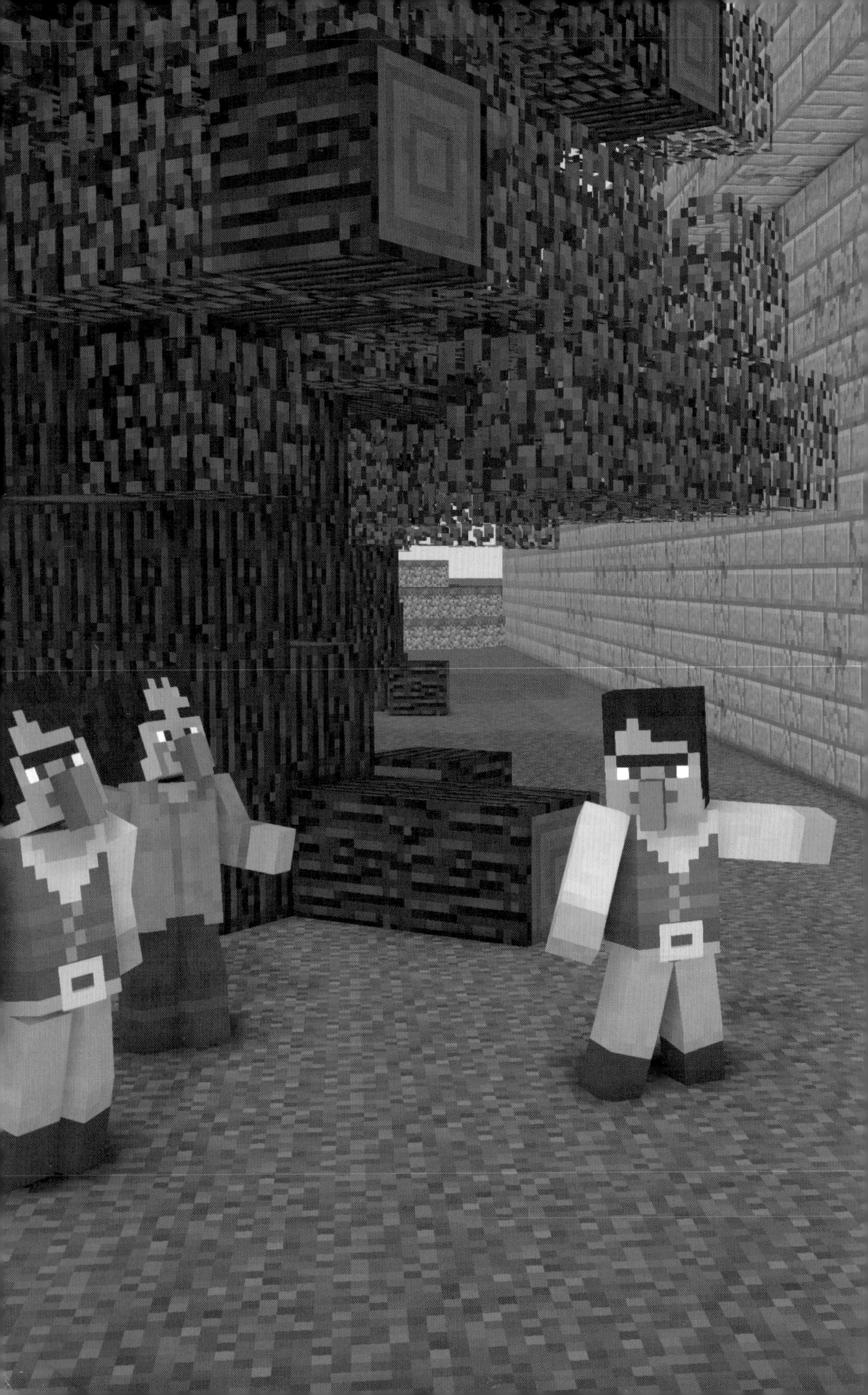

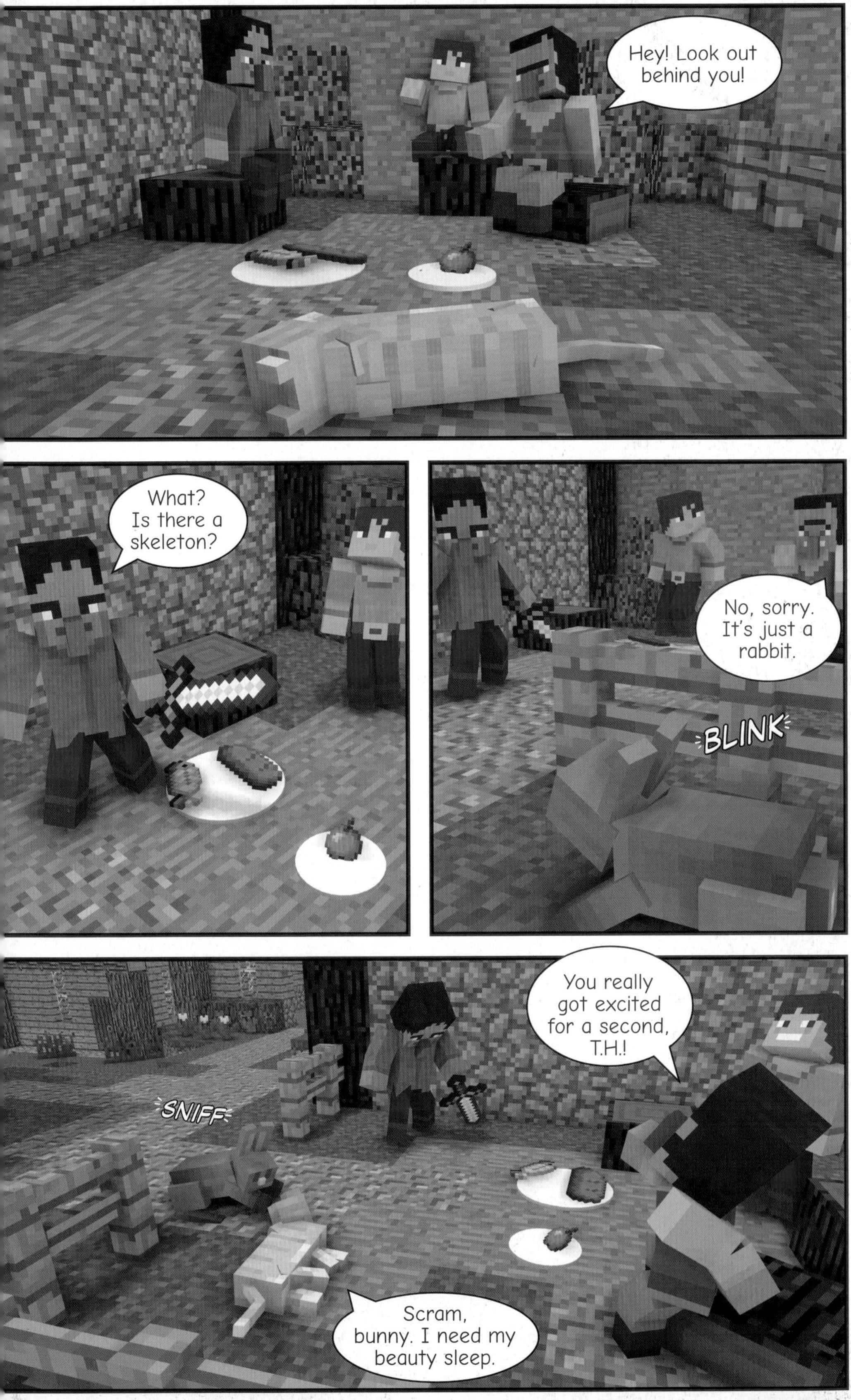
Hey! Look out behind you!
What? Is there a skeleton?
No, sorry. It's just a rabbit.
BLINK
You really got excited for a second, T.H.!
SNIFF
Scram, bunny. I need my beauty sleep.

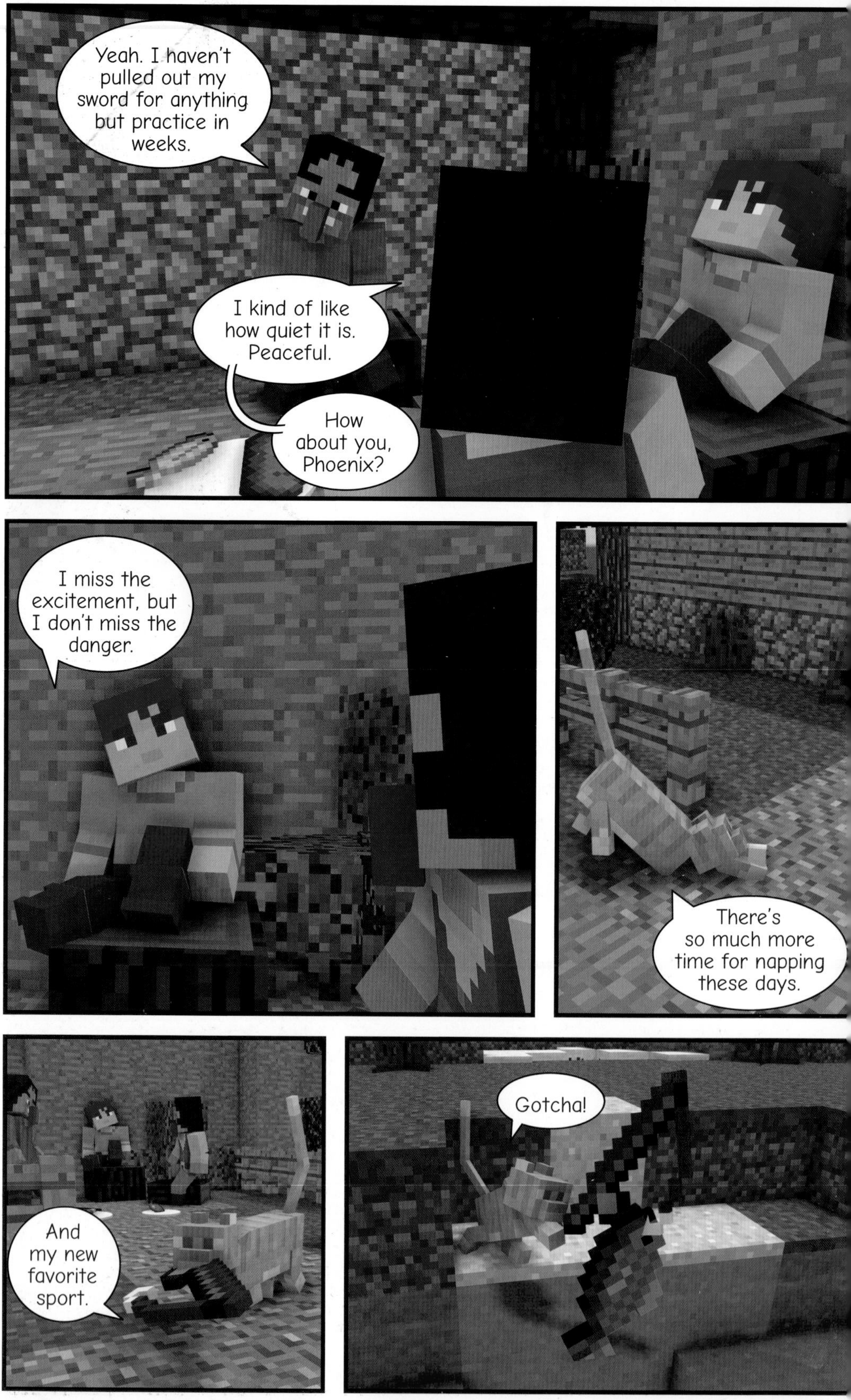
Yeah. I haven't pulled out my sword for anything but practice in weeks.
I kind of like how quiet it is. Peaceful.
How about you, Phoenix?
I miss the excitement, but I don't miss the danger.
There's so much more time for napping these days.
And my new favorite sport.
Gotcha!

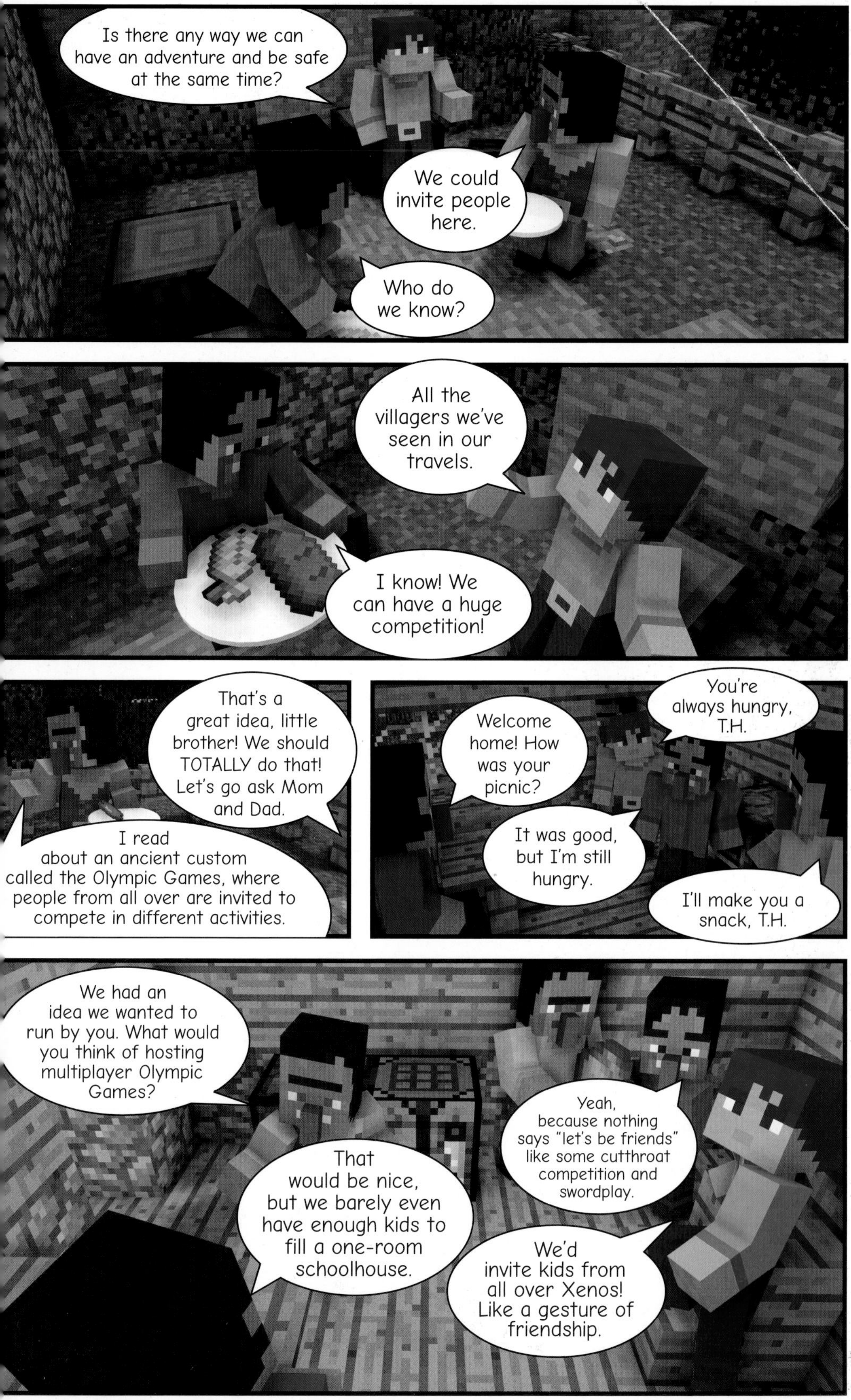

Is there any way we can have an adventure and be safe at the same time?
We could invite people here.
Who do we know?
All the villagers we've seen in our travels.
I know! We can have a huge competition!
I read about an ancient custom called the Olympic Games, where people from all over are invited to compete in different activities.
That's a great idea, little brother! We should TOTALLY do that! Let's go ask Mom and Dad.
Welcome home! How was your picnic?
It was good, but I'm still hungry.
You're always hungry, T.H.
I'll make you a snack, T.H.
We had an idea we wanted to run by you. What would you think of hosting multiplayer Olympic Games?
That would be nice, but we barely even have enough kids to fill a one-room schoolhouse.
Yeah, because nothing says "let's be friends" like some cutthroat competition and swordplay.
We'd invite kids from all over Xenos! Like a gesture of friendship.

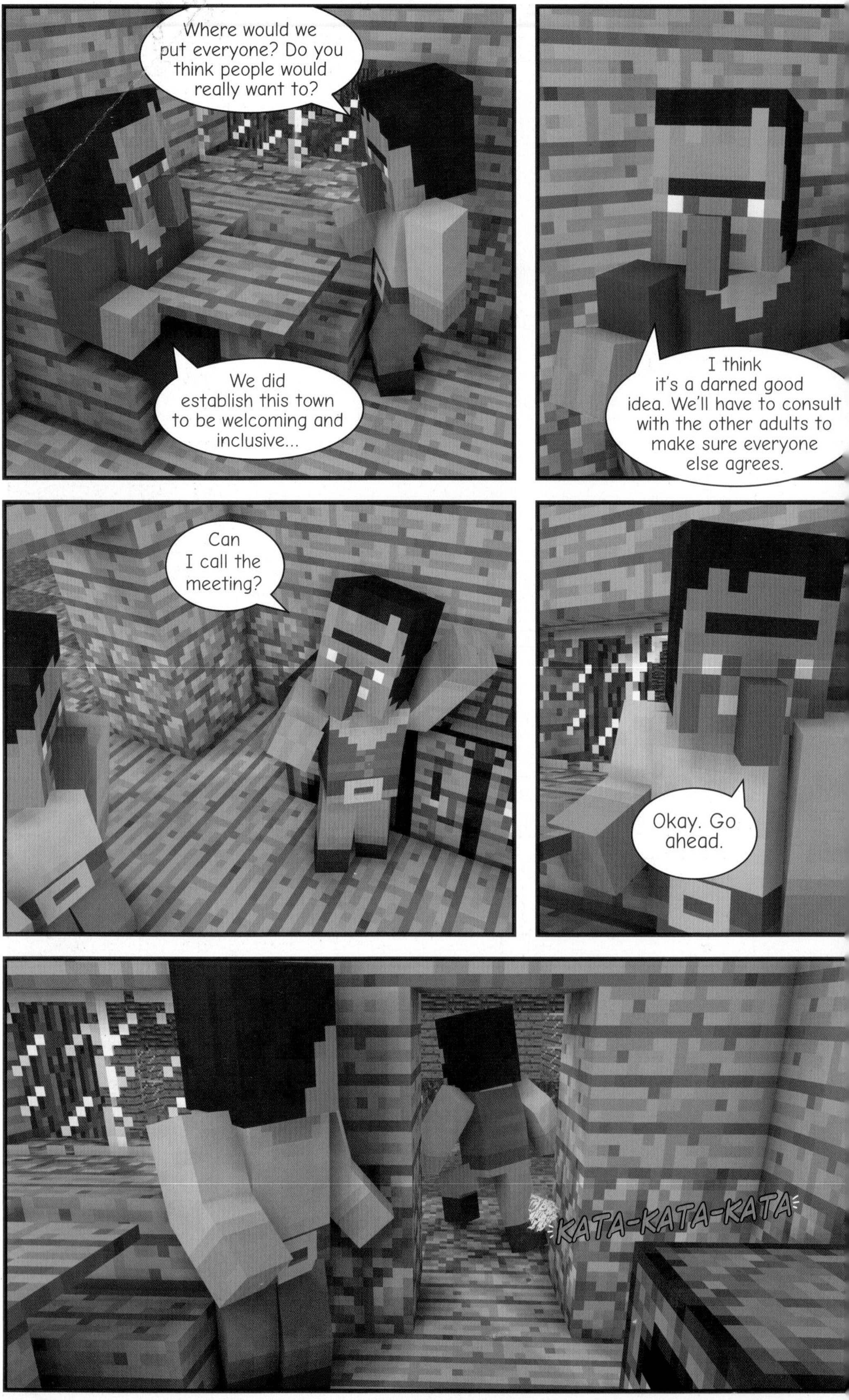
Where would we put everyone? Do you think people would really want to?
We did establish this town to be welcoming and inclusive...
I think it's a darned good idea. We'll have to consult with the other adults to make sure everyone else agrees.
Can I call the meeting?
Okay. Go ahead.
KATA-KATA-KATA

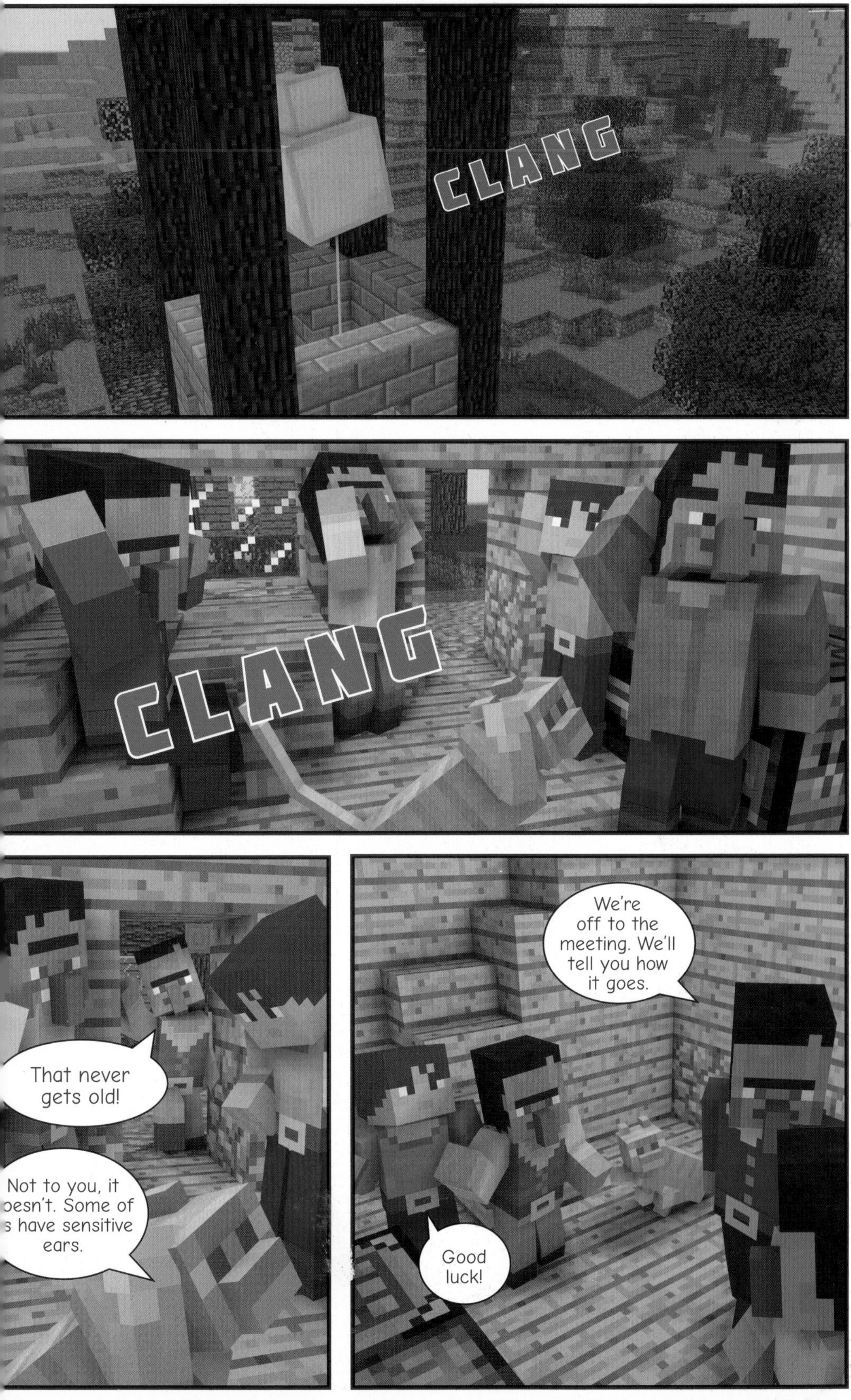

CLANG
CLANG
That never gets old!
Not to you, it oesn't. Some of s have sensitive ears.
We're off to the meeting. We'll tell you how it goes.
Good luck!

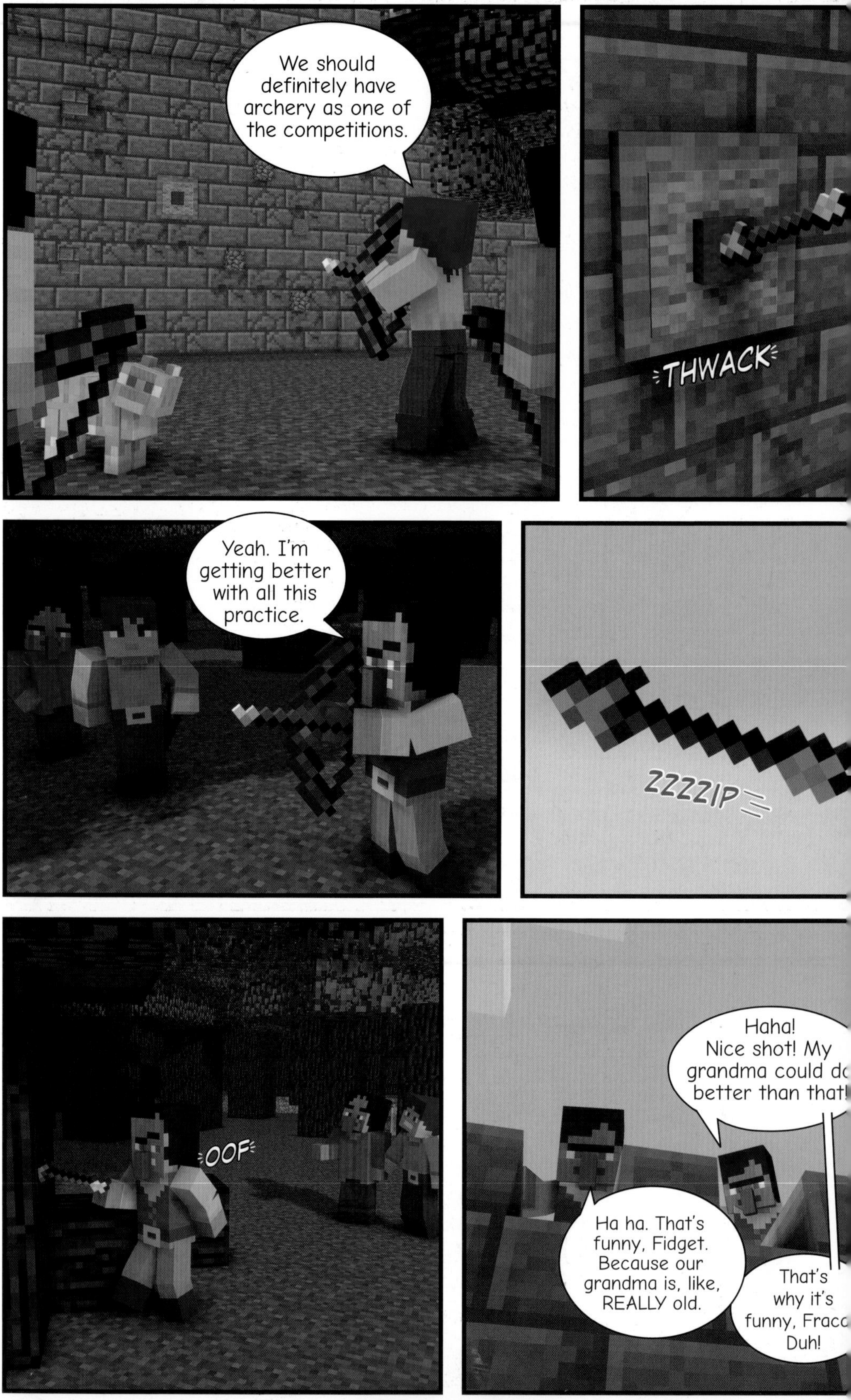
We should definitely have archery as one of the competitions.
THWACK
Yeah. I'm getting better with all this practice.
ZZZZIP
OOF
Haha! Nice shot! My grandma could do better than that!
Ha ha. That's funny, Fidget. Because our grandma is, like, REALLY old.
That's why it's funny, Frac Duh!

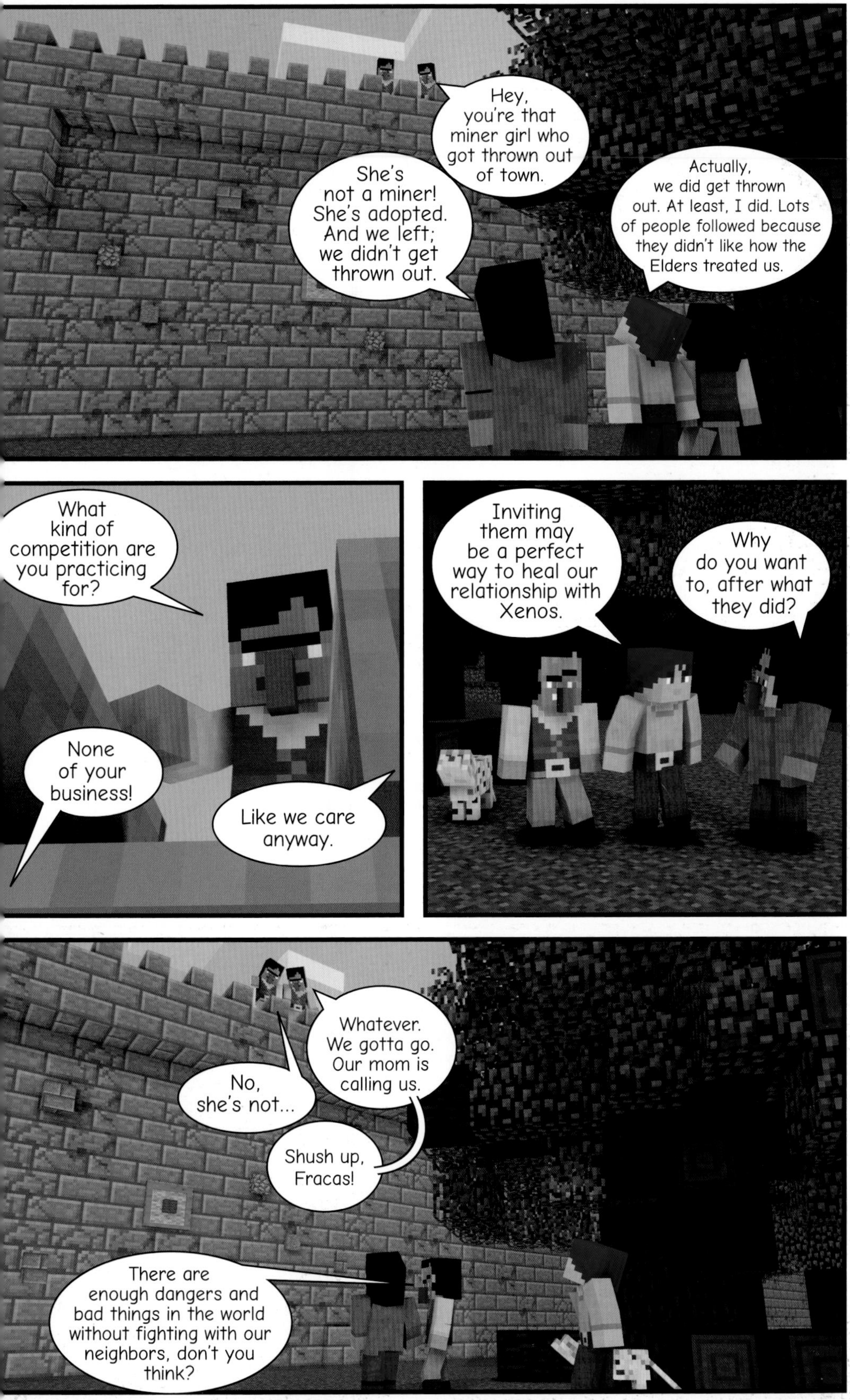
Hey, you're that miner girl who got thrown out of town.
She's not a miner! She's adopted. And we left; we didn't get thrown out.
Actually, we did get thrown out. At least, I did. Lots of people followed because they didn't like how the Elders treated us.
What kind of competition are you practicing for?
None of your business!
Like we care anyway.
Inviting them may be a perfect way to heal our relationship with Xenos.
Why do you want to, after what they did?
Whatever. We gotta go. Our mom is calling us.
No, she's not...
Shush up, Fracas!
There are enough dangers and bad things in the world without fighting with our neighbors, don't you think?

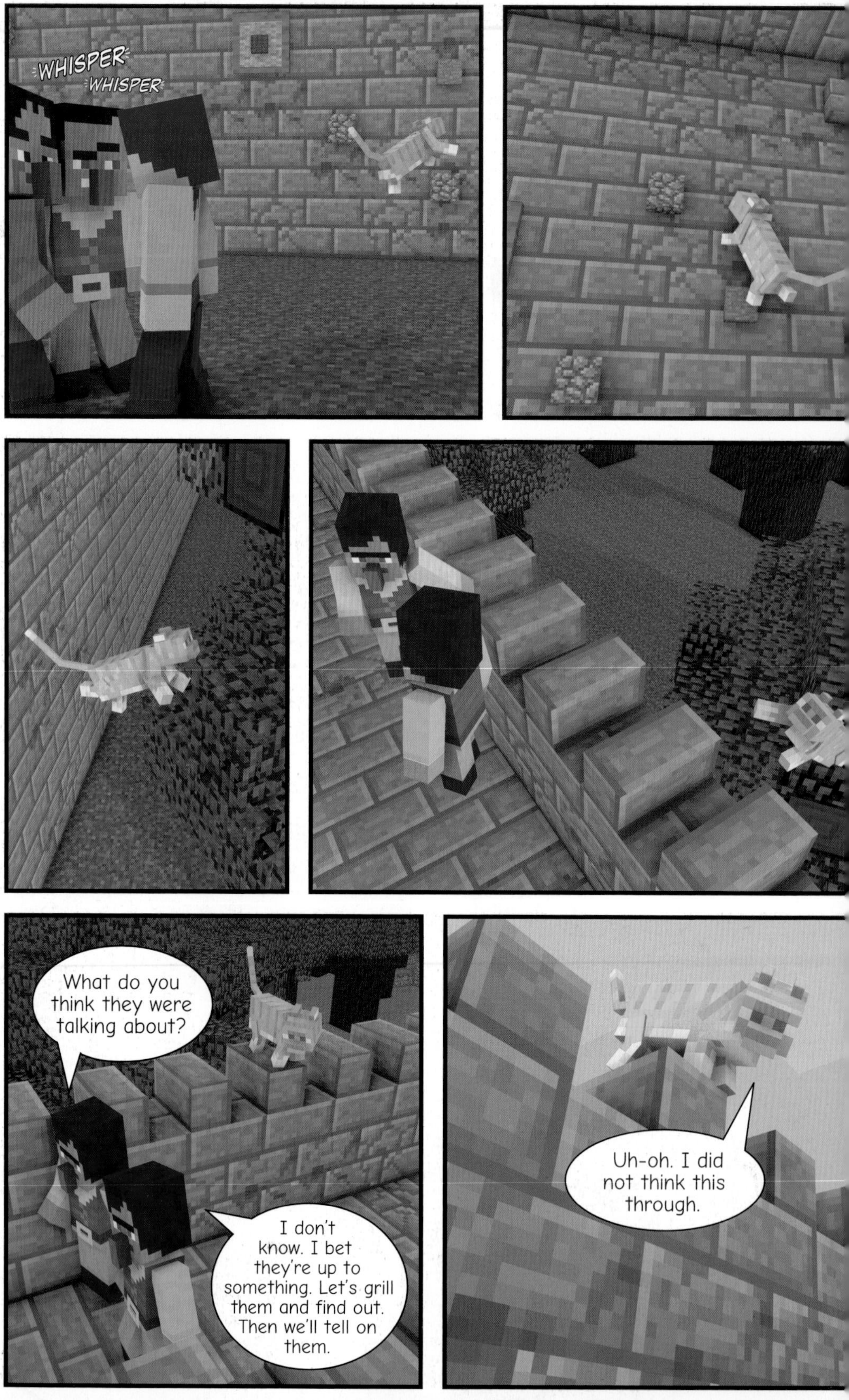
WHISPER
WHISPER
What do you think they were talking about?
I don't know. I bet they're up to something. Let's grill them and find out. Then we'll tell on them.
Uh-oh. I did not think this through.

Whaa?

Busted! I have to get out of here!

What are you doing here?

PANT PANT

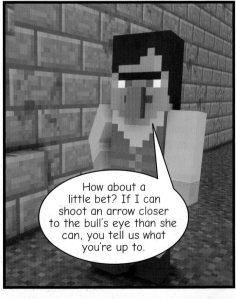

How about a little bet? If I can shoot an arrow closer to the bull's eye than she can, you tell us what you're up to.

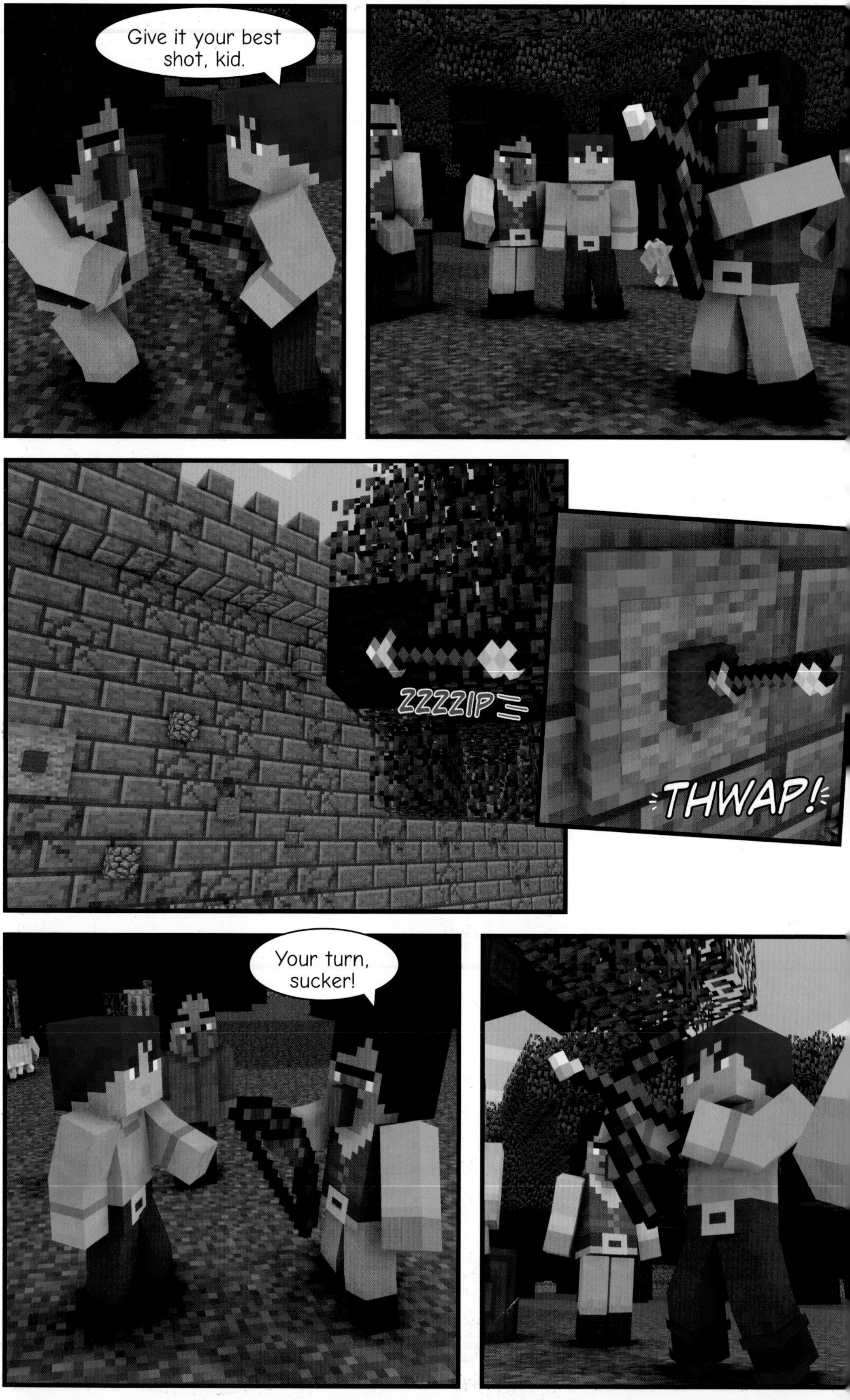
Give it your best shot, kid.
ZZZZIP
THWAP!
Your turn, sucker!

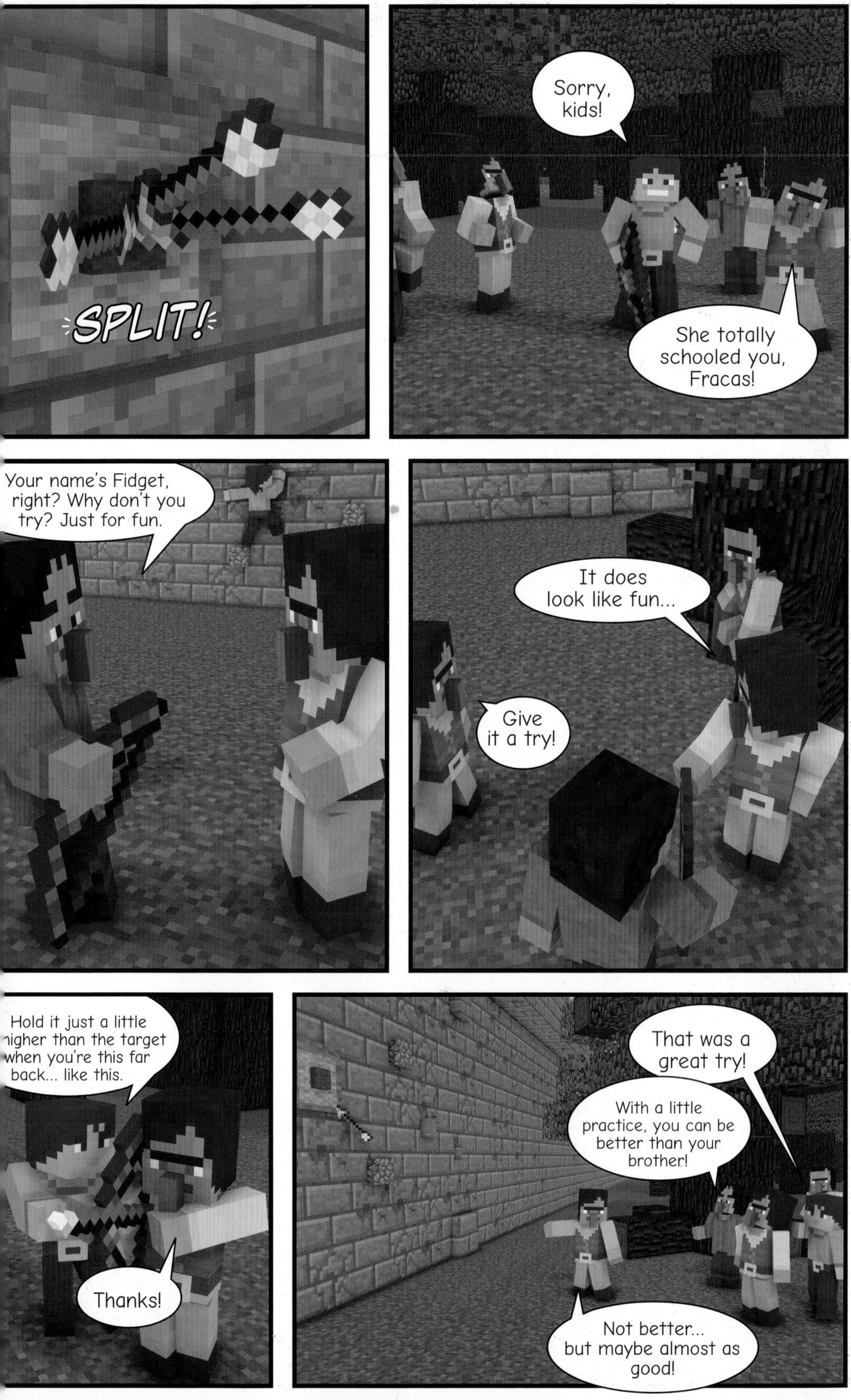
SPLIT!
Sorry, kids!
She totally schooled you, Fracas!
Your name's Fidget, right? Why don't you try? Just for fun.
It does look like fun...
Give it a try!
Hold it just a little
igher than the target
when you're this far
back... like this.
Thanks!
That was a great try!
With a little practice, you can be better than your brother!
Not better... but maybe almost as good!

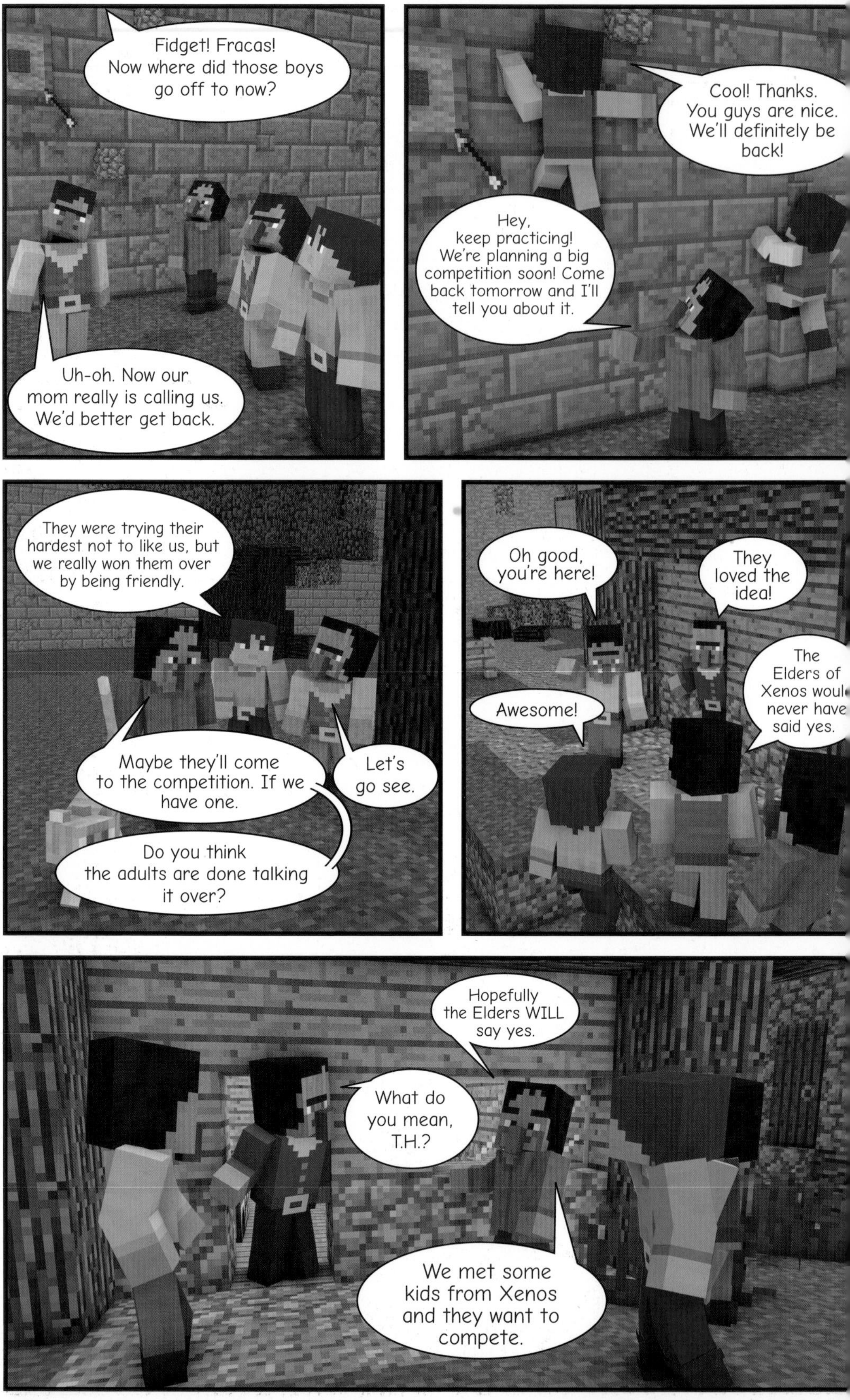
Fidget! Fracas! Now where did those boys go off to now?
Uh-oh. Now our mom really is calling us. We'd better get back.
Cool! Thanks. You guys are nice. We'll definitely be back!
Hey, keep practicing! We're planning a big competition soon! Come back tomorrow and I'll tell you about it.
They were trying their hardest not to like us, but we really won them over by being friendly.
Maybe they'll come to the competition. If we have one.
Let's go see.
Do you think the adults are done talking it over?
Oh good, you're here!
They loved the idea!
Awesome!
The Elders of Xenos woul never have said yes.
Hopefully the Elders WILL say yes.
What do you mean, T.H.?
We met some kids from Xenos and they want to compete.

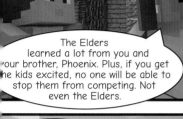

o you think the Elders of Xenos would ever gree to let their kids leave the safety of their town to compete? Their only friends are books. They don't believe in the people. They don't care about them.

The Elders learned a lot from you and our brother, Phoenix. Plus, if you get he kids excited, no one will be able to stop them from competing. Not even the Elders.

YES!

But how do we get the word out to everyone?

Wolfie and his family can deliver invitations

Wolfie and Crystal are coming tonight for the Full Moon Festival. They're the perfect messengers!

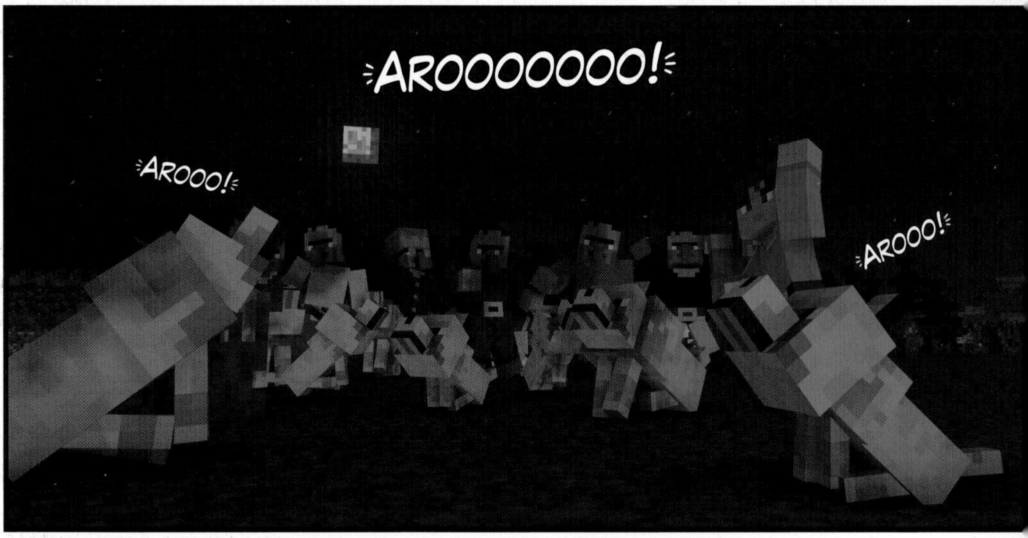
ARROOOOOOO!
AROOO!
AROOO!

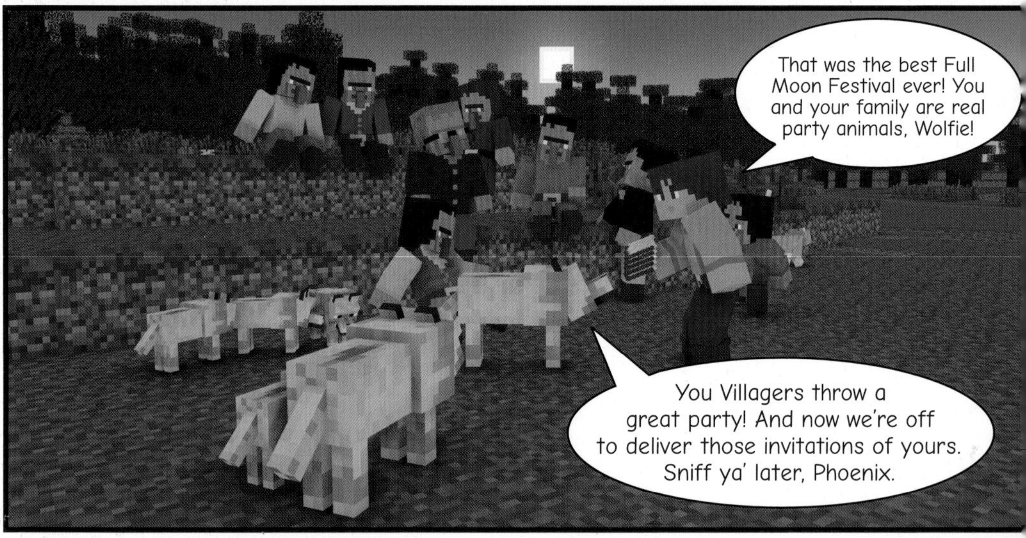
That was the best Full Moon Festival ever! You and your family are real party animals, Wolfie!
You Villagers throw a great party! And now we're off to deliver those invitations of yours. Sniff ya' later, Phoenix.

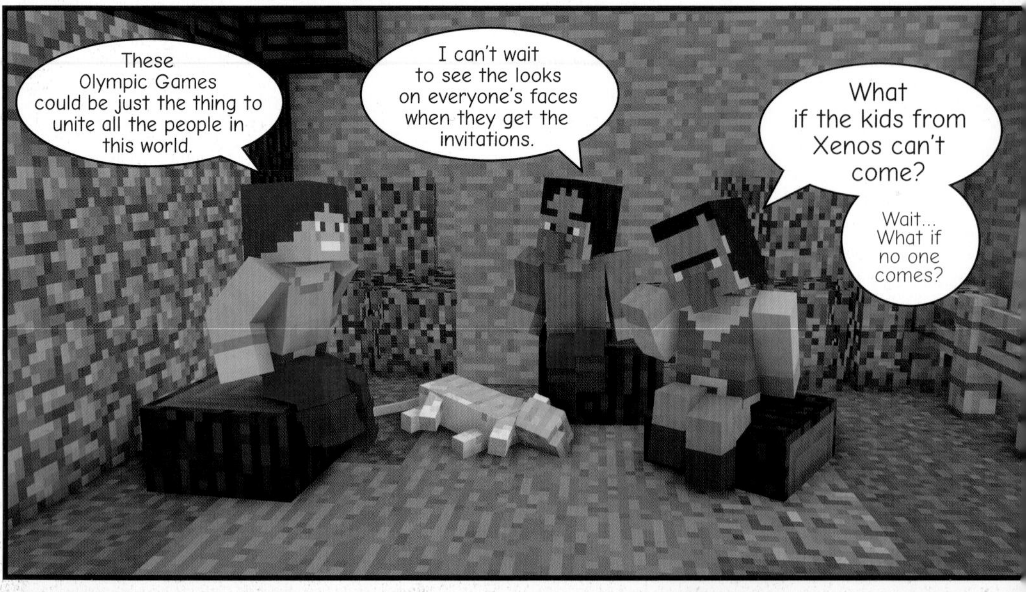
These Olympic Games could be just the thing to unite all the people in this world.
I can't wait to see the looks on everyone's faces when they get the invitations.
What if the kids from Xenos can't come?
Wait... What if no one comes?

CHAPTER 2

THE FIRST OLYMPICS

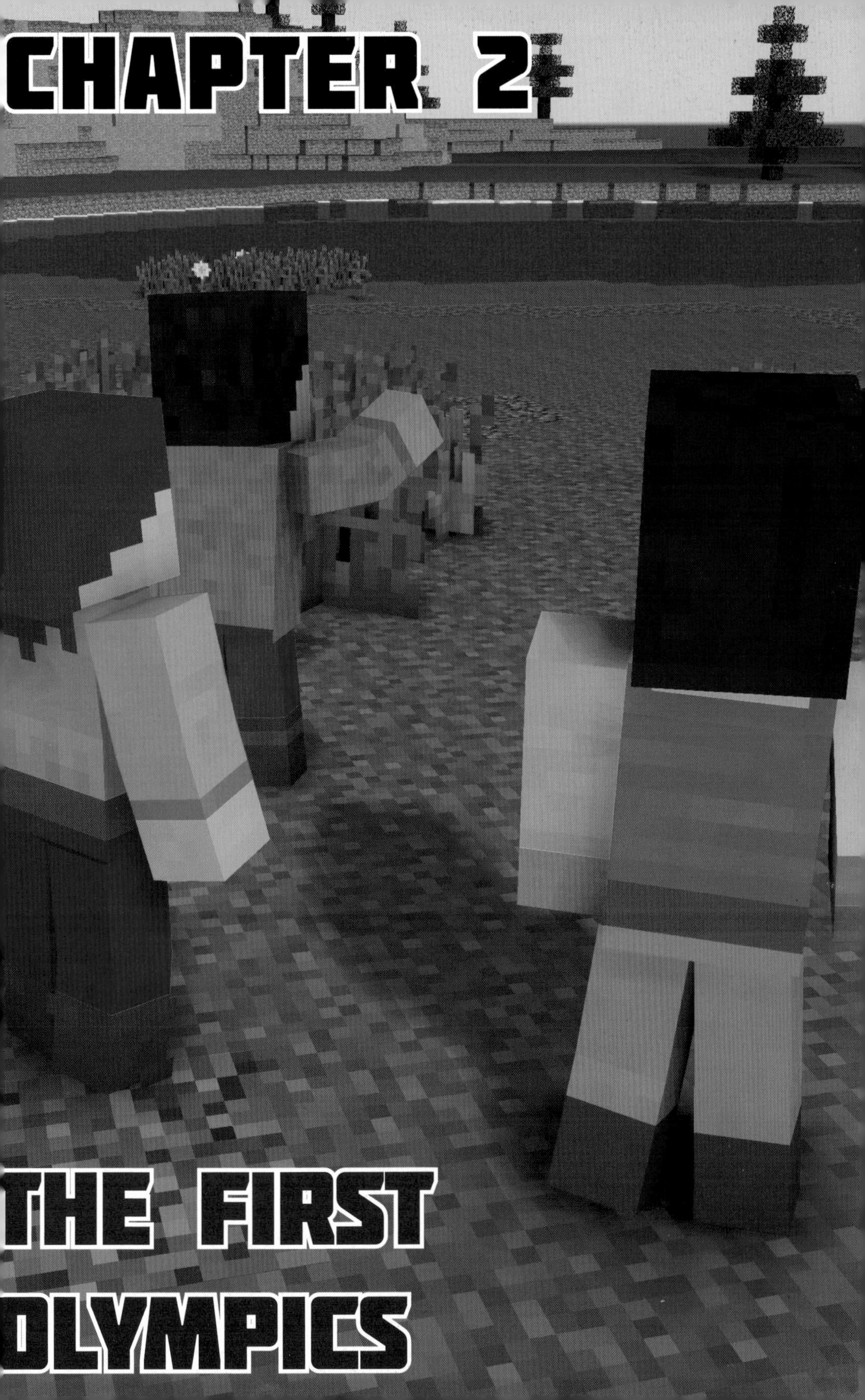

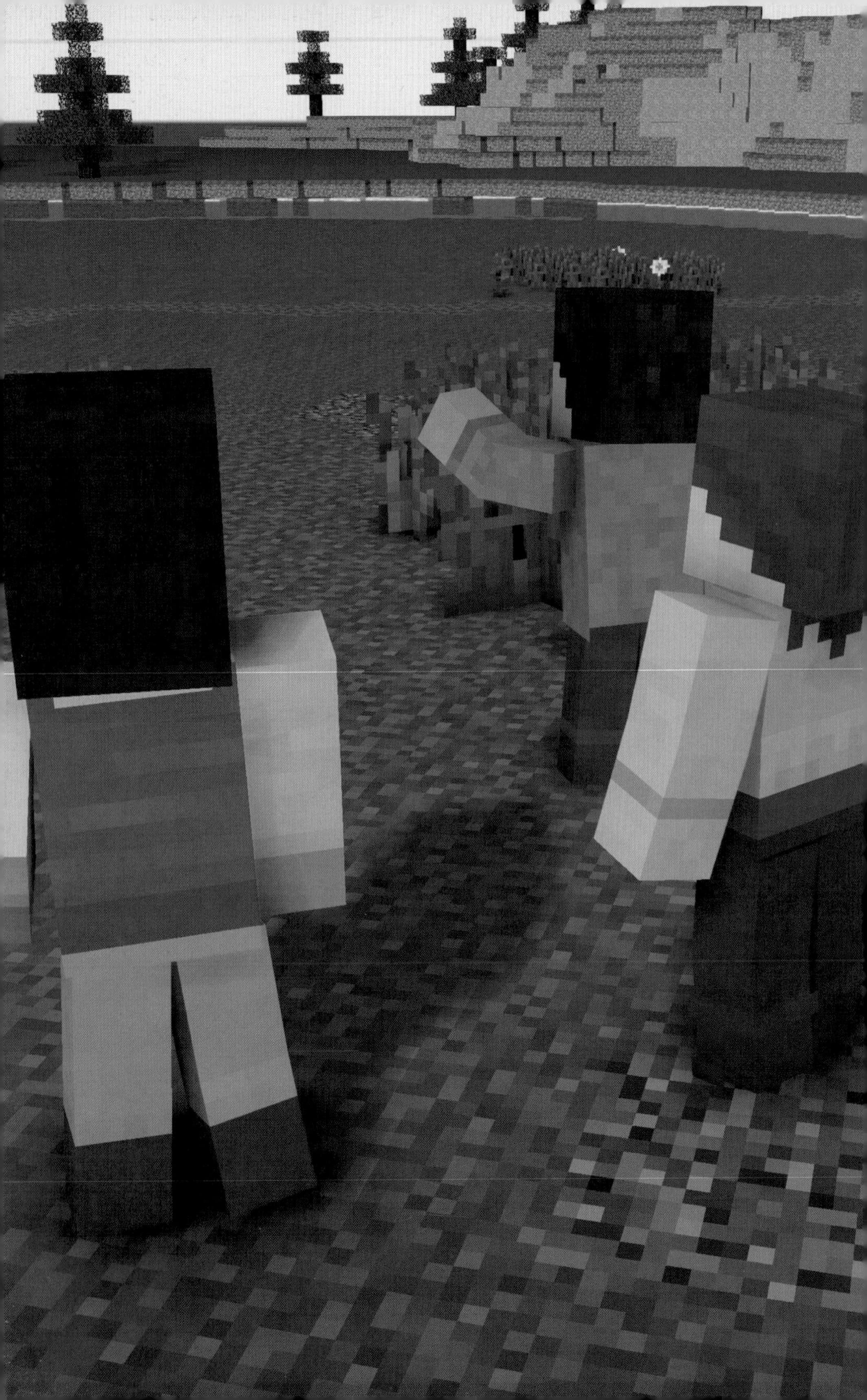

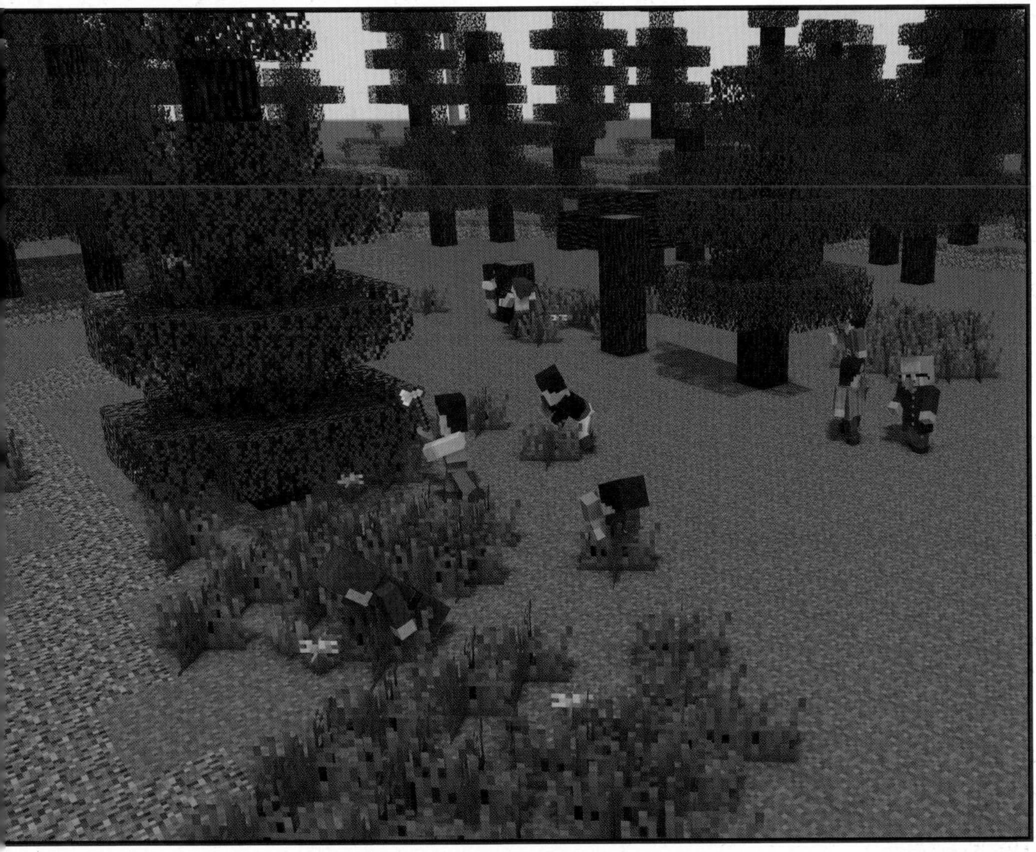

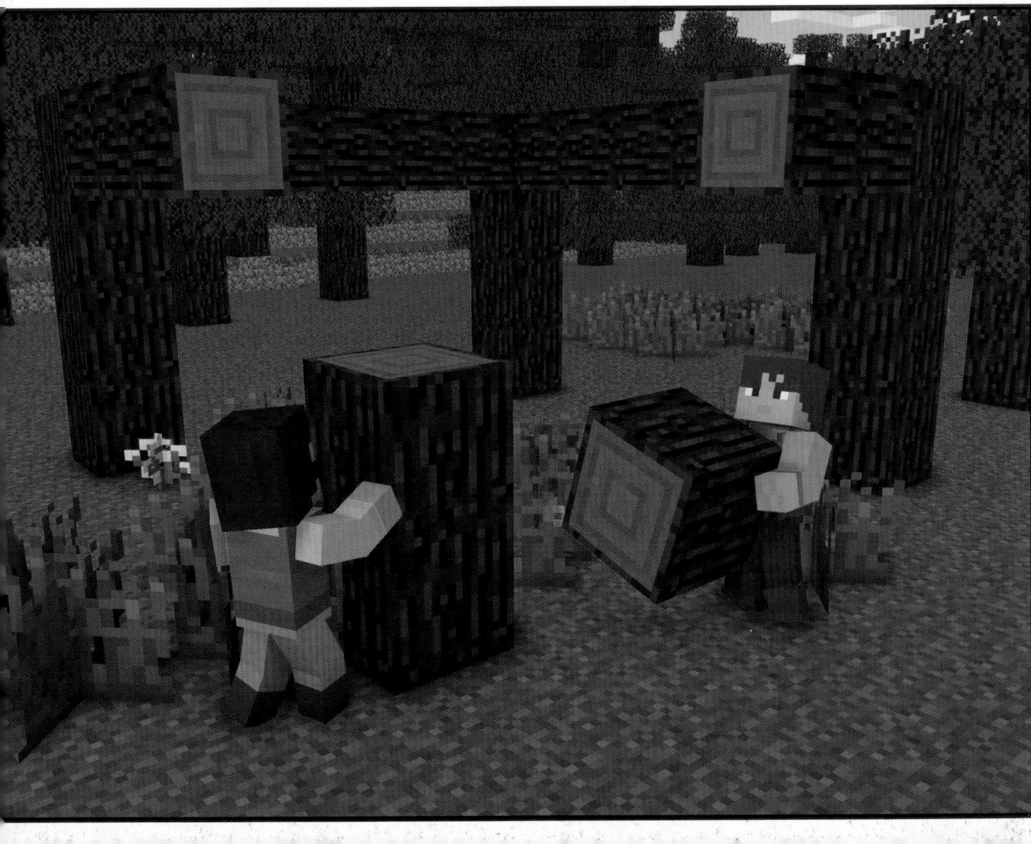

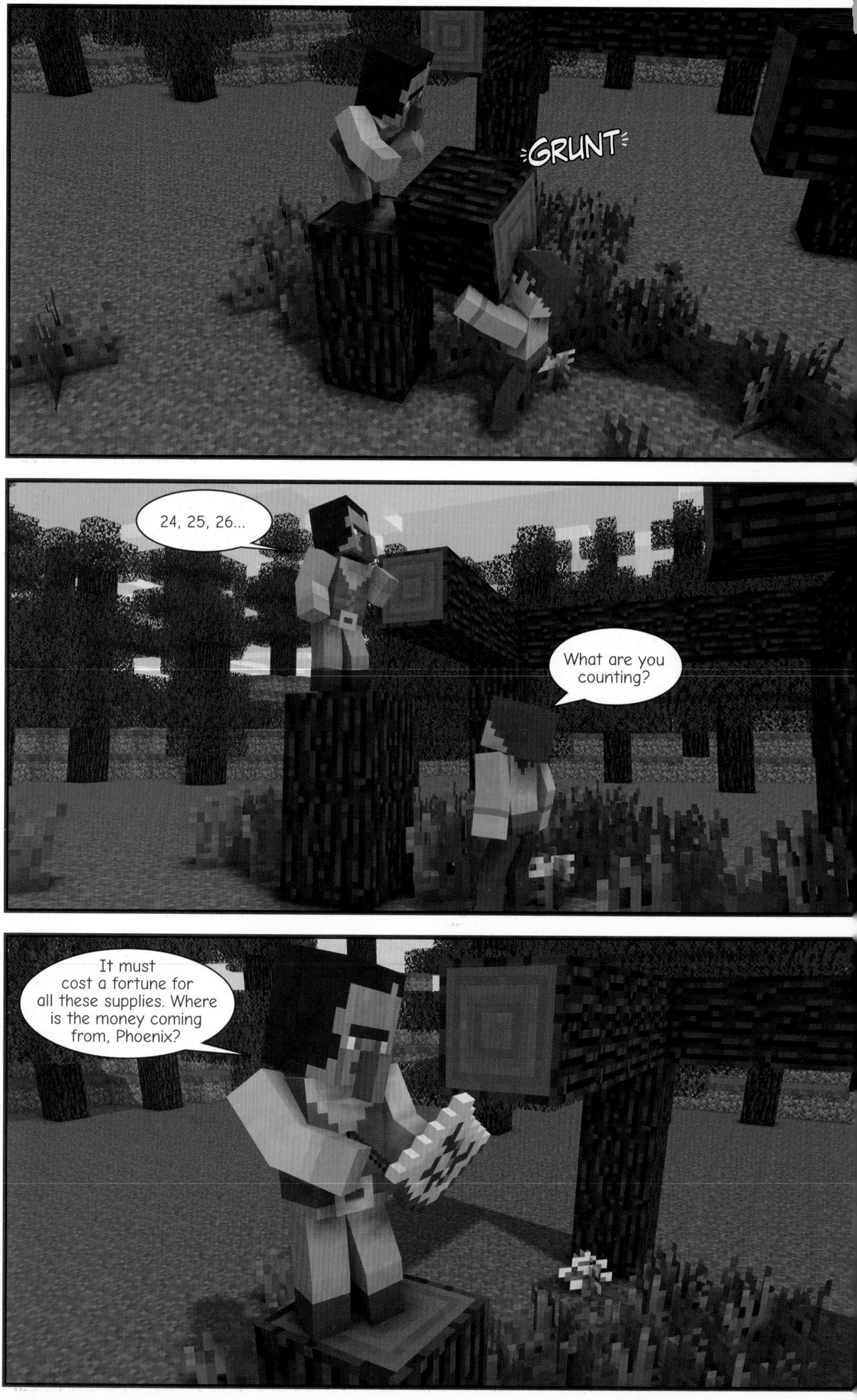
GRUNT
24, 25, 26...
What are you counting?
It must cost a fortune for all these supplies. Where is the money coming from, Phoenix?

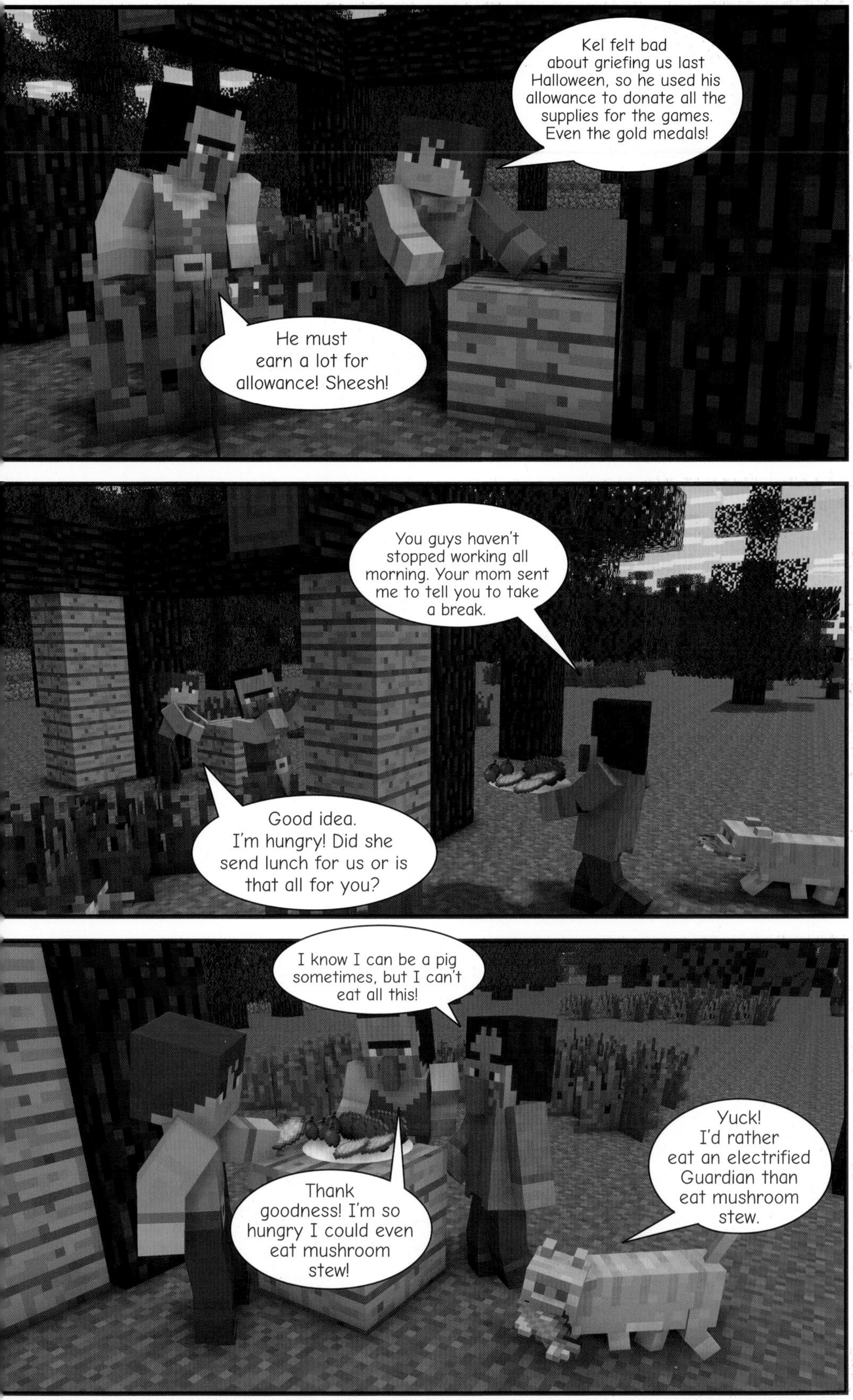
Kel felt bad about griefing us last Halloween, so he used his allowance to donate all the supplies for the games. Even the gold medals!
He must earn a lot for allowance! Sheesh!
You guys haven't stopped working all morning. Your mom sent me to tell you to take a break.
Good idea. I'm hungry! Did she send lunch for us or is that all for you?
I know I can be a pig sometimes, but I can't eat all this!
Thank goodness! I'm so hungry I could even eat mushroom stew!
Yuck! I'd rather eat an electrified Guardian than eat mushroom stew.

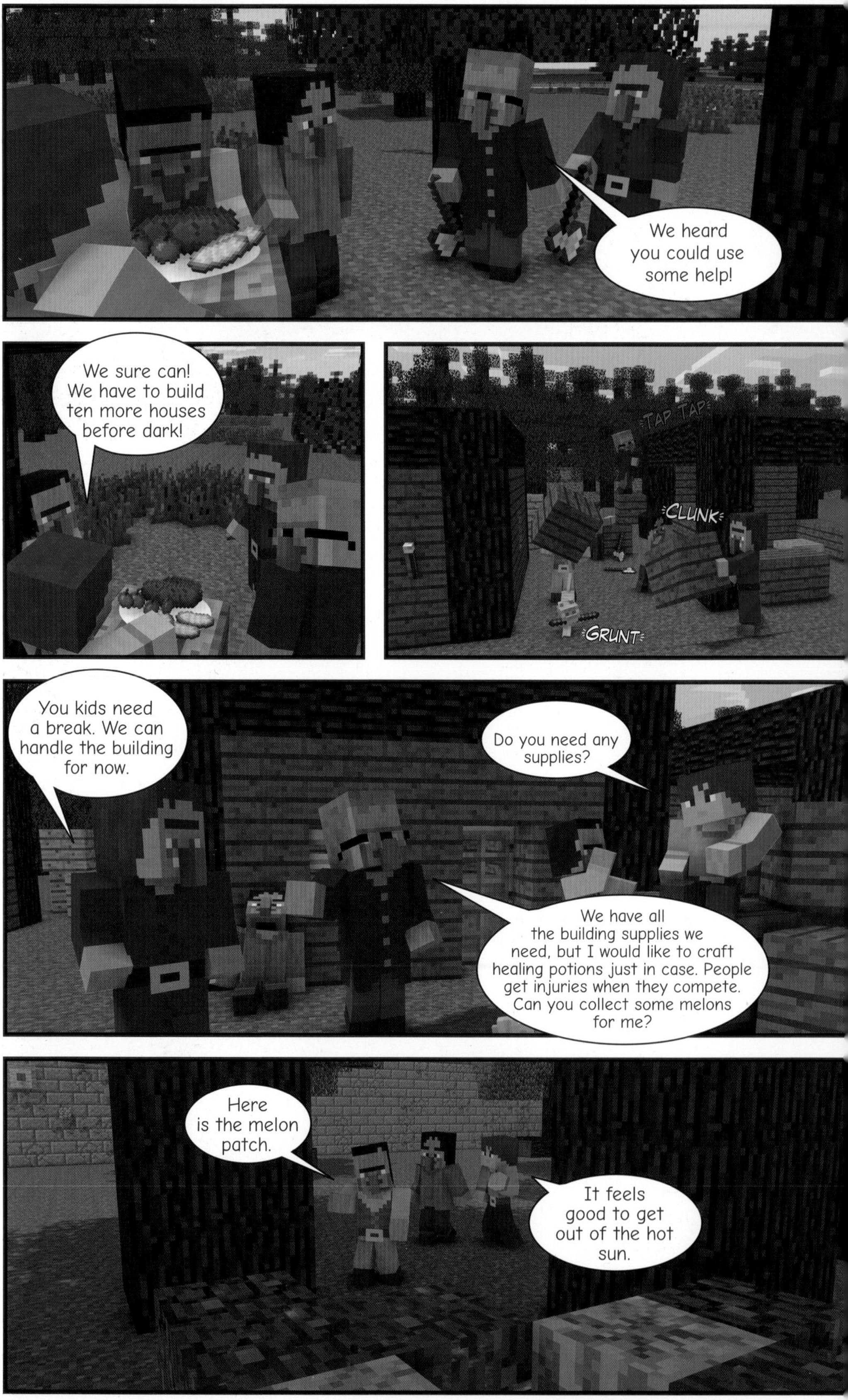
We heard you could use some help!
We sure can! We have to build ten more houses before dark!
TAP TAP
CLUNK
GRUNT
You kids need a break. We can handle the building for now.
Do you need any supplies?
We have all the building supplies we need, but I would like to craft healing potions just in case. People get injuries when they compete. Can you collect some melons for me?
Here is the melon patch.
It feels good to get out of the hot sun.

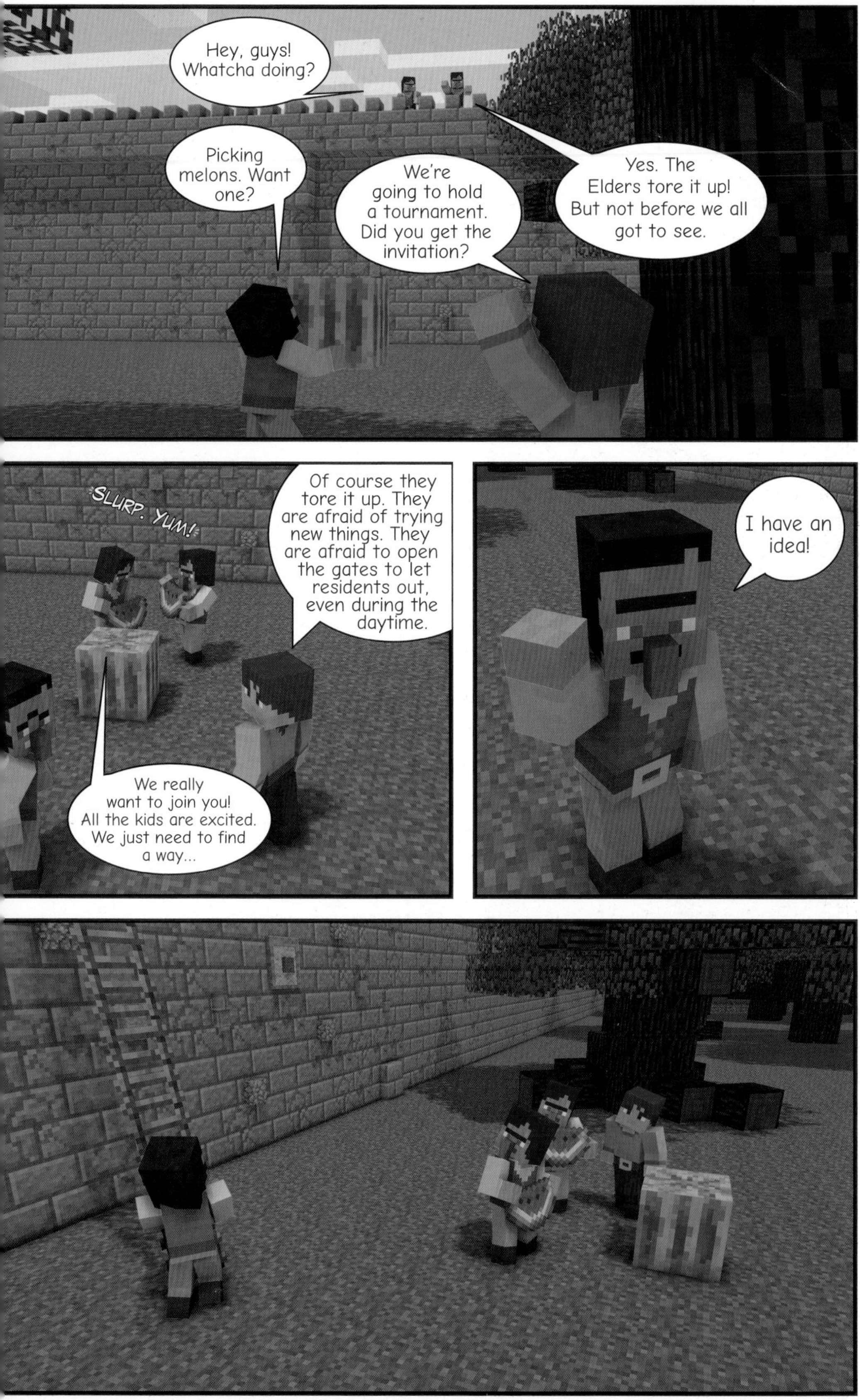
Hey, guys!
Whatcha doing?
Picking melons. Want one?
We're going to hold a tournament. Did you get the invitation?
Yes. The Elders tore it up! But not before we all got to see.
SLURP. YUM!
Of course they tore it up. They are afraid of trying new things. They are afraid to open the gates to let residents out, even during the daytime.
We really want to join you! All the kids are excited. We just need to find a way...
I have an idea!

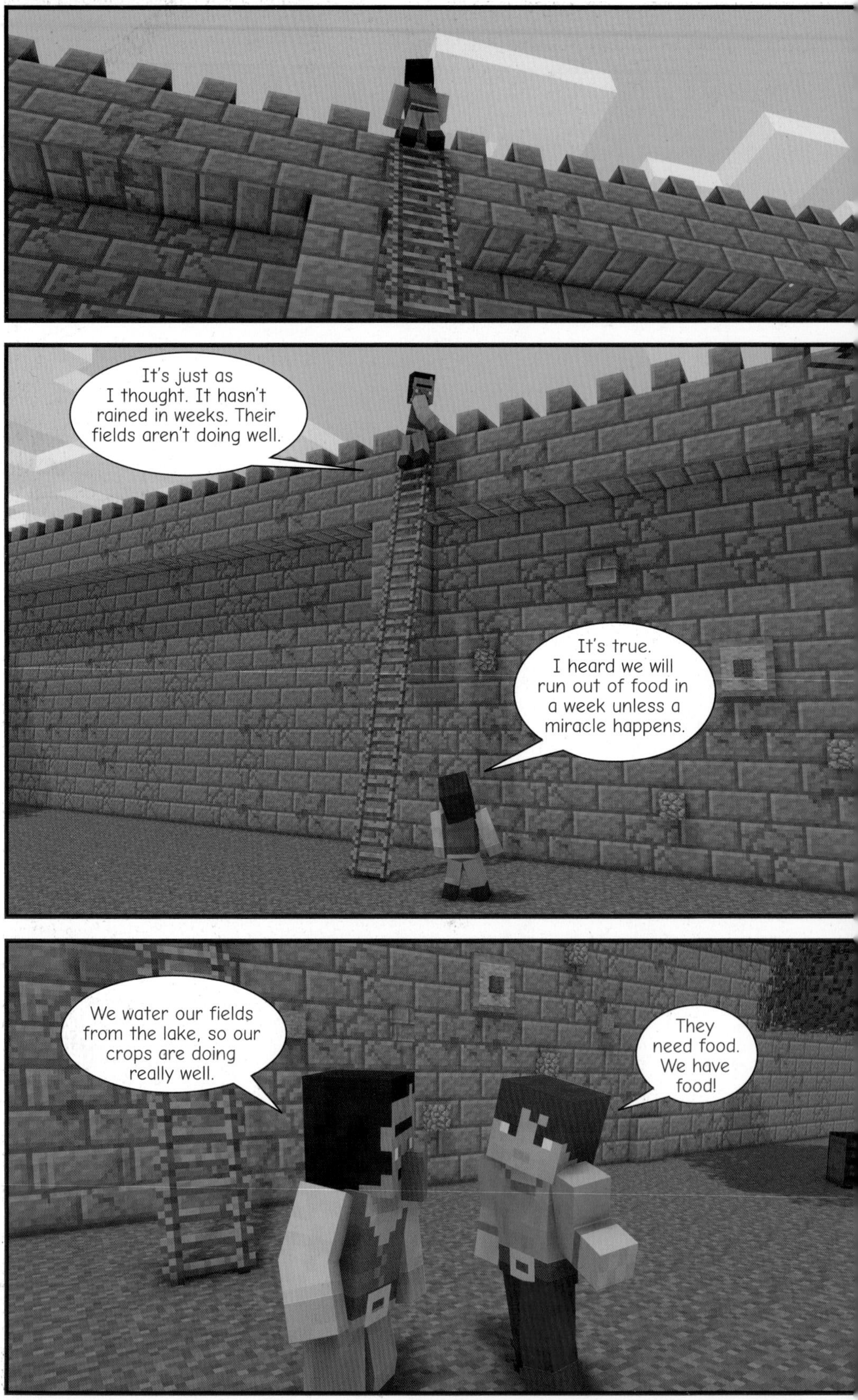
It's just as I thought. It hasn't rained in weeks. Their fields aren't doing well.
It's true. I heard we will run out of food in a week unless a miracle happens.
We water our fields from the lake, so our crops are doing really well.
They need food. We have food!

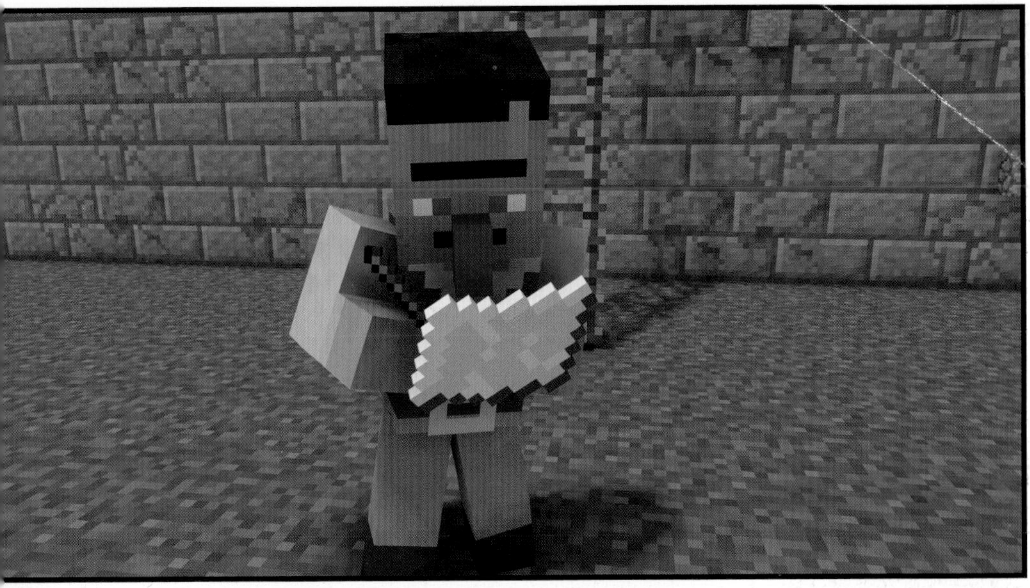

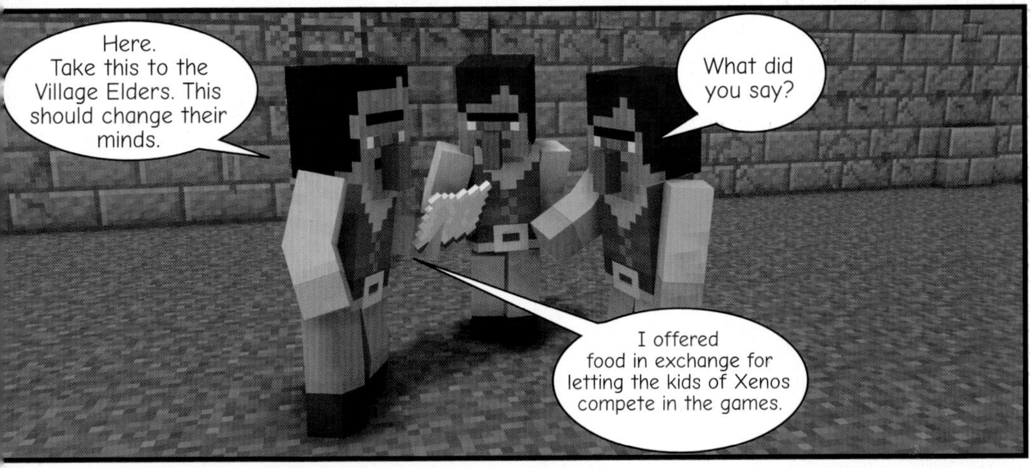
Here. Take this to the Village Elders. This should change their minds.
What did you say?
I offered food in exchange for letting the kids of Xenos compete in the games.

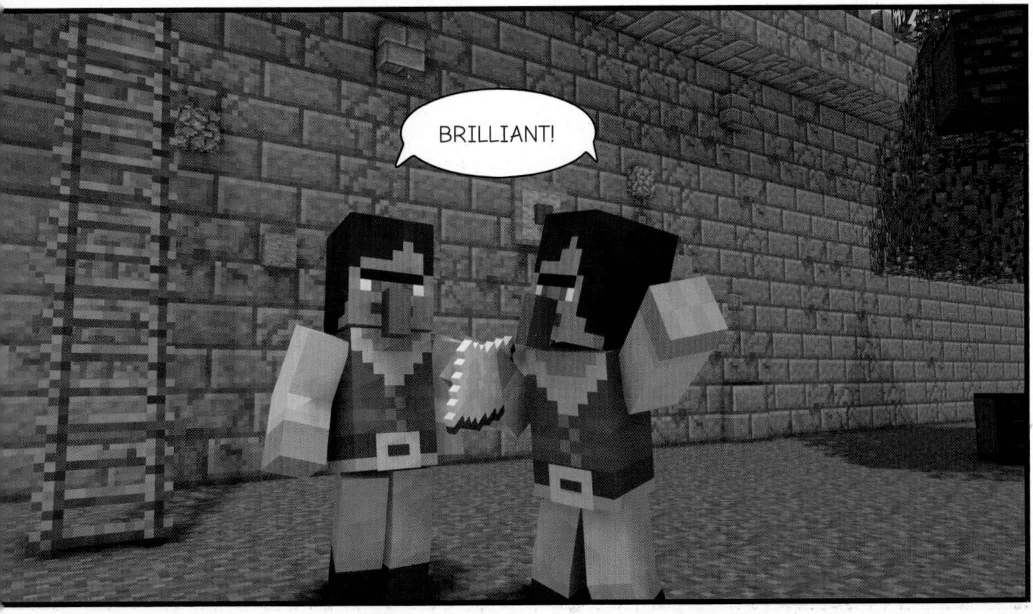
BRILLIANT!

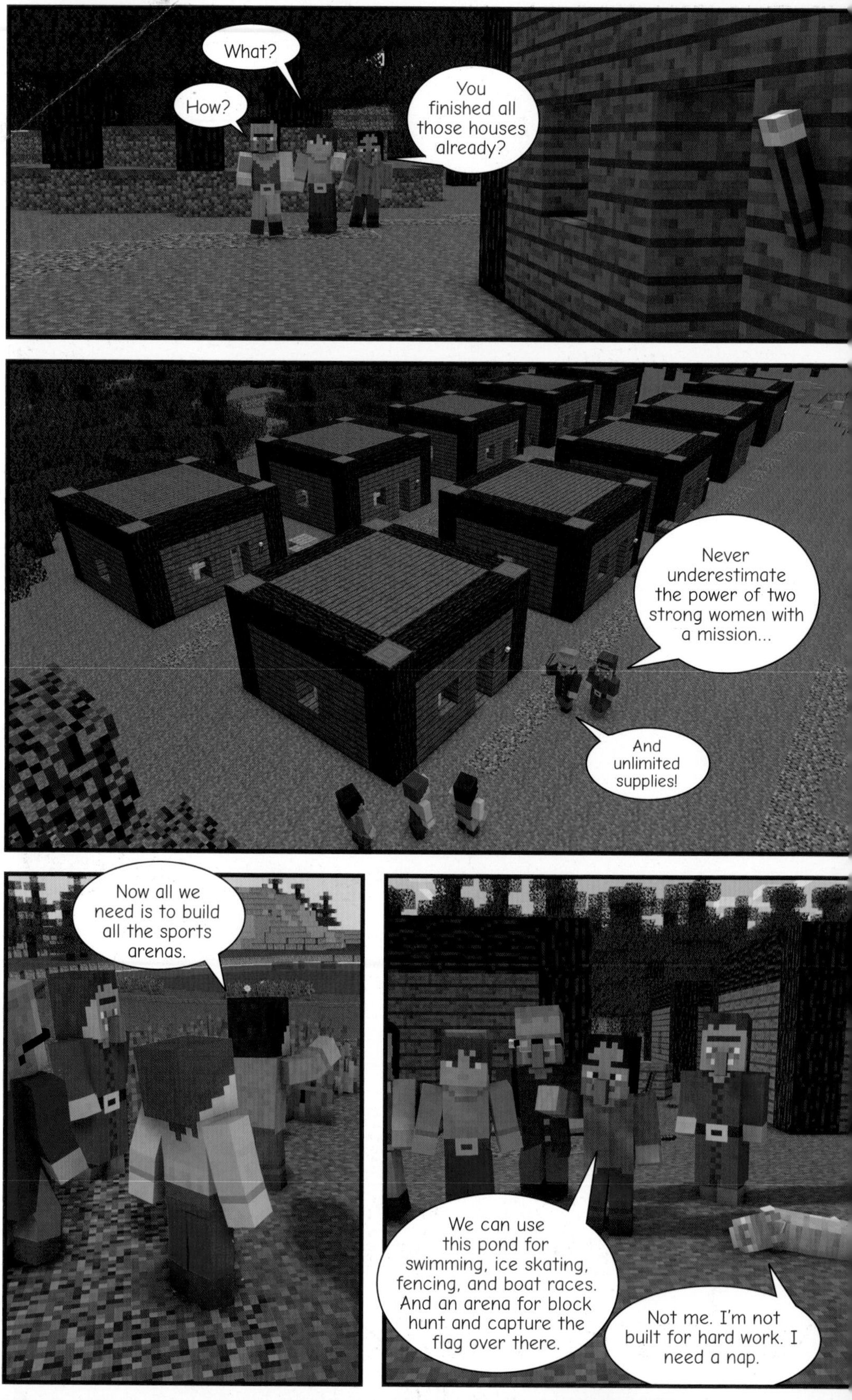
How?
What?
You finished all those houses already?
Never underestimate the power of two strong women with a mission...
And unlimited supplies!
Now all we need is to build all the sports arenas.
We can use this pond for swimming, ice skating, fencing, and boat races. And an arena for block hunt and capture the flag over there.
Not me. I'm not built for hard work. I need a nap.

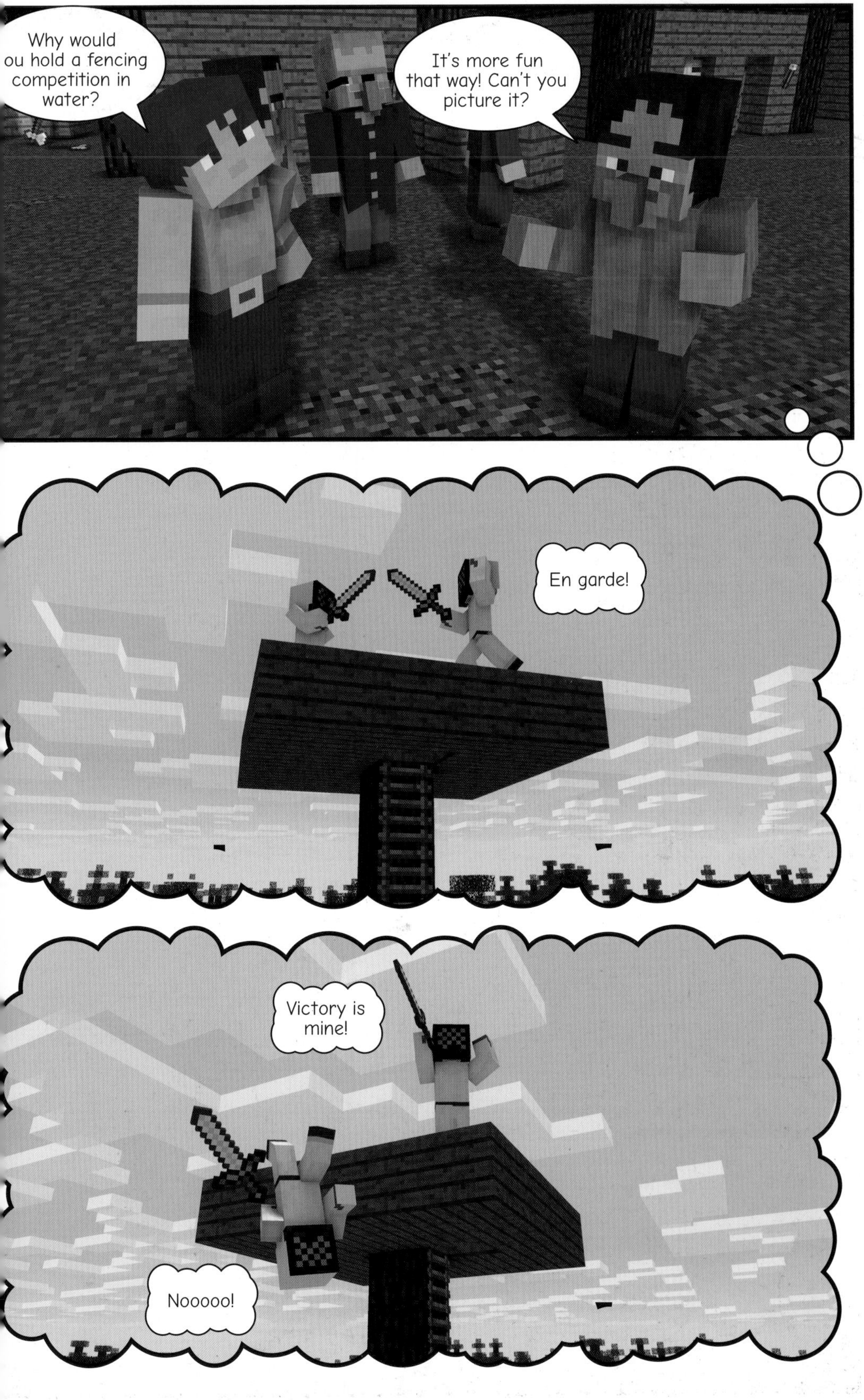
Why would ou hold a fencing competition in water?
It's more fun that way! Can't you picture it?
En garde!
Victory is mine!
Nooooo!

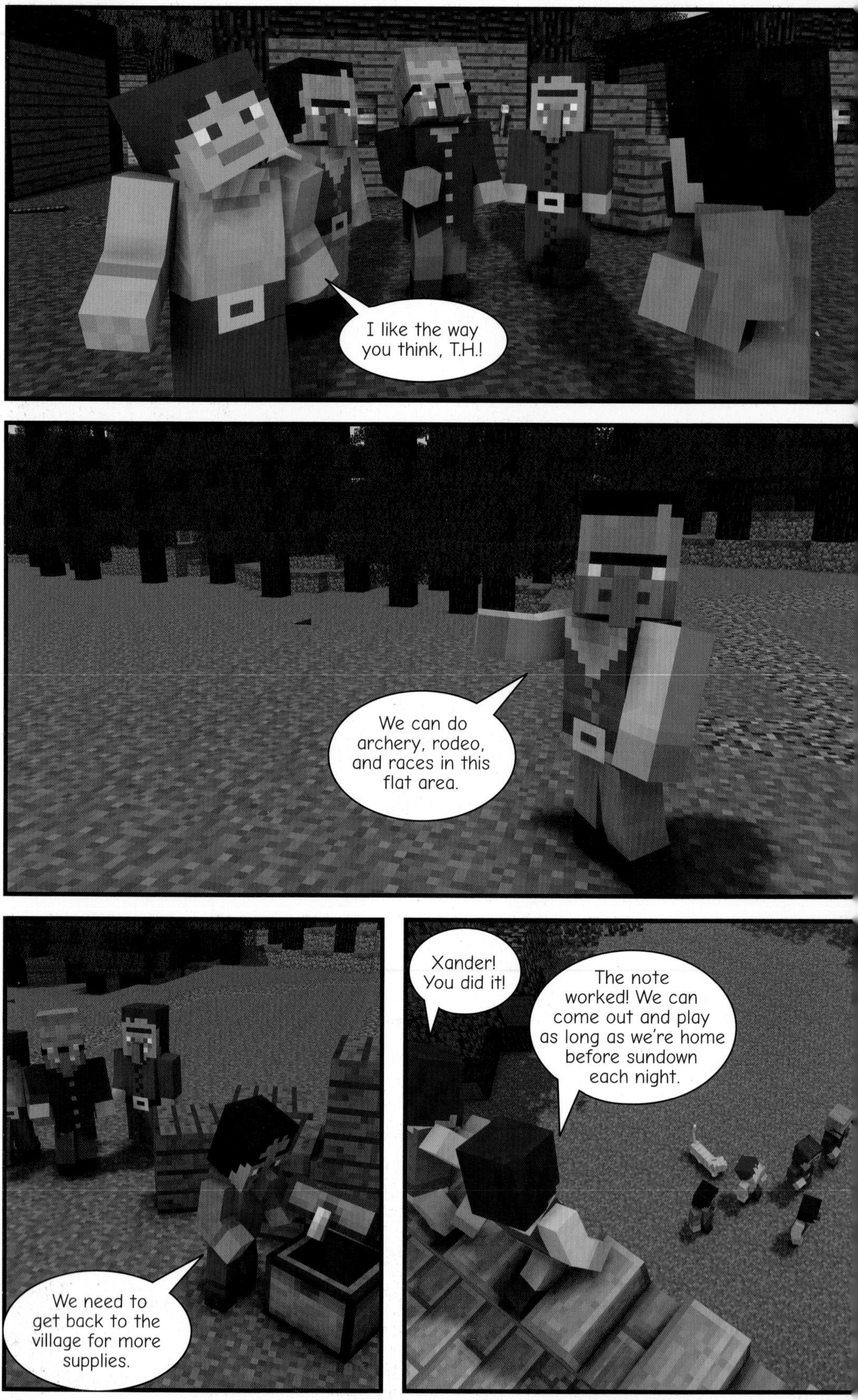
I like the way you think, T.H.!
We can do archery, rodeo, and races in this flat area.
We need to get back to the village for more supplies.
Xander! You did it!
The note worked! We can come out and play as long as we're home before sundown each night.

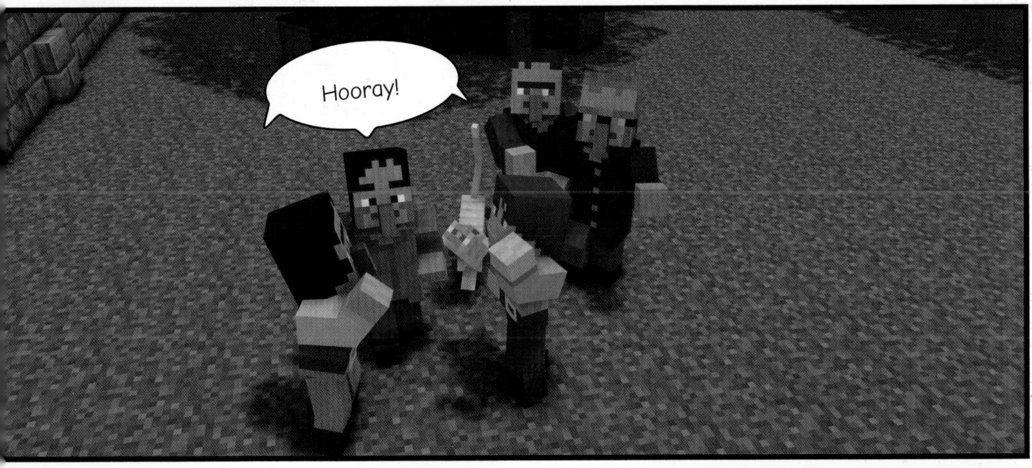
Hooray!

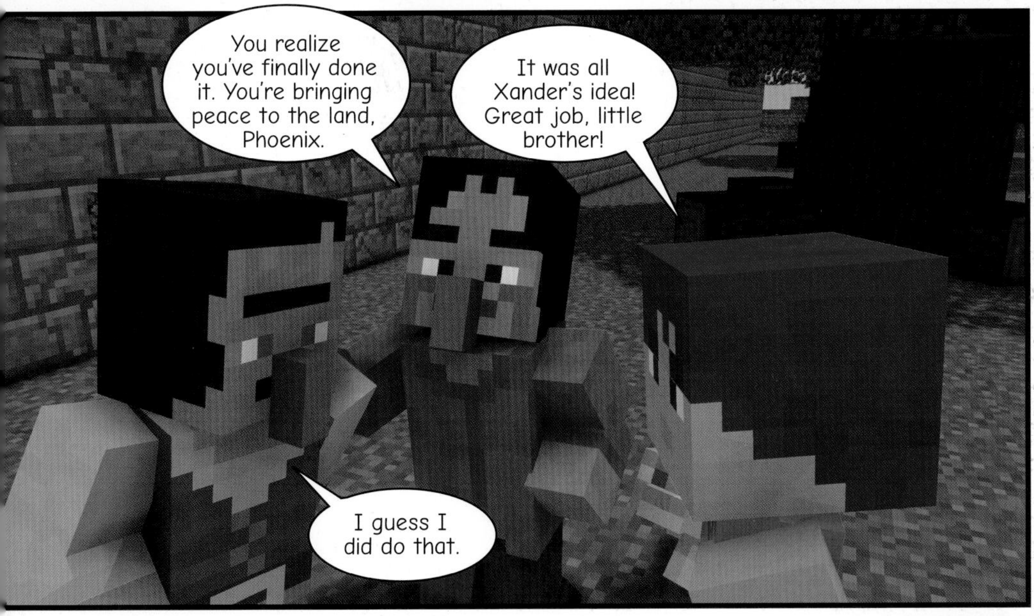
You realize you've finally done it. You're bringing peace to the land, Phoenix.
It was all Xander's idea! Great job, little brother!
I guess I did do that.

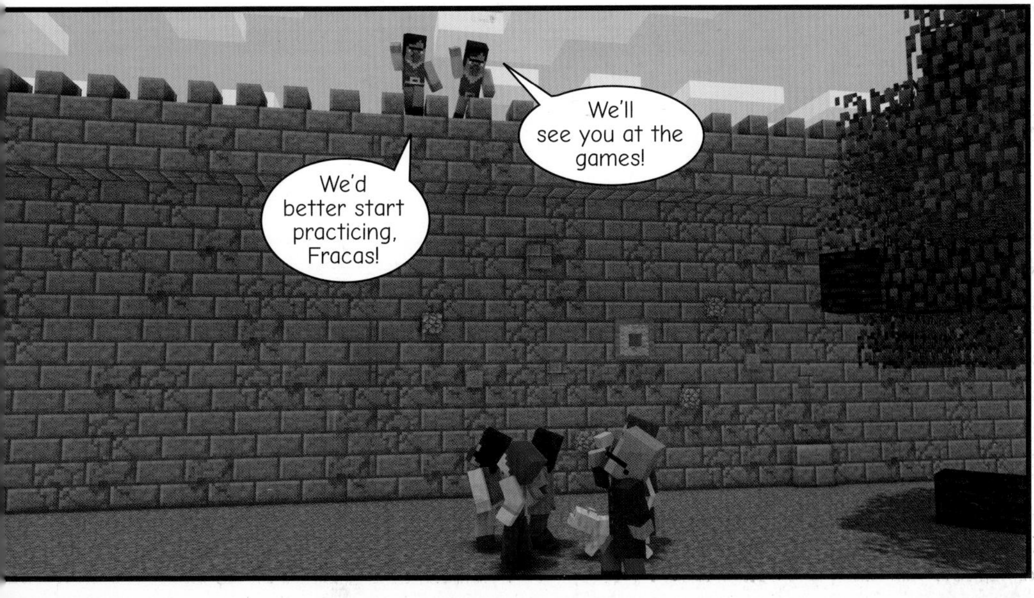
We'll see you at the games!
We'd better start practicing, Fracas!

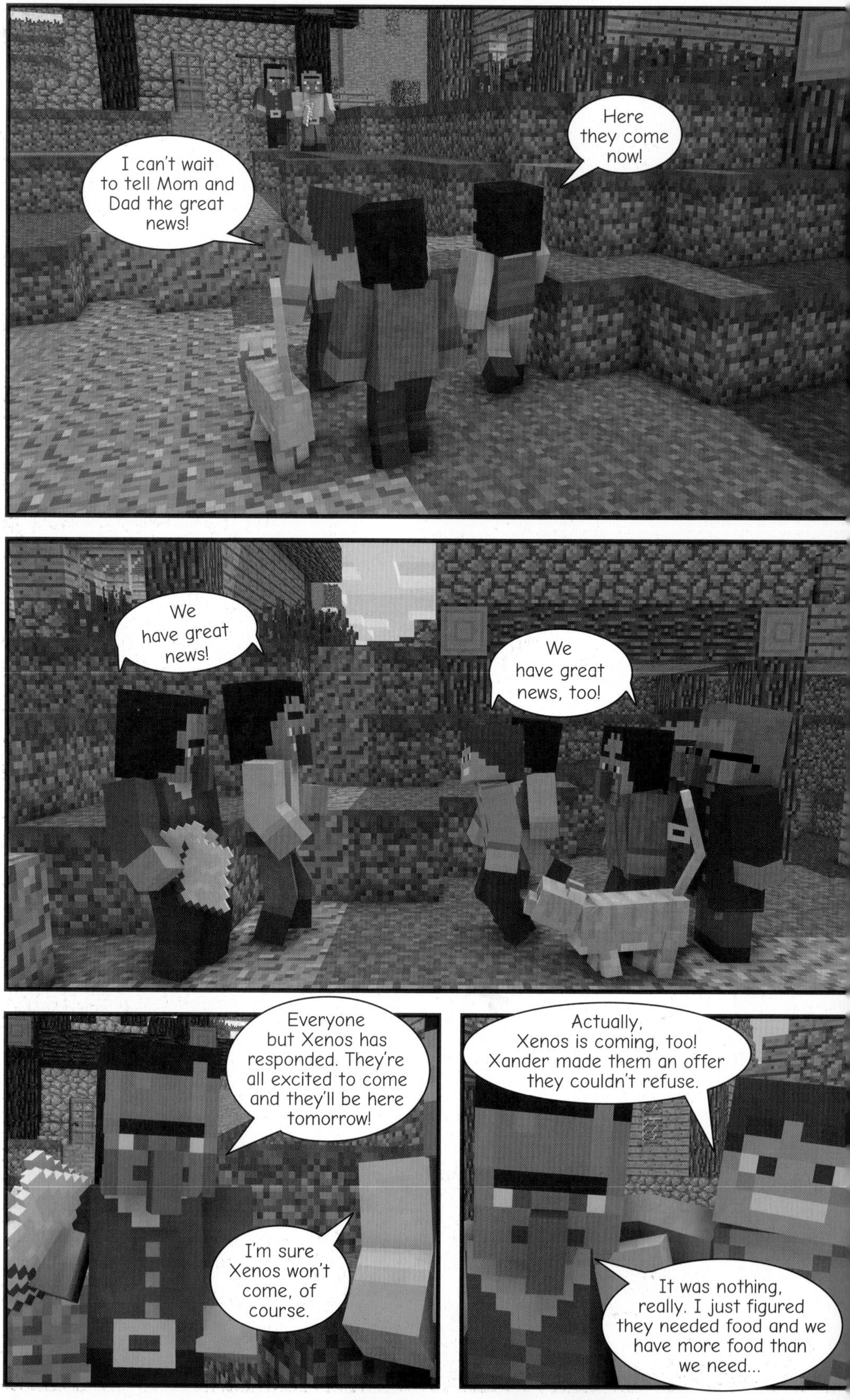
I can't wait to tell Mom and Dad the great news!
Here they come now!
We have great news!
We have great news, too!
Everyone but Xenos has responded. They're all excited to come and they'll be here tomorrow!
I'm sure Xenos won't come, of course.
Actually, Xenos is coming, too! Xander made them an offer they couldn't refuse.
It was nothing, really. I just figured they needed food and we have more food than we need...

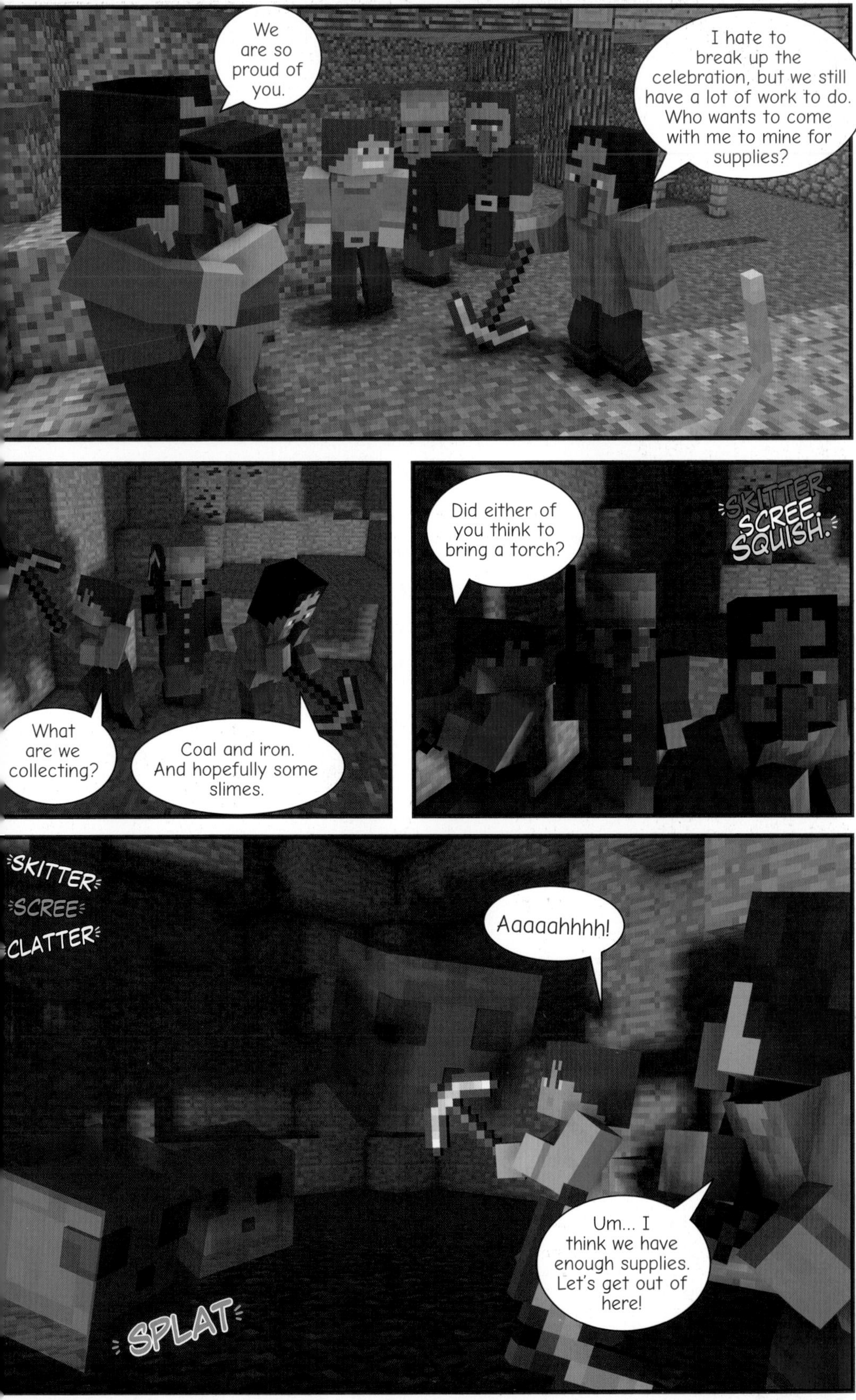

We are so proud of you.
I hate to break up the celebration, but we still have a lot of work to do. Who wants to come with me to mine for supplies?
What are we collecting?
Coal and iron. And hopefully some slimes.
Did either of you think to bring a torch?
SKITTER. SCREE. SQUISH.
SKITTER
SCREE
CLATTER
Aaaaahhhh!
SPLAT
Um... I think we have enough supplies. Let's get out of here!

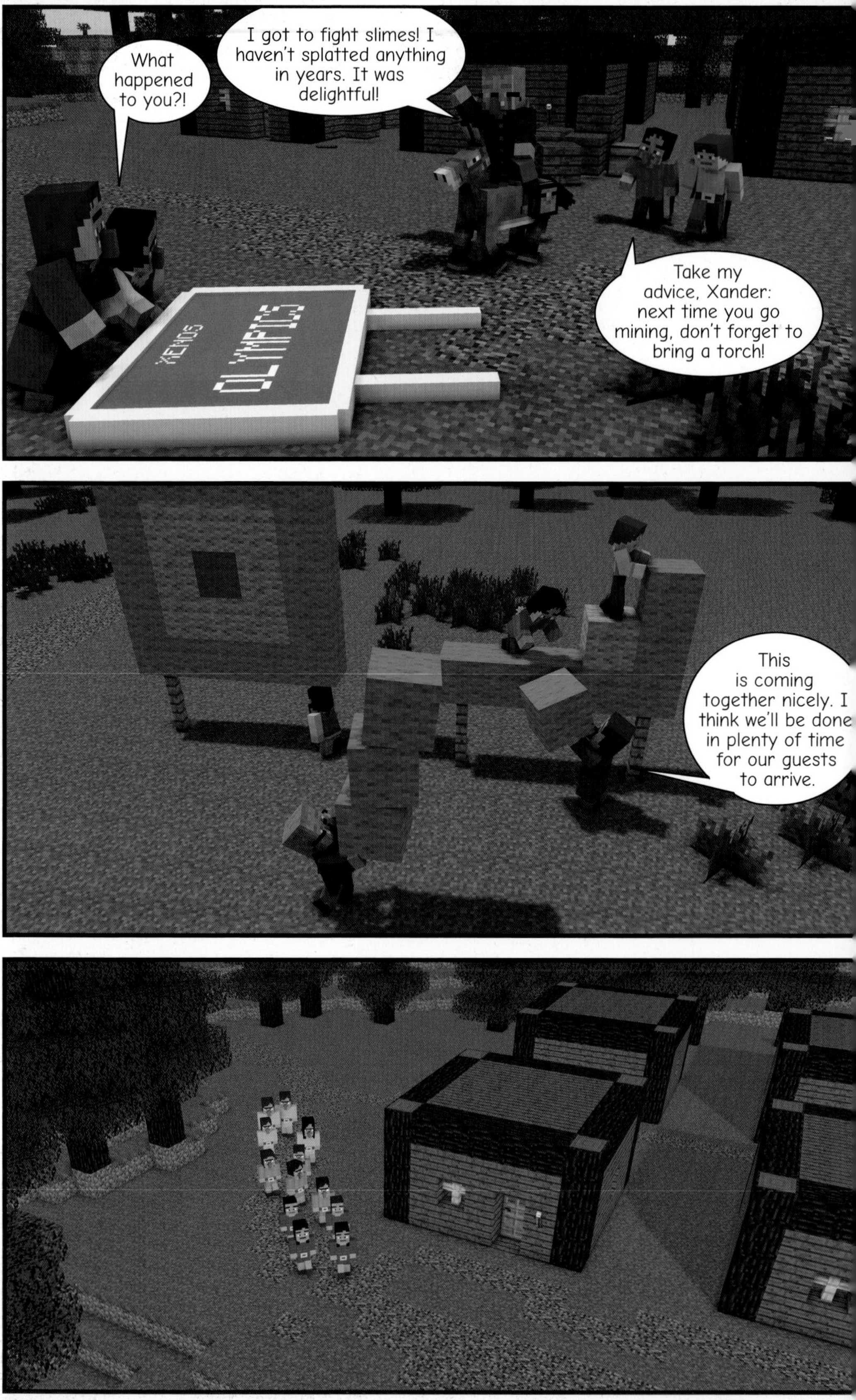
What happened to you?!
I got to fight slimes! I haven't splatted anything in years. It was delightful!
XENOS
OLYMPICS
Take my advice, Xander: next time you go mining, don't forget to bring a torch!
This is coming together nicely. I think we'll be done in plenty of time for our guests to arrive.

CHAPTER 3

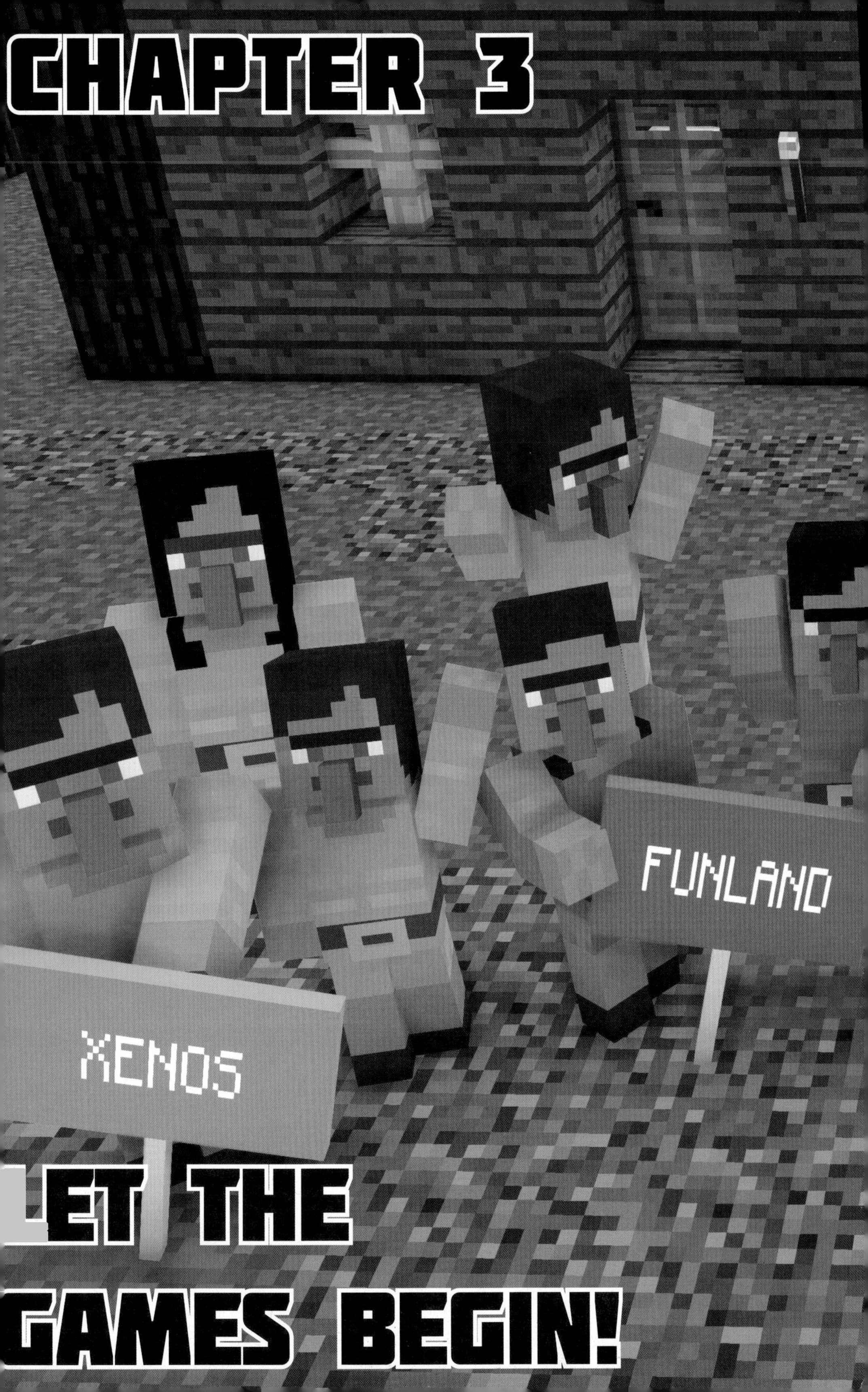
FUNLAND
XENOS

LET THE GAMES BEGIN!

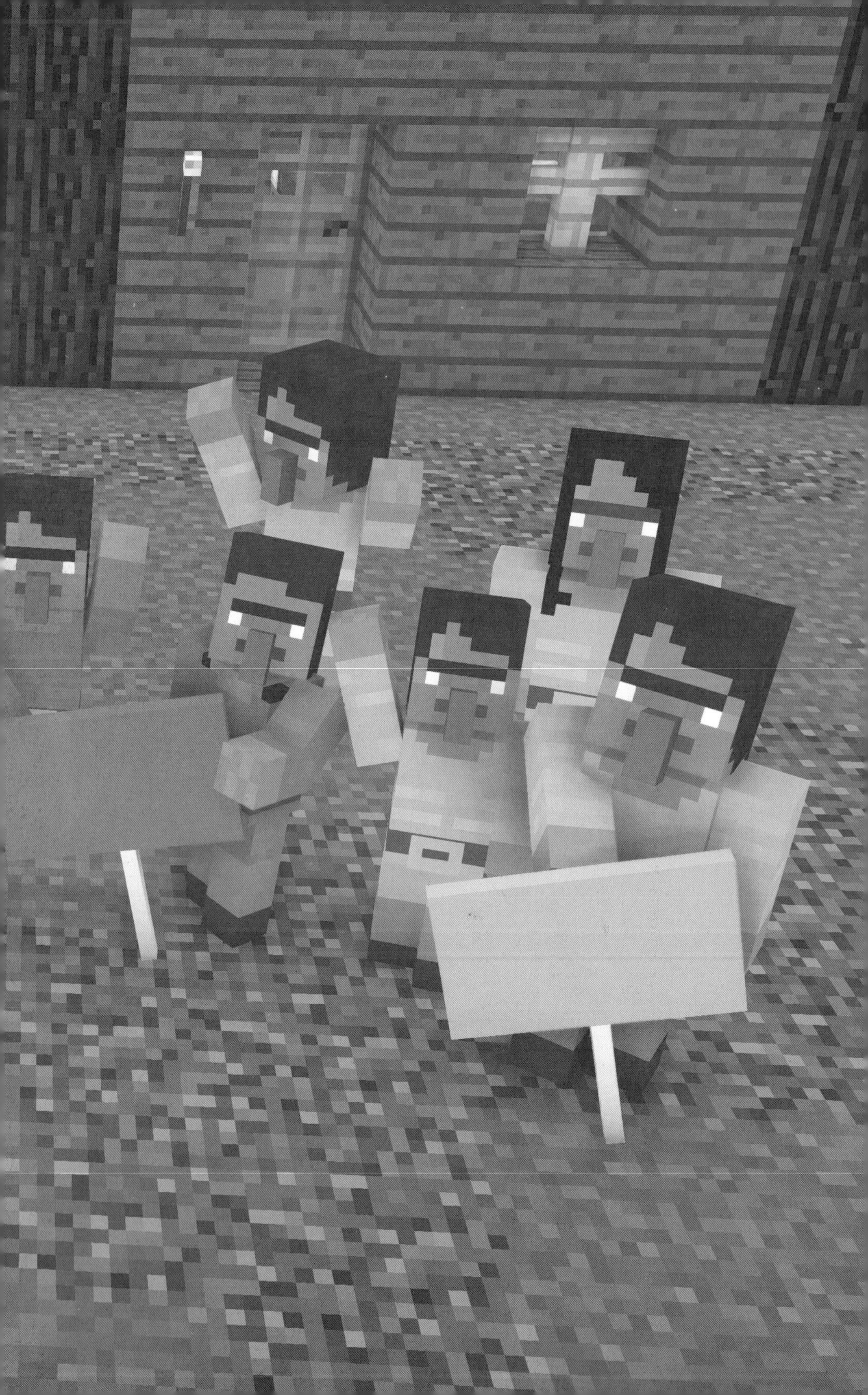

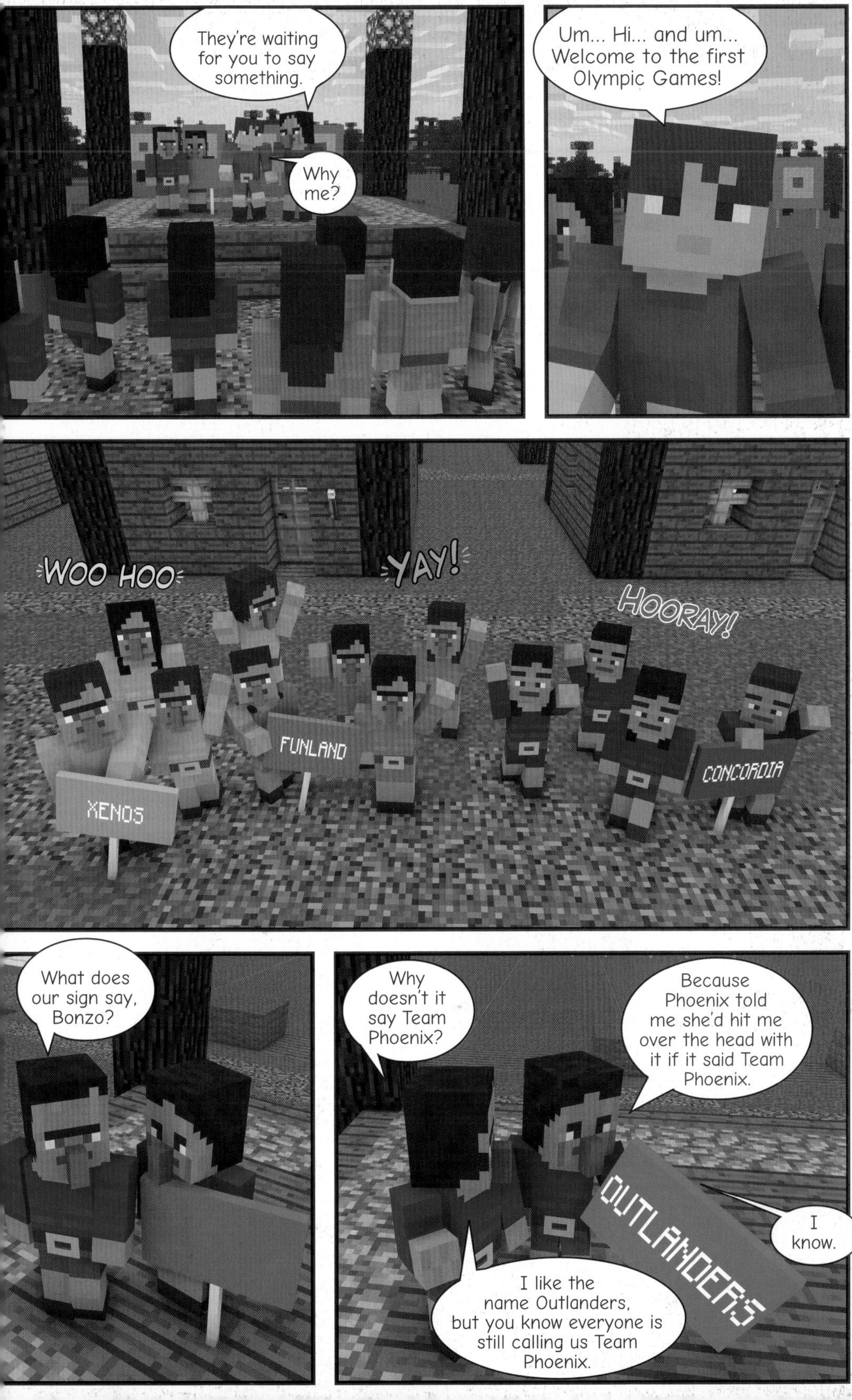
They're waiting for you to say something.
Why me?
Um... Hi... and um... Welcome to the first Olympic Games!
WOO HOO
YAY!
HOORAY!
XENOS
FUNLAND
CONCORDIA
What does our sign say, Bonzo?
Why doesn't it say Team Phoenix?
Because Phoenix told me she'd hit me over the head with it if it said Team Phoenix.
OUTLANDERS
I know.
I like the name Outlanders, but you know everyone is still calling us Team Phoenix.

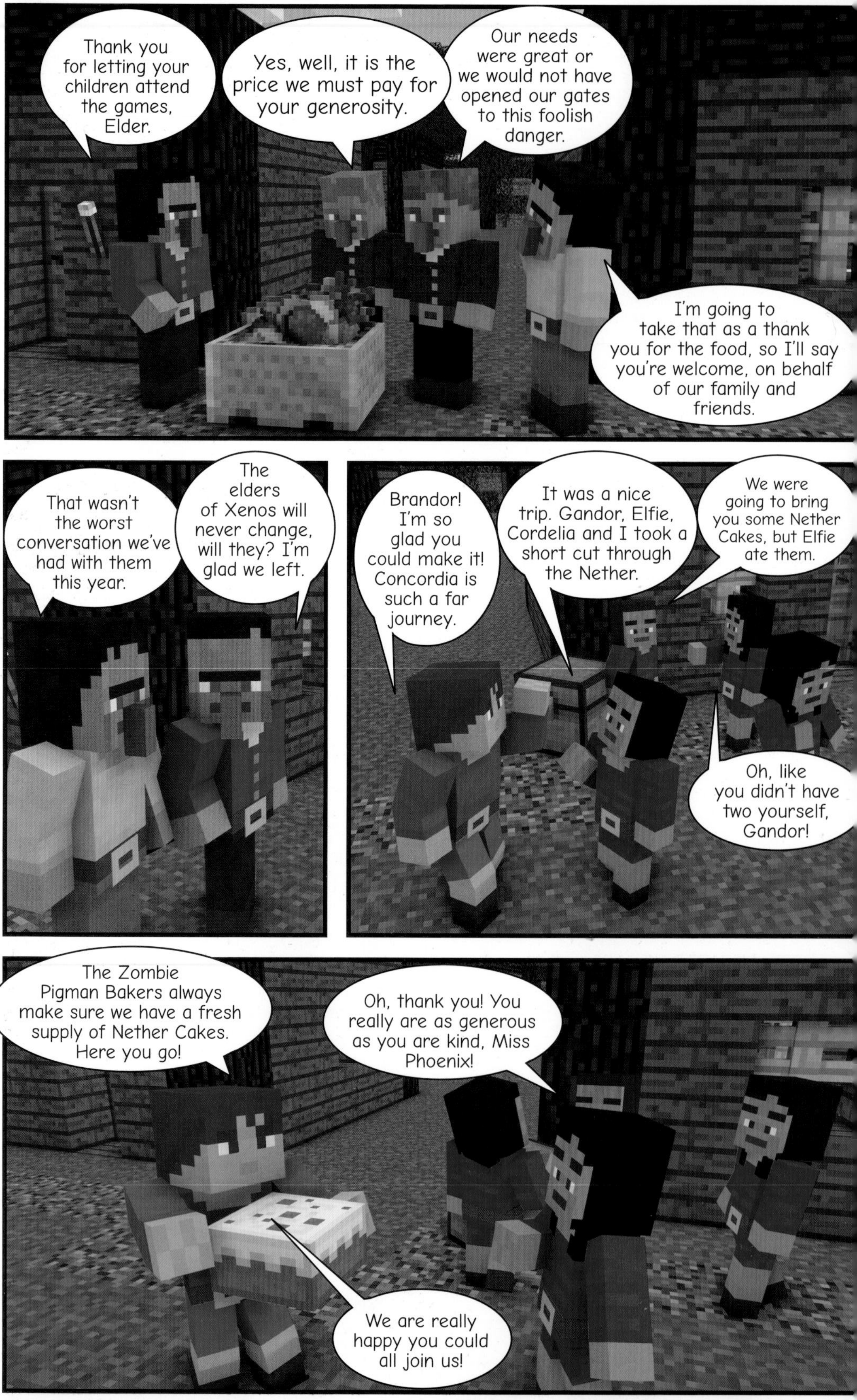
Thank you for letting your children attend the games, Elder.
Yes, well, it is the price we must pay for your generosity.
Our needs were great or we would not have opened our gates to this foolish danger.
I'm going to take that as a thank you for the food, so I'll say you're welcome, on behalf of our family and friends.
That wasn't the worst conversation we've had with them this year.
The elders of Xenos will never change, will they? I'm glad we left.
Brandor! I'm so glad you could make it! Concordia is such a far journey.
It was a nice trip. Gandor, Elfie, Cordelia and I took a short cut through the Nether.
We were going to bring you some Nether Cakes, but Elfie ate them.
Oh, like you didn't have two yourself, Gandor!
The Zombie Pigman Bakers always make sure we have a fresh supply of Nether Cakes. Here you go!
Oh, thank you! You really are as generous as you are kind, Miss Phoenix!
We are really happy you could all join us!

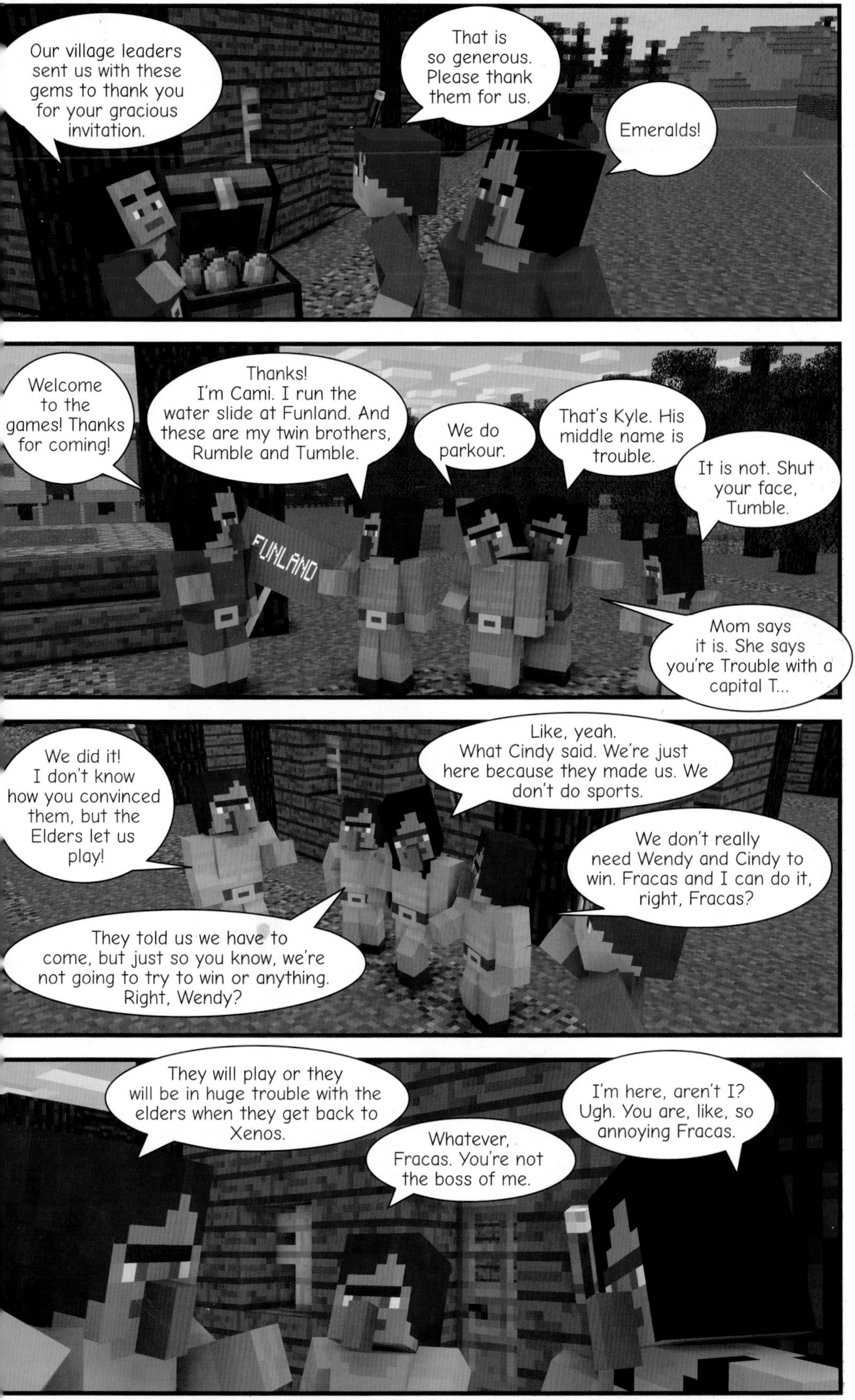
Our village leaders sent us with these gems to thank you for your gracious invitation.
That is so generous. Please thank them for us.
Emeralds!
Welcome to the games! Thanks for coming!
Thanks! I'm Cami. I run the water slide at Funland. And these are my twin brothers, Rumble and Tumble.
FUNLAND
We do parkour.
That's Kyle. His middle name is trouble.
It is not. Shut your face, Tumble.
Mom says it is. She says you're Trouble with a capital T...
We did it! I don't know how you convinced them, but the Elders let us play!
Like, yeah. What Cindy said. We're just here because they made us. We don't do sports.
We don't really need Wendy and Cindy to win. Fracas and I can do it, right, Fracas?
They told us we have to come, but just so you know, we're not going to try to win or anything. Right, Wendy?
They will play or they will be in huge trouble with the elders when they get back to Xenos.
Whatever, Fracas. You're not the boss of me.
I'm here, aren't I? Ugh. You are, like, so annoying Fracas.

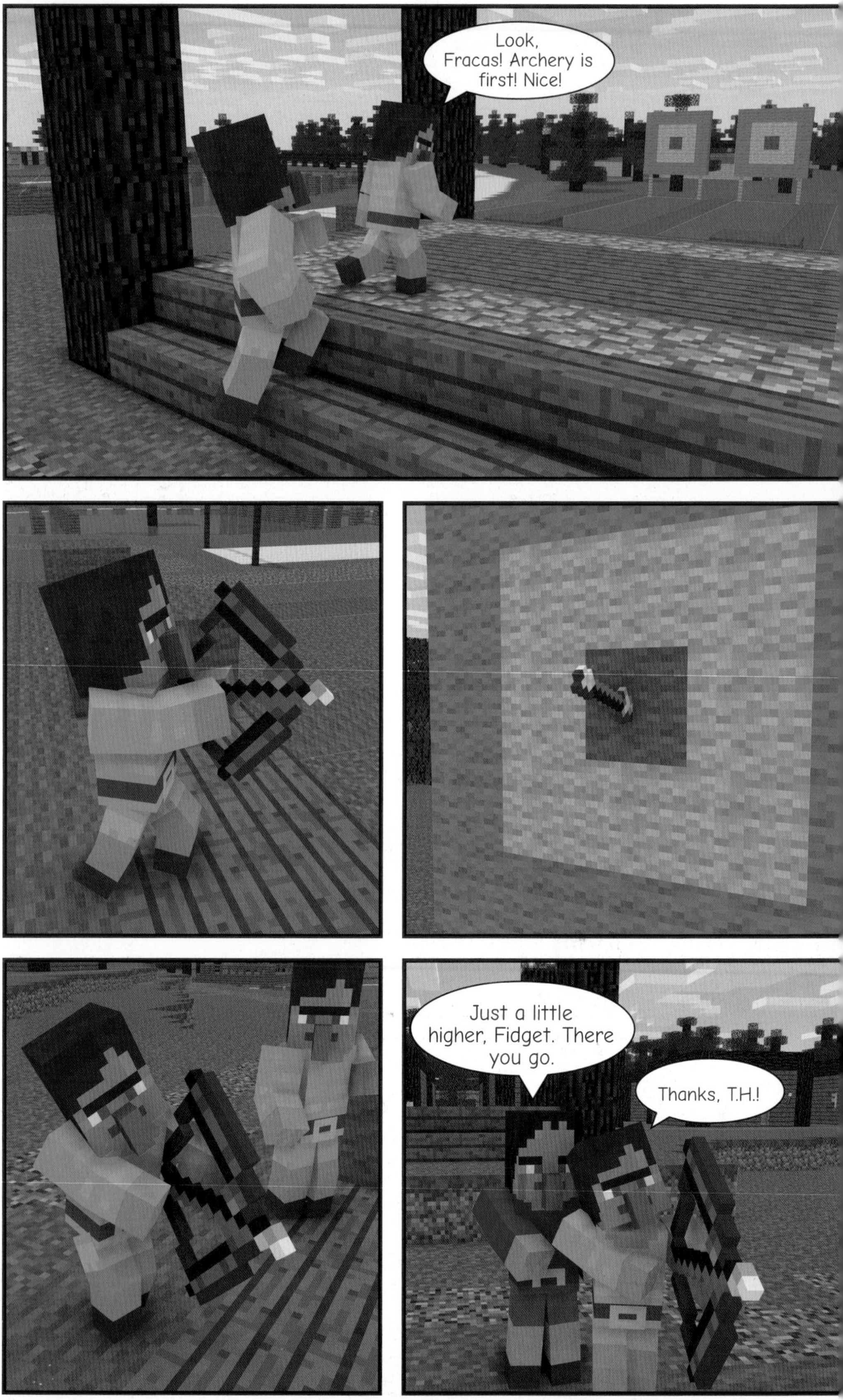
Look, Fracas! Archery is first! Nice!
Just a little higher, Fidget. There you go.
Thanks, T.H.!

Did you see that? I hit the target! Woo-hoo!
One...
Two...
CONCORDIA
Three...
Twenty points for Concordia!
Yay!
Yay!
CONCORDIA
FUNLAND
Ready, Kyle?

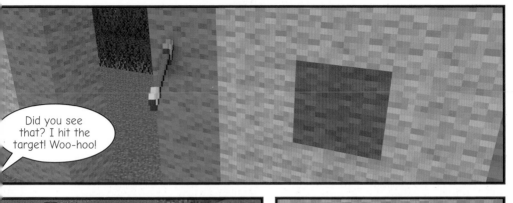

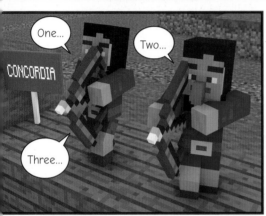

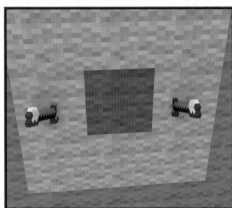

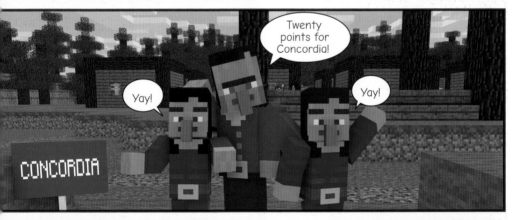

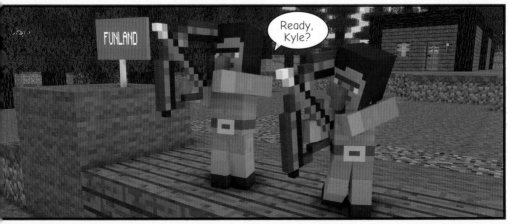

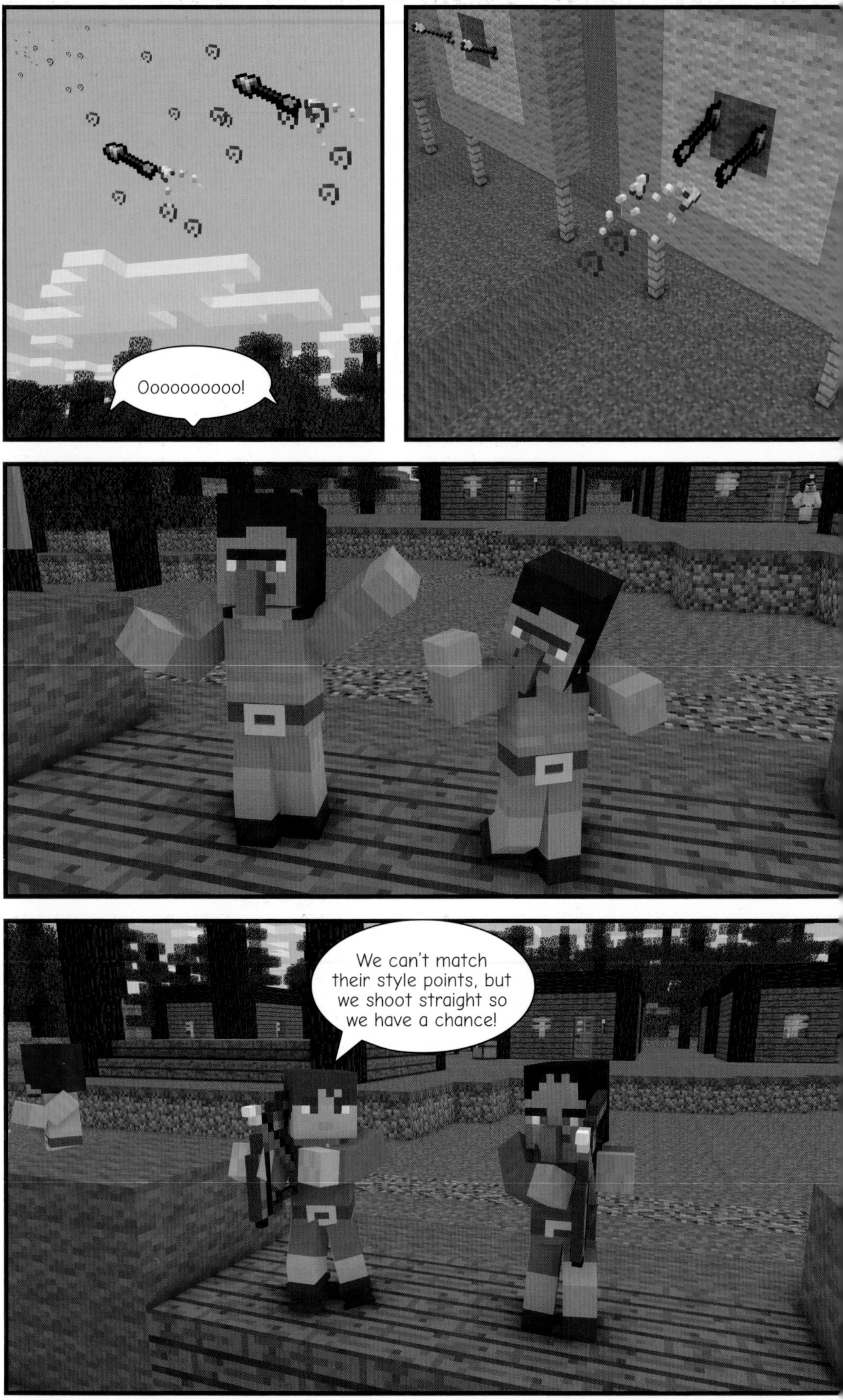
Oooooooooo!
We can't match their style points, but we shoot straight so we have a chance!

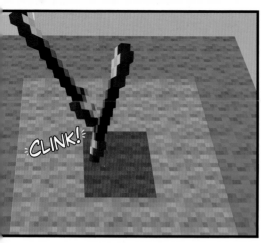

CLINK!

I didn't expect that to happen, but it looks like we came in last place on this event!

We won Capture the Flag!

Did you win at archery? Of course you did.

That's great, but... um, you know you're not supposed to KEEP the flags, right?

I'm so proud of you guys!

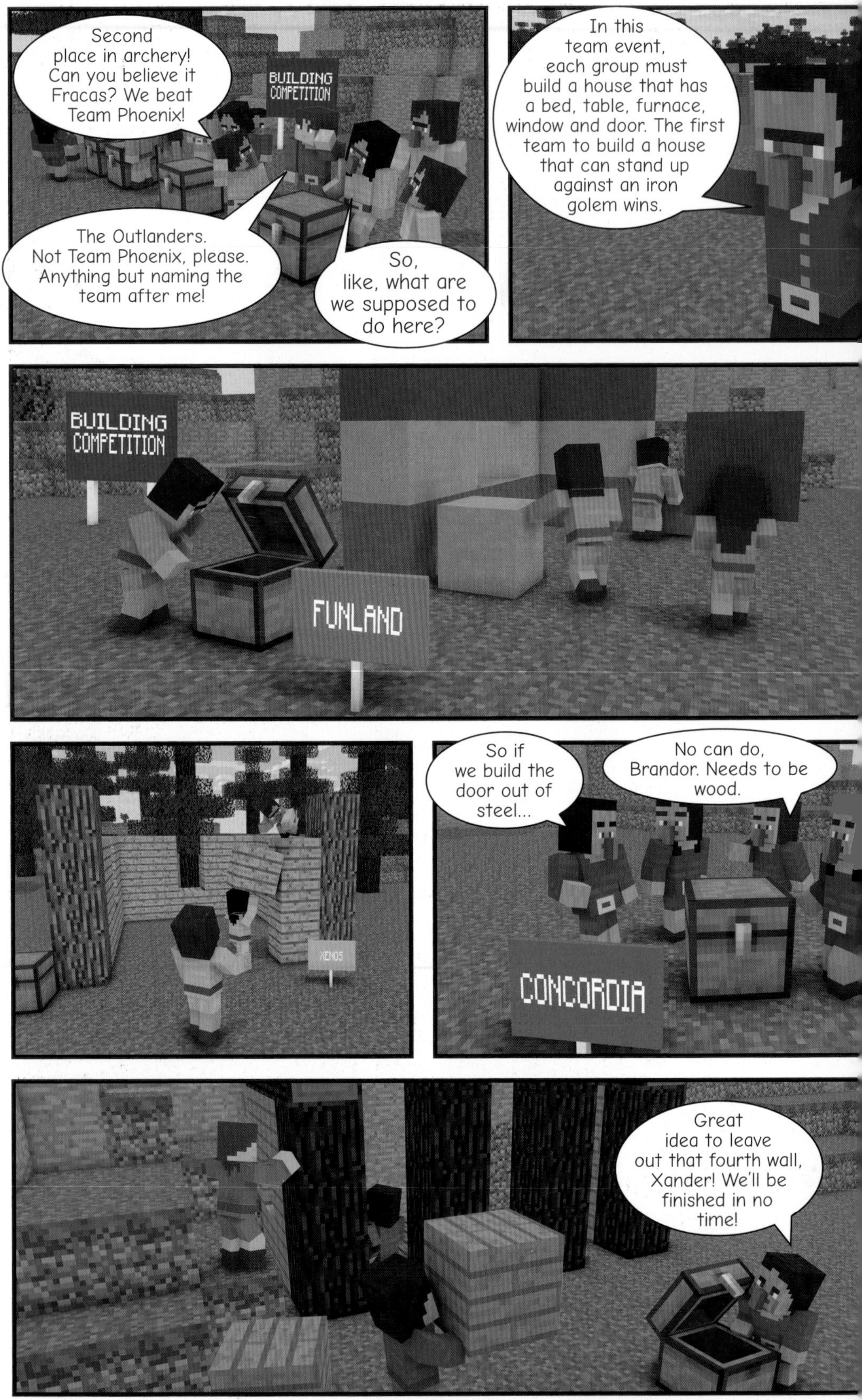

Second place in archery! Can you believe it Fracas? We beat Team Phoenix!
BUILDING COMPETITION
The Outlanders. Not Team Phoenix, please. Anything but naming the team after me!
So, like, what are we supposed to do here?
In this team event, each group must build a house that has a bed, table, furnace, window and door. The first team to build a house that can stand up against an iron golem wins.
BUILDING COMPETITION
FUNLAND
XENOS
So if we build the door out of steel...
No can do, Brandor. Needs to be wood.
CONCORDIA
Great idea to leave out that fourth wall, Xander! We'll be finished in no time!

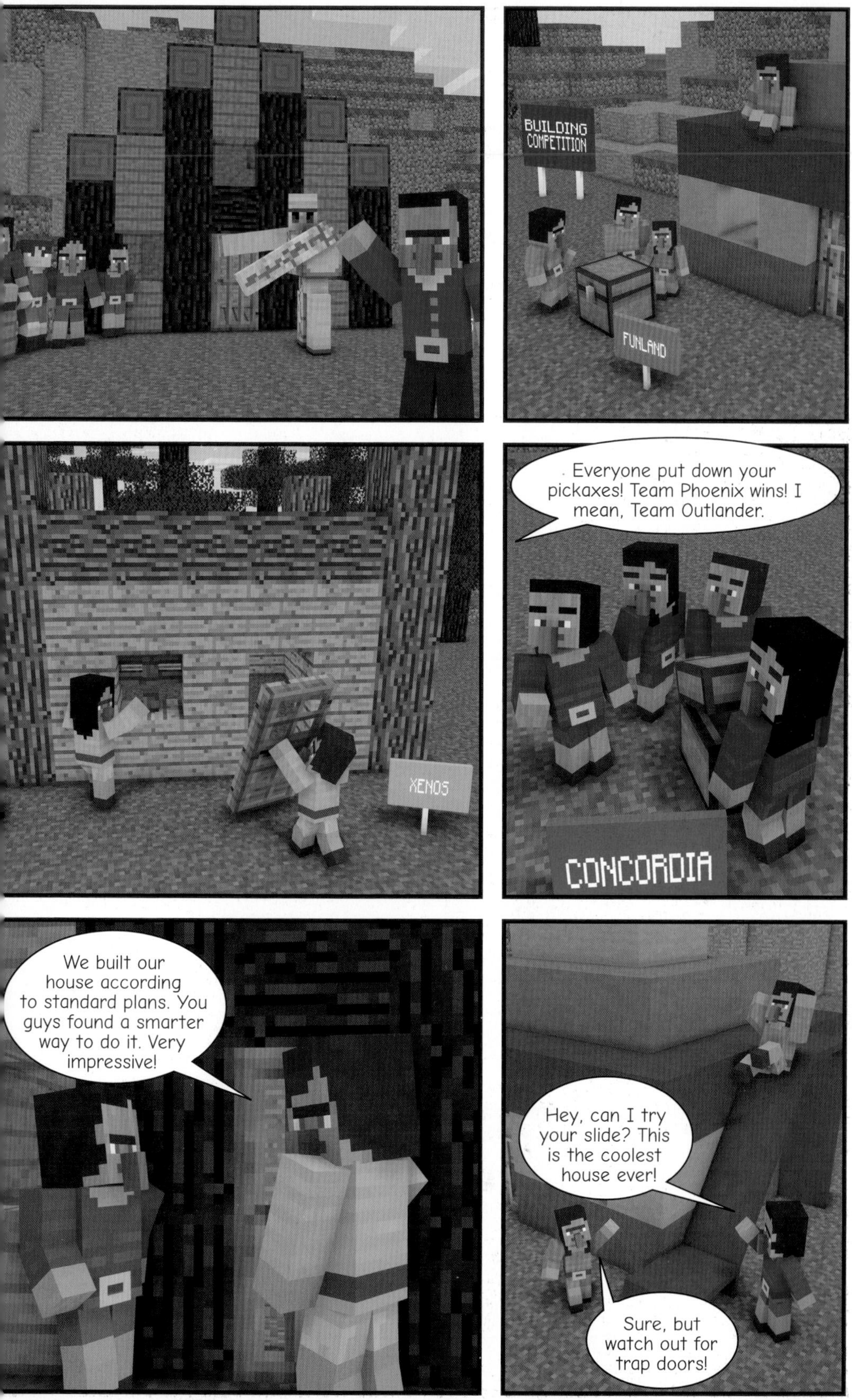
BUILDING COMPETITION
FUNLAND
XENOS
Everyone put down your pickaxes! Team Phoenix wins! I mean, Team Outlander.
CONCORDIA
We built our house according to standard plans. You guys found a smarter way to do it. Very impressive!
Hey, can I try your slide? This is the coolest house ever!
Sure, but watch out for trap doors!

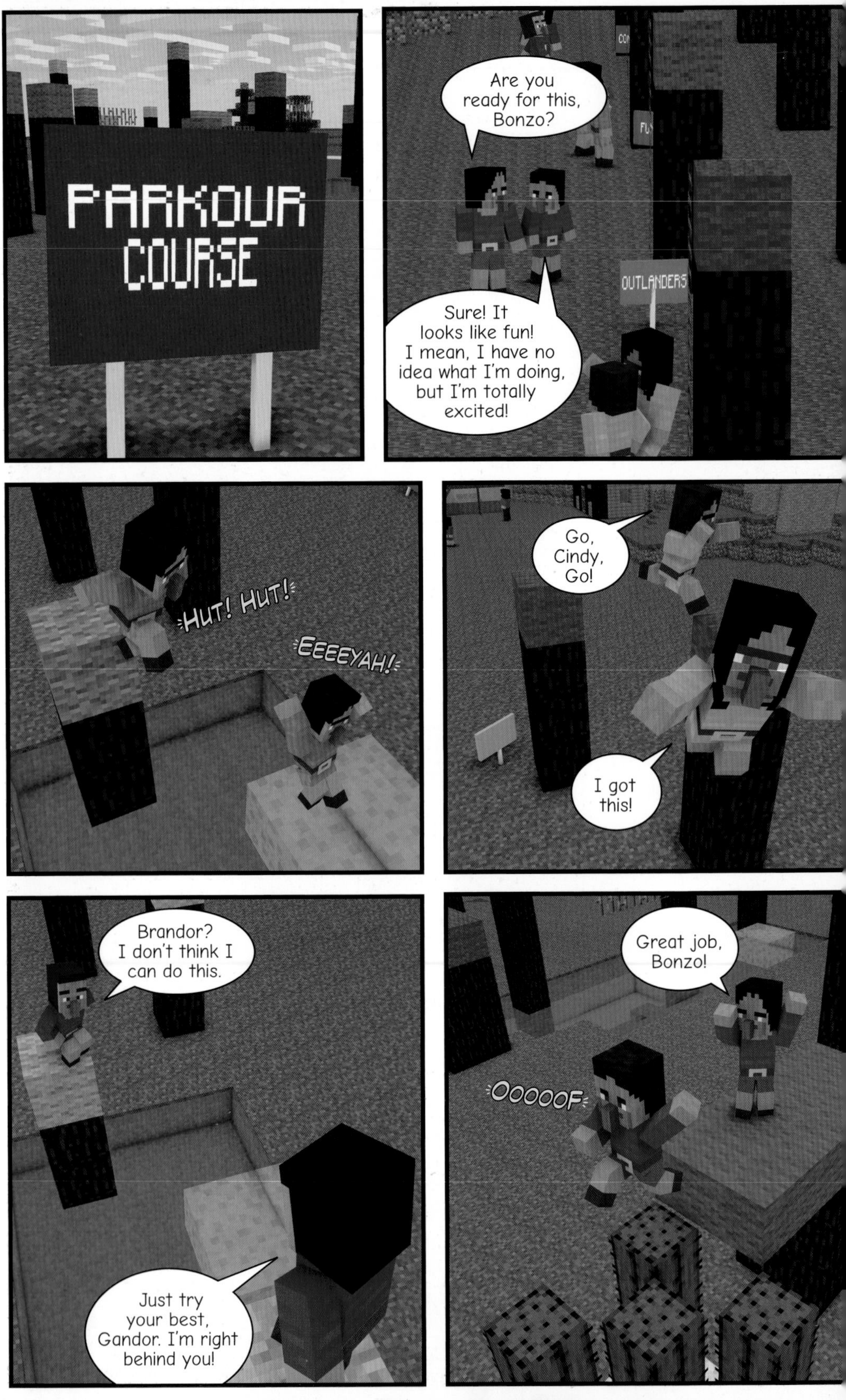
PARKOUR
COURSE
Are you ready for this, Bonzo?
Sure! It looks like fun! I mean, I have no idea what I'm doing, but I'm totally excited!
OUTLANDERS
HUT! HUT!
EEEEYAH!
Go, Cindy, Go!
I got this!
Brandor? I don't think I can do this.
Just try your best, Gandor. I'm right behind you!
Great job, Bonzo!
OOOOOF

AAAAaaahhhhhh!

Ow. I think I broke my butt.

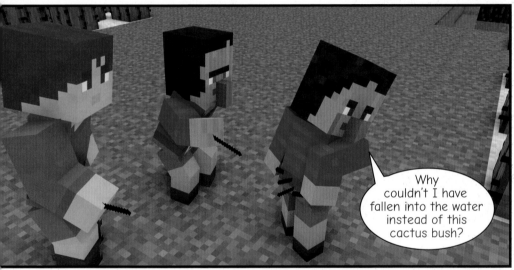

Why couldn't I have fallen into the water instead of this cactus bush?

Can we try, Dad? Please?

Please? Please? Please? Can we?

Okay, pups. But be careful!

WHEE! YAY! BEST DAY EVER!

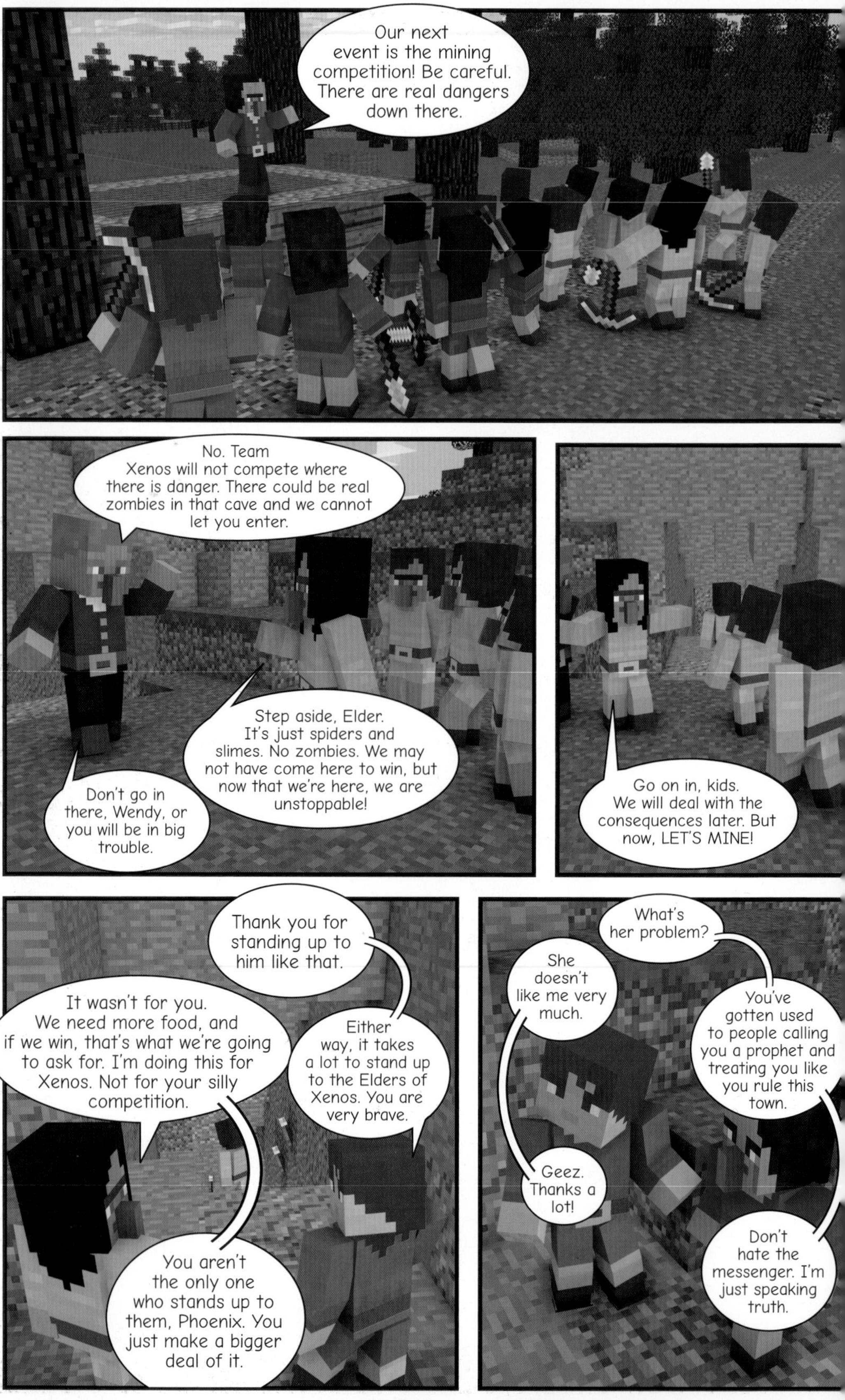

Our next event is the mining competition! Be careful. There are real dangers down there.
No. Team Xenos will not compete where there is danger. There could be real zombies in that cave and we cannot let you enter.
Step aside, Elder. It's just spiders and slimes. No zombies. We may not have come here to win, but now that we're here, we are unstoppable!
Don't go in there, Wendy, or you will be in big trouble.
Go on in, kids. We will deal with the consequences later. But now, LET'S MINE!
Thank you for standing up to him like that.
It wasn't for you. We need more food, and if we win, that's what we're going to ask for. I'm doing this for Xenos. Not for your silly competition.
Either way, it takes a lot to stand up to the Elders of Xenos. You are very brave.
You aren't the only one who stands up to them, Phoenix. You just make a bigger deal of it.
What's her problem?
She doesn't like me very much.
You've gotten used to people calling you a prophet and treating you like you rule this town.
Geez. Thanks a lot!
Don't hate the messenger. I'm just speaking truth.

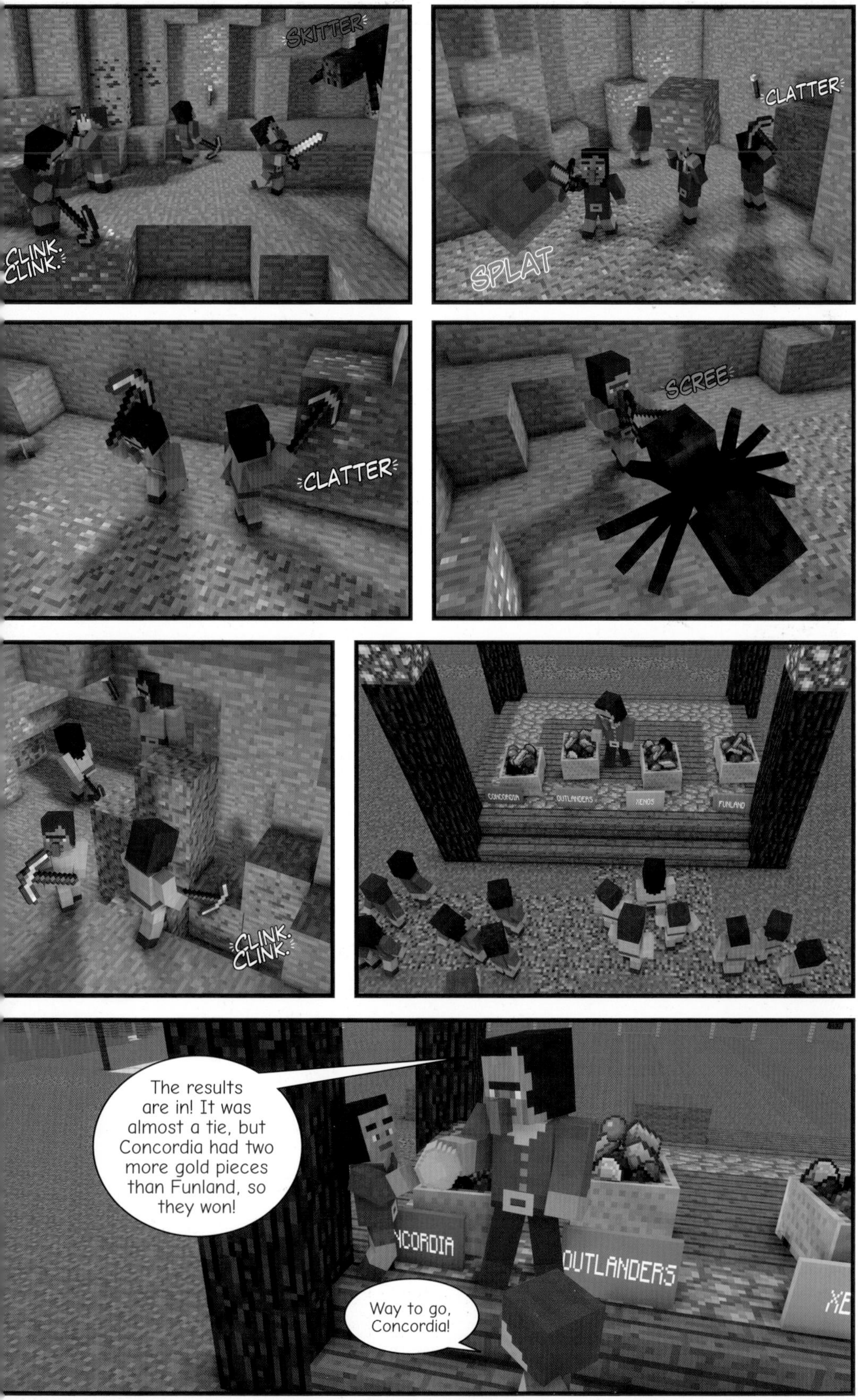

SKITTER
CLINK. CLINK.
CLATTER
SPLAT
CLATTER
SCREE
CLINK. CLINK.
CONCORDIA
OUTLANDERS
XENOS
FUNLAND
The results are in! It was almost a tie, but Concordia had two more gold pieces than Funland, so they won!
OUTLANDERS
Way to go, Concordia!

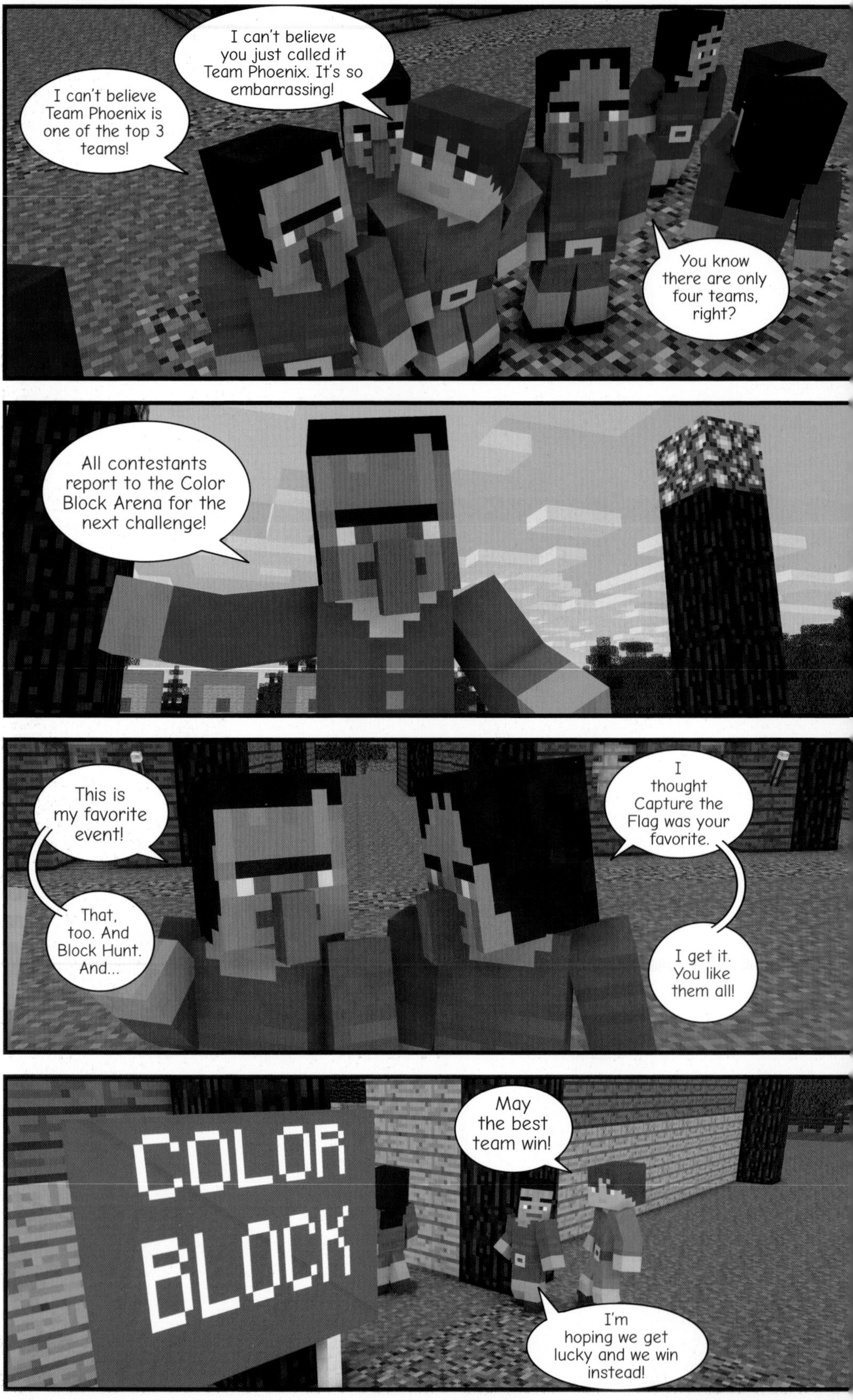
I can't believe Team Phoenix is one of the top 3 teams!
I can't believe you just called it Team Phoenix. It's so embarrassing!
You know there are only four teams, right?
All contestants report to the Color Block Arena for the next challenge!
This is my favorite event!
I thought Capture the Flag was your favorite.
That, too. And Block Hunt. And...
I get it. You like them all!
COLOR BLOCK
May the best team win!
I'm hoping we get lucky and we win instead!

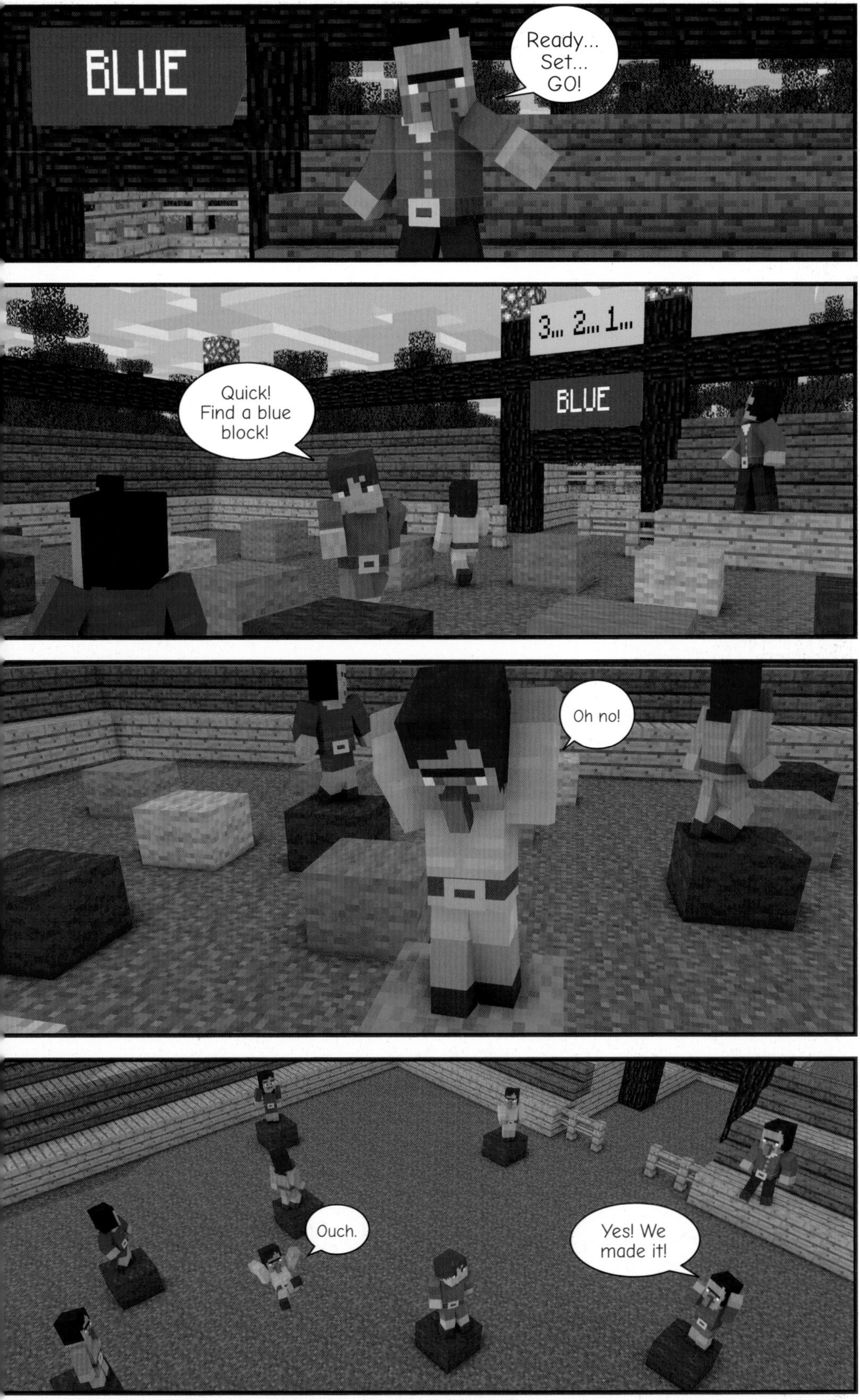
BLUE
Ready... Set... GO!
3... 2... 1...
BLUE
Quick! Find a blue block!
Oh no!
Ouch.
Yes! We made it!

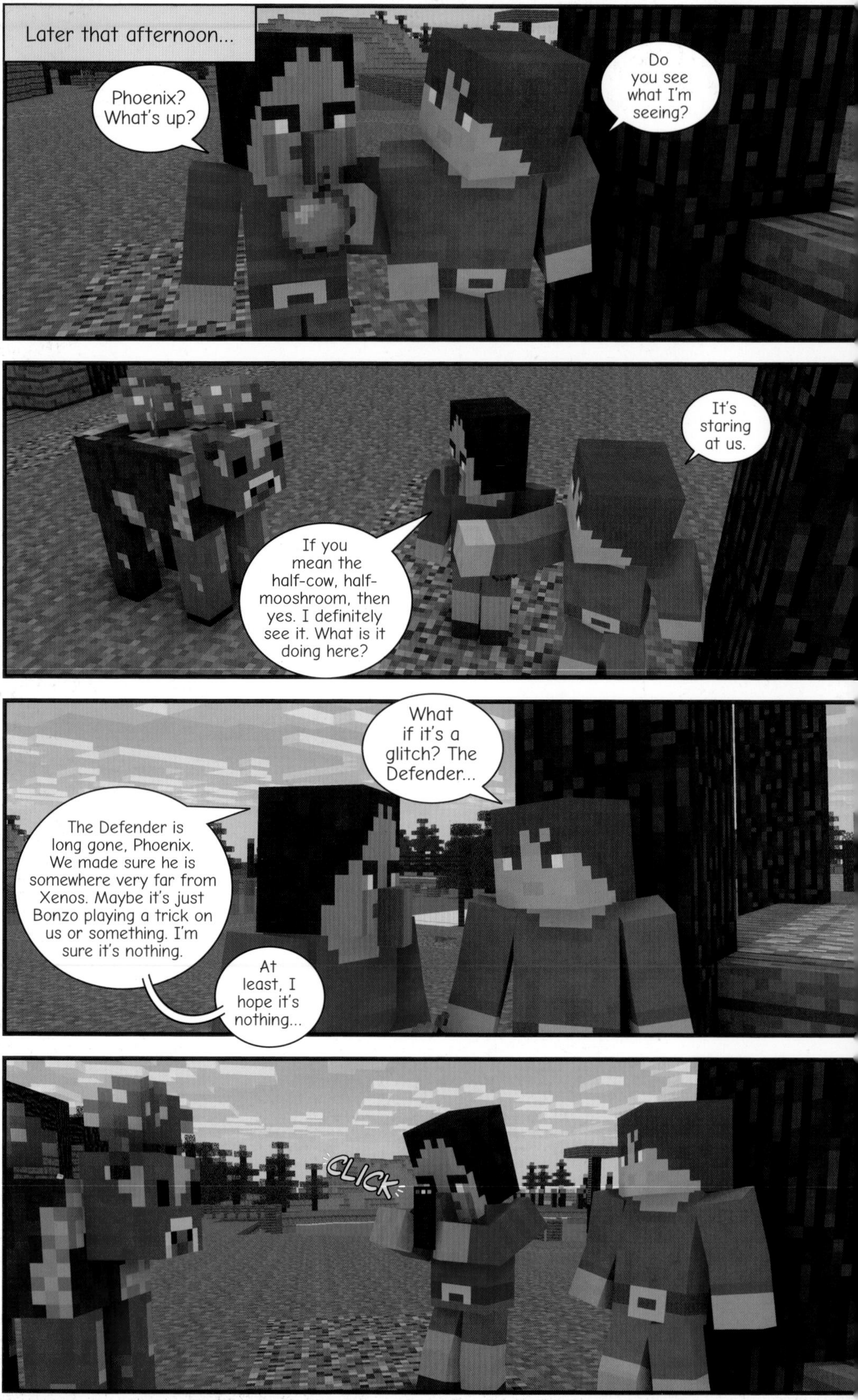
Later that afternoon...
Phoenix? What's up?
Do you see what I'm seeing?
It's staring at us.
If you mean the half-cow, half-mooshroom, then yes. I definitely see it. What is it doing here?
What if it's a glitch? The Defender...
The Defender is long gone, Phoenix. We made sure he is somewhere very far from Xenos. Maybe it's just Bonzo playing a trick on us or something. I'm sure it's nothing.
At least, I hope it's nothing...
CLICK

CHAPTER 4

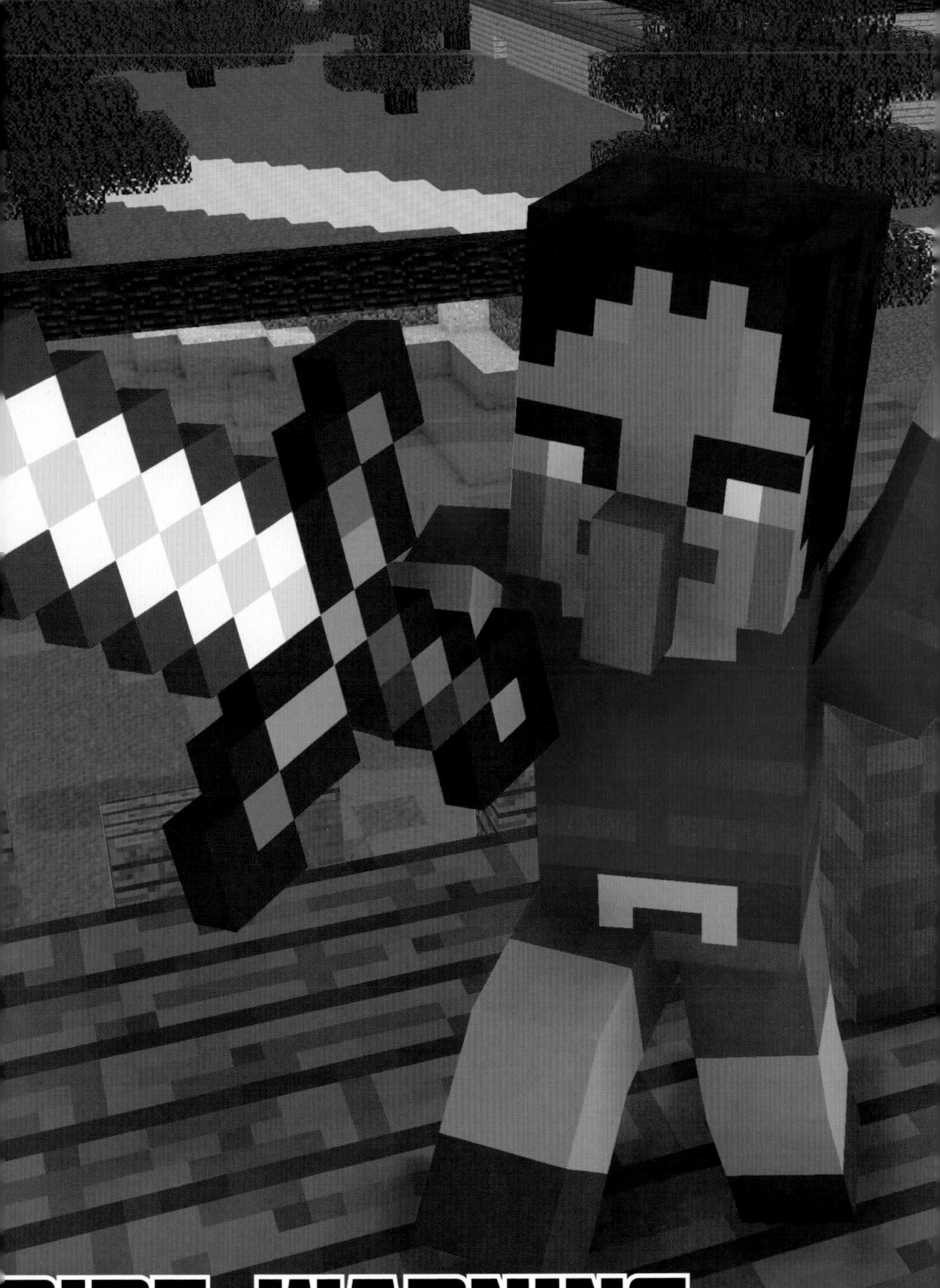

DIRE WARNING

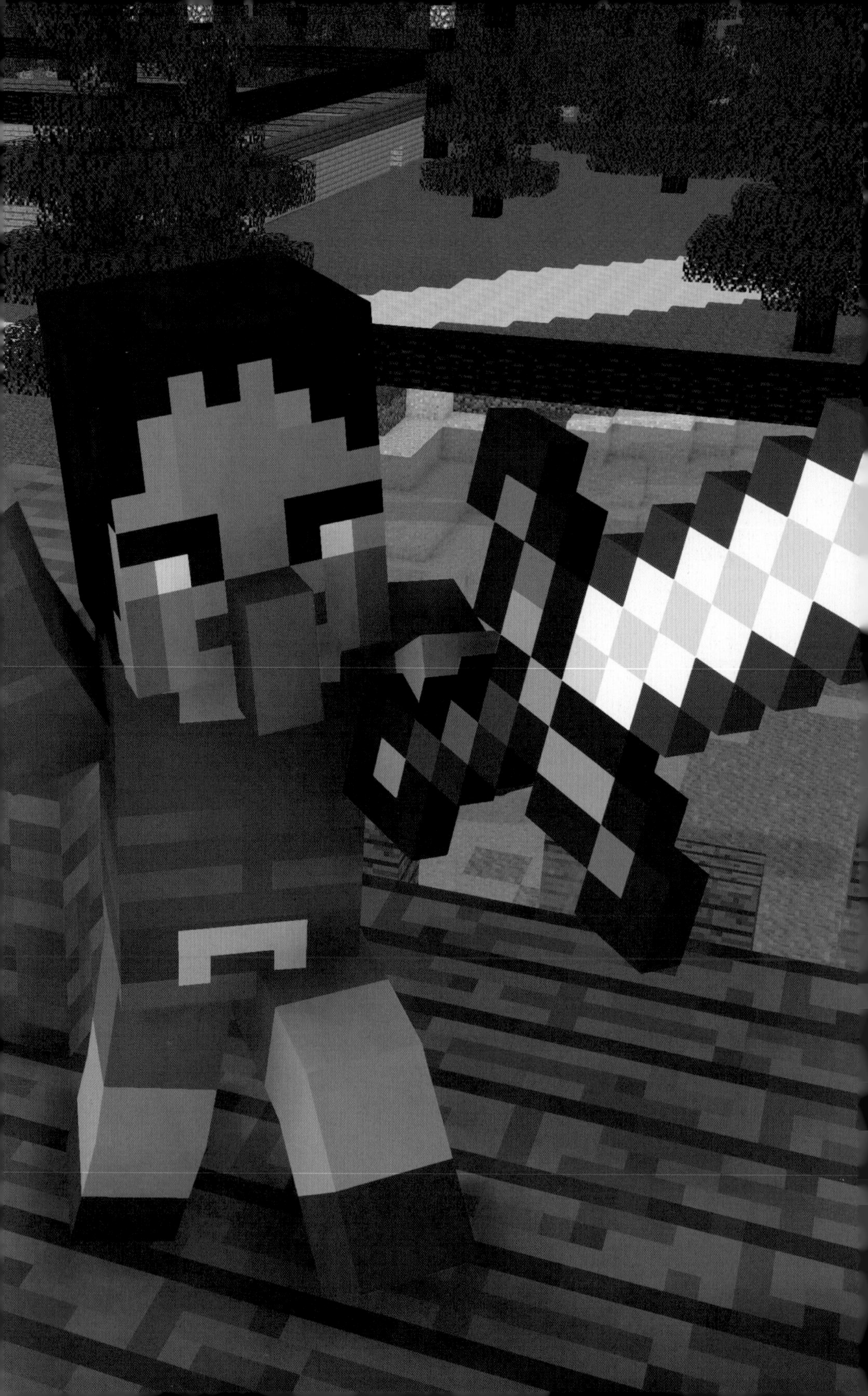

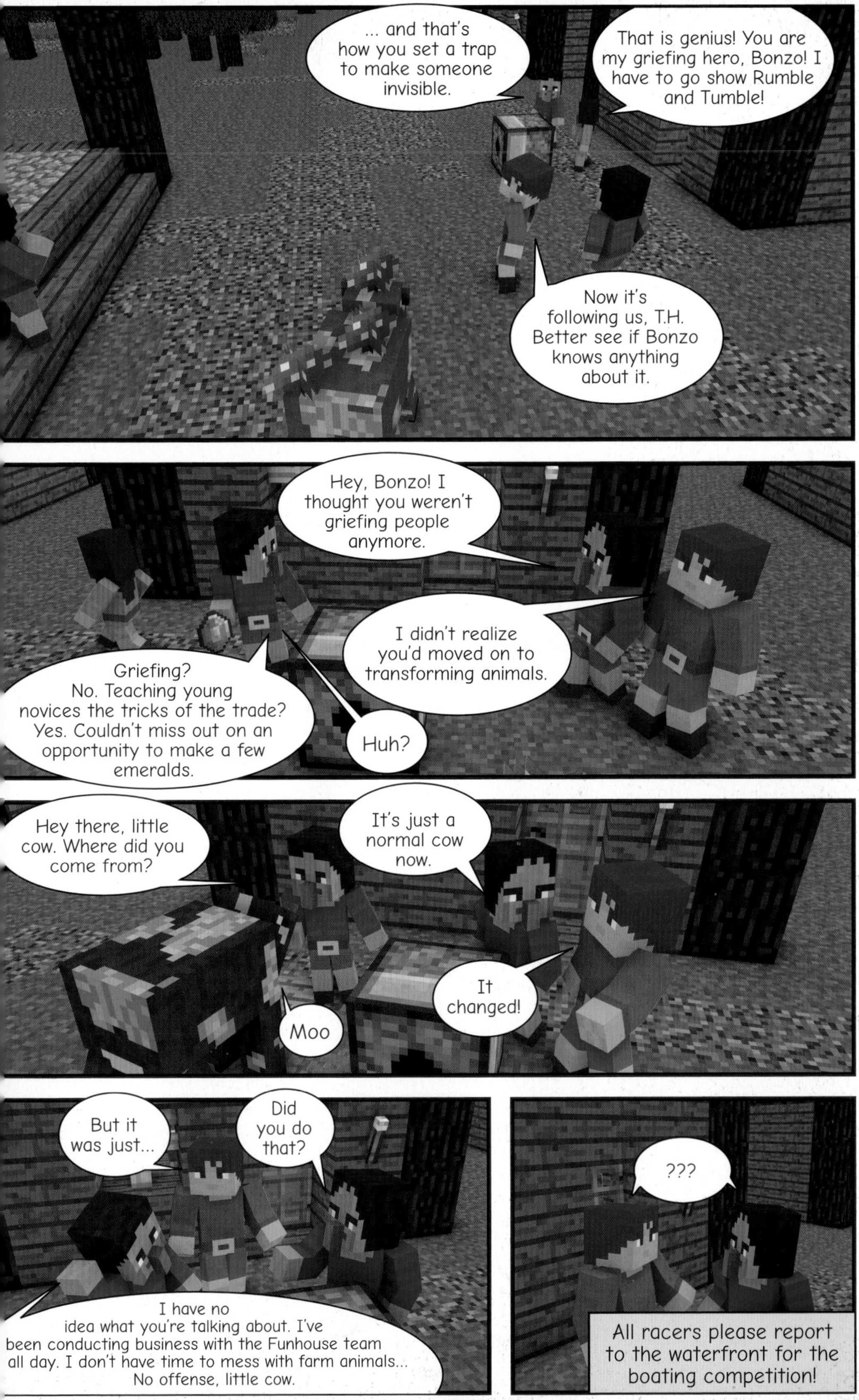
... and that's how you set a trap to make someone invisible.
That is genius! You are my griefing hero, Bonzo! I have to go show Rumble and Tumble!
Now it's following us, T.H. Better see if Bonzo knows anything about it.
Hey, Bonzo! I thought you weren't griefing people anymore.
I didn't realize you'd moved on to transforming animals.
Griefing? No. Teaching young novices the tricks of the trade? Yes. Couldn't miss out on an opportunity to make a few emeralds.
Huh?
Hey there, little cow. Where did you come from?
It's just a normal cow now.
It changed!
Moo
But it was just...
Did you do that?
I have no idea what you're talking about. I've been conducting business with the Funhouse team all day. I don't have time to mess with farm animals... No offense, little cow.
???
All racers please report to the waterfront for the boating competition!

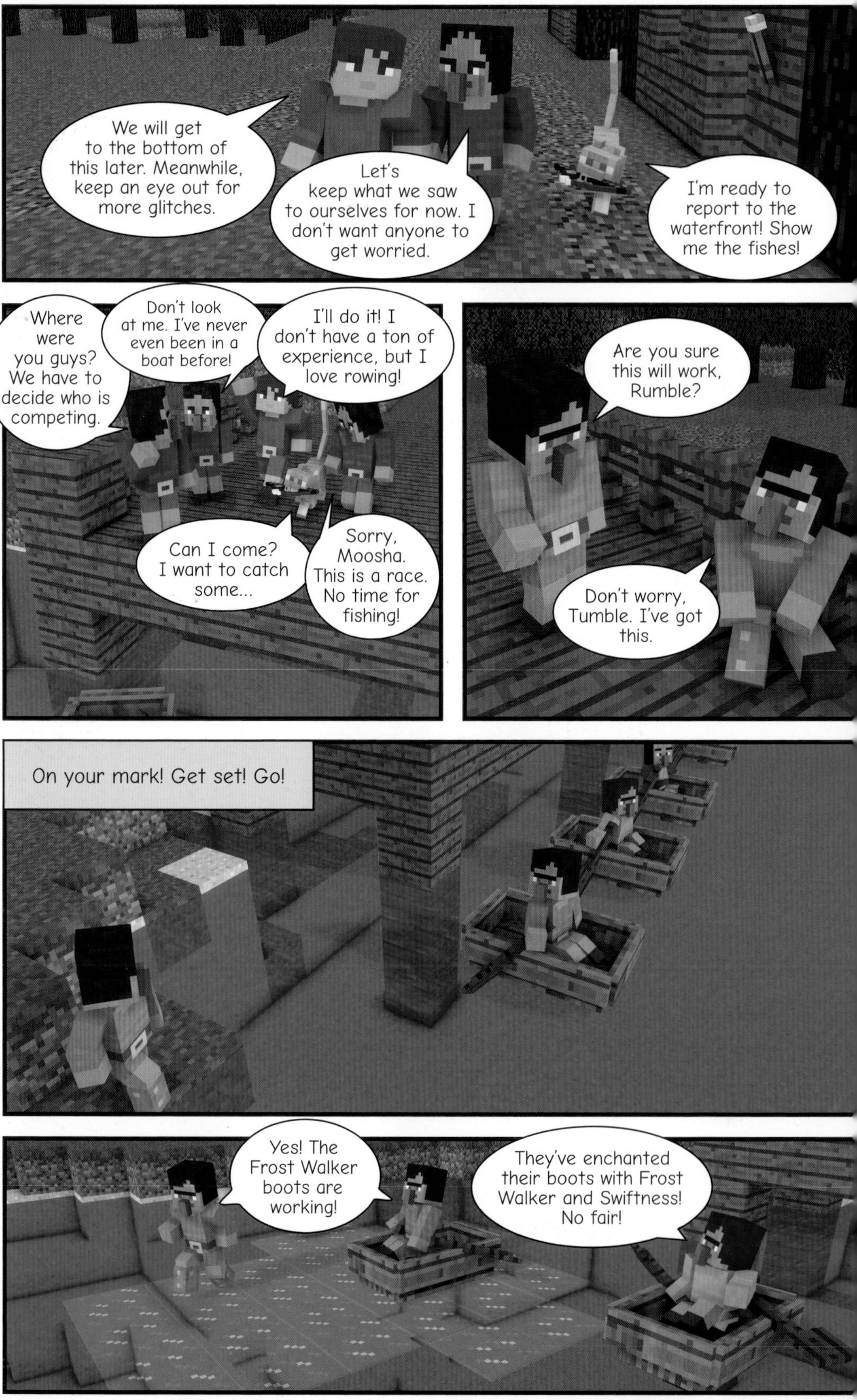
We will get to the bottom of this later. Meanwhile, keep an eye out for more glitches.
Let's keep what we saw to ourselves for now. I don't want anyone to get worried.
I'm ready to report to the waterfront! Show me the fishes!
Where were you guys? We have to decide who is competing.
Don't look at me. I've never even been in a boat before!
I'll do it! I don't have a ton of experience, but I love rowing!
Can I come? I want to catch some...
Sorry, Moosha. This is a race. No time for fishing!
Are you sure this will work, Rumble?
Don't worry, Tumble. I've got this.
On your mark! Get set! Go!
Yes! The Frost Walker boots are working!
They've enchanted their boots with Frost Walker and Swiftness! No fair!

They can't do that, can they?

Absolutely! That was a brilliant idea!

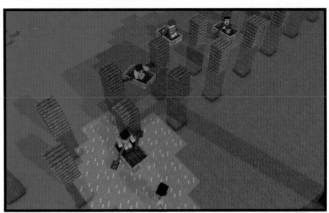

Yes!

SLAP

Well played, Rumble! That was good thinking!

Team Funland is the clear winner! Next event is fishing!

FISHING!

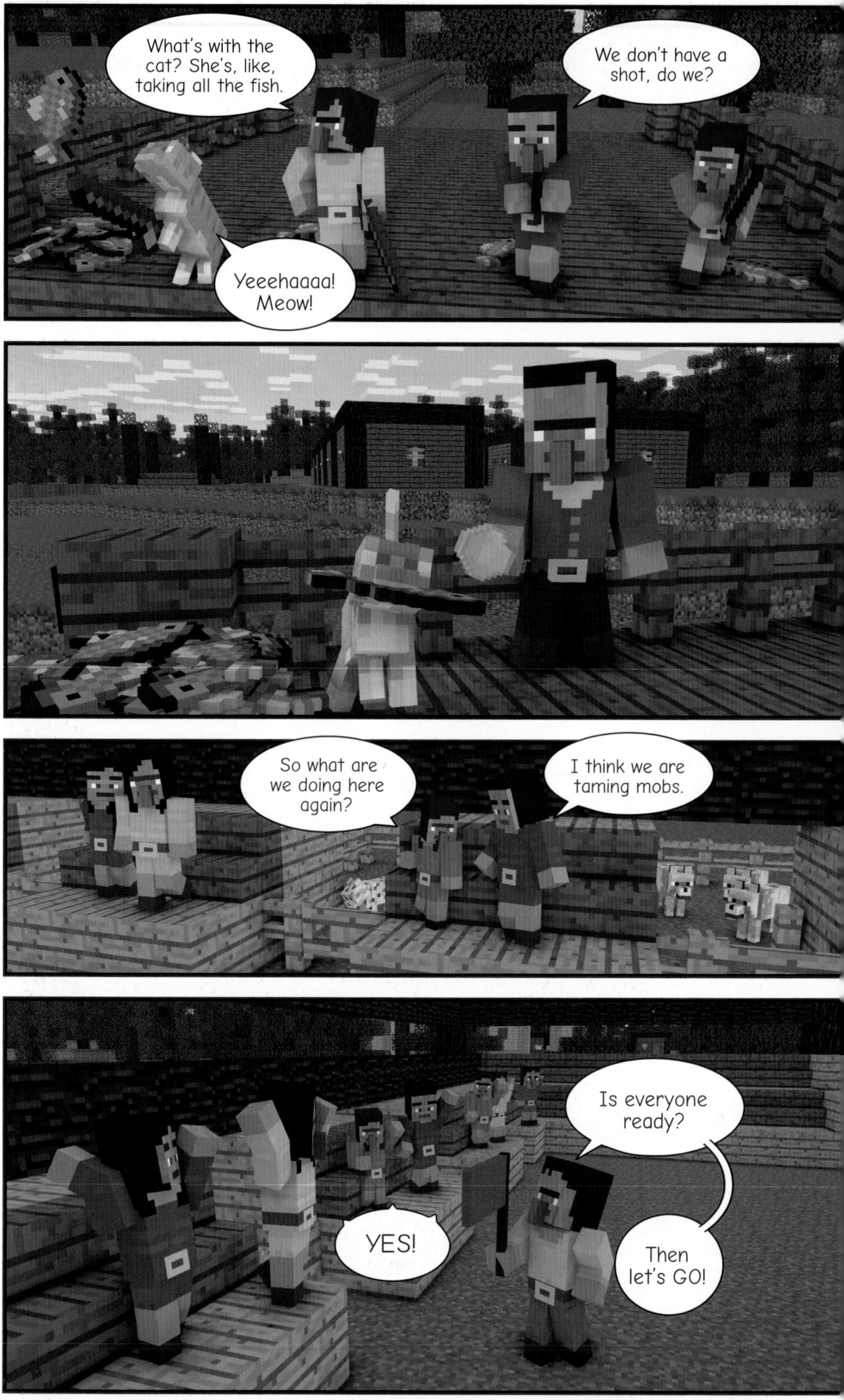
What's with the cat? She's, like, taking all the fish.
We don't have a shot, do we?
Yeeehaaaa! Meow!
So what are we doing here again?
I think we are taming mobs.
Is everyone ready?
YES!
Then let's GO!

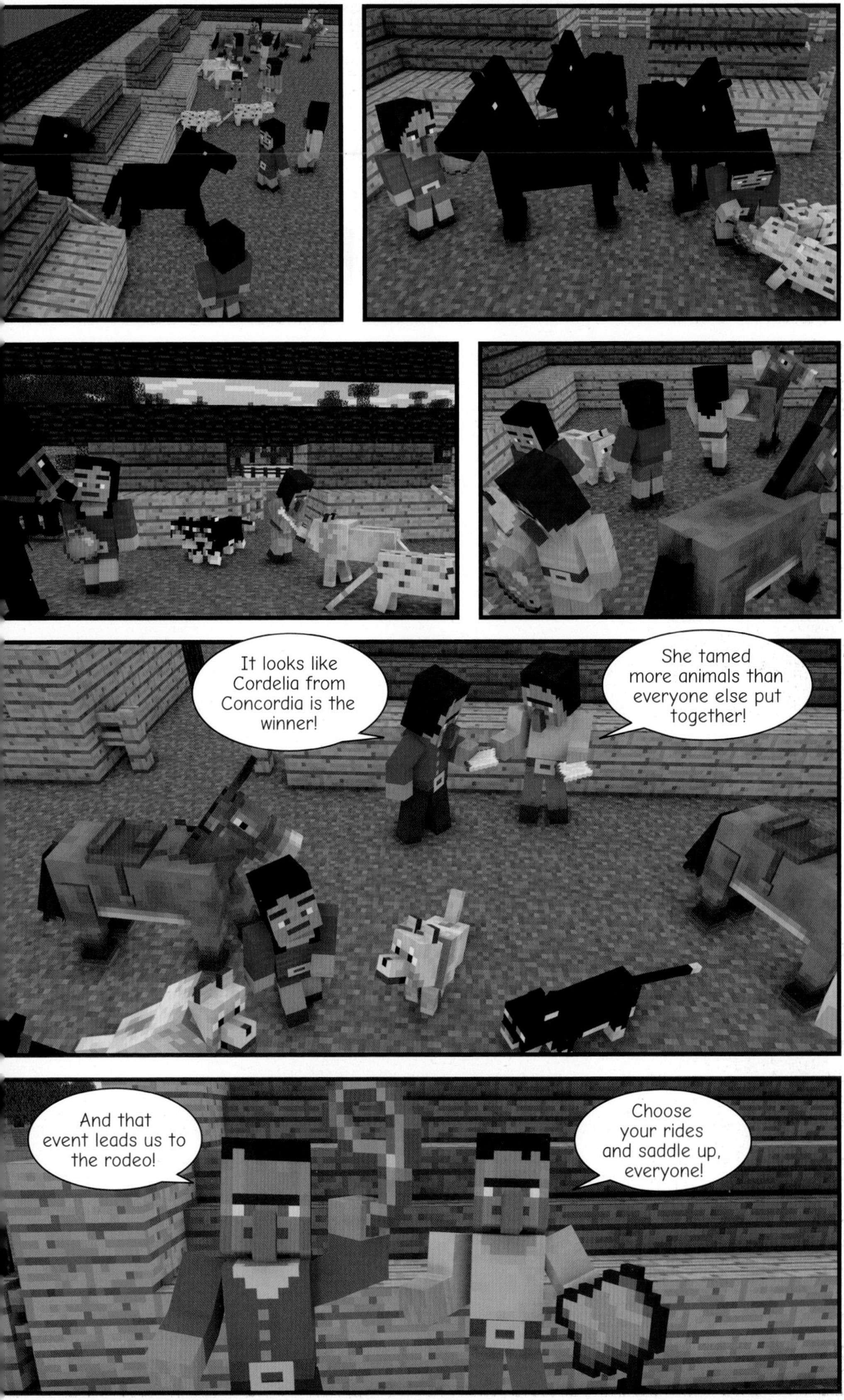
It looks like Cordelia from Concordia is the winner!
She tamed more animals than everyone else put together!
And that event leads us to the rodeo!
Choose your rides and saddle up, everyone!

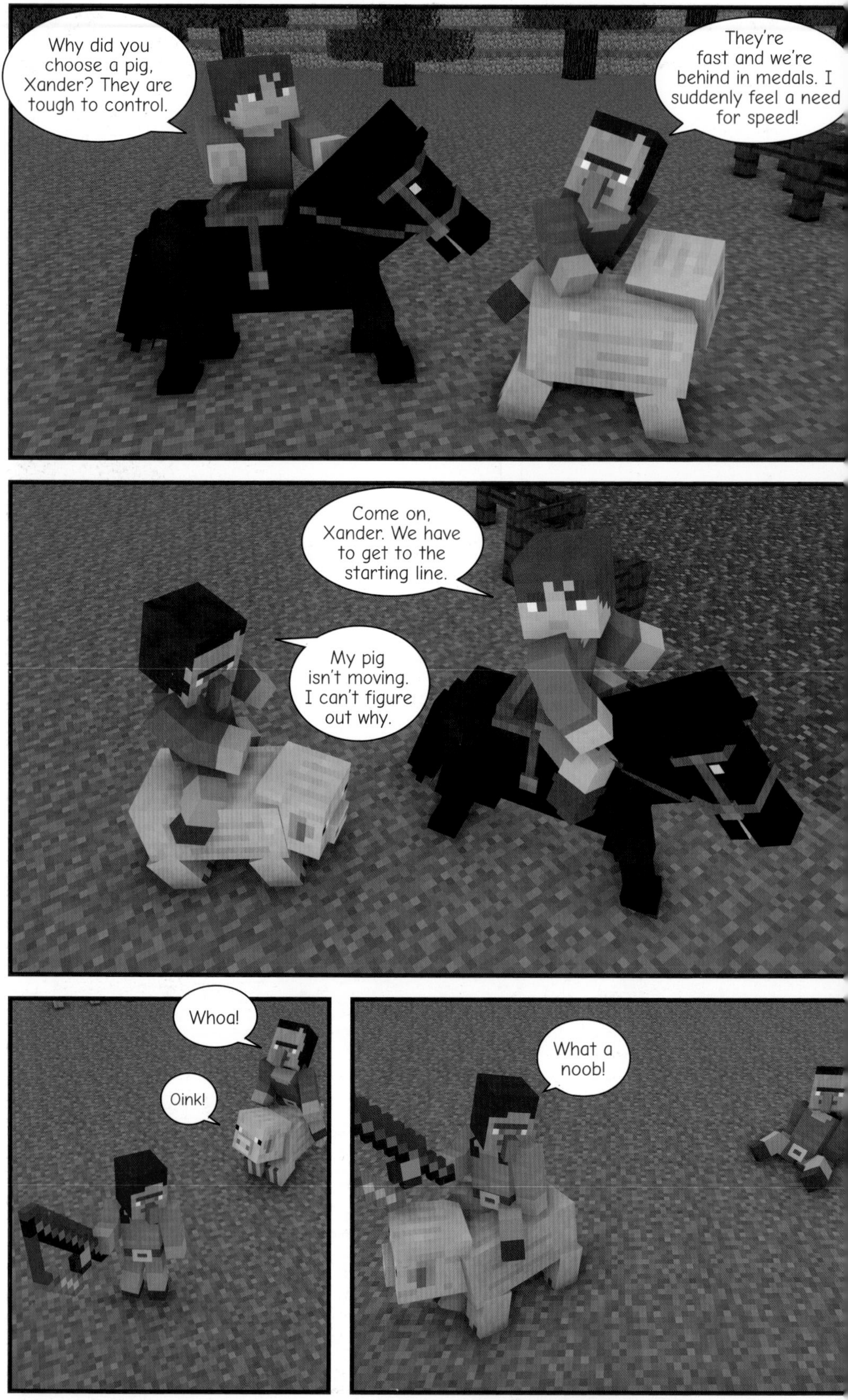
Why did you choose a pig, Xander? They are tough to control.
They're fast and we're behind in medals. I suddenly feel a need for speed!
Come on, Xander. We have to get to the starting line.
My pig isn't moving. I can't figure out why.
Whoa!
Oink!
What a noob!

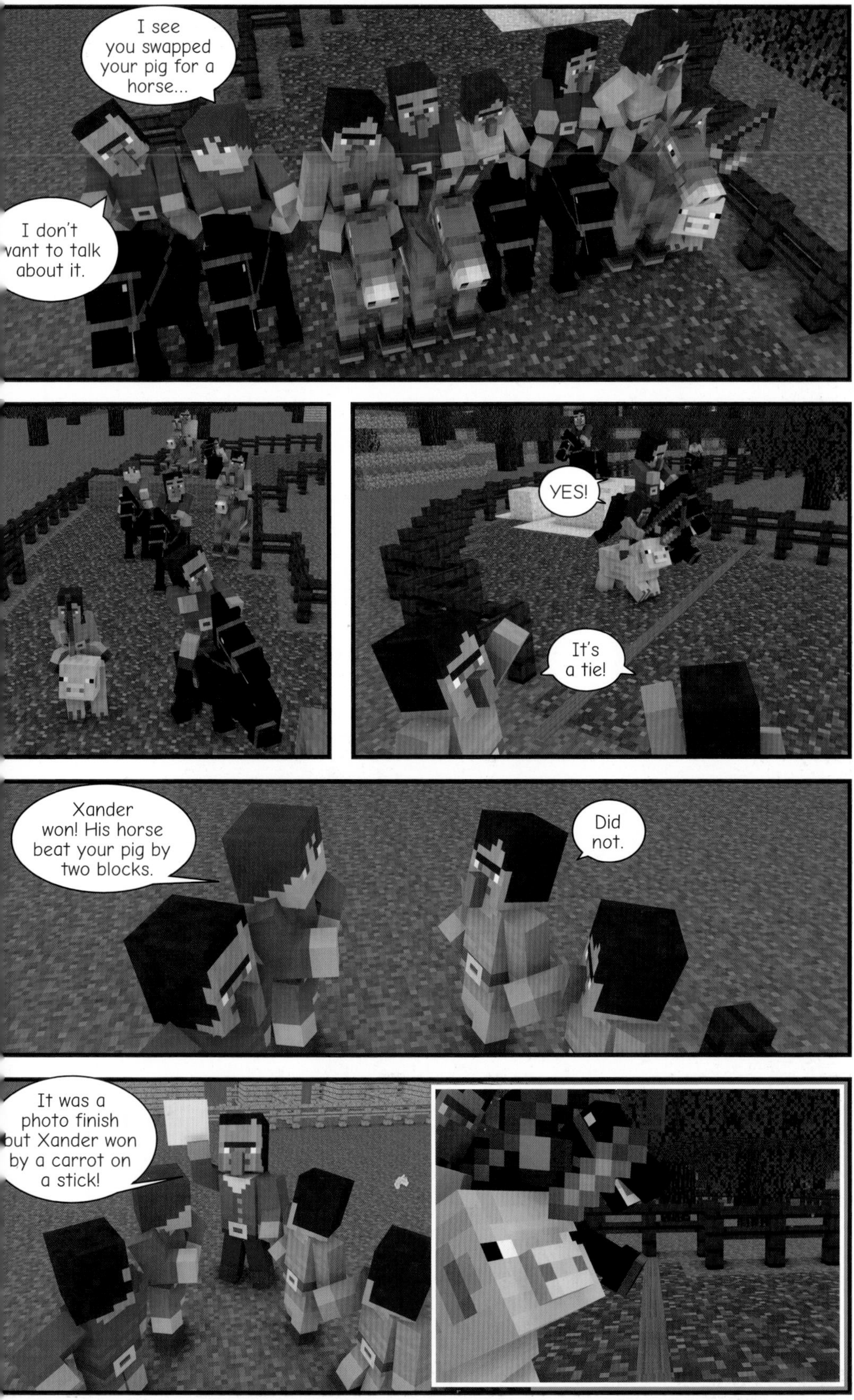
I see you swapped your pig for a horse...
I don't vant to talk about it.
YES!
It's a tie!
Xander won! His horse beat your pig by two blocks.
Did not.
It was a photo finish but Xander won by a carrot on a stick!

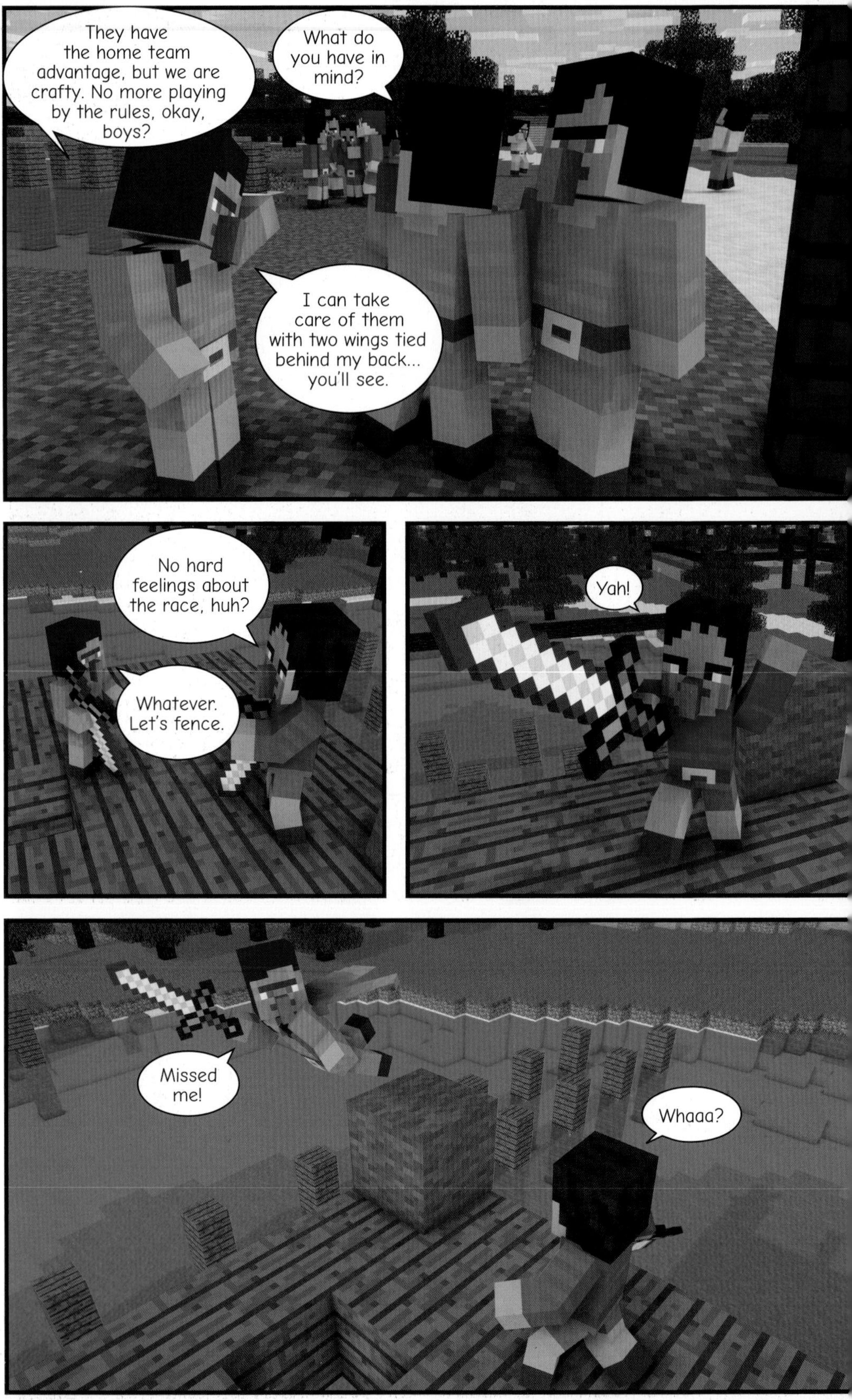
They have the home team advantage, but we are crafty. No more playing by the rules, okay, boys?
What do you have in mind?
I can take care of them with two wings tied behind my back... you'll see.
No hard feelings about the race, huh?
Whatever. Let's fence.
Yah!
Missed me!
Whaaa?

Whoooaaaa

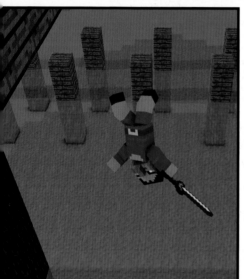

Ha ha! You're all wet!

I should have known you'd try something like that.

Sorry, T.H. When I suggested Water Fencing as an activity, I guess I didn't think it through.

Next time we play, let's fence over a nice cushion of slime blocks!

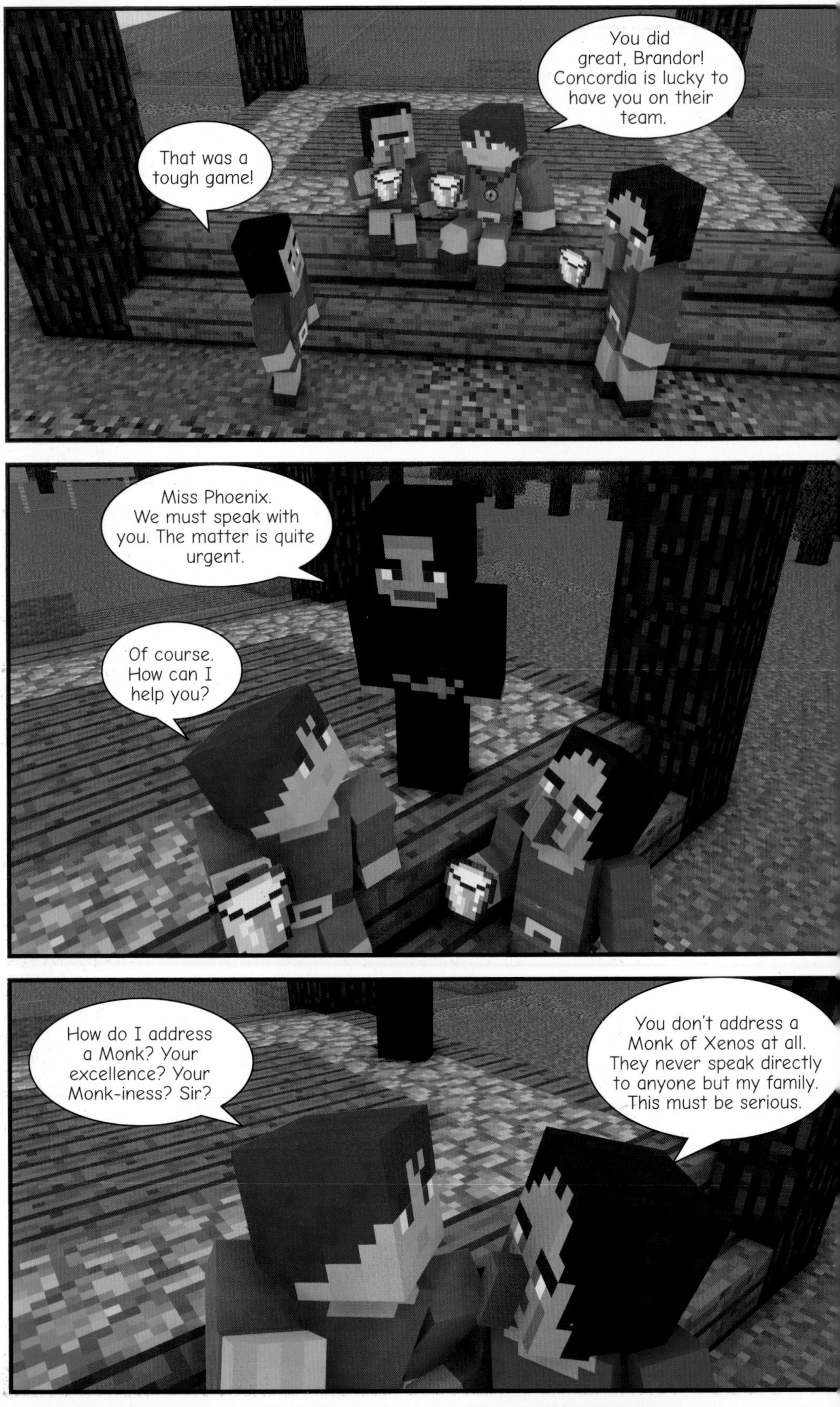
You did great, Brandor! Concordia is lucky to have you on their team.
That was a tough game!
Miss Phoenix. We must speak with you. The matter is quite urgent.
Of course. How can I help you?
How do I address a Monk? Your excellence? Your Monk-iness? Sir?
You don't address a Monk of Xenos at all. They never speak directly to anyone but my family. This must be serious.

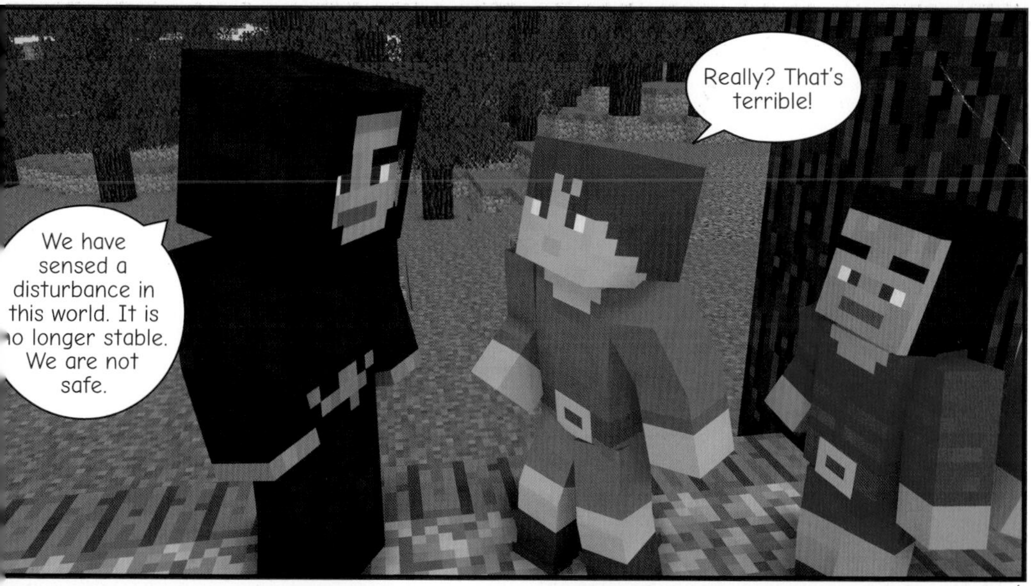
We have sensed a disturbance in this world. It is no longer stable. We are not safe.
Really? That's terrible!

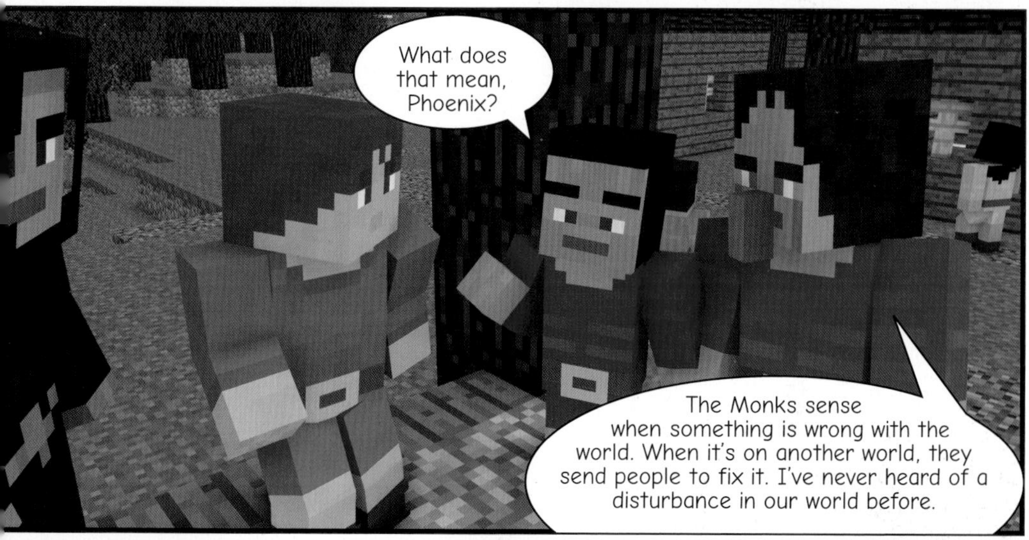
What does that mean, Phoenix?
The Monks sense when something is wrong with the world. When it's on another world, they send people to fix it. I've never heard of a disturbance in our world before.

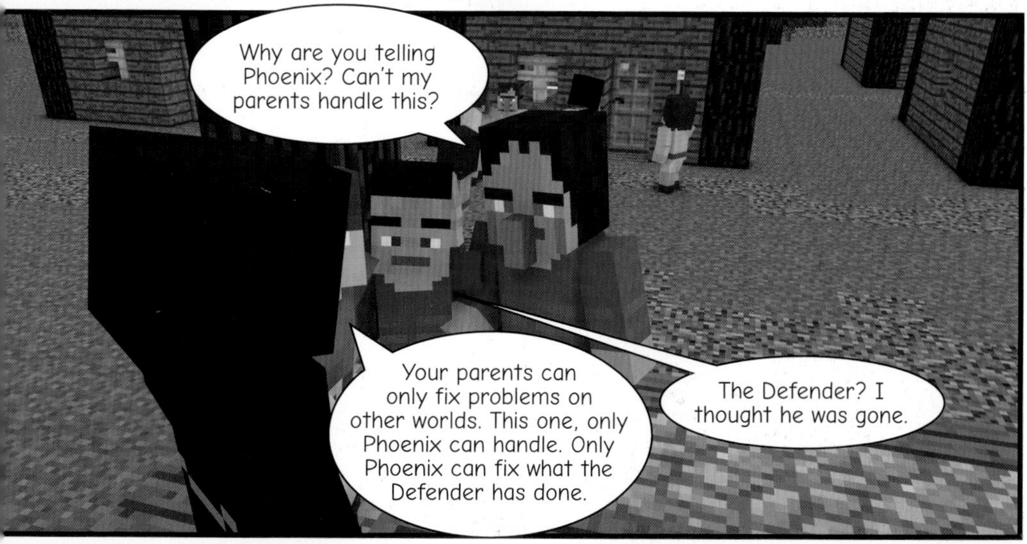
Why are you telling Phoenix? Can't my parents handle this?
Your parents can only fix problems on other worlds. This one, only Phoenix can handle. Only Phoenix can fix what the Defender has done.
The Defender? I thought he was gone.

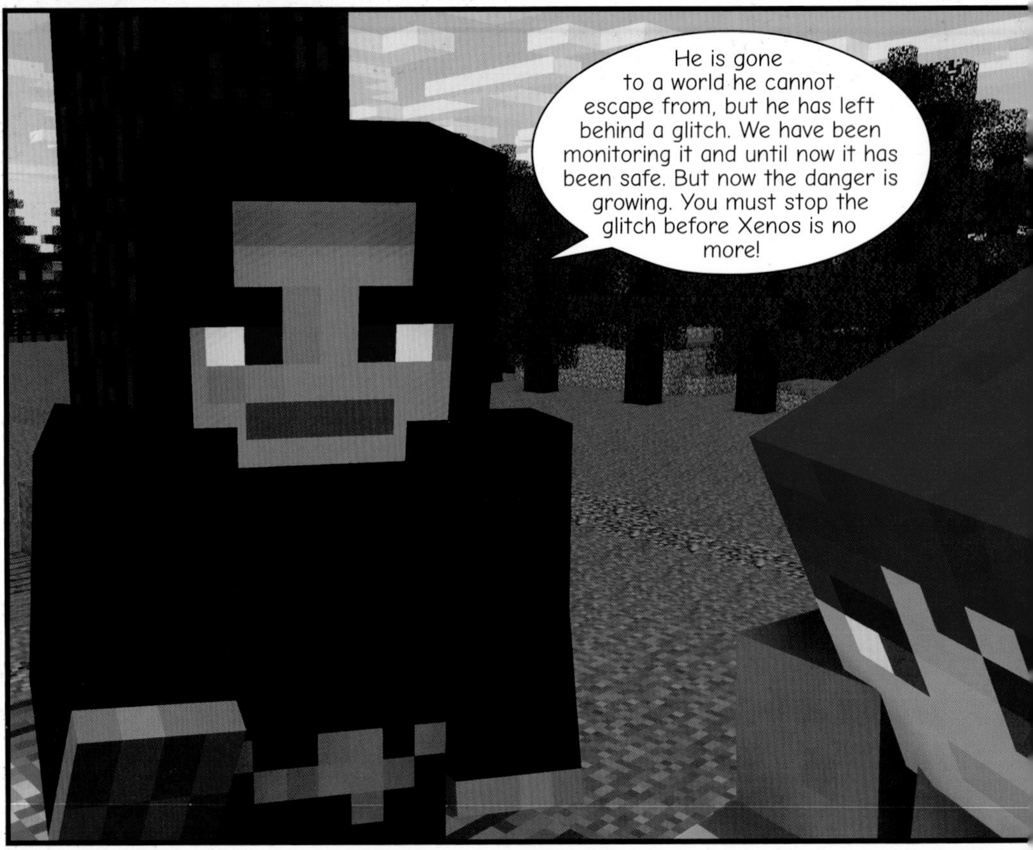
He is gone to a world he cannot escape from, but he has left behind a glitch. We have been monitoring it and until now it has been safe. But now the danger is growing. You must stop the glitch before Xenos is no more!

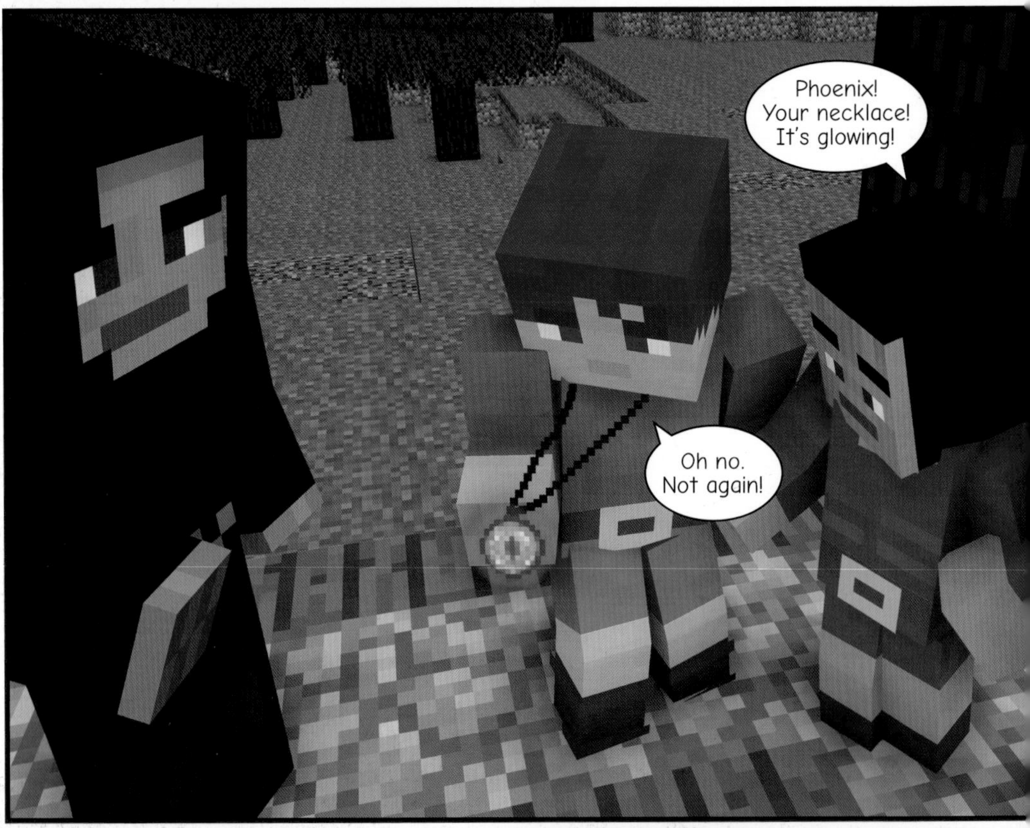
Phoenix! Your necklace! It's glowing!
Oh no. Not again!

CHAPTER 5

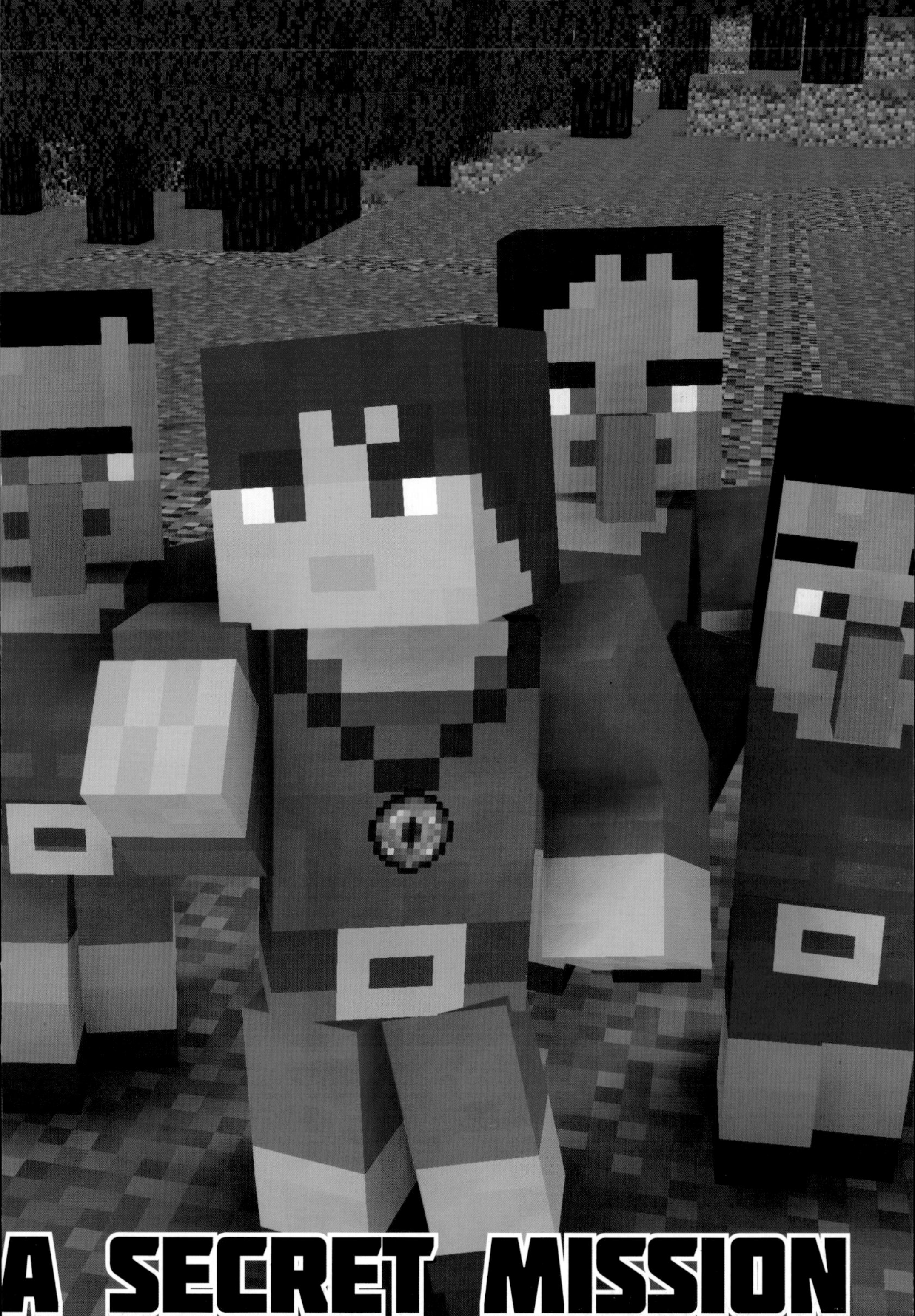

A SECRET MISSION

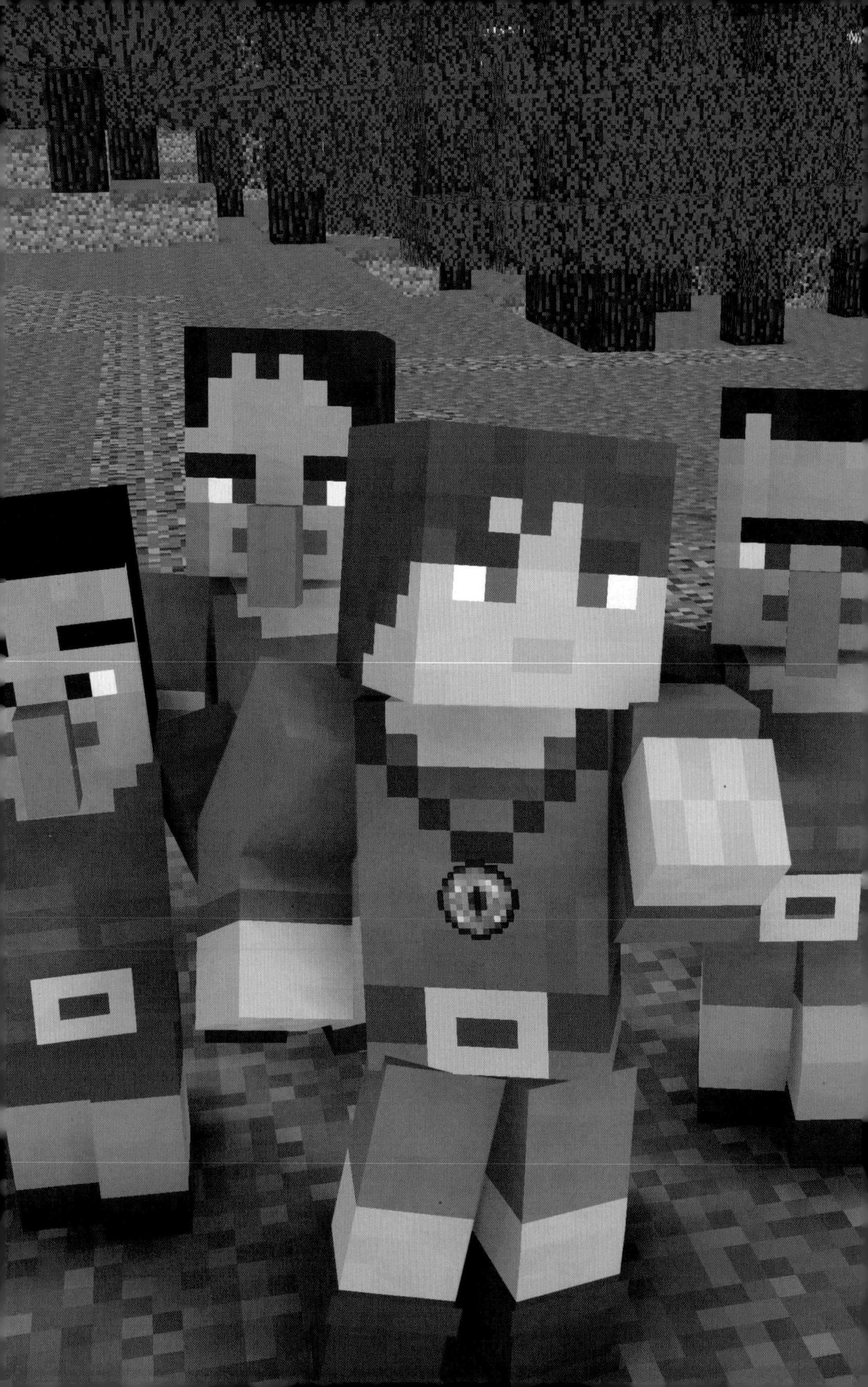

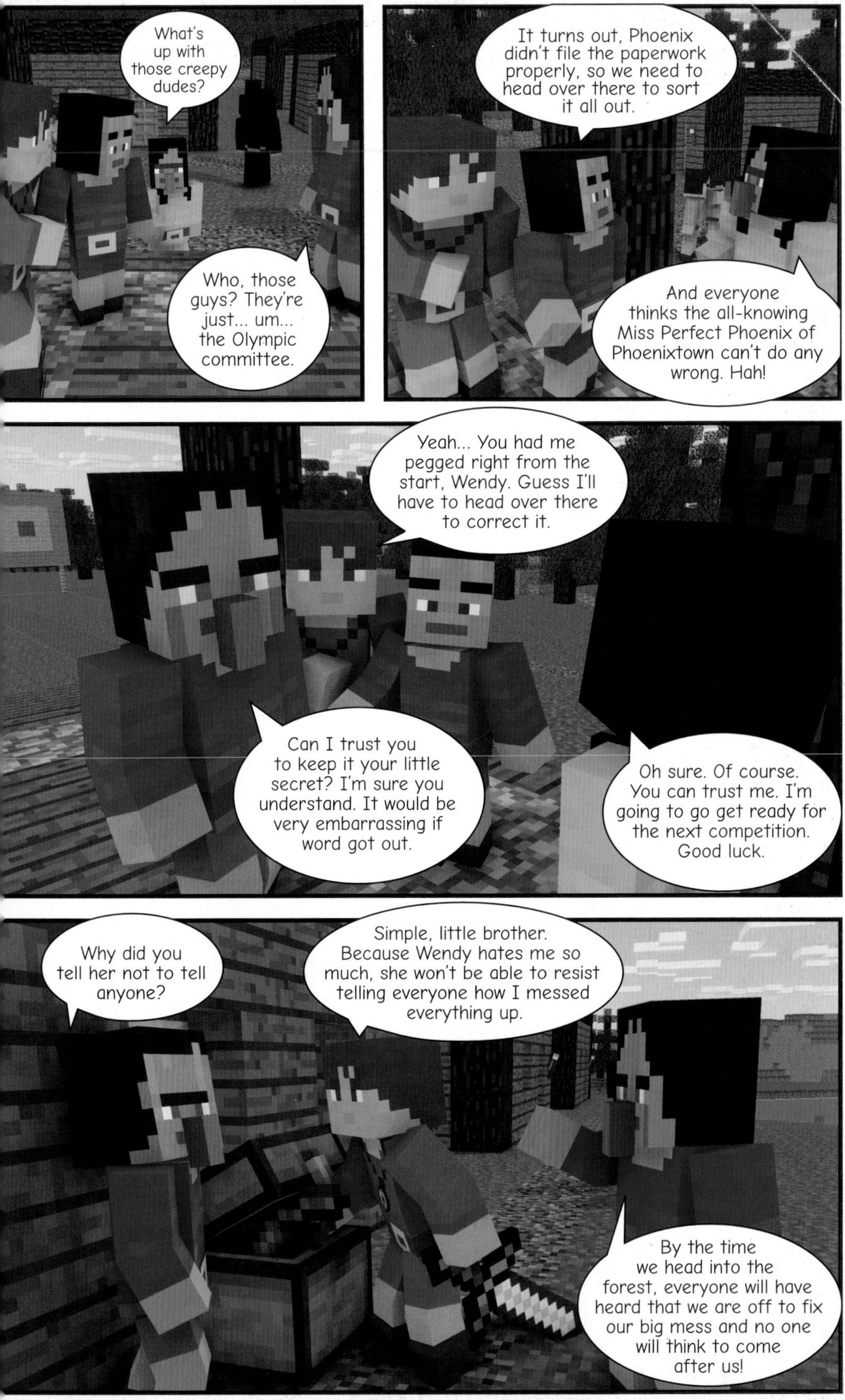
What's up with those creepy dudes?
Who, those guys? They're just... um... the Olympic committee.
It turns out, Phoenix didn't file the paperwork properly, so we need to head over there to sort it all out.
And everyone thinks the all-knowing Miss Perfect Phoenix of Phoenixtown can't do any wrong. Hah!
Yeah... You had me pegged right from the start, Wendy. Guess I'll have to head over there to correct it.
Can I trust you to keep it your little secret? I'm sure you understand. It would be very embarrassing if word got out.
Oh sure. Of course. You can trust me. I'm going to go get ready for the next competition. Good luck.
Why did you tell her not to tell anyone?
Simple, little brother. Because Wendy hates me so much, she won't be able to resist telling everyone how I messed everything up.
By the time we head into the forest, everyone will have heard that we are off to fix our big mess and no one will think to come after us!

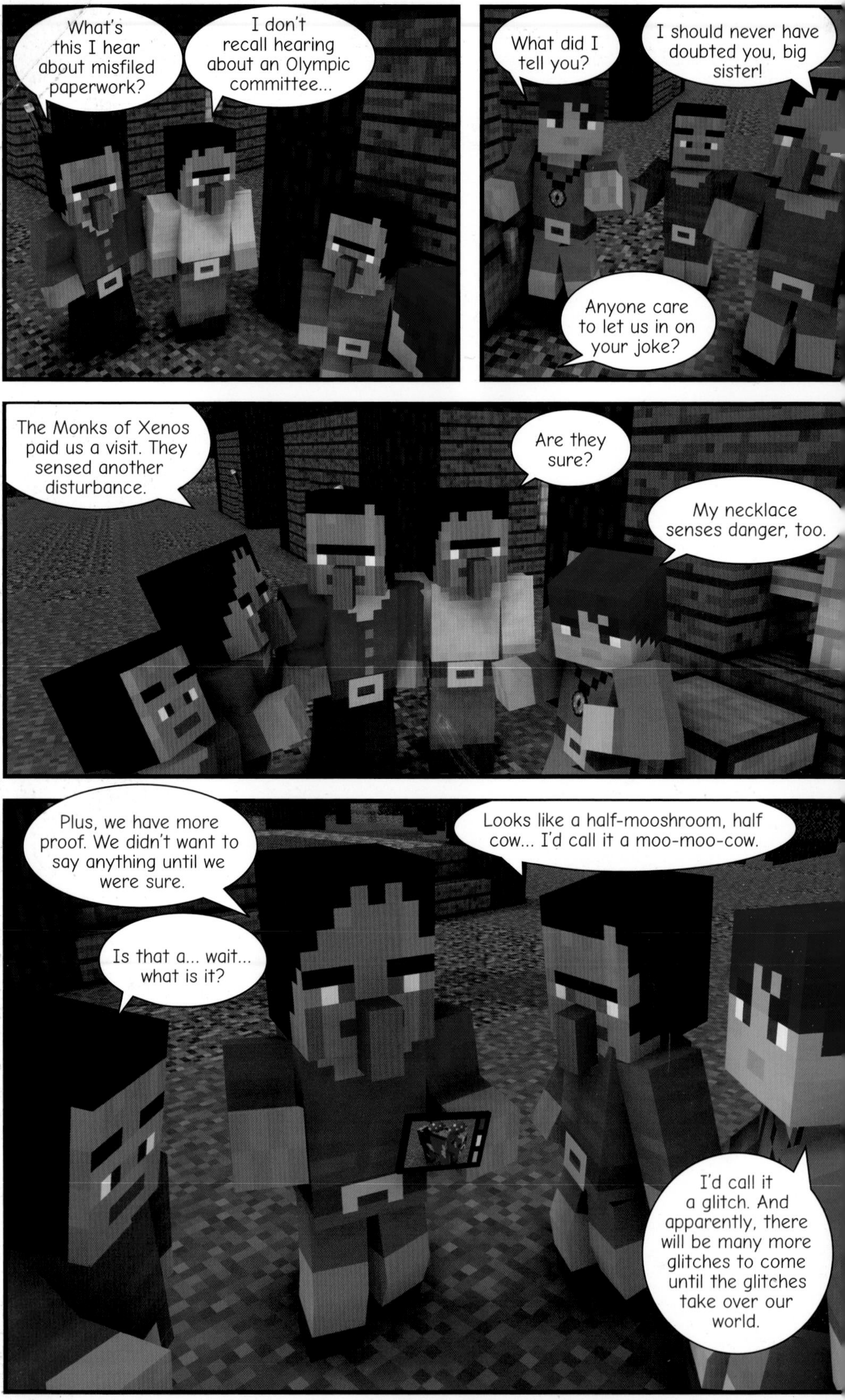
What's this I hear about misfiled paperwork?
I don't recall hearing about an Olympic committee...
What did I tell you?
I should never have doubted you, big sister!
Anyone care to let us in on your joke?
The Monks of Xenos paid us a visit. They sensed another disturbance.
Are they sure?
My necklace senses danger, too.
Plus, we have more proof. We didn't want to say anything until we were sure.
Is that a... wait... what is it?
Looks like a half-mooshroom, half cow... I'd call it a moo-moo-cow.
I'd call it a glitch. And apparently, there will be many more glitches to come until the glitches take over our world.

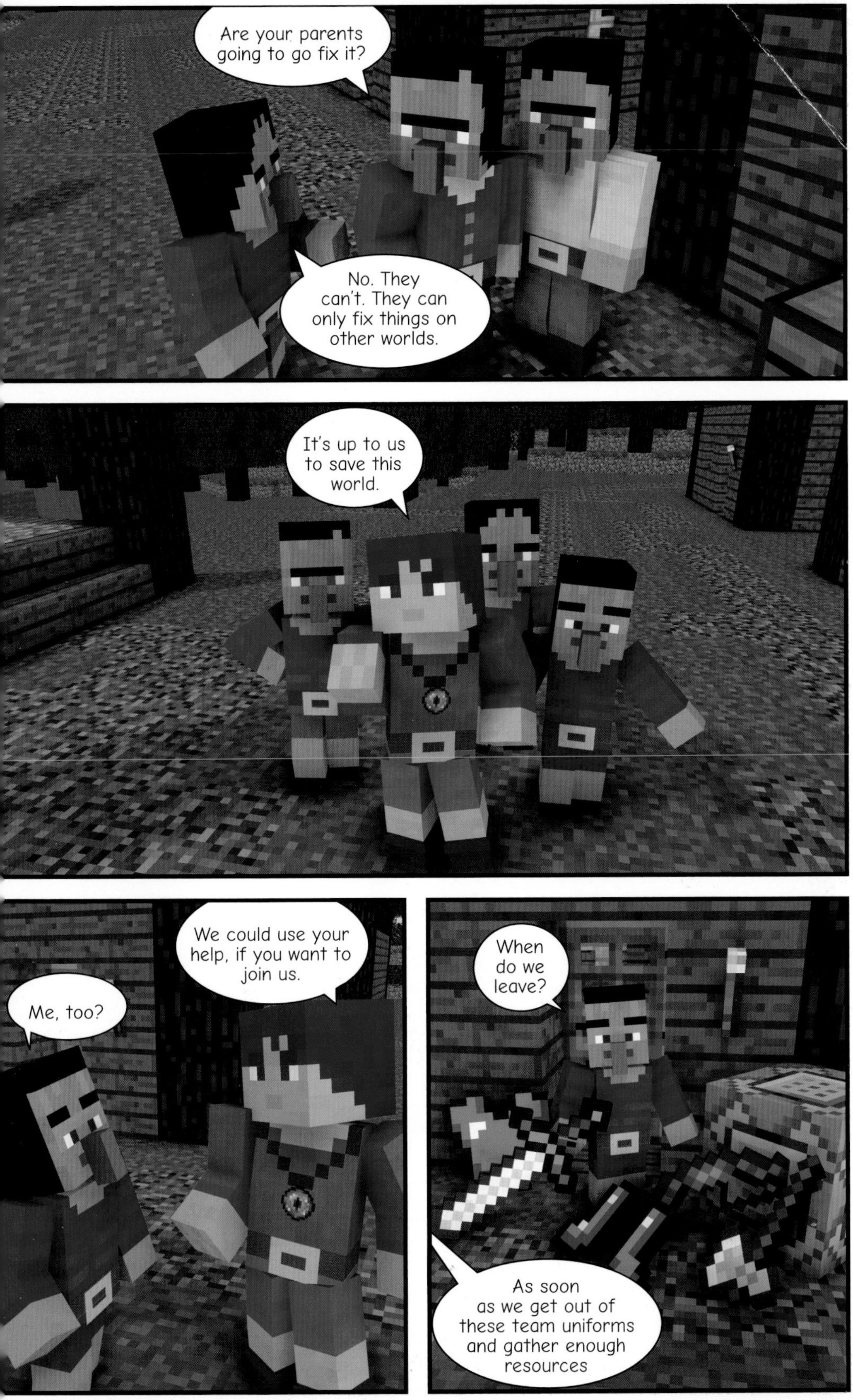
Are your parents going to go fix it?
No. They can't. They can only fix things on other worlds.
It's up to us to save this world.
We could use your help, if you want to join us.
Me, too?
When do we leave?
As soon as we get out of these team uniforms and gather enough resources

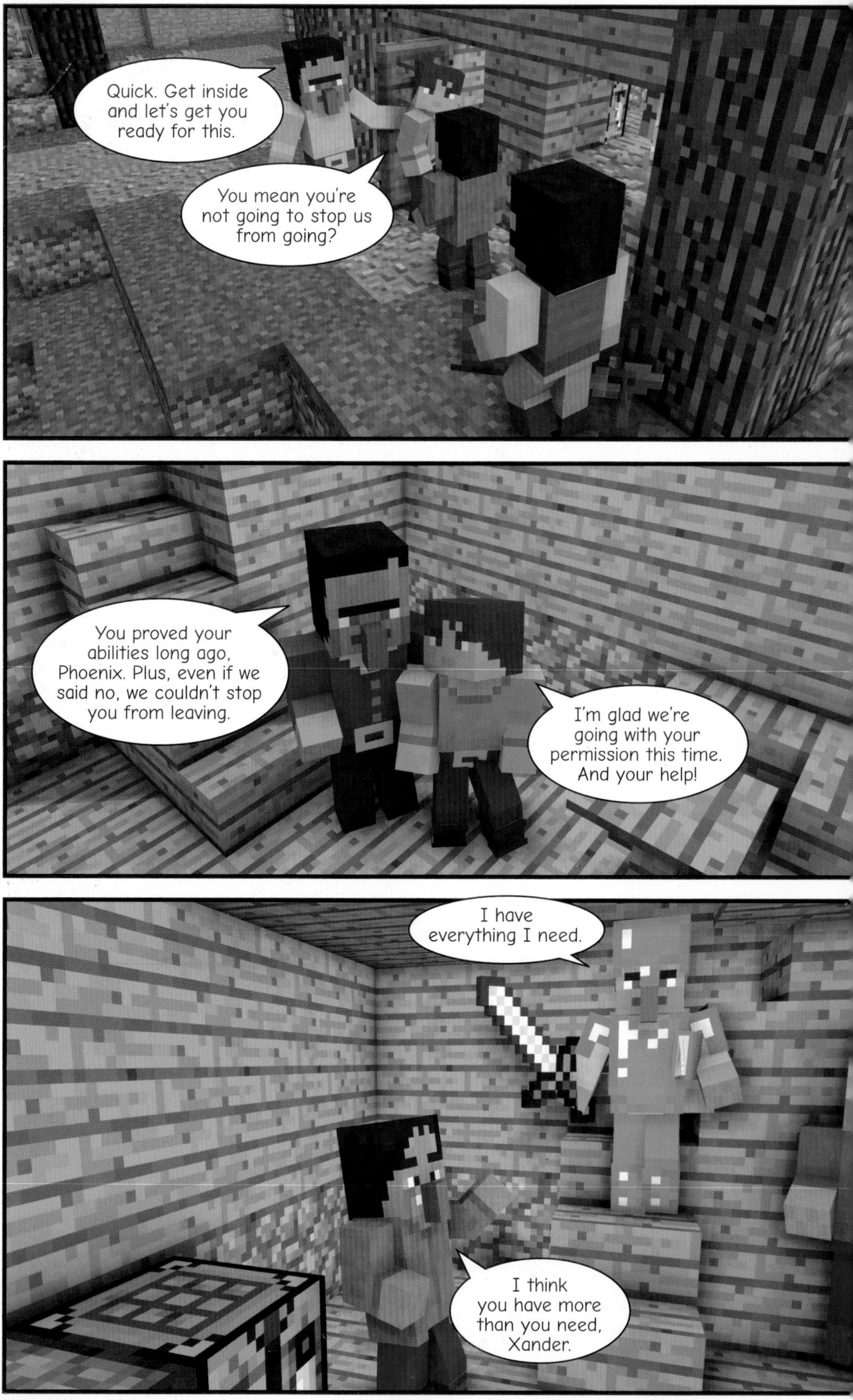
Quick. Get inside and let's get you ready for this.
You mean you're not going to stop us from going?
You proved your abilities long ago, Phoenix. Plus, even if we said no, we couldn't stop you from leaving.
I'm glad we're going with your permission this time. And your help!
I have everything I need.
I think you have more than you need, Xander.

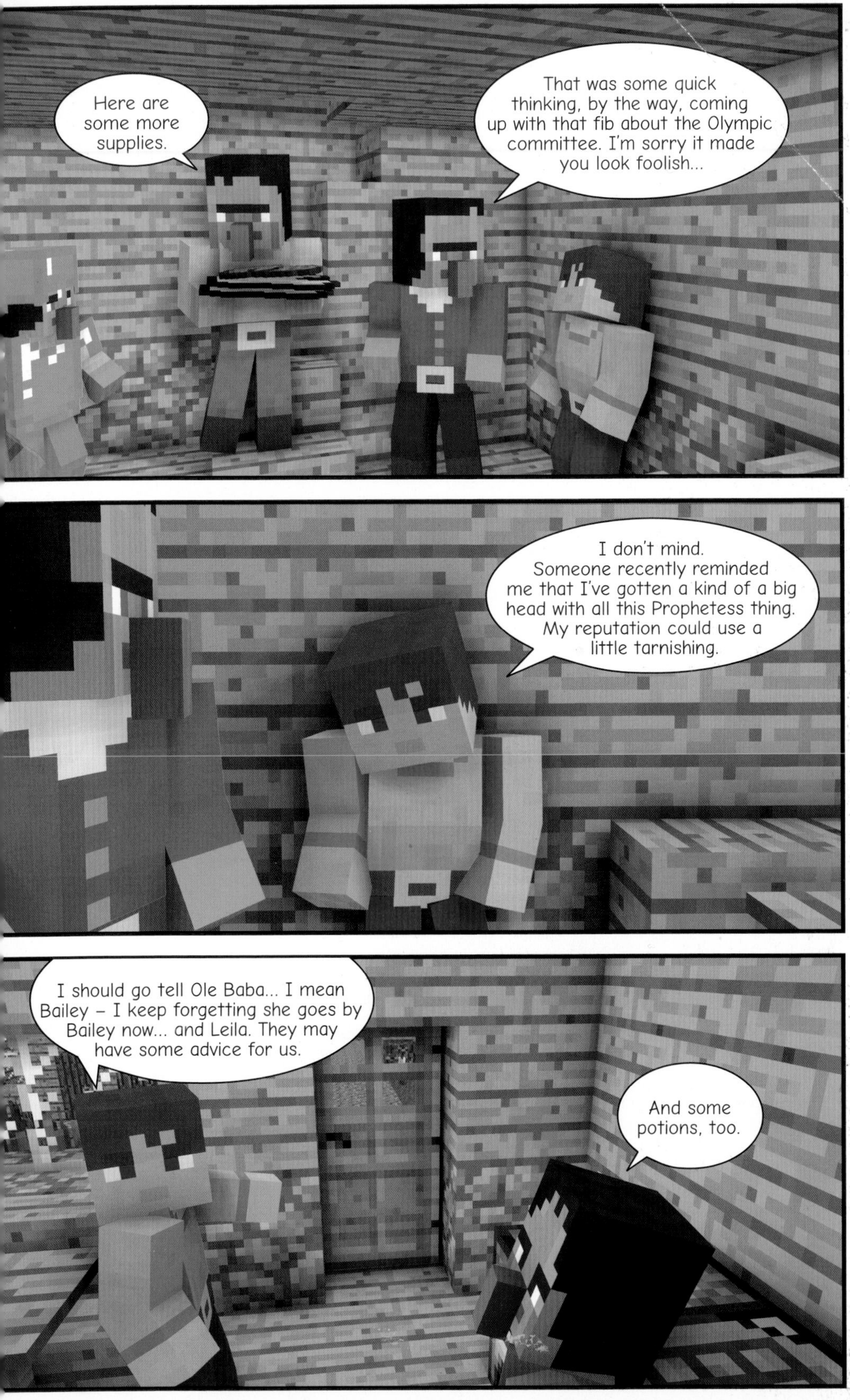
Here are some more supplies.
That was some quick thinking, by the way, coming up with that fib about the Olympic committee. I'm sorry it made you look foolish...
I don't mind. Someone recently reminded me that I've gotten a kind of a big head with all this Prophetess thing. My reputation could use a little tarnishing.
I should go tell Ole Baba... I mean Bailey – I keep forgetting she goes by Bailey now... and Leila. They may have some advice for us.
And some potions, too.

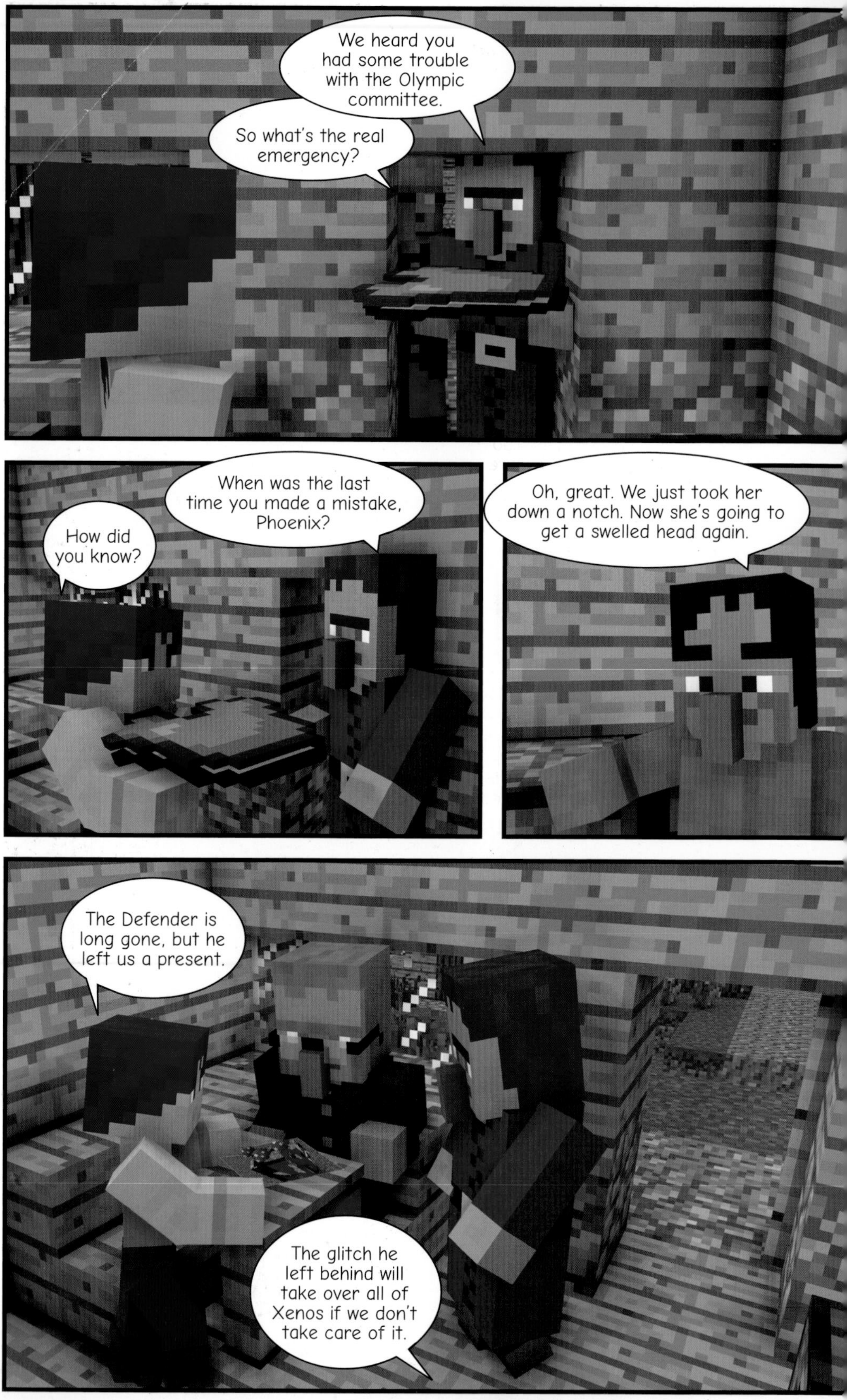

We heard you had some trouble with the Olympic committee.
So what's the real emergency?
When was the last time you made a mistake, Phoenix?
How did you know?
Oh, great. We just took her down a notch. Now she's going to get a swelled head again.
The Defender is long gone, but he left us a present.
The glitch he left behind will take over all of Xenos if we don't take care of it.

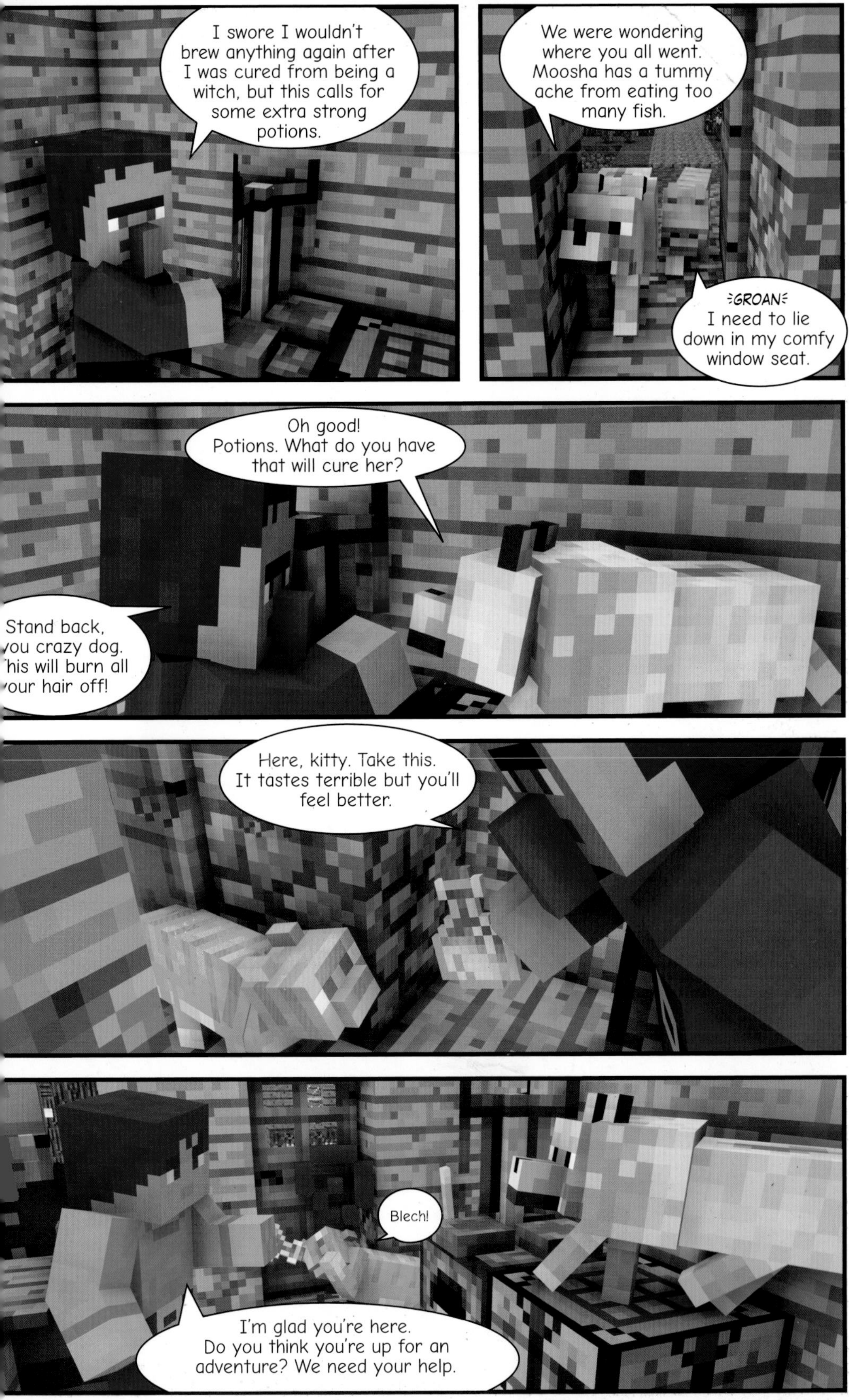

I swore I wouldn't brew anything again after I was cured from being a witch, but this calls for some extra strong potions.
We were wondering where you all went. Moosha has a tummy ache from eating too many fish.
GROAN
I need to lie down in my comfy window seat.
Oh good! Potions. What do you have that will cure her?
Stand back, ou crazy dog. his will burn all our hair off!
Here, kitty. Take this. It tastes terrible but you'll feel better.
Blech!
I'm glad you're here. Do you think you're up for an adventure? We need your help.

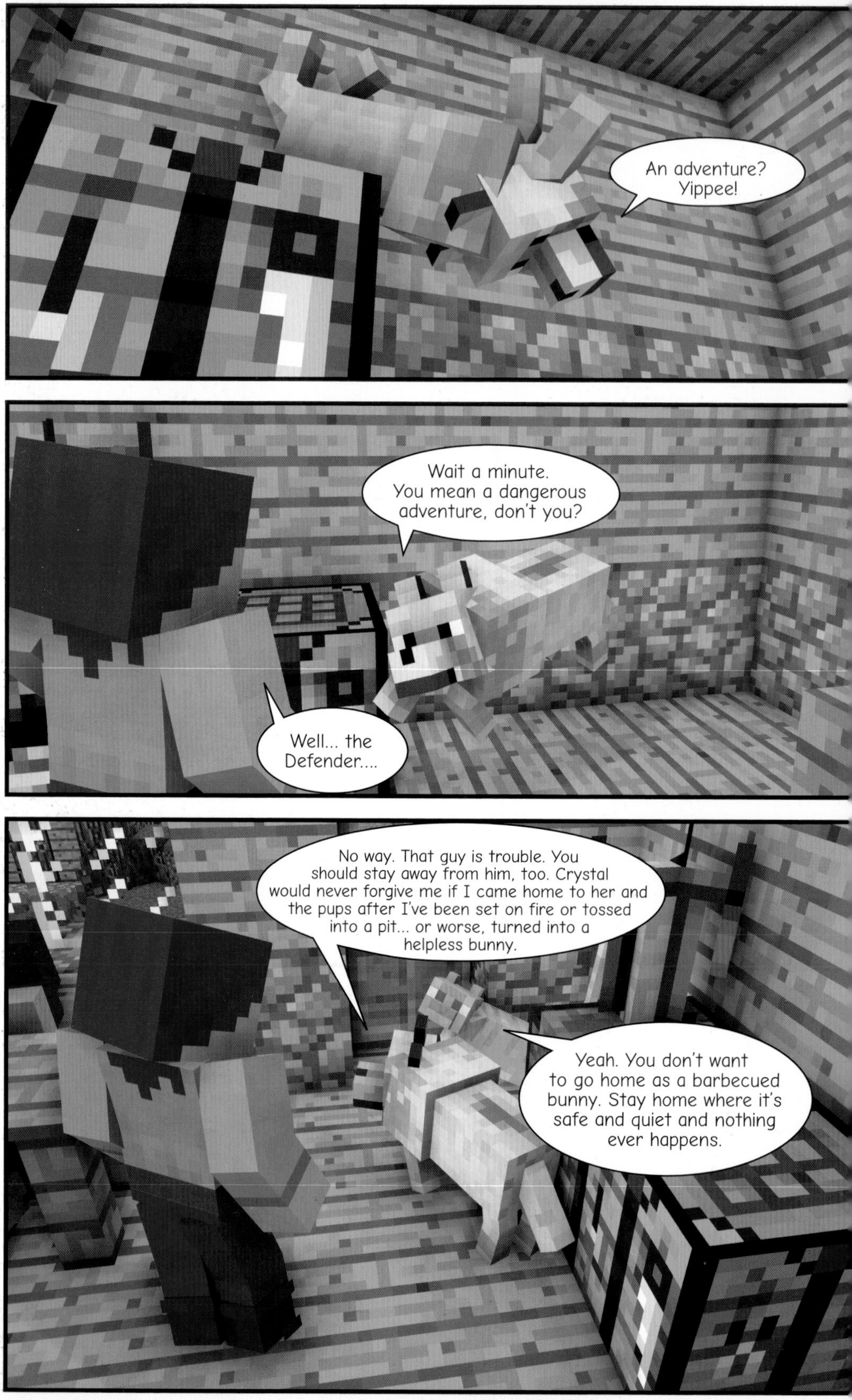
An adventure? Yippee!
Wait a minute. You mean a dangerous adventure, don't you?
Well... the Defender....
No way. That guy is trouble. You should stay away from him, too. Crystal would never forgive me if I came home to her and the pups after I've been set on fire or tossed into a pit... or worse, turned into a helpless bunny.
Yeah. You don't want to go home as a barbecued bunny. Stay home where it's safe and quiet and nothing ever happens.

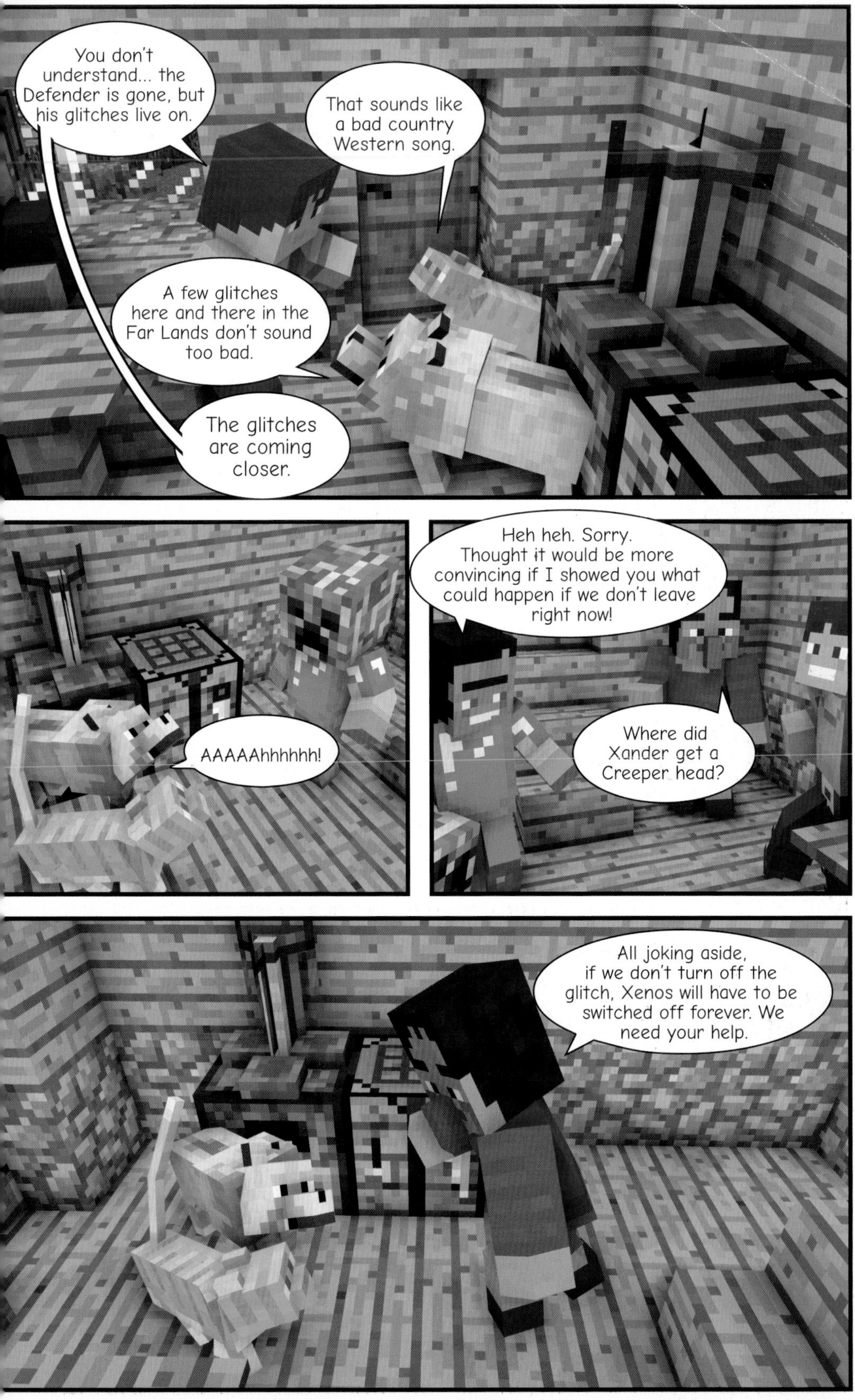
You don't understand... the Defender is gone, but his glitches live on.
That sounds like a bad country Western song.
A few glitches here and there in the Far Lands don't sound too bad.
The glitches are coming closer.
AAAAAhhhhhh!
Heh heh. Sorry. Thought it would be more convincing if I showed you what could happen if we don't leave right now!
Where did Xander get a Creeper head?
All joking aside, if we don't turn off the glitch, Xenos will have to be switched off forever. We need your help.

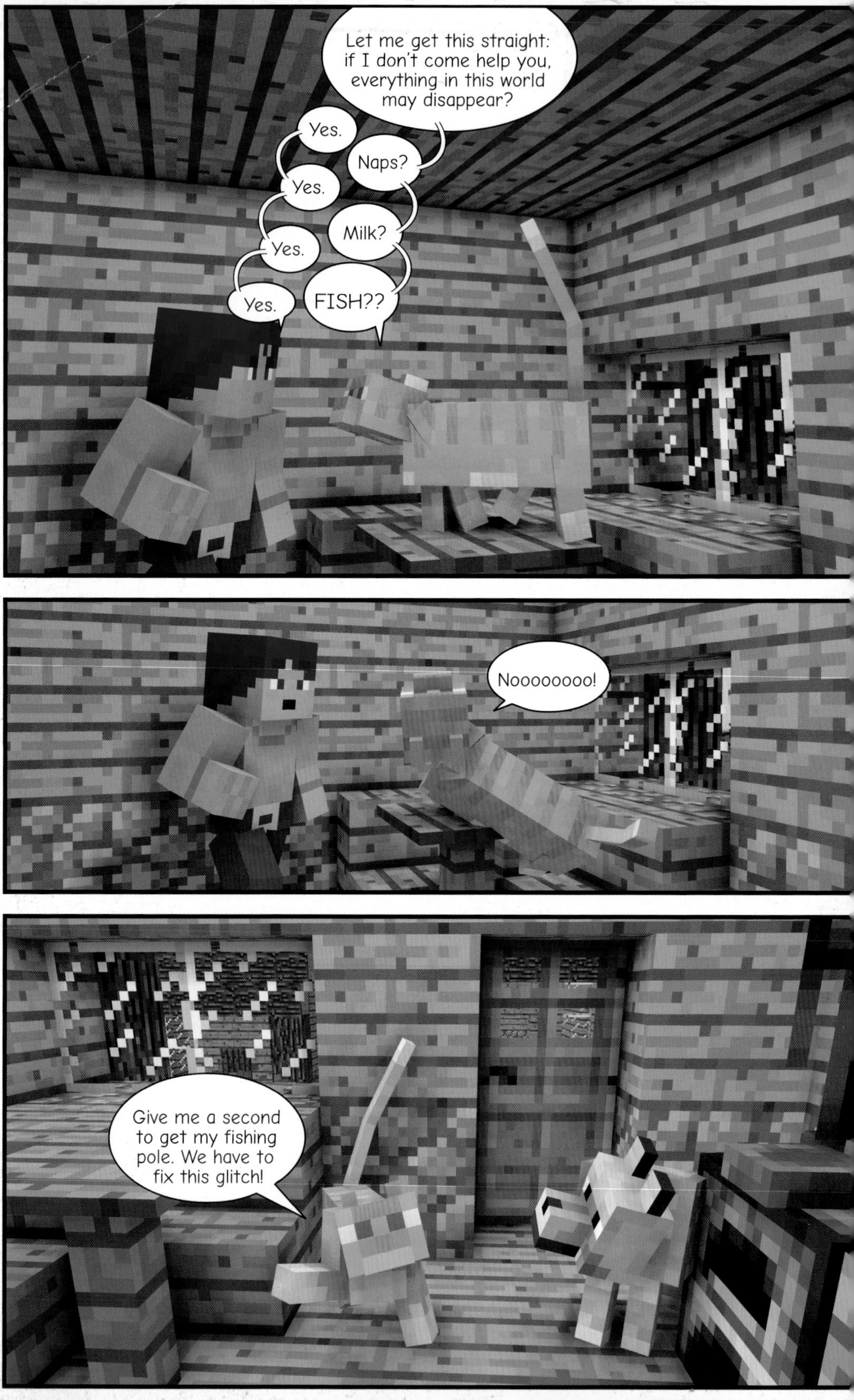

Let me get this straight: if I don't come help you, everything in this world may disappear?
Yes.
Naps?
Yes.
Milk?
Yes.
FISH??
Yes.
Noooooooo!
Give me a second to get my fishing pole. We have to fix this glitch!

CHAPTER 6

ZOMBIES IN THE NIGHT

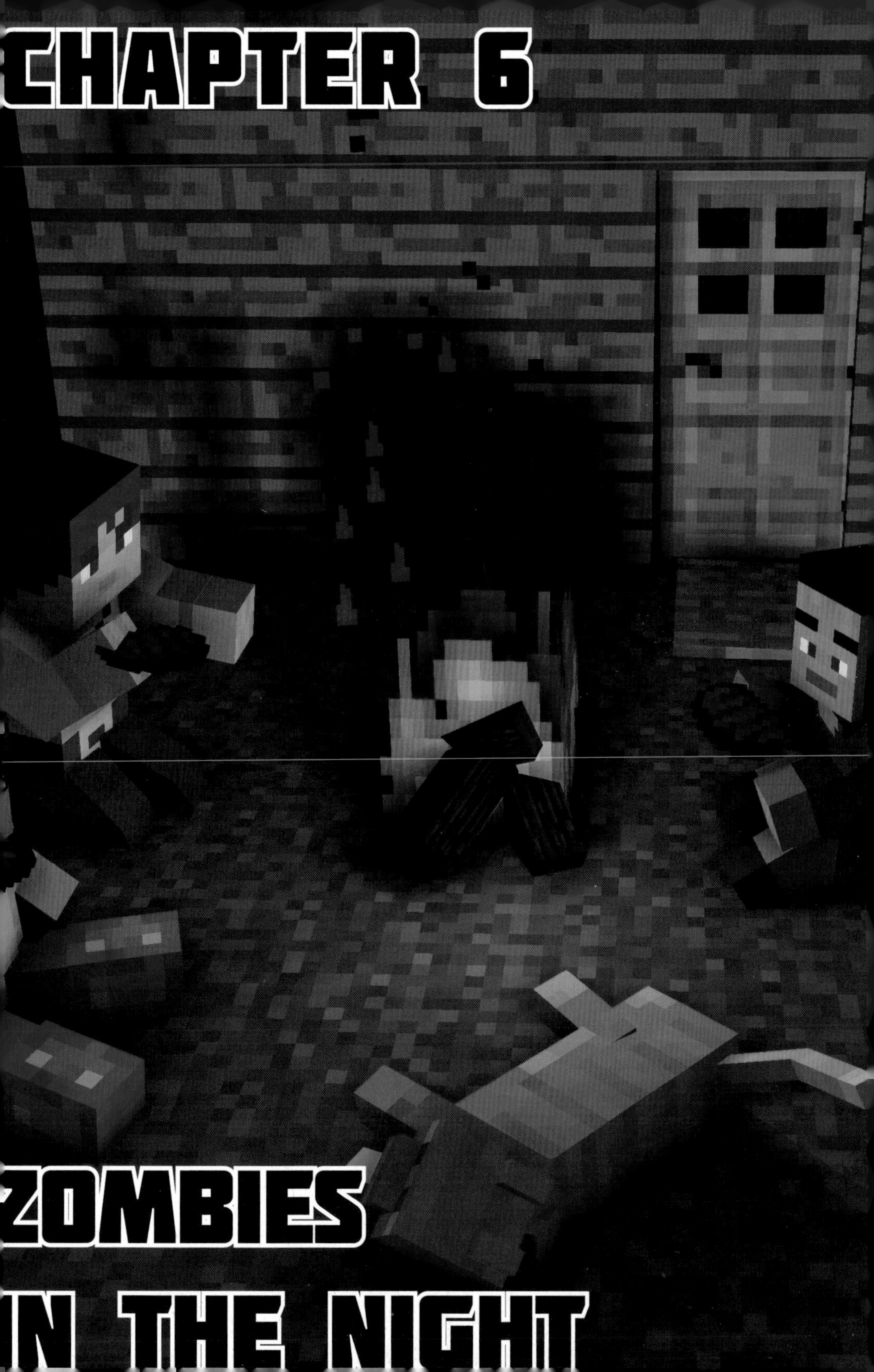

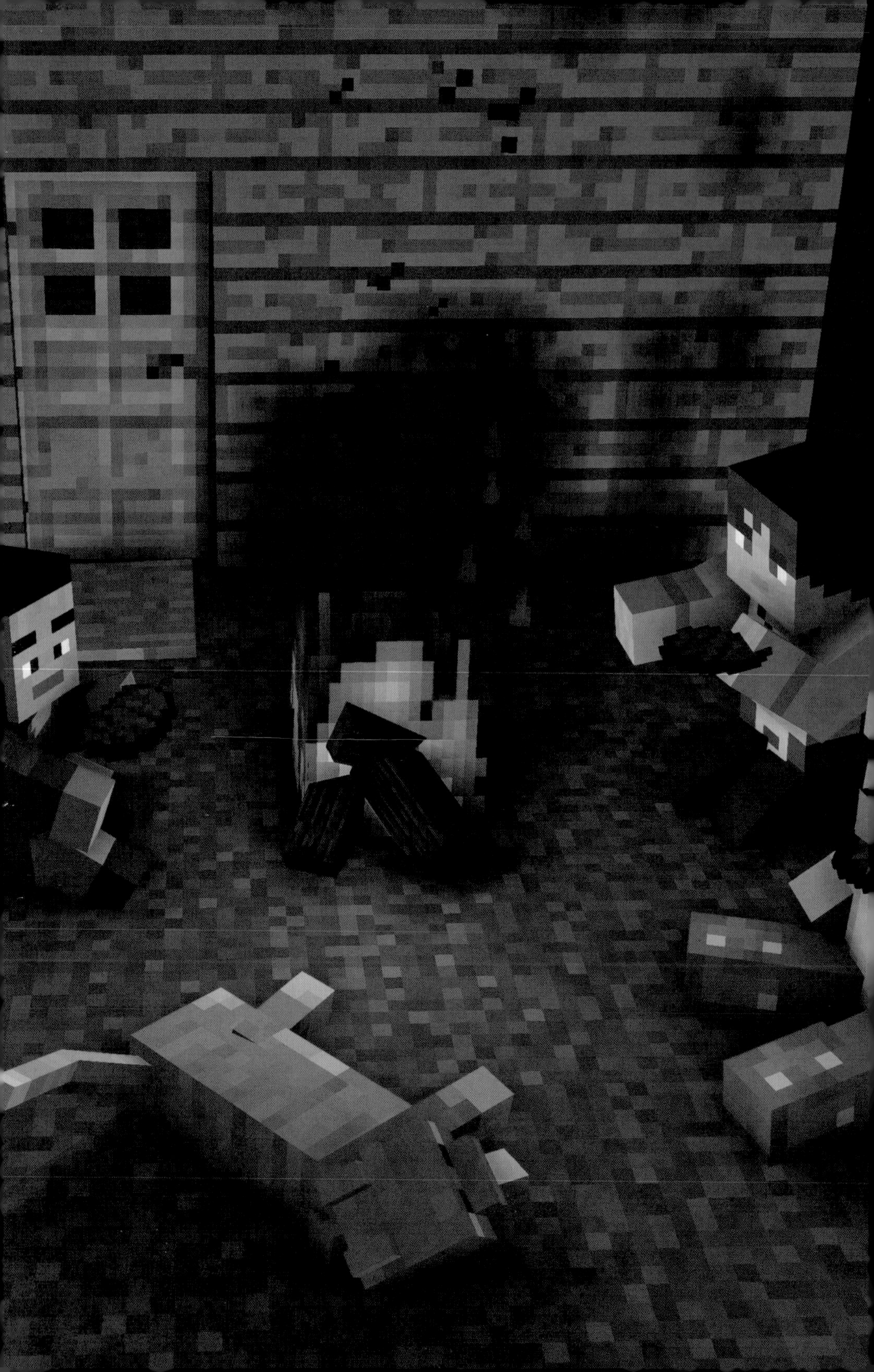

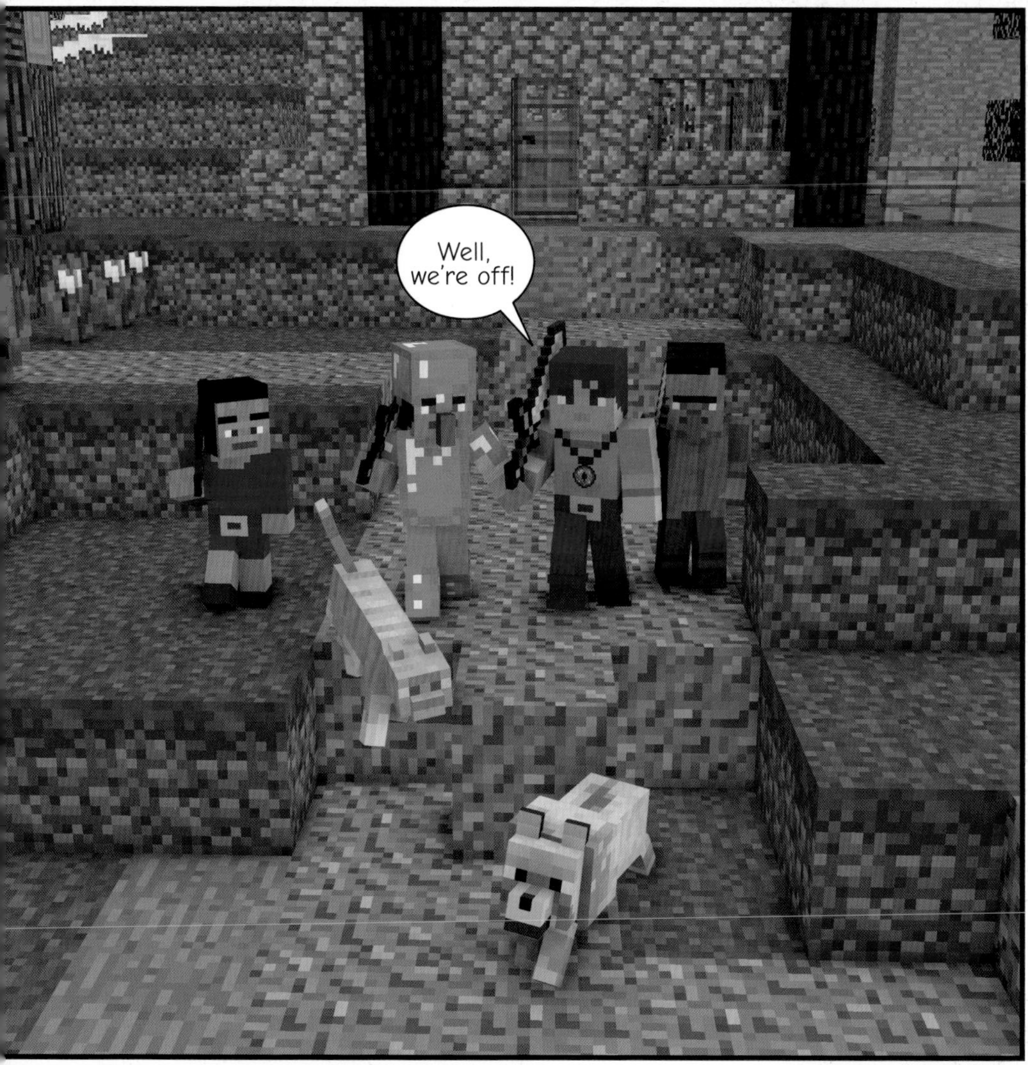
Well, we're off!

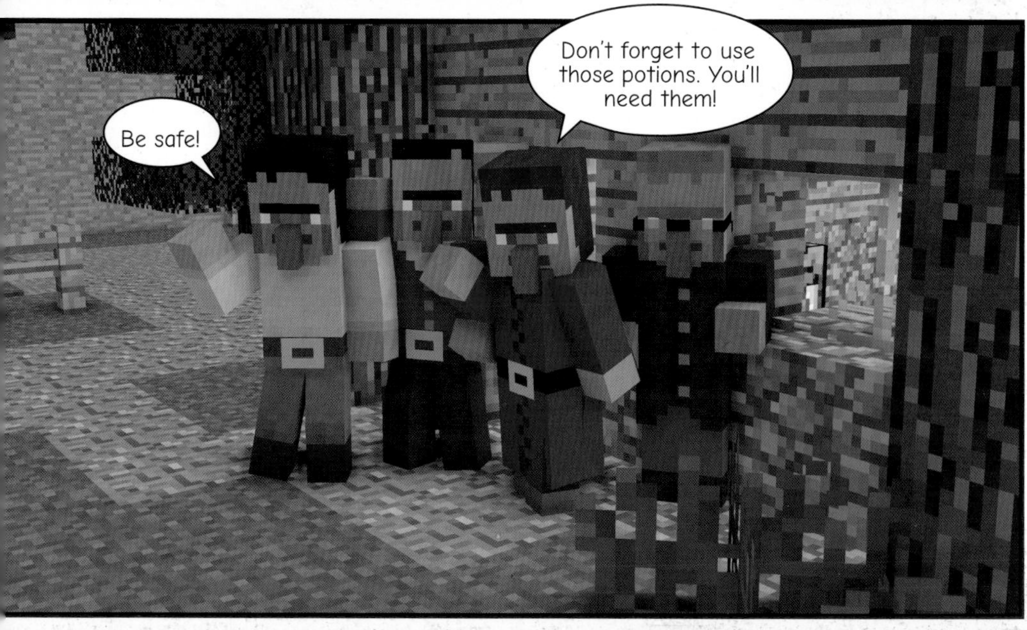
Be safe!
Don't forget to use those potions. You'll need them!

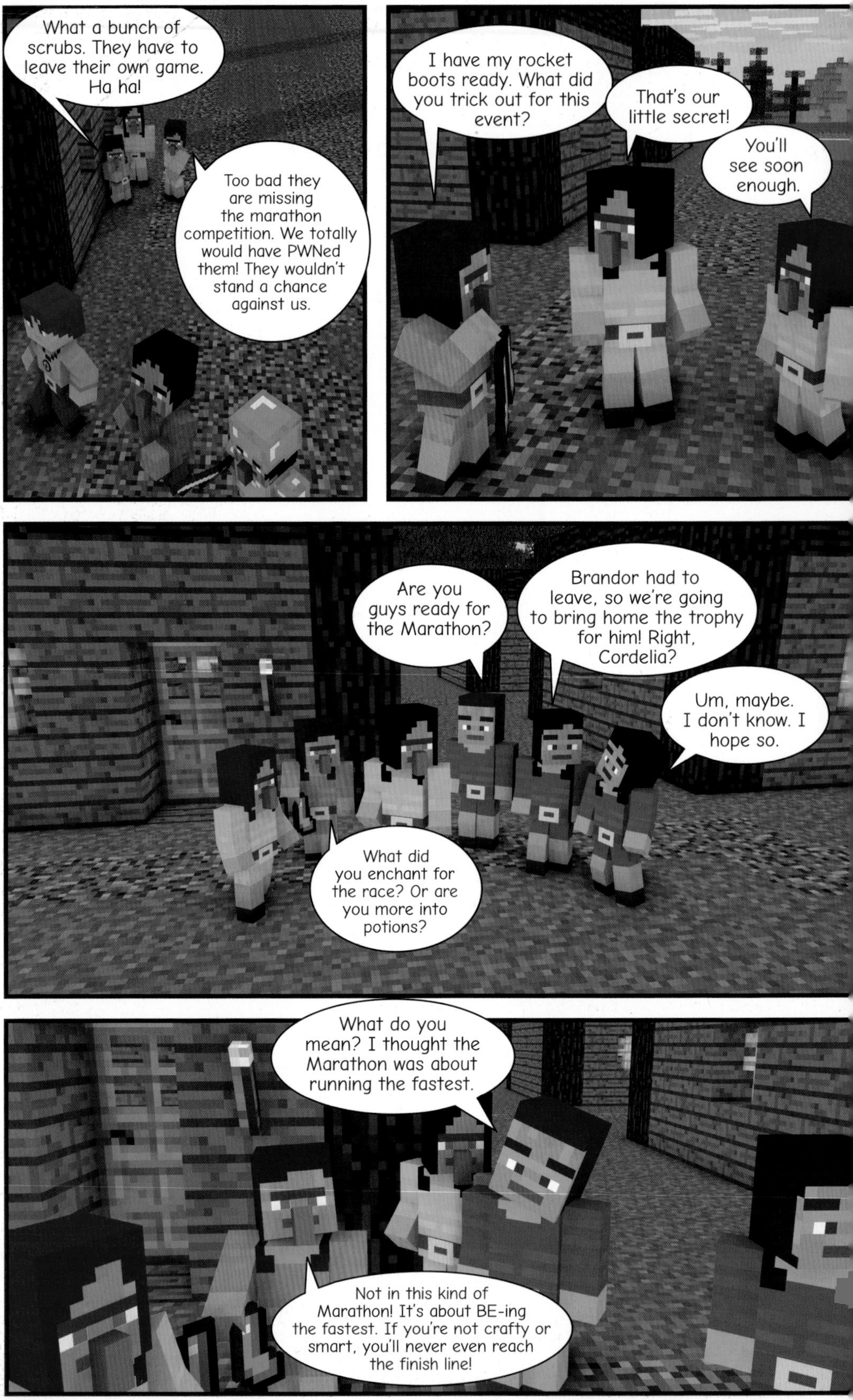
What a bunch of scrubs. They have to leave their own game. Ha ha!
Too bad they are missing the marathon competition. We totally would have PWNed them! They wouldn't stand a chance against us.
I have my rocket boots ready. What did you trick out for this event?
That's our little secret!
You'll see soon enough.
Are you guys ready for the Marathon?
Brandor had to leave, so we're going to bring home the trophy for him! Right, Cordelia?
Um, maybe. I don't know. I hope so.
What did you enchant for the race? Or are you more into potions?
What do you mean? I thought the Marathon was about running the fastest.
Not in this kind of Marathon! It's about BE-ing the fastest. If you're not crafty or smart, you'll never even reach the finish line!

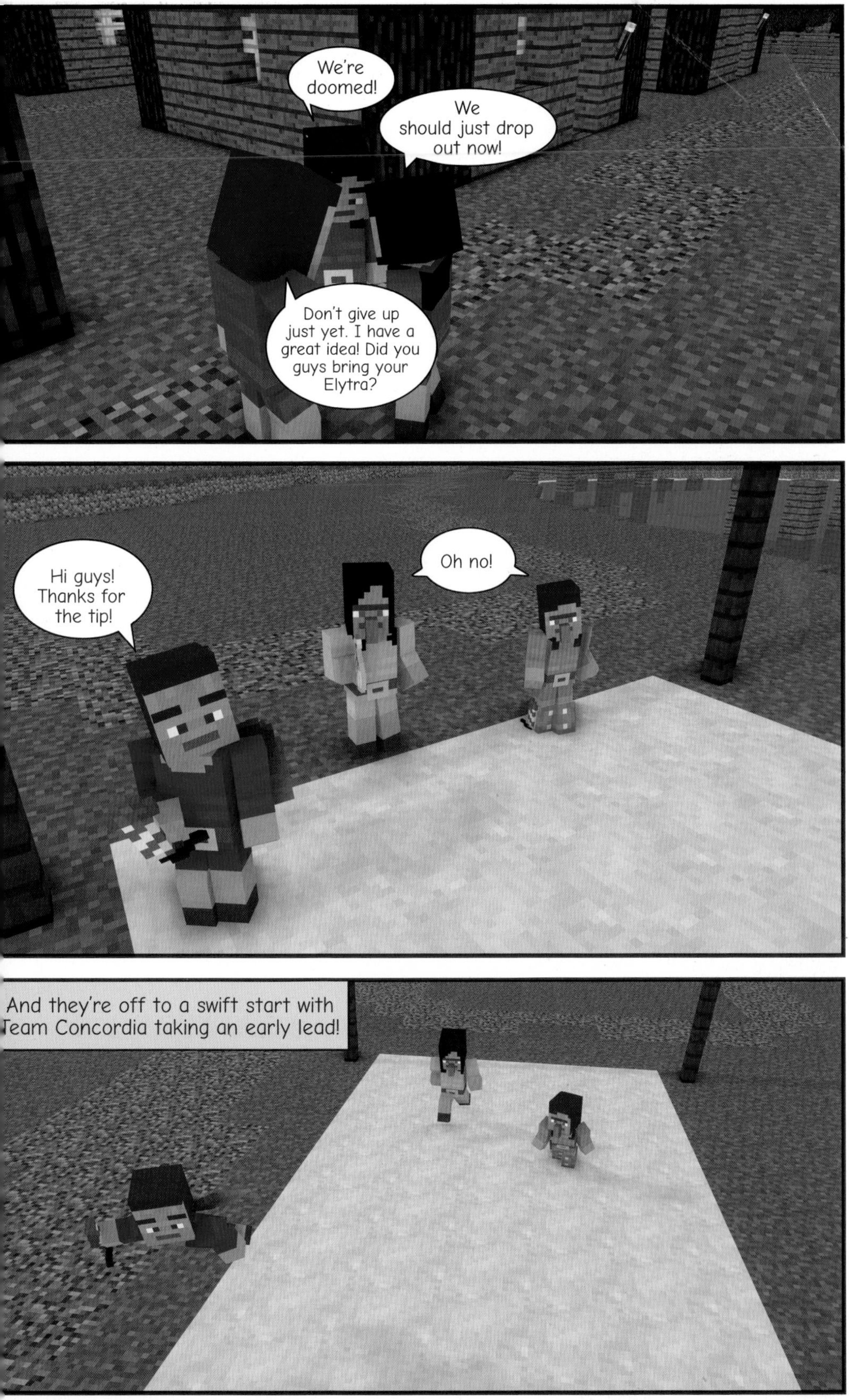
We're doomed!
We should just drop out now!
Don't give up just yet. I have a great idea! Did you guys bring your Elytra?
Hi guys! Thanks for the tip!
Oh no!
And they're off to a swift start with Team Concordia taking an early lead!

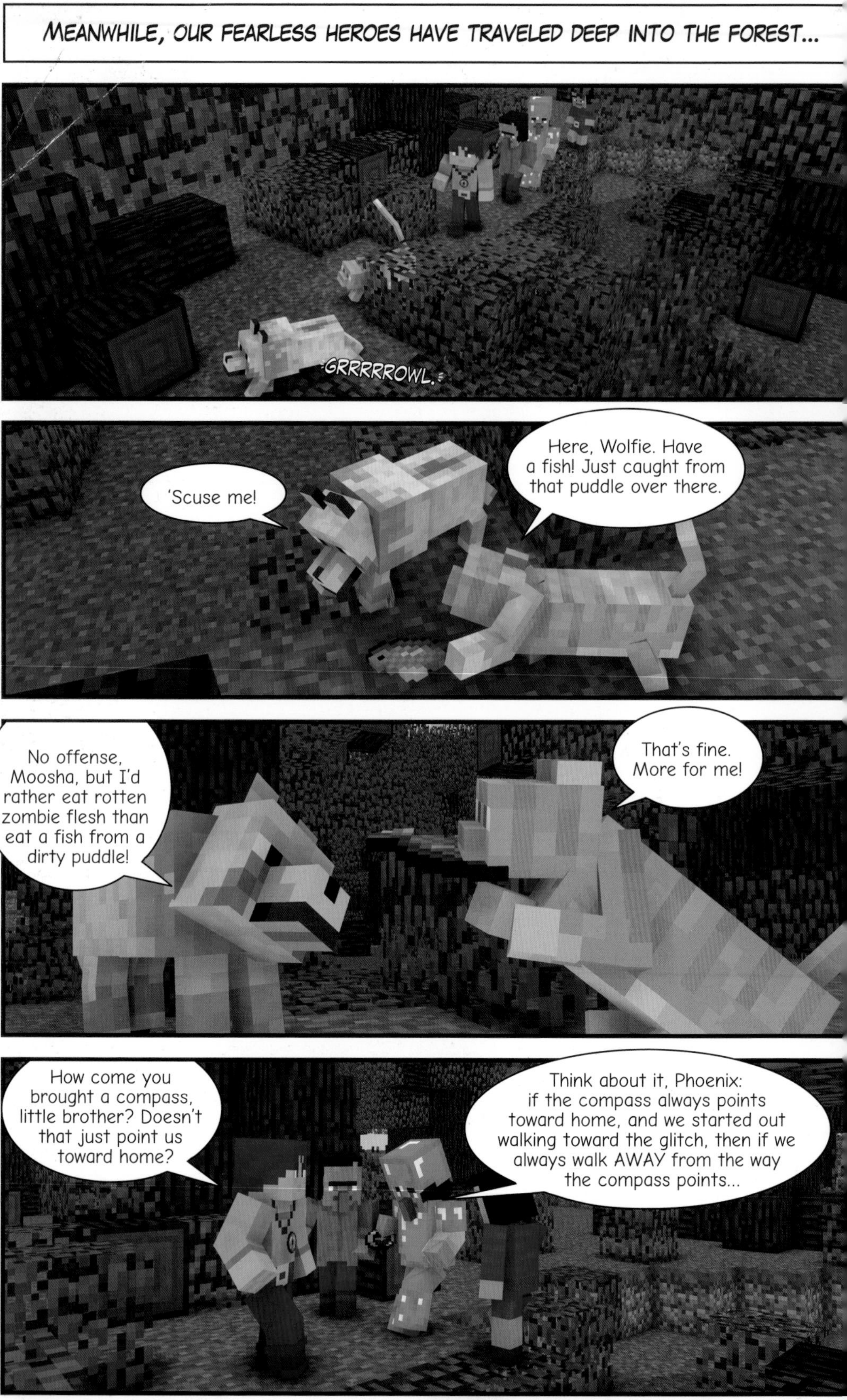
MEANWHILE, OUR FEARLESS HEROES HAVE TRAVELED DEEP INTO THE FOREST...
GRRRRROWL.
'Scuse me!
Here, Wolfie. Have a fish! Just caught from that puddle over there.
No offense, Moosha, but I'd rather eat rotten zombie flesh than eat a fish from a dirty puddle!
That's fine. More for me!
How come you brought a compass, little brother? Doesn't that just point us toward home?
Think about it, Phoenix: if the compass always points toward home, and we started out walking toward the glitch, then if we always walk AWAY from the way the compass points...

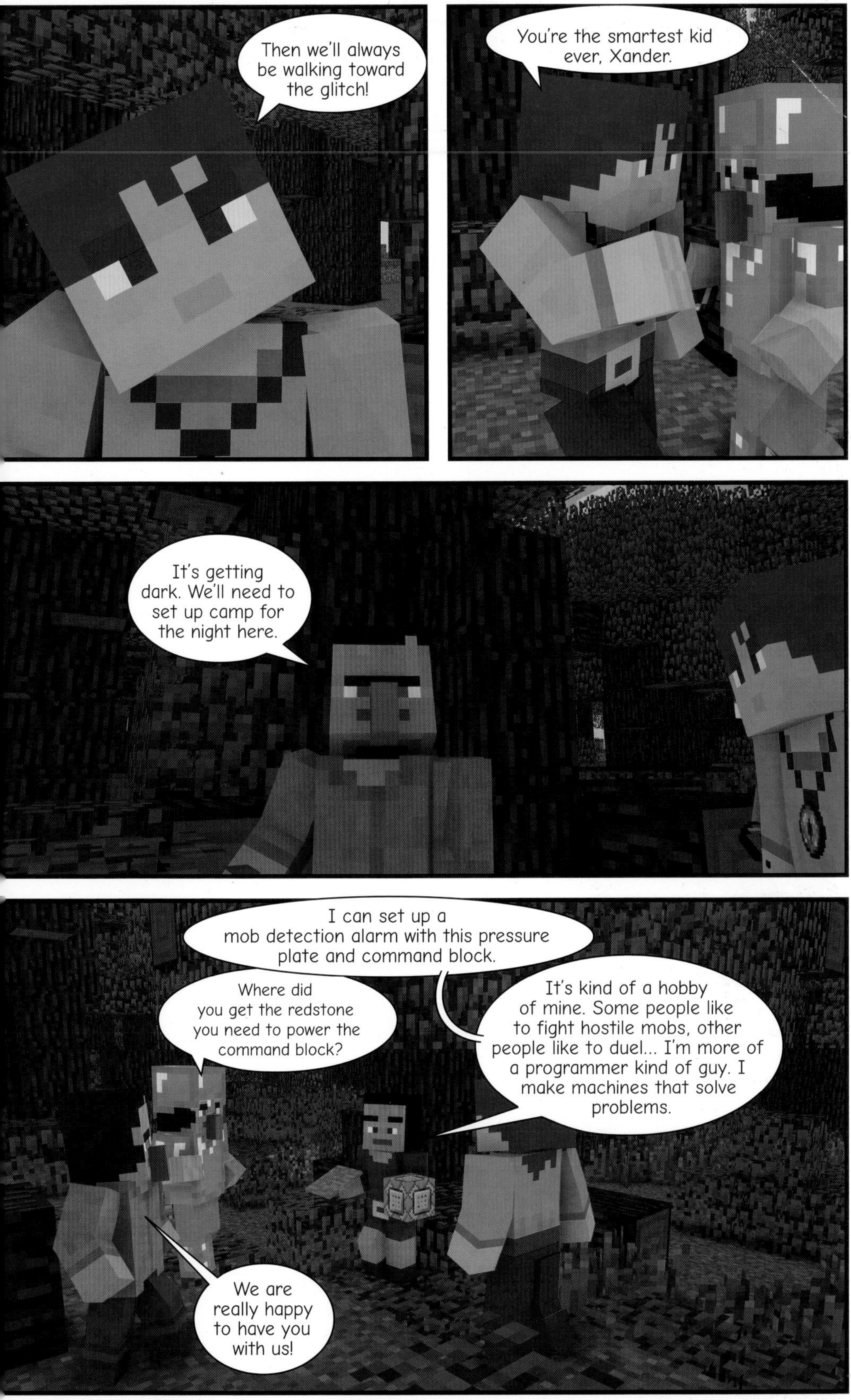
Then we'll always be walking toward the glitch!
You're the smartest kid ever, Xander.
It's getting dark. We'll need to set up camp for the night here.
I can set up a mob detection alarm with this pressure plate and command block.
Where did you get the redstone you need to power the command block?
It's kind of a hobby of mine. Some people like to fight hostile mobs, other people like to duel... I'm more of a programmer kind of guy. I make machines that solve problems.
We are really happy to have you with us!

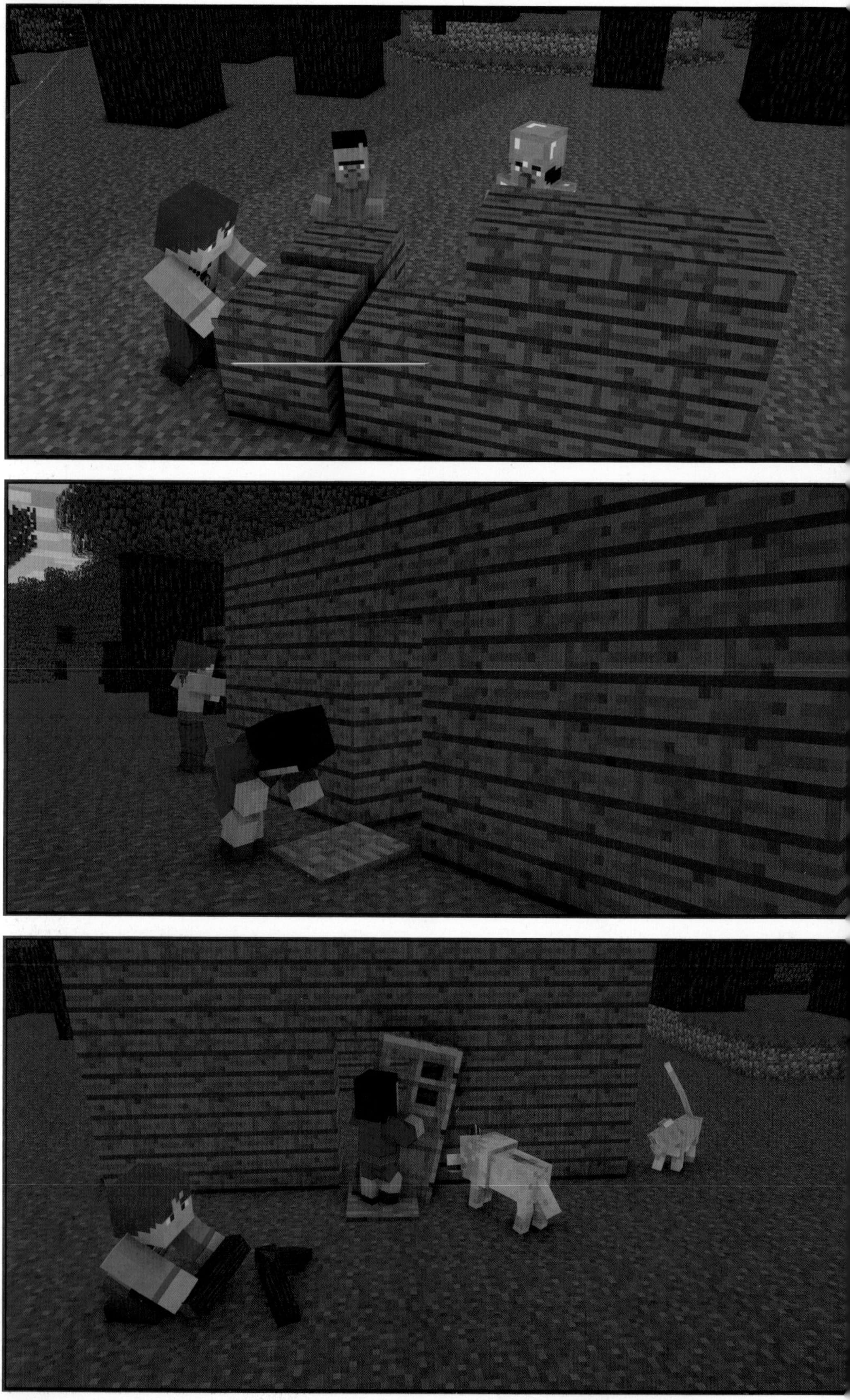

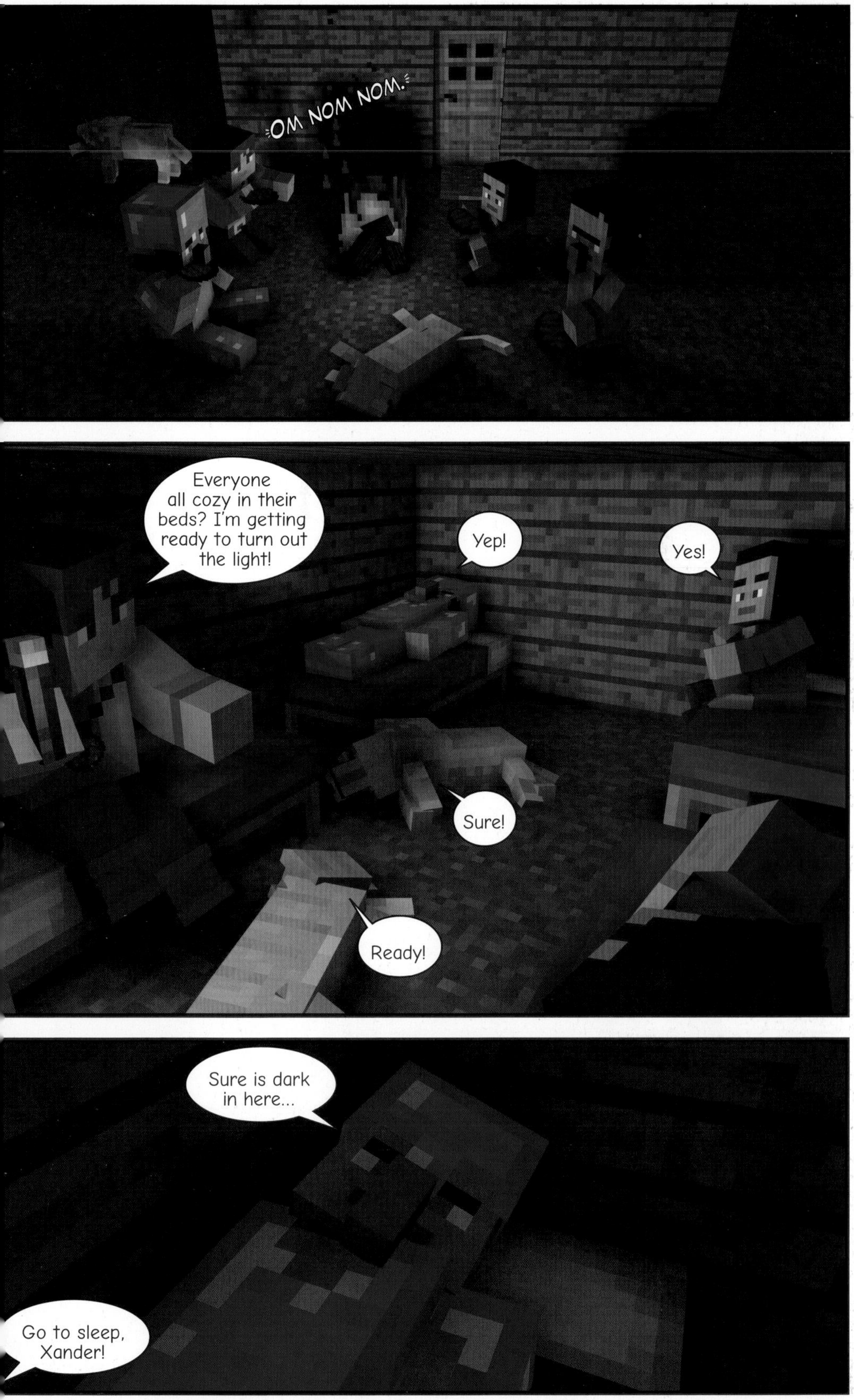
OM NOM NOM.
Everyone all cozy in their beds? I'm getting ready to turn out the light!
Yep!
Yes!
Sure!
Ready!
Sure is dark in here...
Go to sleep, Xander!

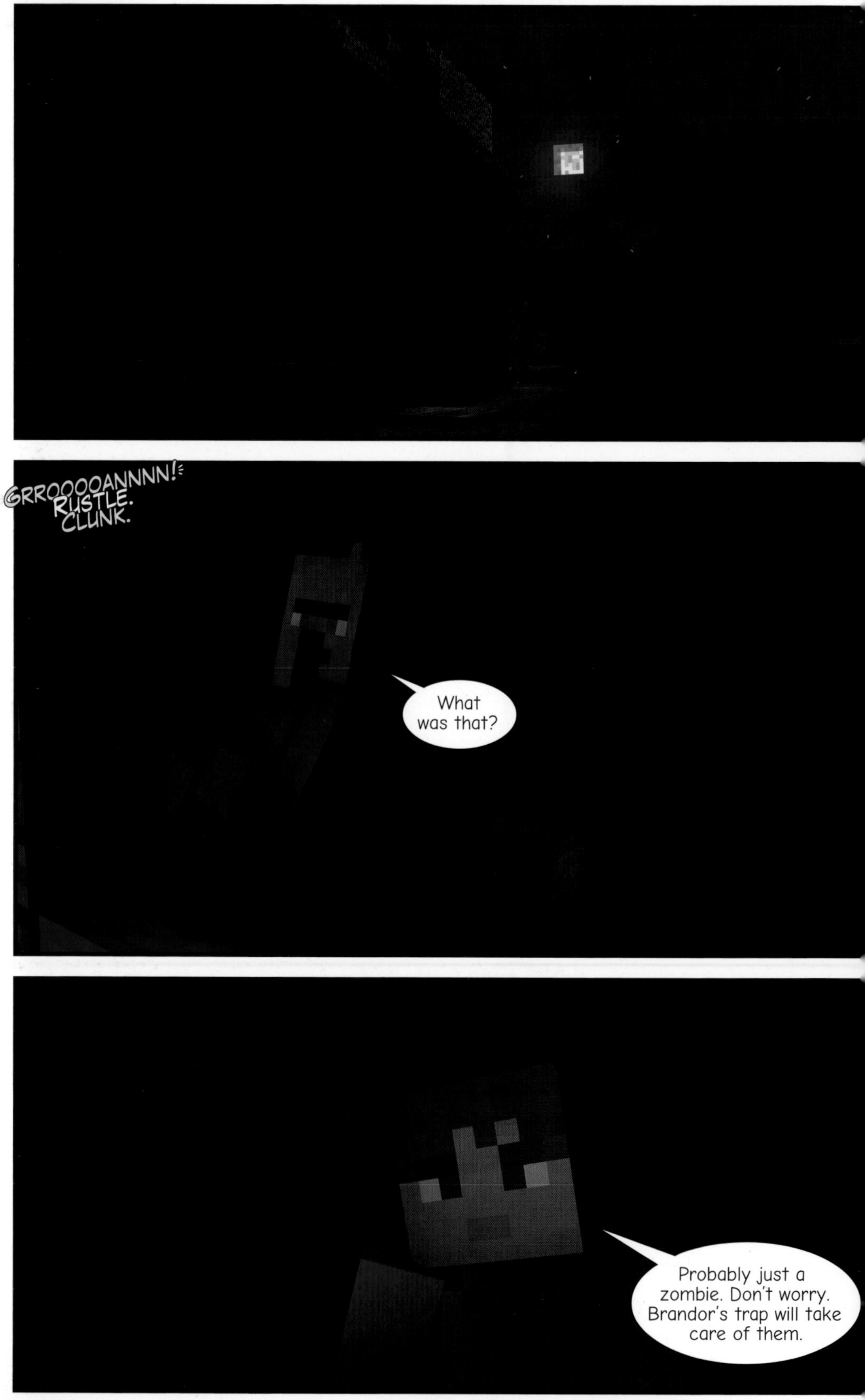
GRROOOOOANNNN!
RUSTLE.
CLUNK.
What was that?
Probably just a zombie. Don't worry. Brandor's trap will take care of them.

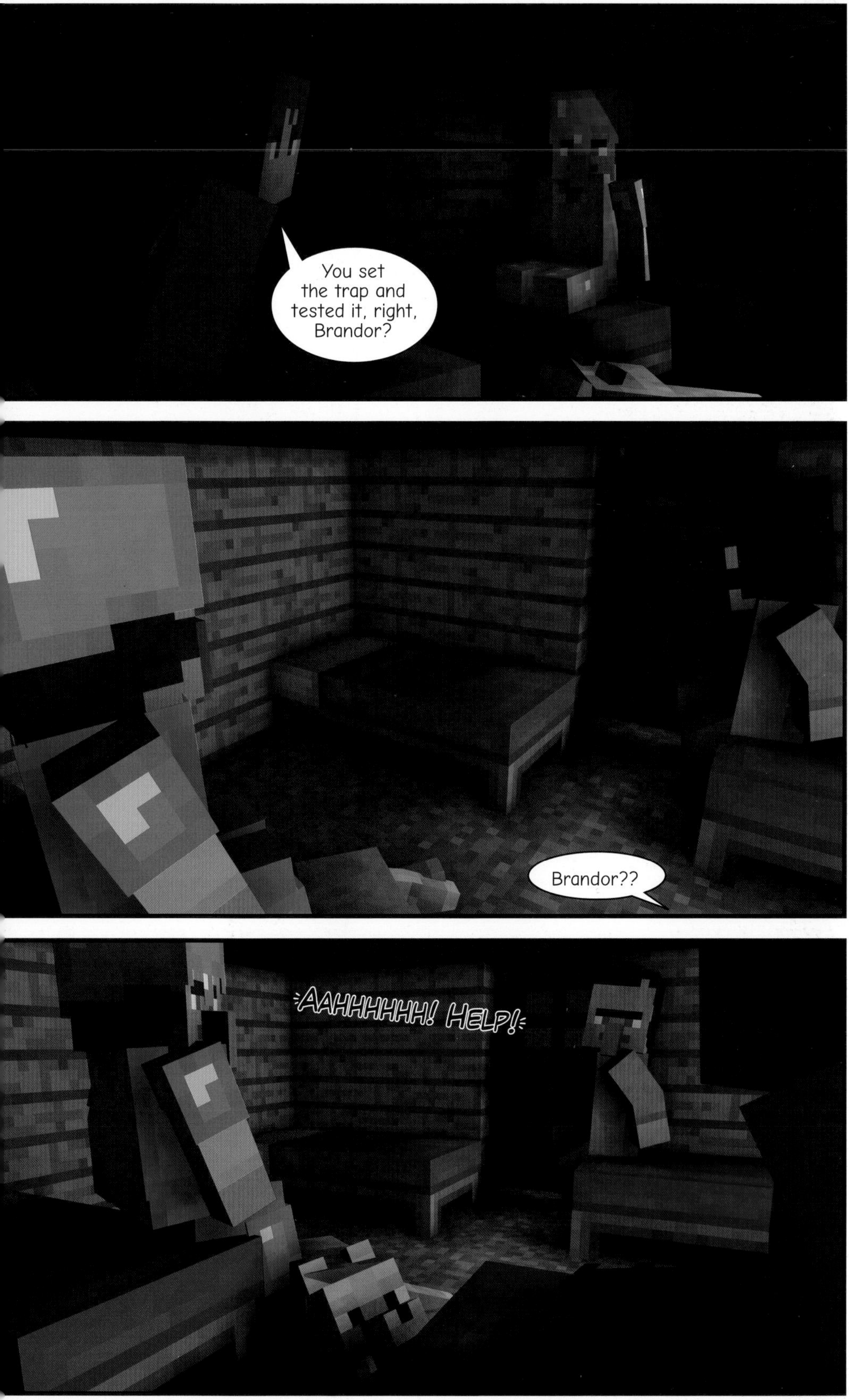
You set the trap and tested it, right, Brandor?
Brandor??
AAHHHHHHH! HELP!

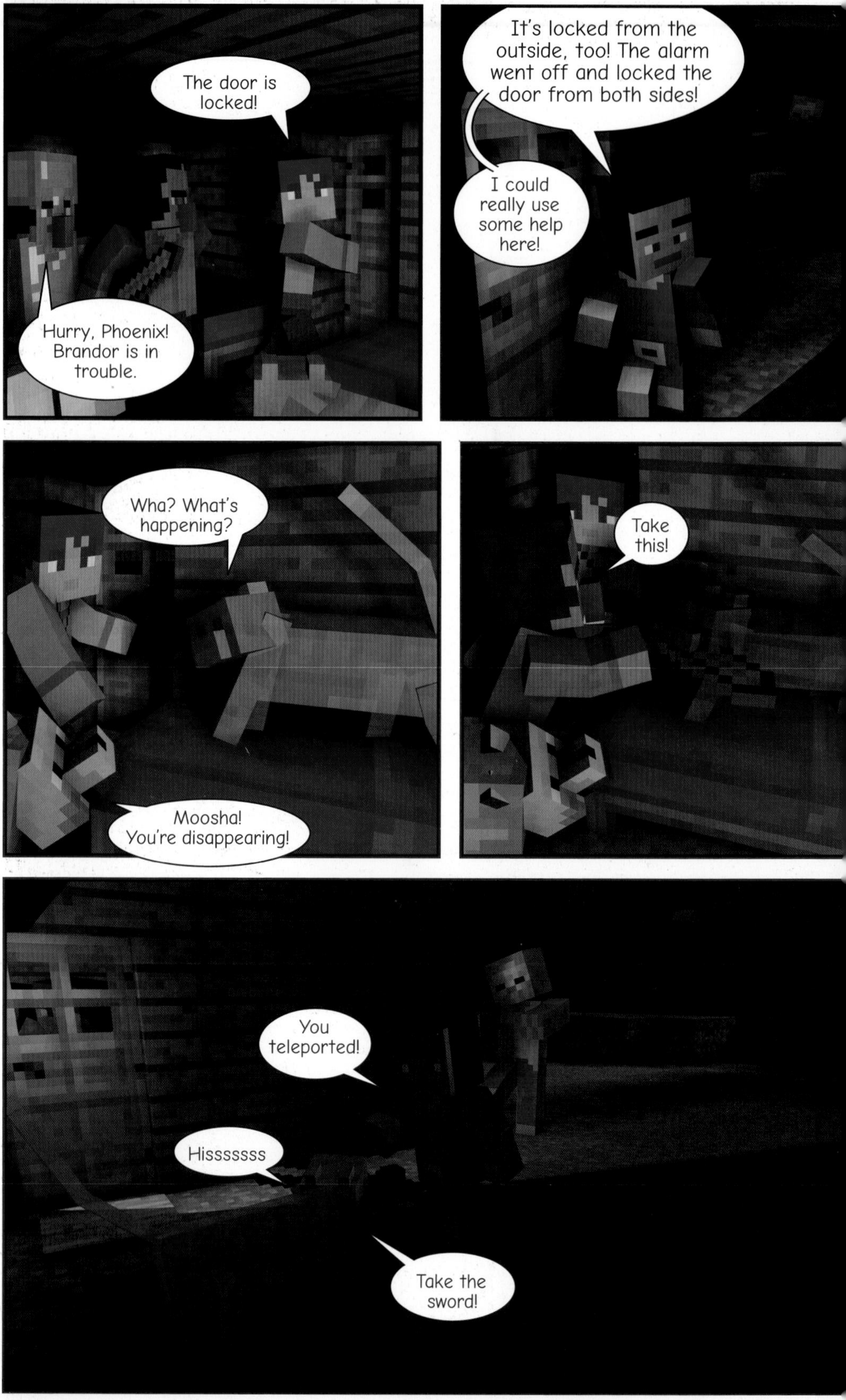
The door is locked!
Hurry, Phoenix! Brandor is in trouble.
It's locked from the outside, too! The alarm went off and locked the door from both sides!
I could really use some help here!
Wha? What's happening?
Moosha! You're disappearing!
Take this!
You teleported!
Hisssssss
Take the sword!

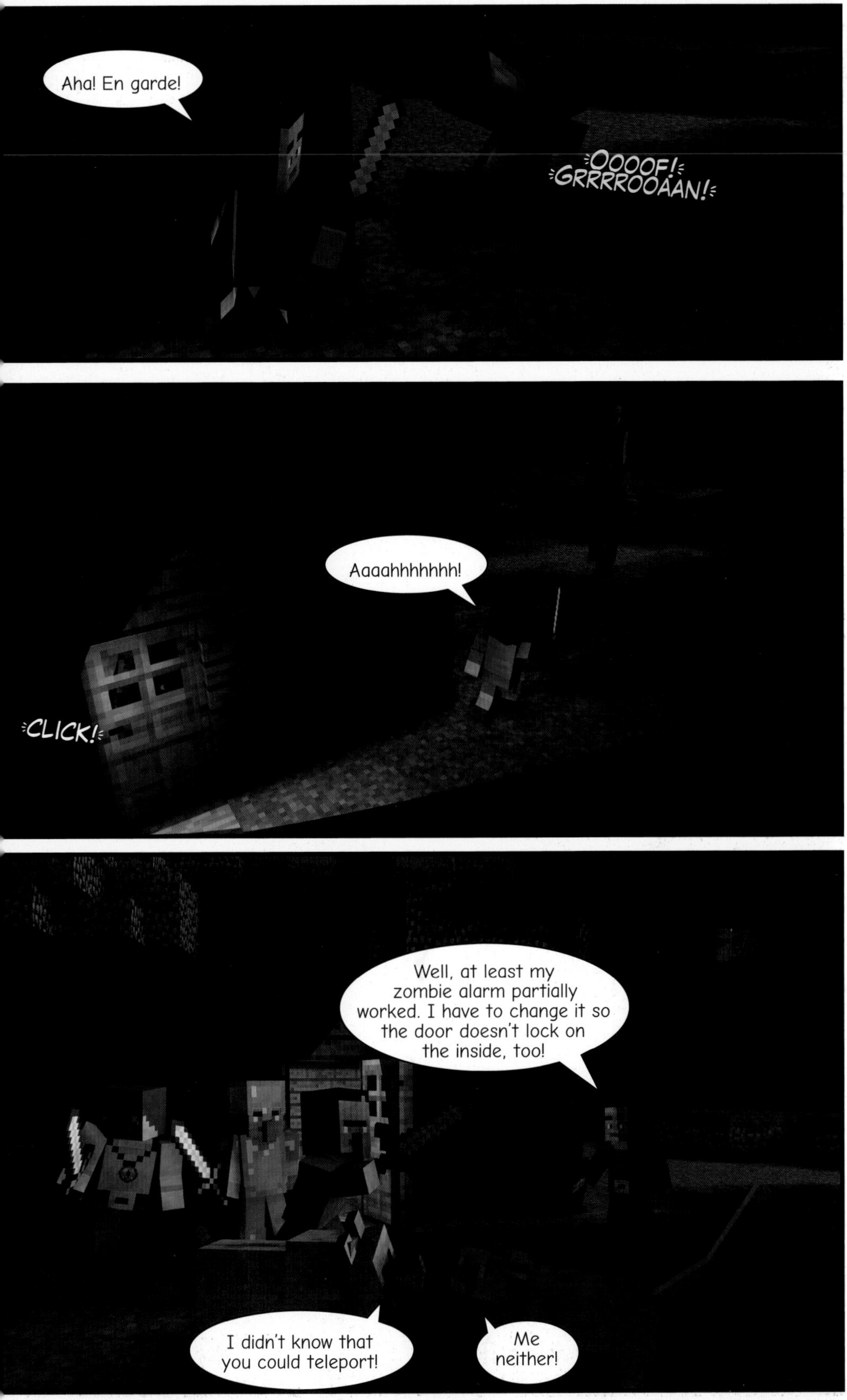
Aha! En garde!
OOOOF!
GRRRROOAAN!
Aaaahhhhhh!
CLICK!
Well, at least my zombie alarm partially worked. I have to change it so the door doesn't lock on the inside, too!
I didn't know that you could teleport!
Me neither!

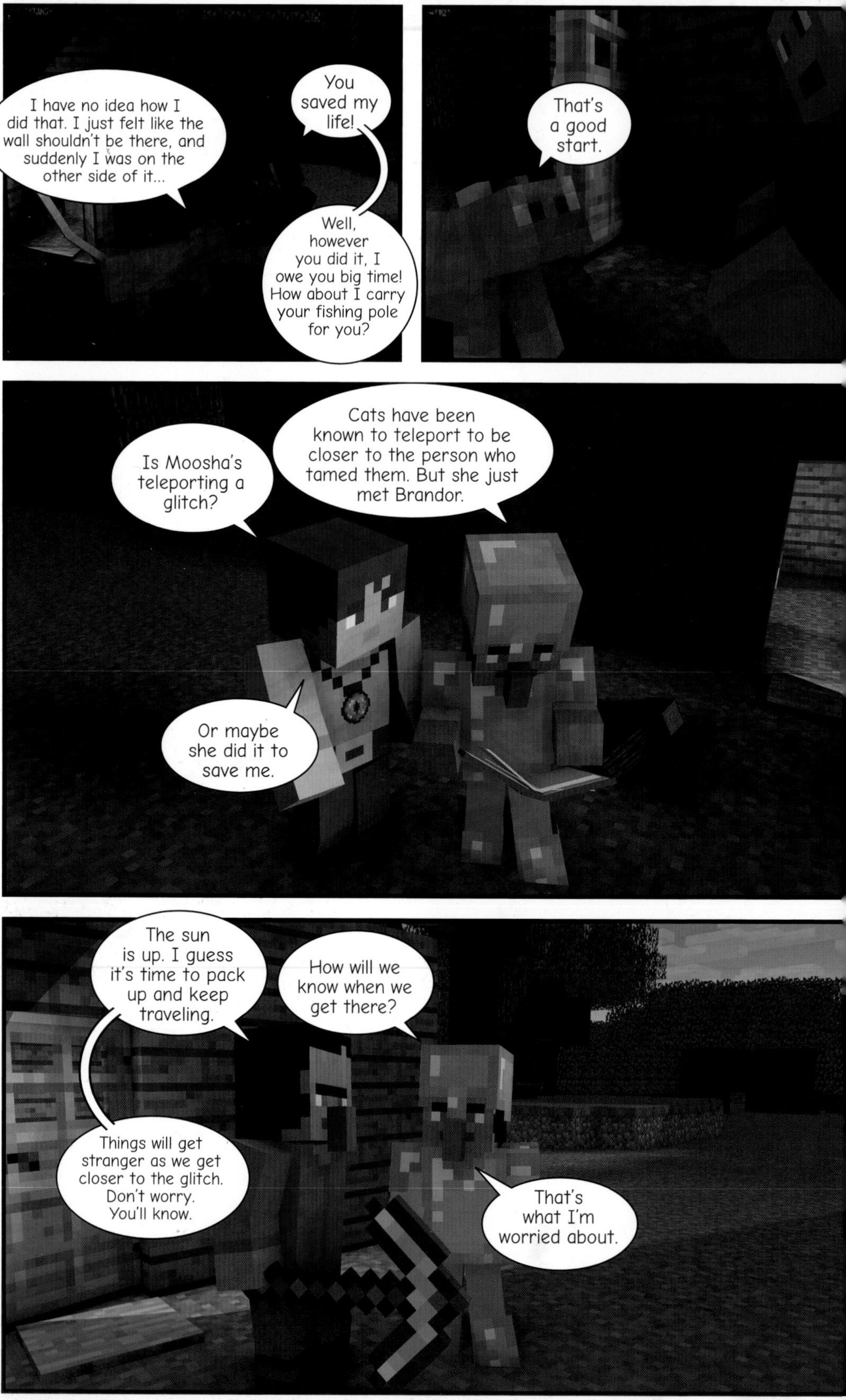
I have no idea how I did that. I just felt like the wall shouldn't be there, and suddenly I was on the other side of it...
You saved my life!
Well, however you did it, I owe you big time! How about I carry your fishing pole for you?
That's a good start.
Is Moosha's teleporting a glitch?
Cats have been known to teleport to be closer to the person who tamed them. But she just met Brandor.
Or maybe she did it to save me.
The sun is up. I guess it's time to pack up and keep traveling.
How will we know when we get there?
Things will get stranger as we get closer to the glitch. Don't worry. You'll know.
That's what I'm worried about.

CHAPTER 7

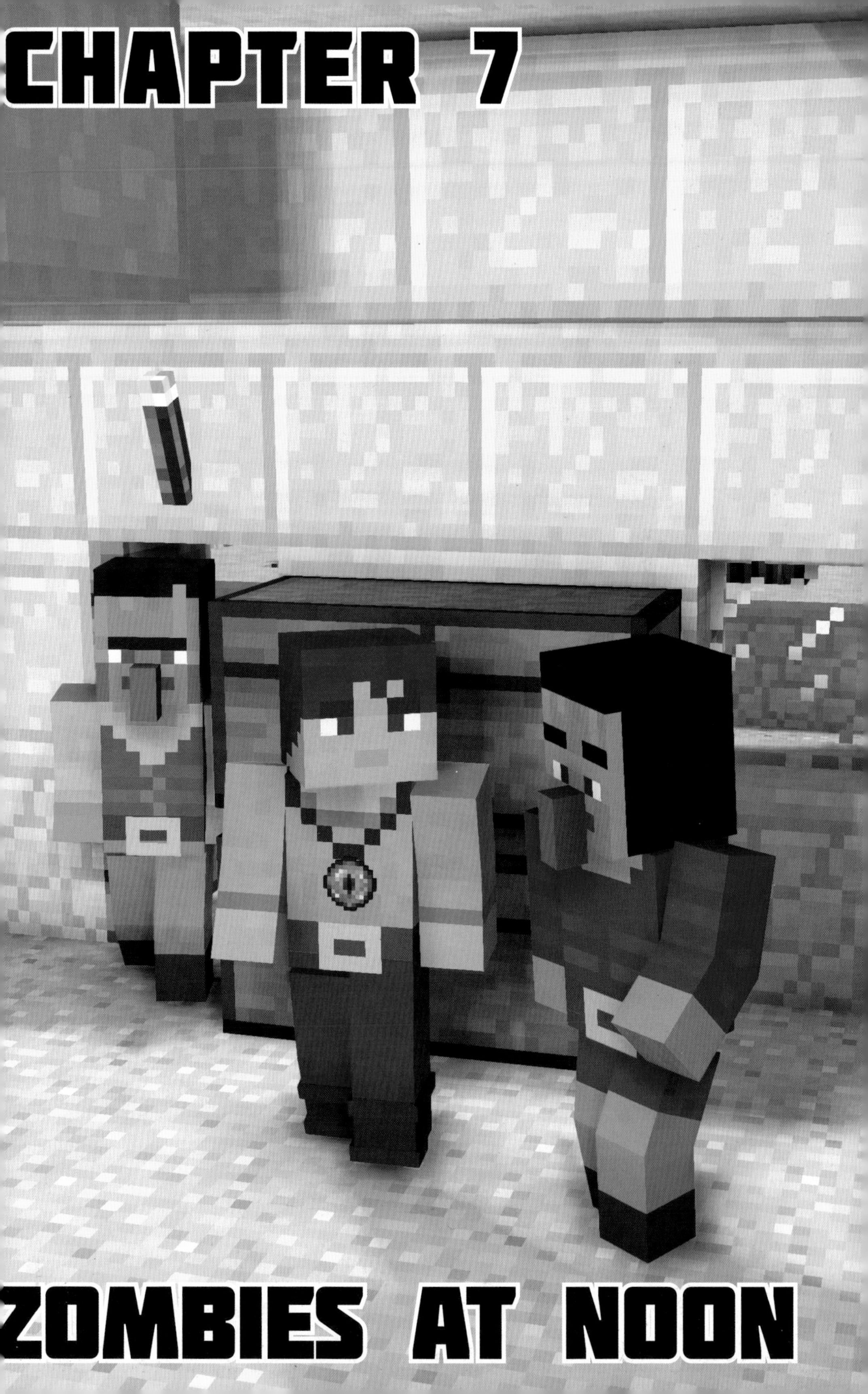

ZOMBIES AT NOON

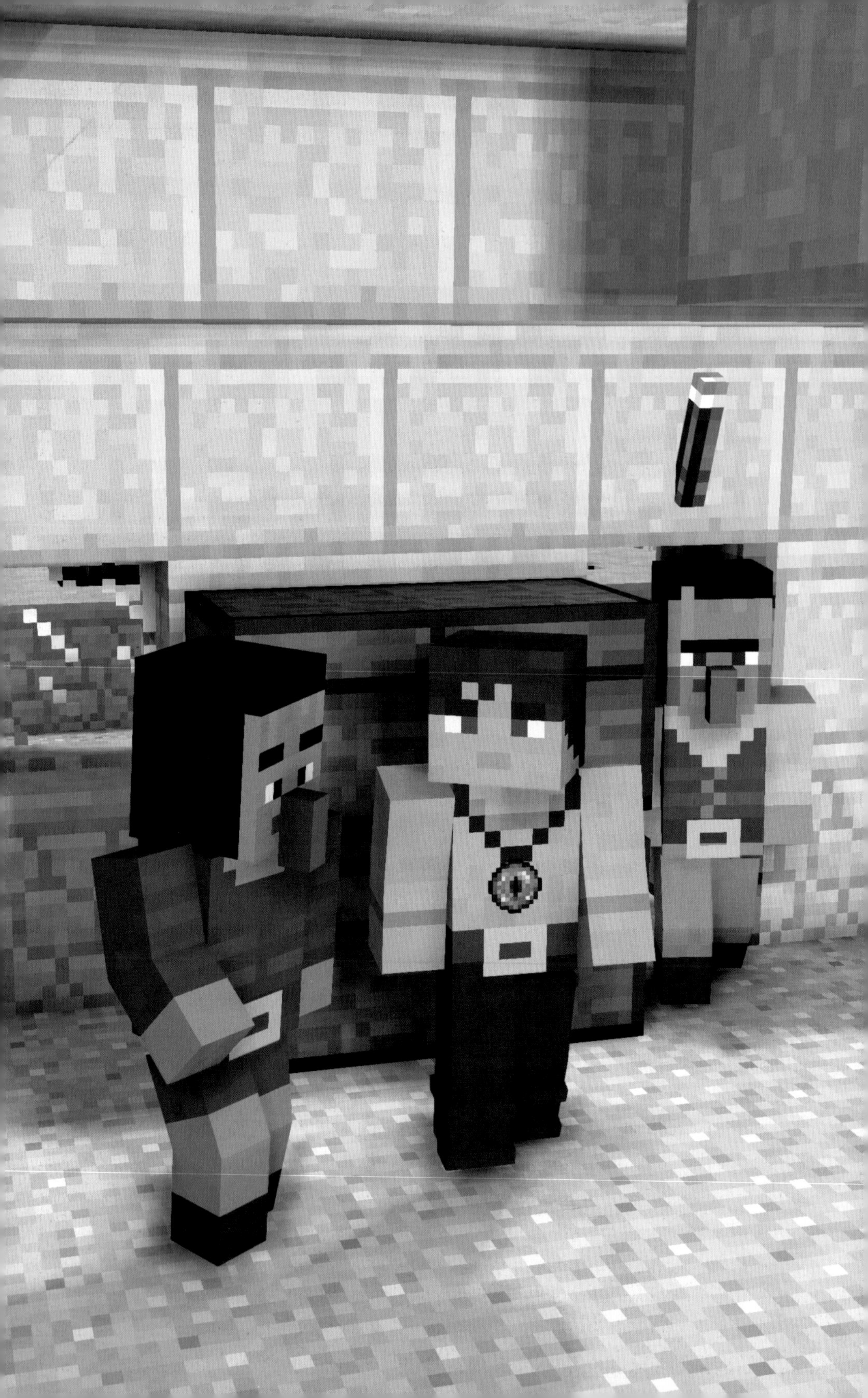

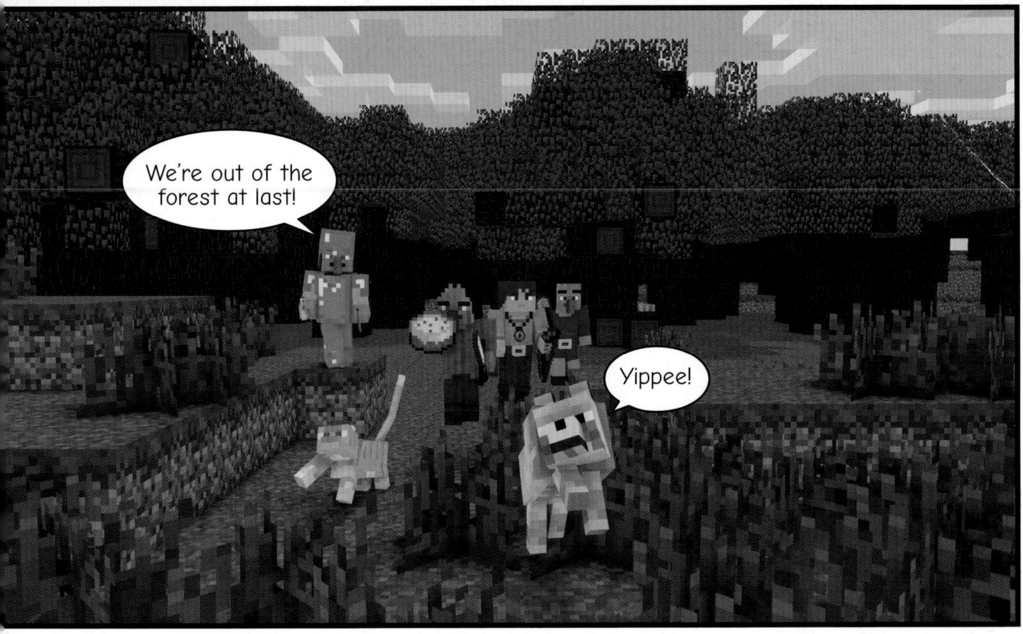
We're out of the forest at last!
Yippee!

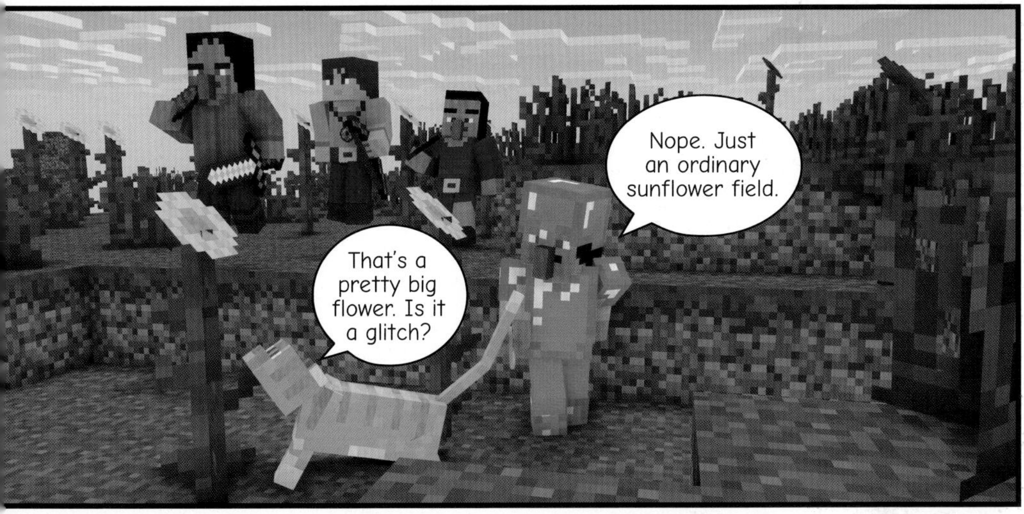
That's a pretty big flower. Is it a glitch?
Nope. Just an ordinary sunflower field.

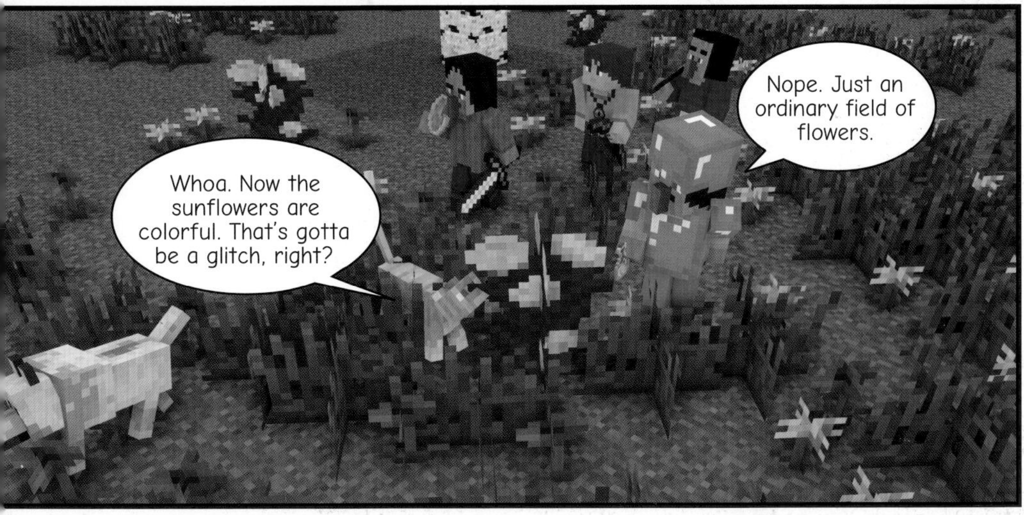
Whoa. Now the sunflowers are colorful. That's gotta be a glitch, right?
Nope. Just an ordinary field of flowers.

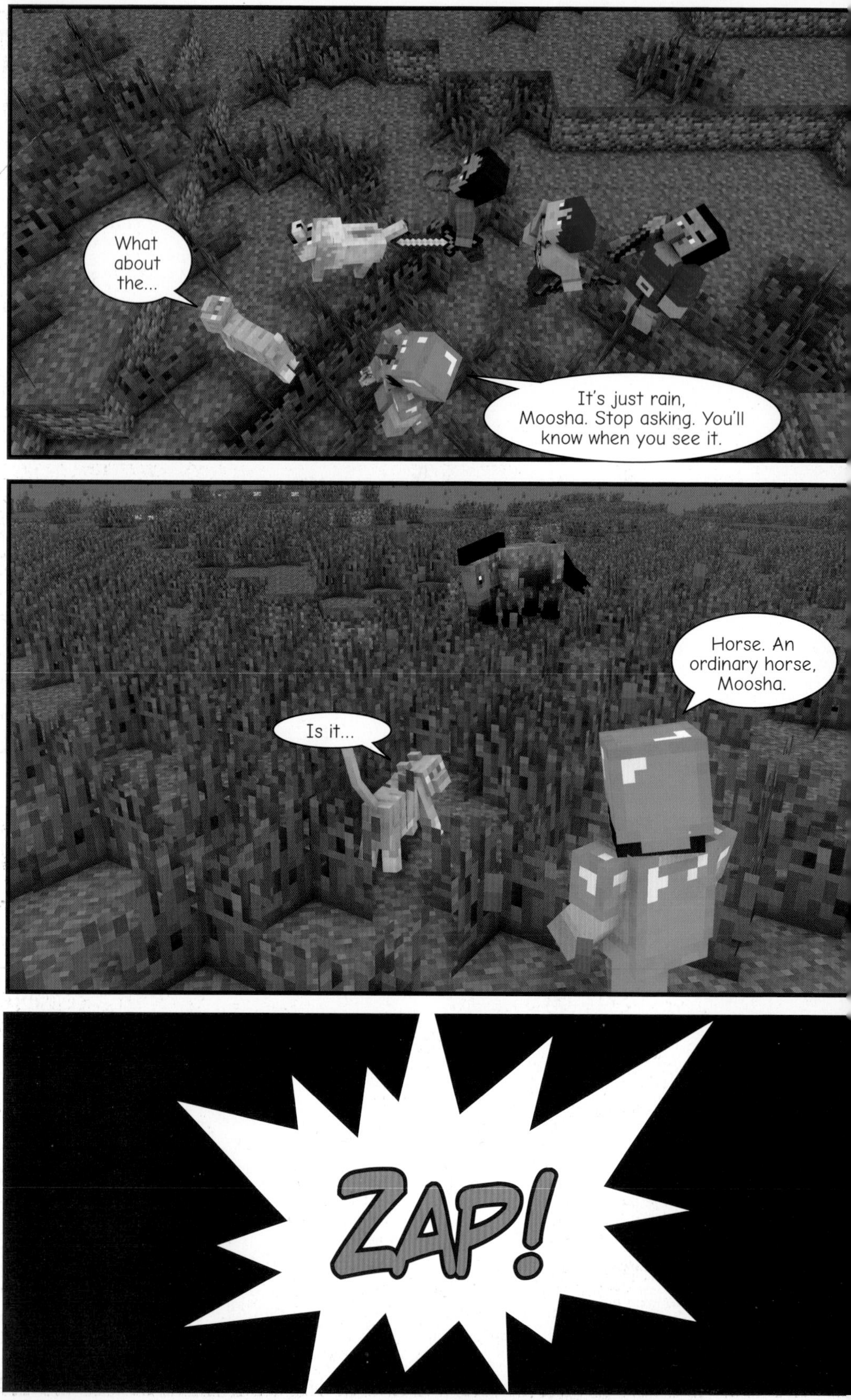
What about the...
It's just rain, Moosha. Stop asking. You'll know when you see it.
Horse. An ordinary horse, Moosha.
Is it...
ZAP!

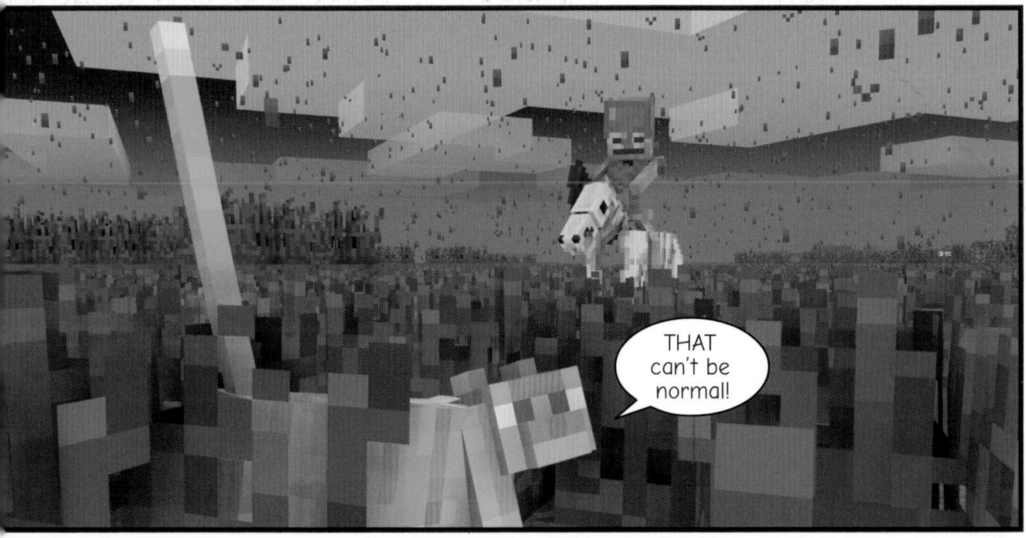
THAT can't be normal!

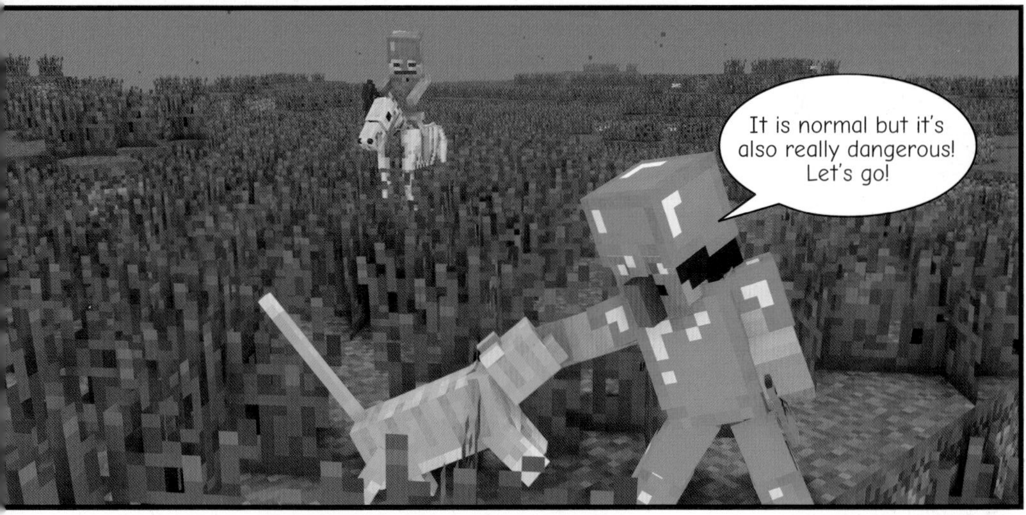
It is normal but it's also really dangerous! Let's go!

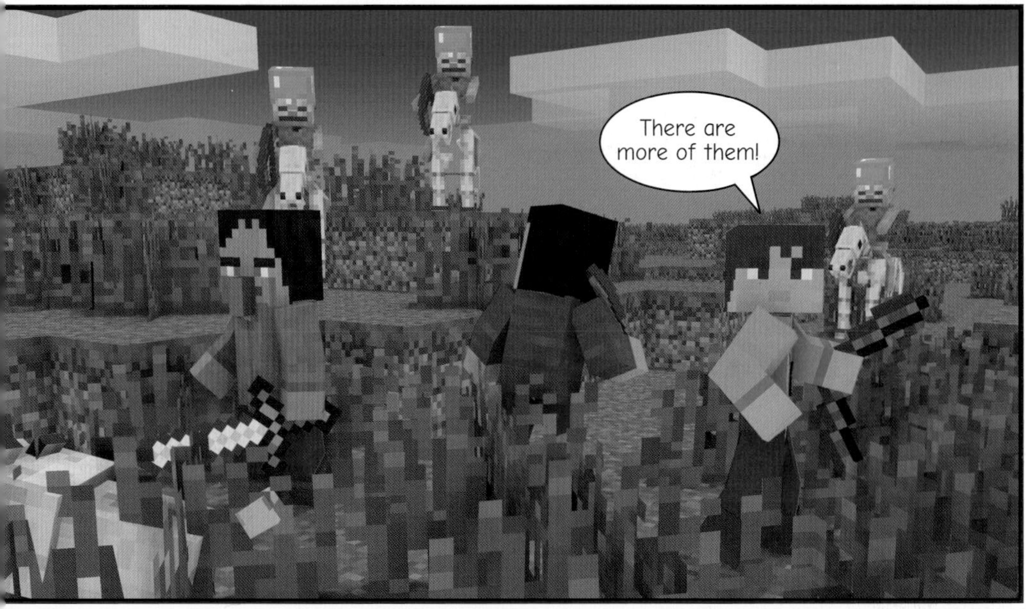
There are more of them!

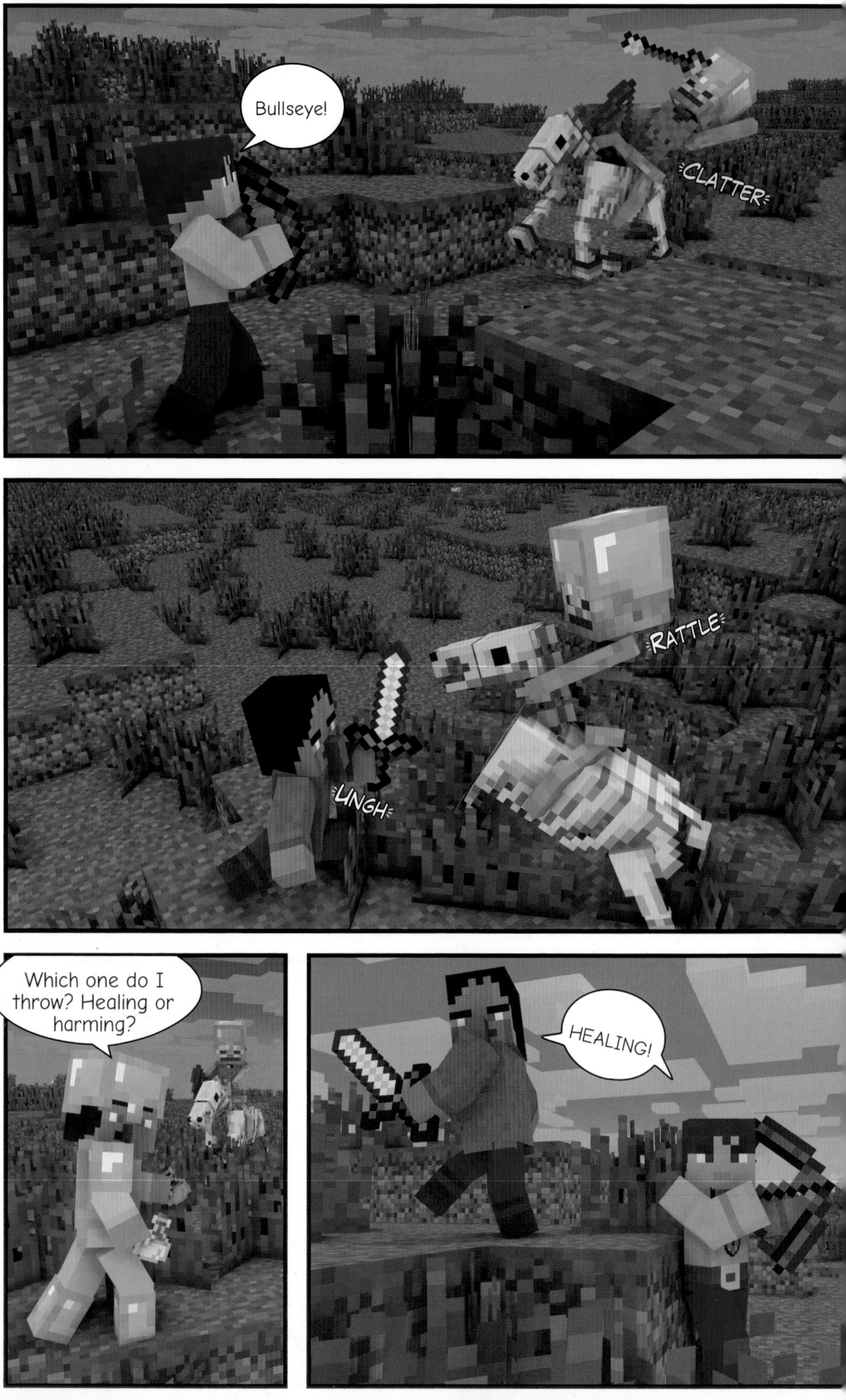
Bullseye!
CLATTER
RATTLE
UNGH
Which one do I throw? Healing or harming?
HEALING!

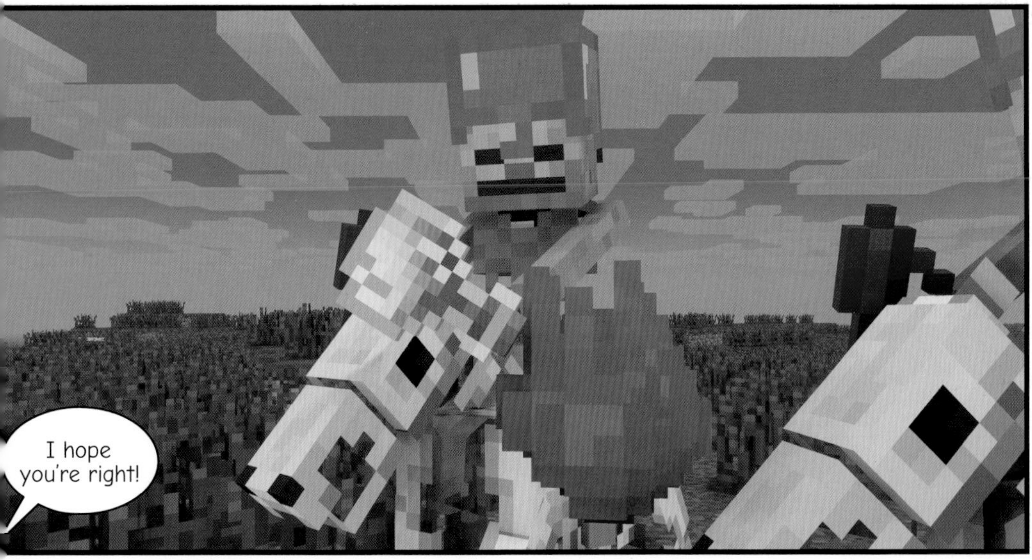
I hope you're right!

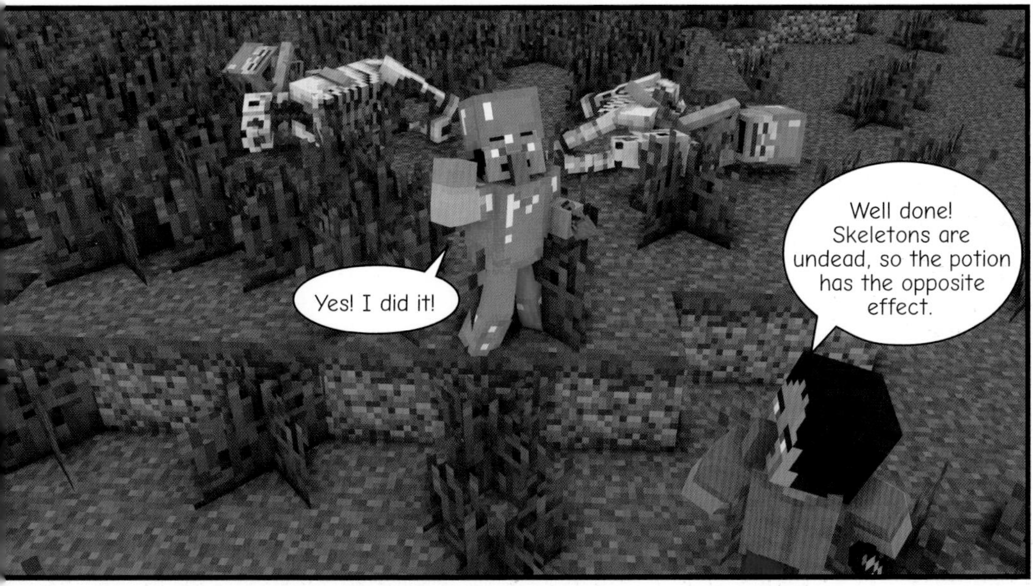
Yes! I did it!
Well done! Skeletons are undead, so the potion has the opposite effect.

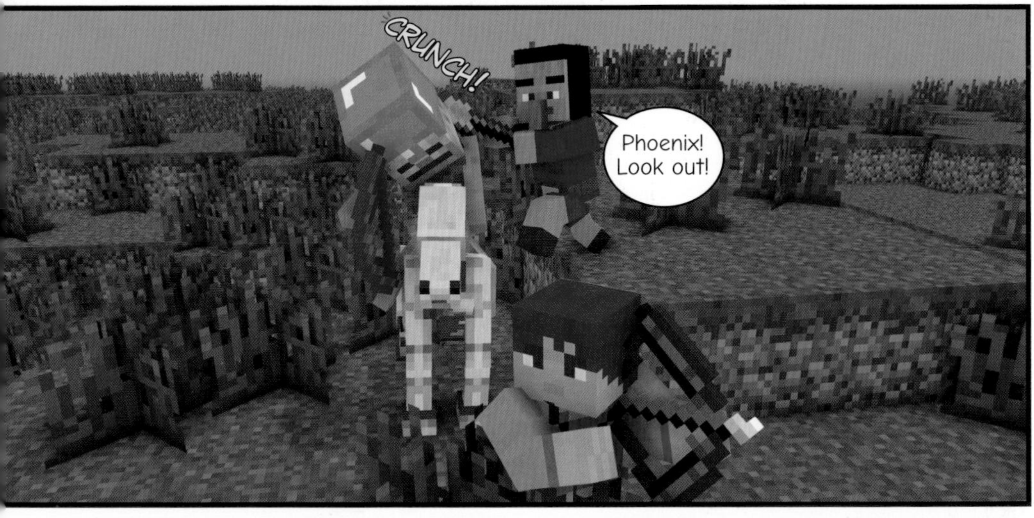
CRUNCH!
Phoenix! Look out!

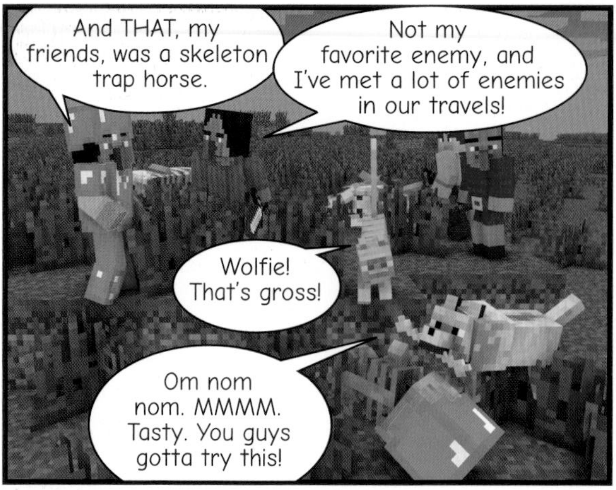
And THAT, my friends, was a skeleton trap horse.
Not my favorite enemy, and I've met a lot of enemies in our travels!
Wolfie! That's gross!
Om nom nom. MMMM. Tasty. You guys gotta try this!

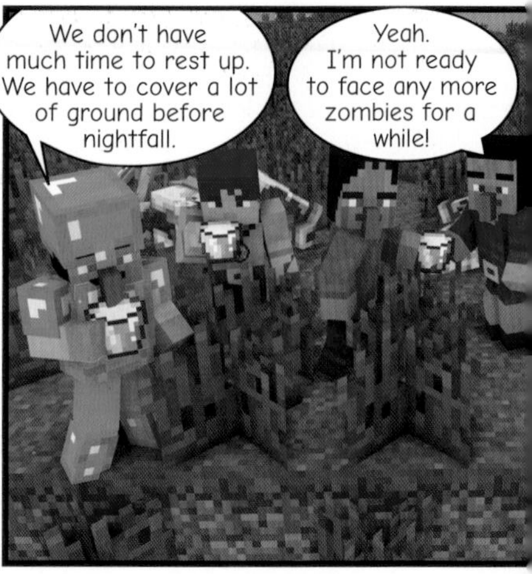
We don't have much time to rest up. We have to cover a lot of ground before nightfall.
Yeah. I'm not ready to face any more zombies for a while!

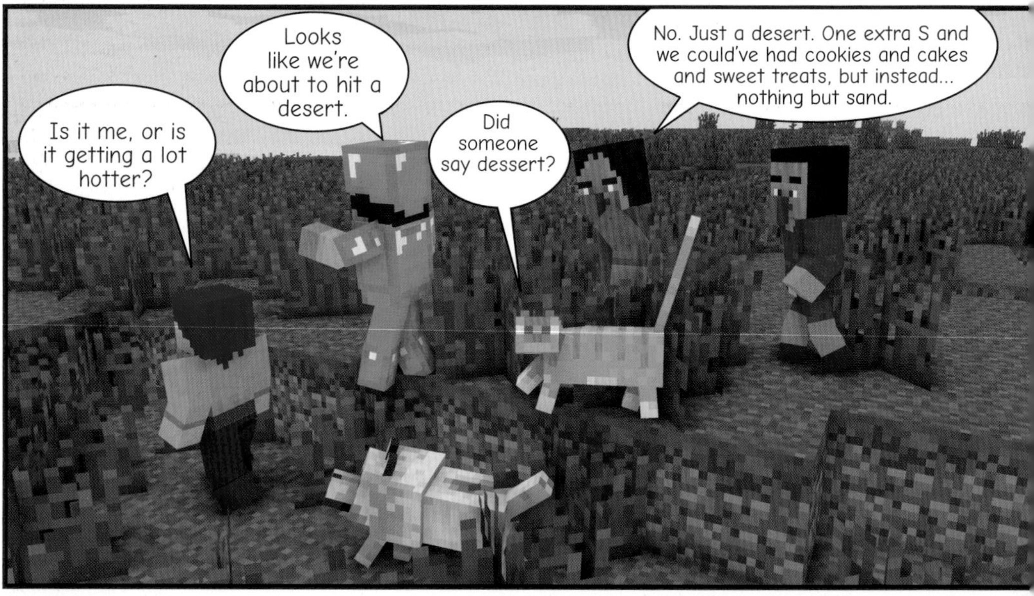
Is it me, or is it getting a lot hotter?
Looks like we're about to hit a desert.
Did someone say dessert?
No. Just a desert. One extra S and we could've had cookies and cakes and sweet treats, but instead... nothing but sand.

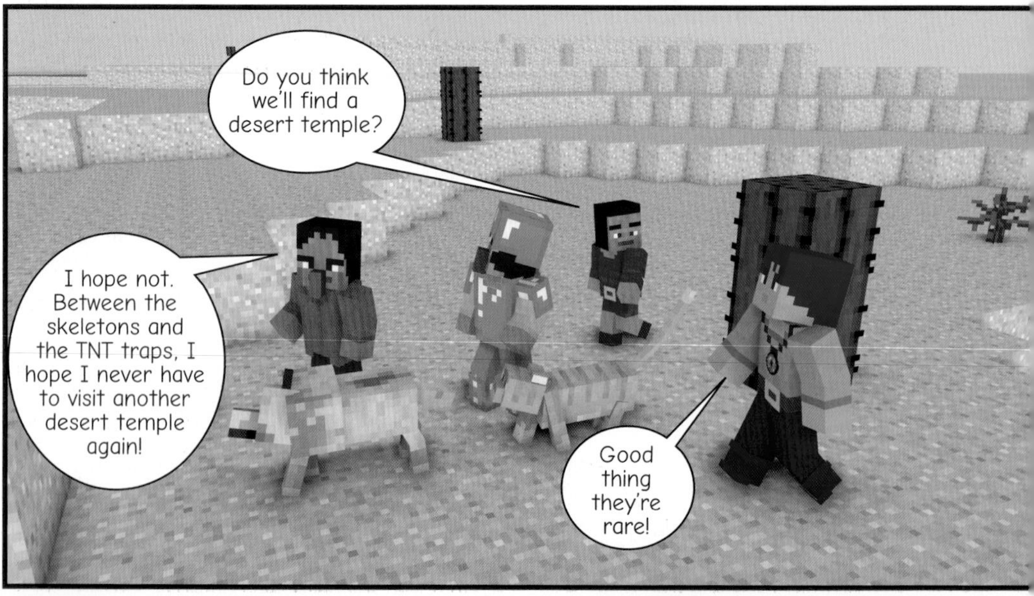
Do you think we'll find a desert temple?
I hope not. Between the skeletons and the TNT traps, I hope I never have to visit another desert temple again!
Good thing they're rare!

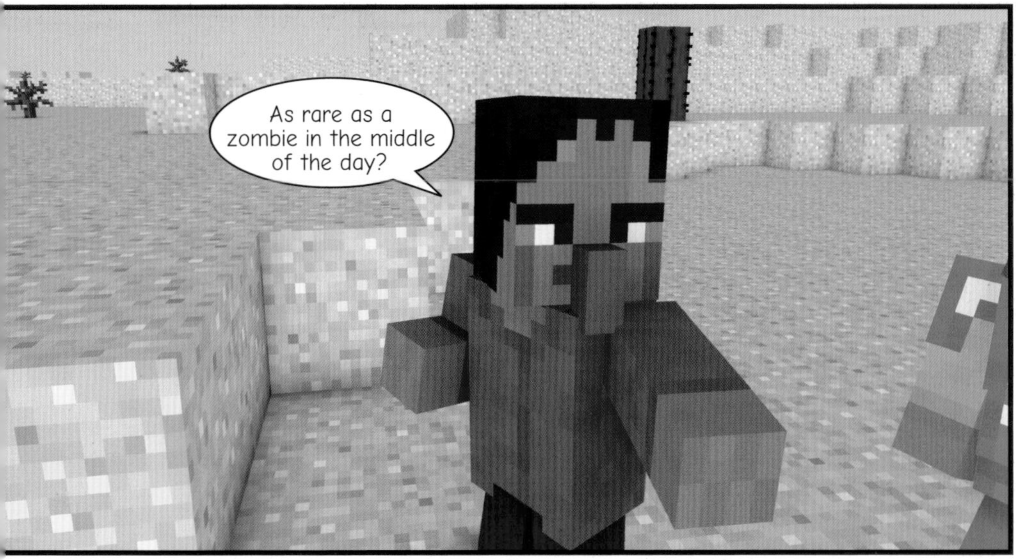
As rare as a zombie in the middle of the day?

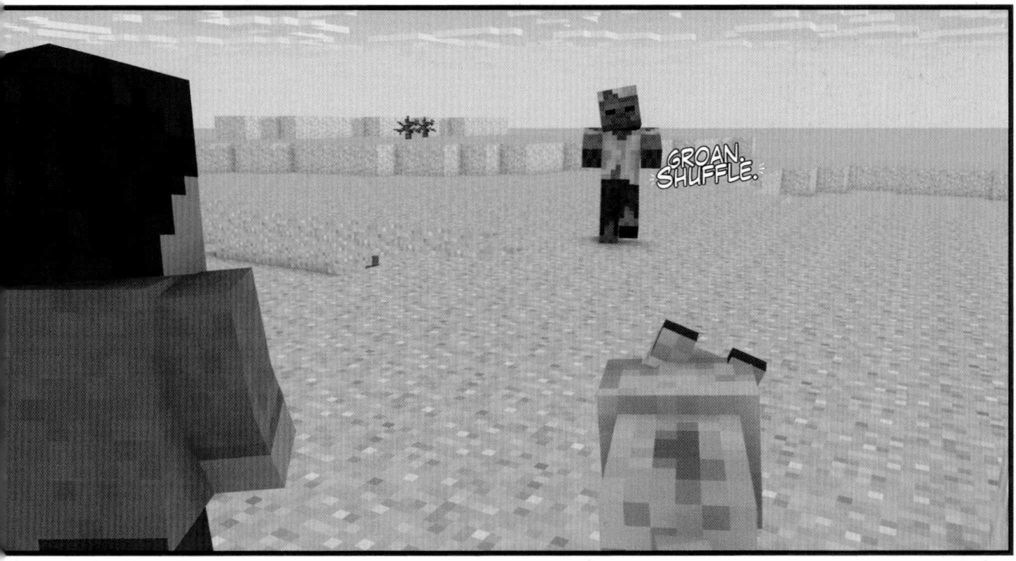
GROAN.
SHUFFLE.

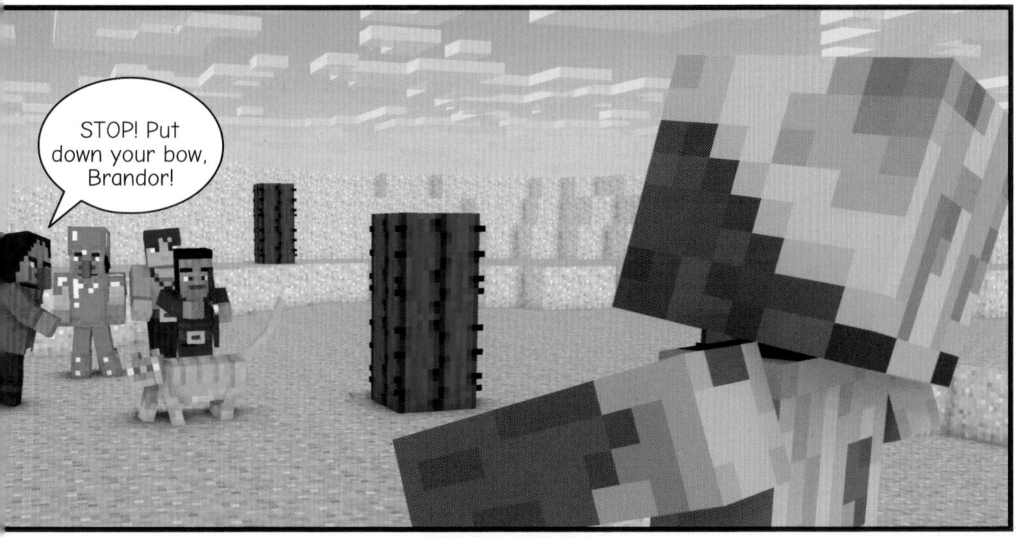
STOP! Put down your bow, Brandor!

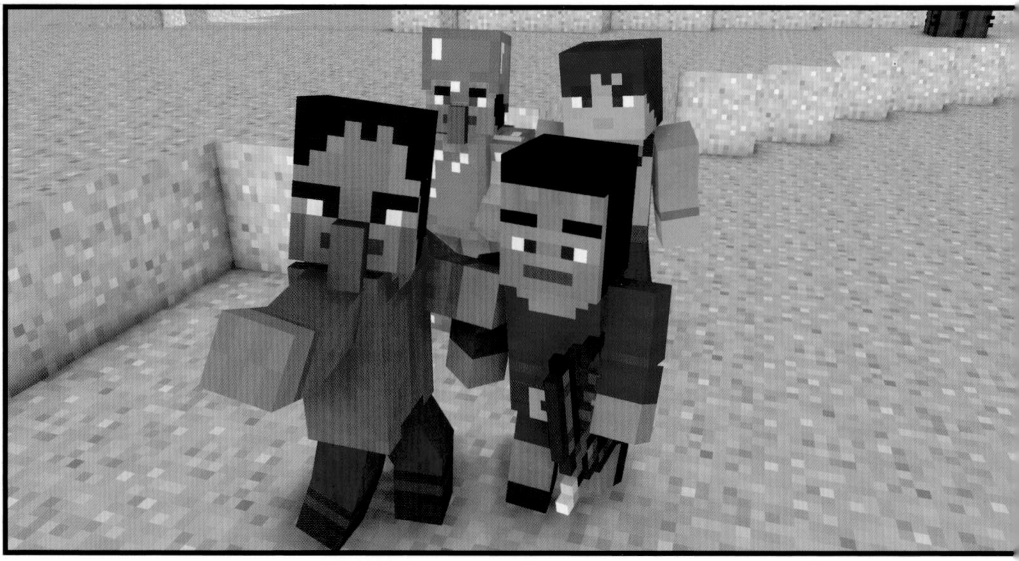

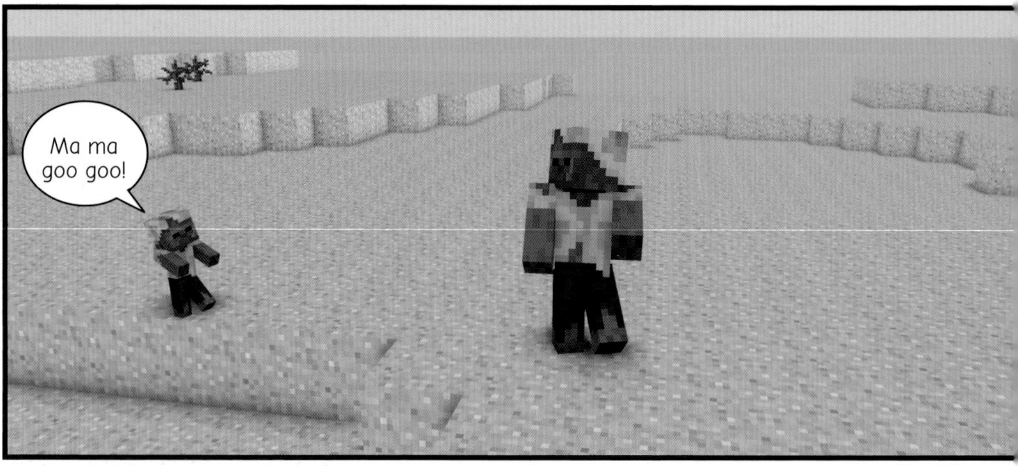

Ma ma goo goo!

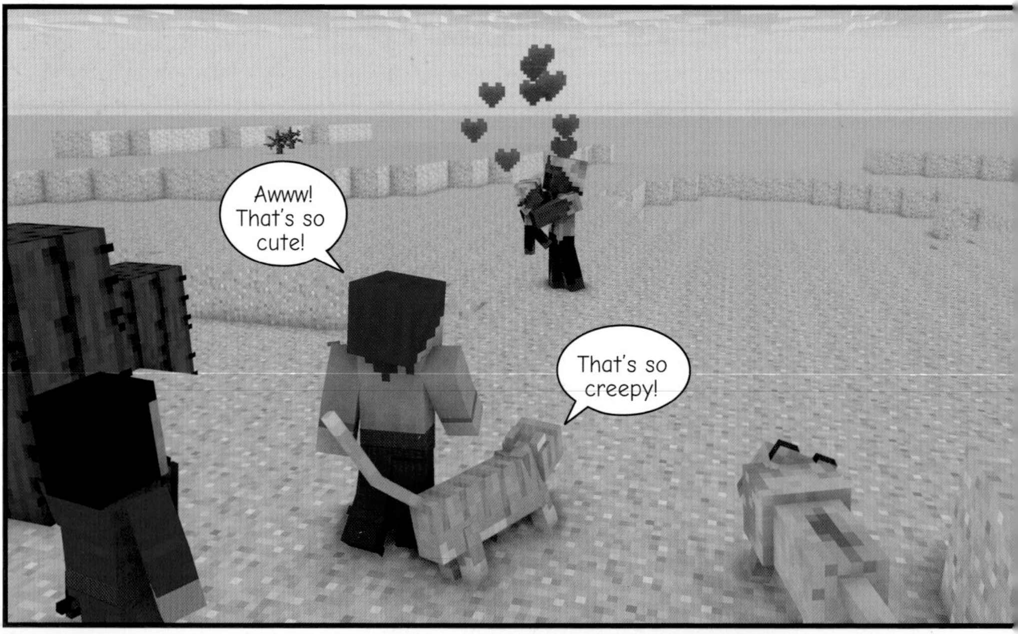

Awww! That's so cute!
That's so creepy!

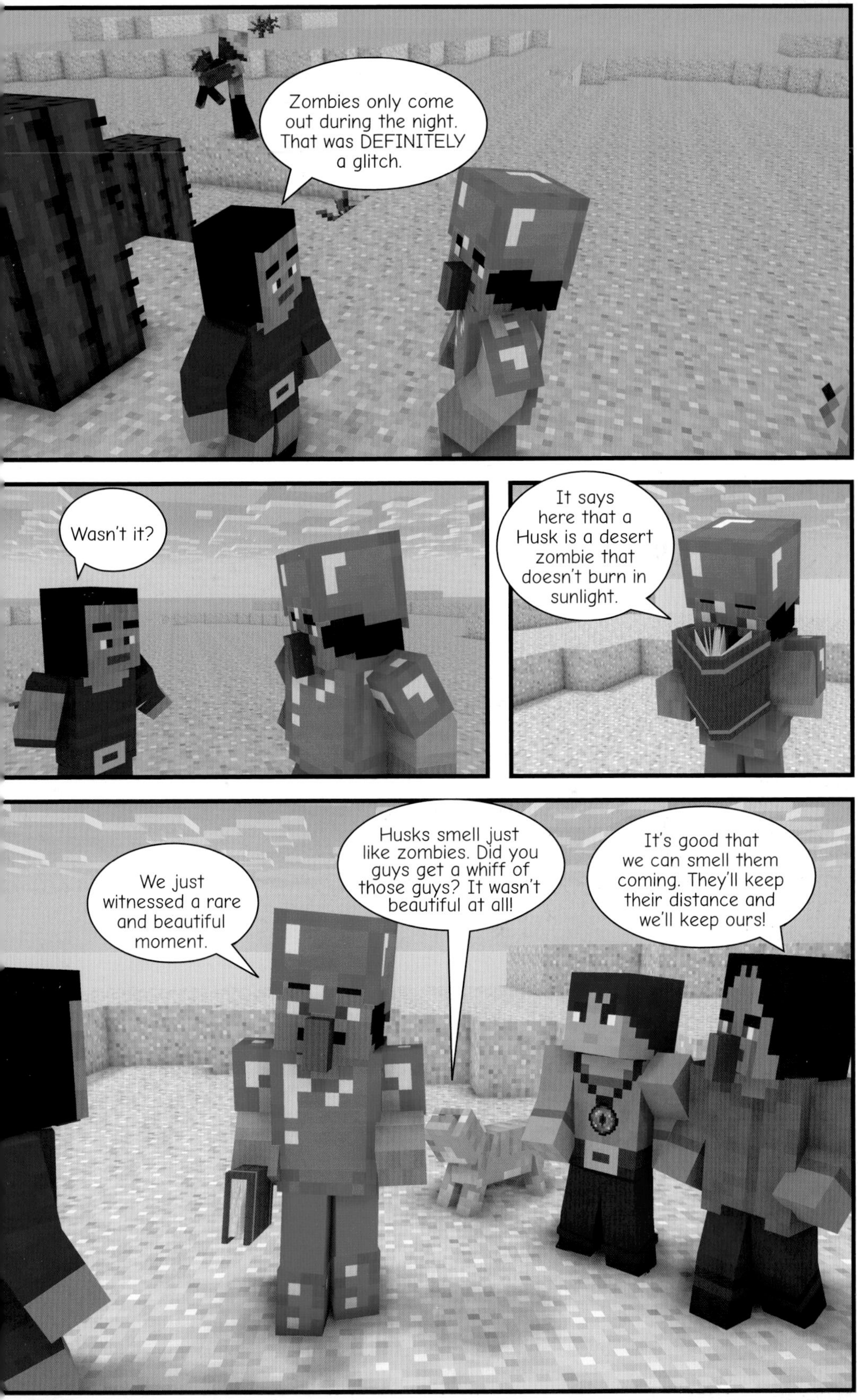
Zombies only come out during the night. That was DEFINITELY a glitch.
Wasn't it?
It says here that a Husk is a desert zombie that doesn't burn in sunlight.
We just witnessed a rare and beautiful moment.
Husks smell just like zombies. Did you guys get a whiff of those guys? It wasn't beautiful at all!
It's good that we can smell them coming. They'll keep their distance and we'll keep ours!

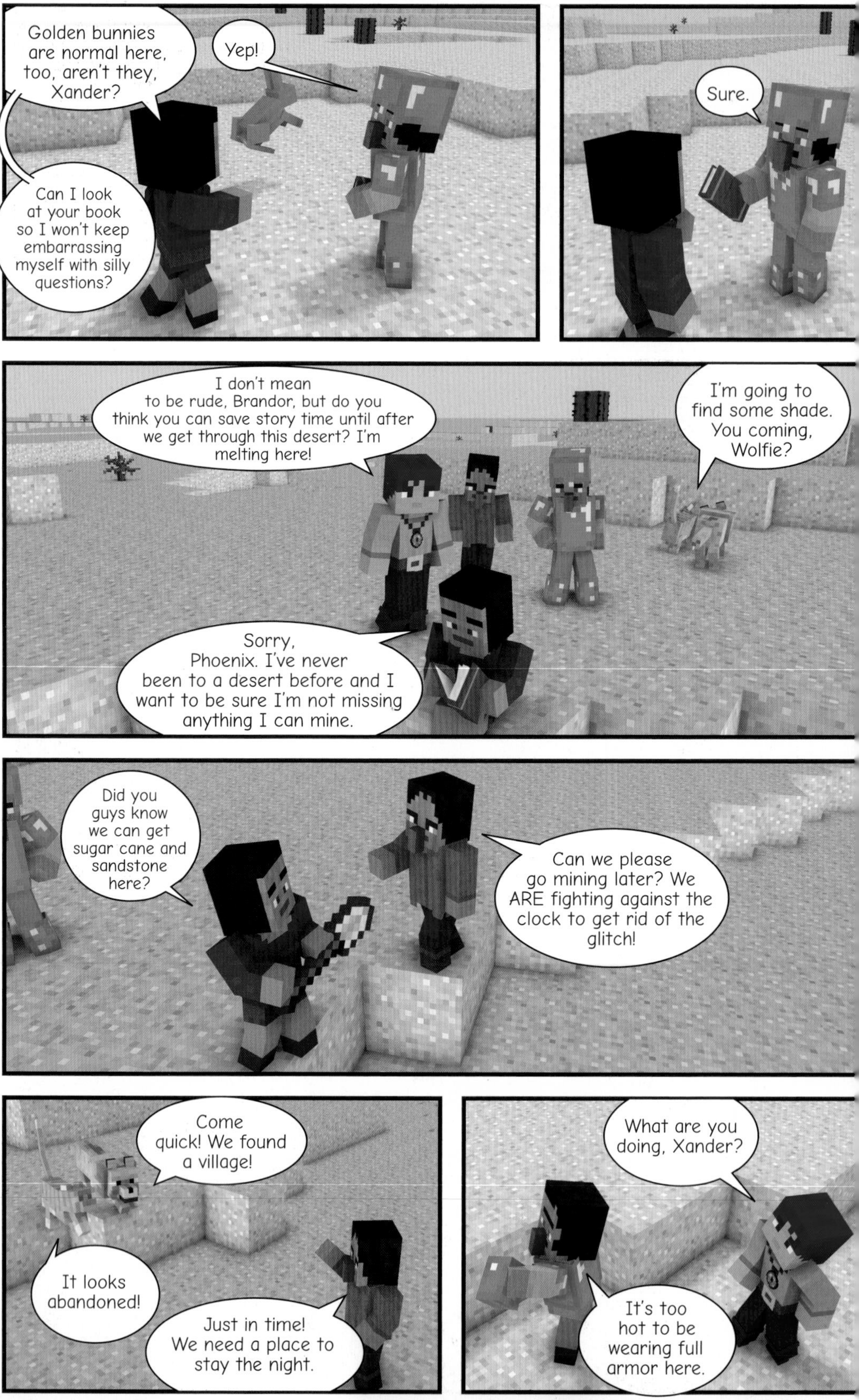
Golden bunnies are normal here, too, aren't they, Xander?
Yep!
Can I look at your book so I won't keep embarrassing myself with silly questions?
Sure.
I don't mean to be rude, Brandor, but do you think you can save story time until after we get through this desert? I'm melting here!
I'm going to find some shade. You coming, Wolfie?
Sorry, Phoenix. I've never been to a desert before and I want to be sure I'm not missing anything I can mine.
Did you guys know we can get sugar cane and sandstone here?
Can we please go mining later? We ARE fighting against the clock to get rid of the glitch!
Come quick! We found a village!
It looks abandoned!
Just in time! We need a place to stay the night.
What are you doing, Xander?
It's too hot to be wearing full armor here.

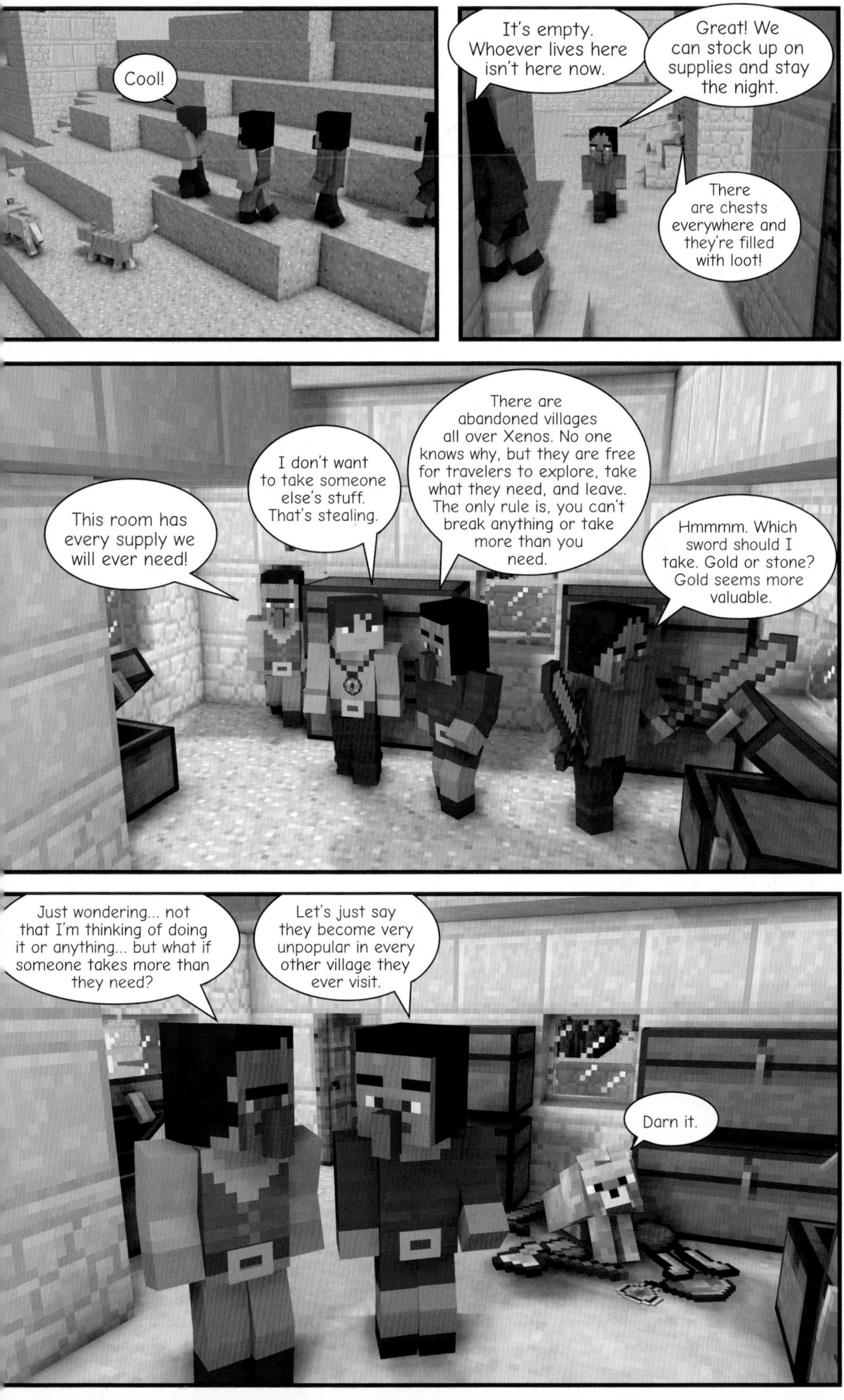
Cool!
It's empty. Whoever lives here isn't here now.
Great! We can stock up on supplies and stay the night.
There are chests everywhere and they're filled with loot!
This room has every supply we will ever need!
I don't want to take someone else's stuff. That's stealing.
There are abandoned villages all over Xenos. No one knows why, but they are free for travelers to explore, take what they need, and leave. The only rule is, you can't break anything or take more than you need.
Hmmmm. Which sword should I take. Gold or stone? Gold seems more valuable.
Just wondering... not that I'm thinking of doing it or anything... but what if someone takes more than they need?
Let's just say they become very unpopular in every other village they ever visit.
Darn it.

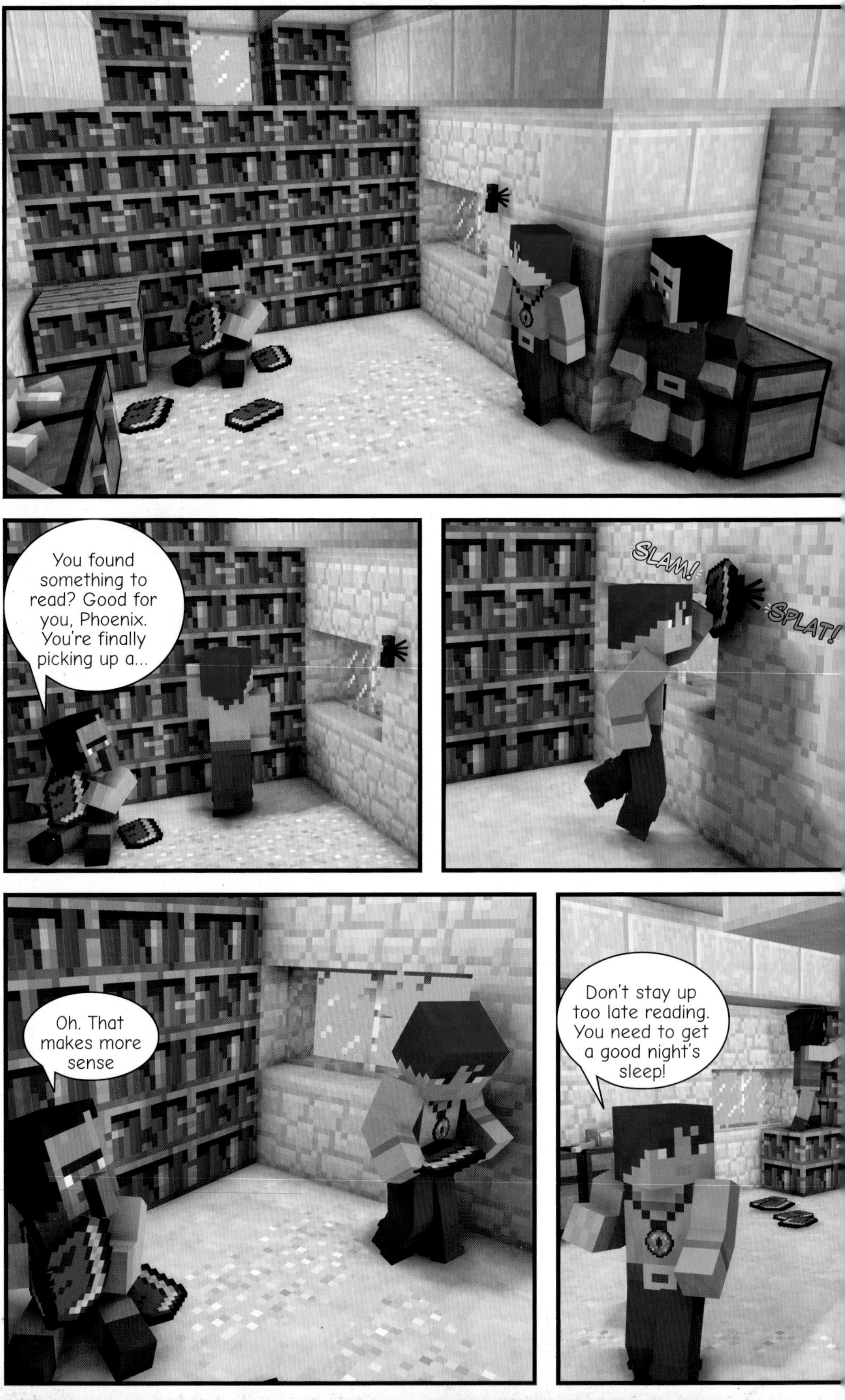
You found something to read? Good for you, Phoenix. You're finally picking up a...
SLAM!
SPLAT!
Oh. That makes more sense
Don't stay up too late reading. You need to get a good night's sleep!

CHAPTER 8

LLAGERS

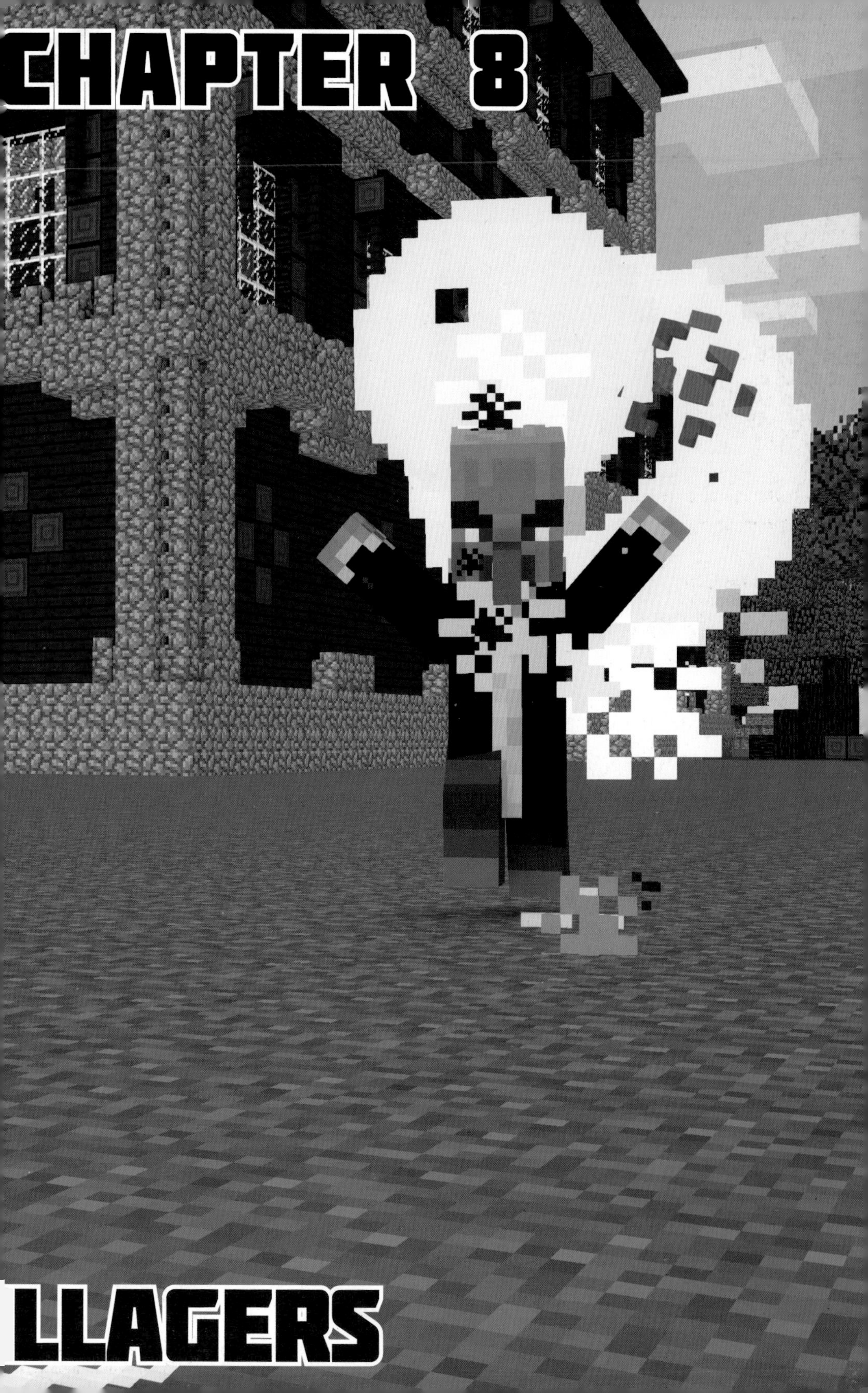

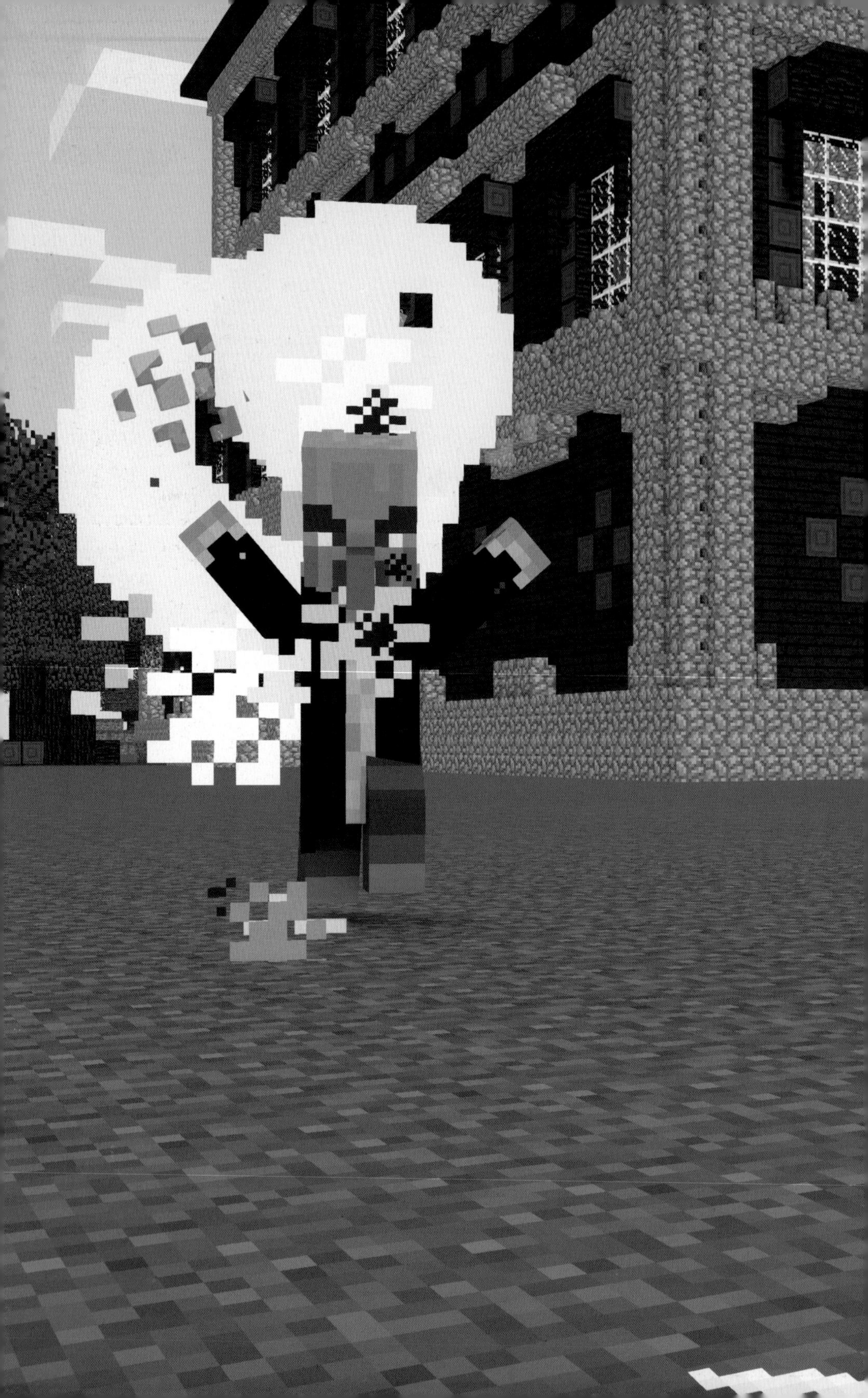

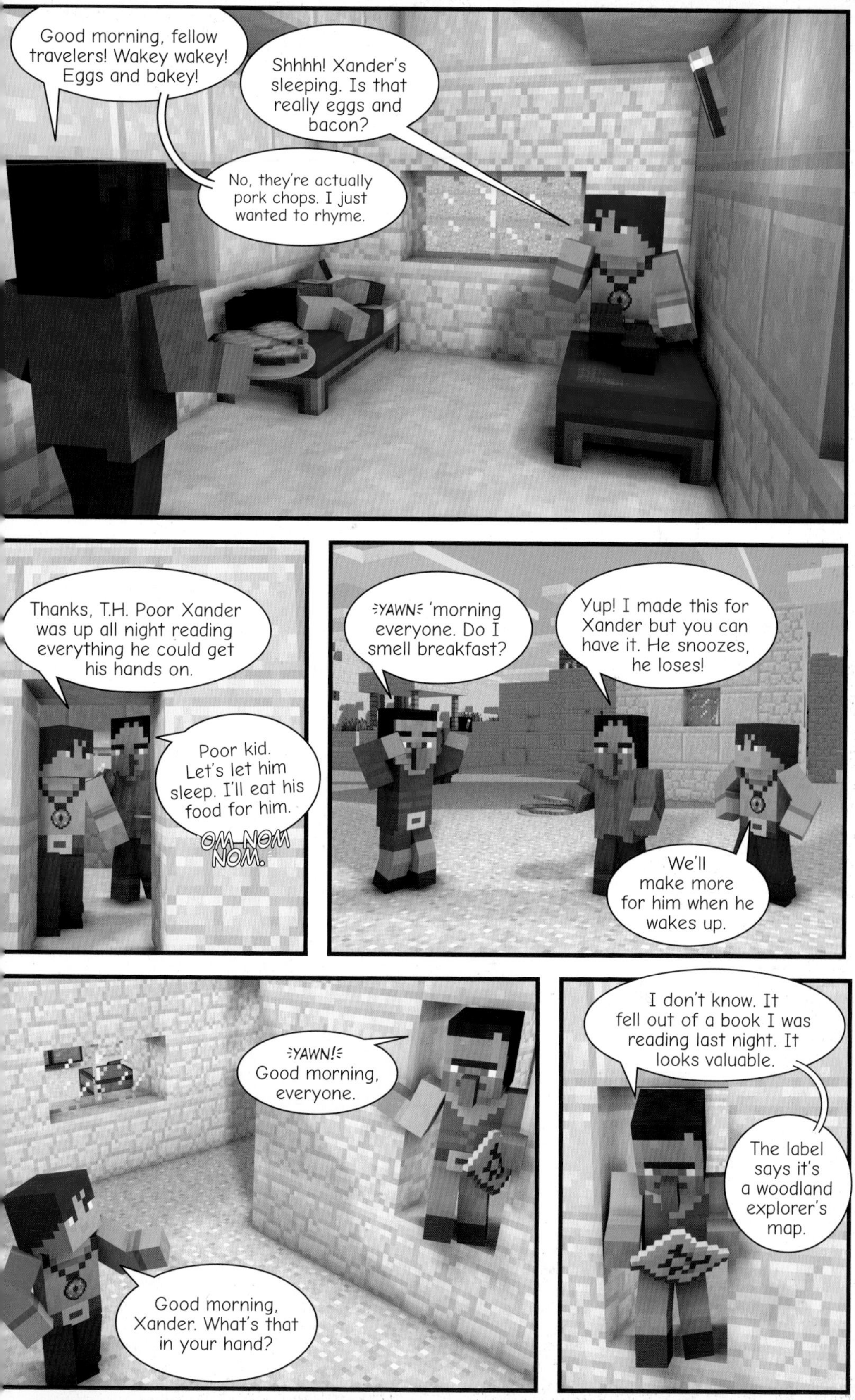
Good morning, fellow travelers! Wakey wakey! Eggs and bakey!
Shhhh! Xander's sleeping. Is that really eggs and bacon?
No, they're actually pork chops. I just wanted to rhyme.
Thanks, T.H. Poor Xander was up all night reading everything he could get his hands on.
Poor kid. Let's let him sleep. I'll eat his food for him.
OM NOM NOM.
YAWN 'morning everyone. Do I smell breakfast?
Yup! I made this for Xander but you can have it. He snoozes, he loses!
We'll make more for him when he wakes up.
YAWN!
Good morning, everyone.
Good morning, Xander. What's that in your hand?
I don't know. It fell out of a book I was reading last night. It looks valuable.
The label says it's a woodland explorer's map.

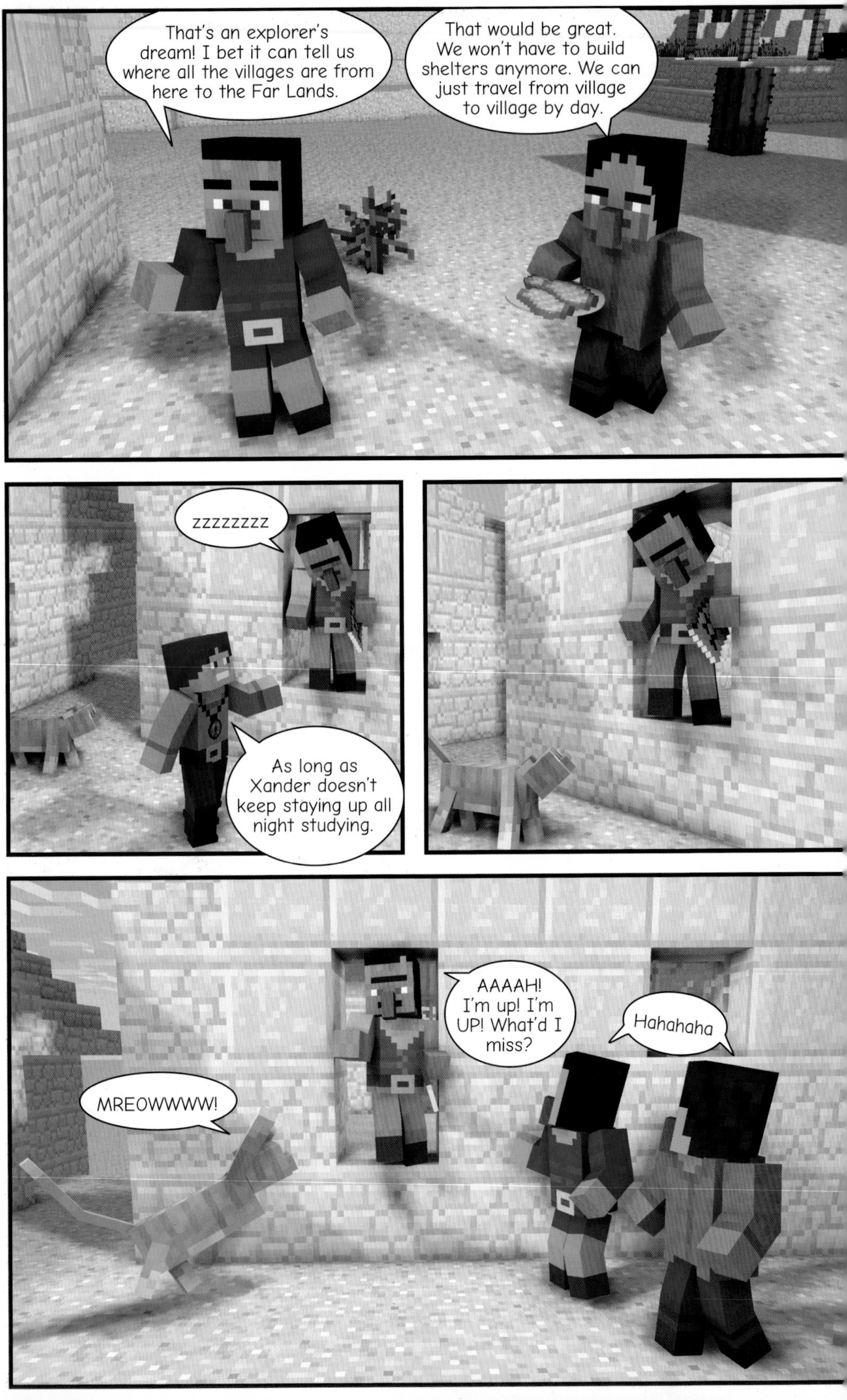
That's an explorer's dream! I bet it can tell us where all the villages are from here to the Far Lands.
That would be great. We won't have to build shelters anymore. We can just travel from village to village by day.
ZZZZZZZZ
As long as Xander doesn't keep staying up all night studying.
MREOWWWW!
AAAAH! I'm up! I'm UP! What'd I miss?
Hahahaha

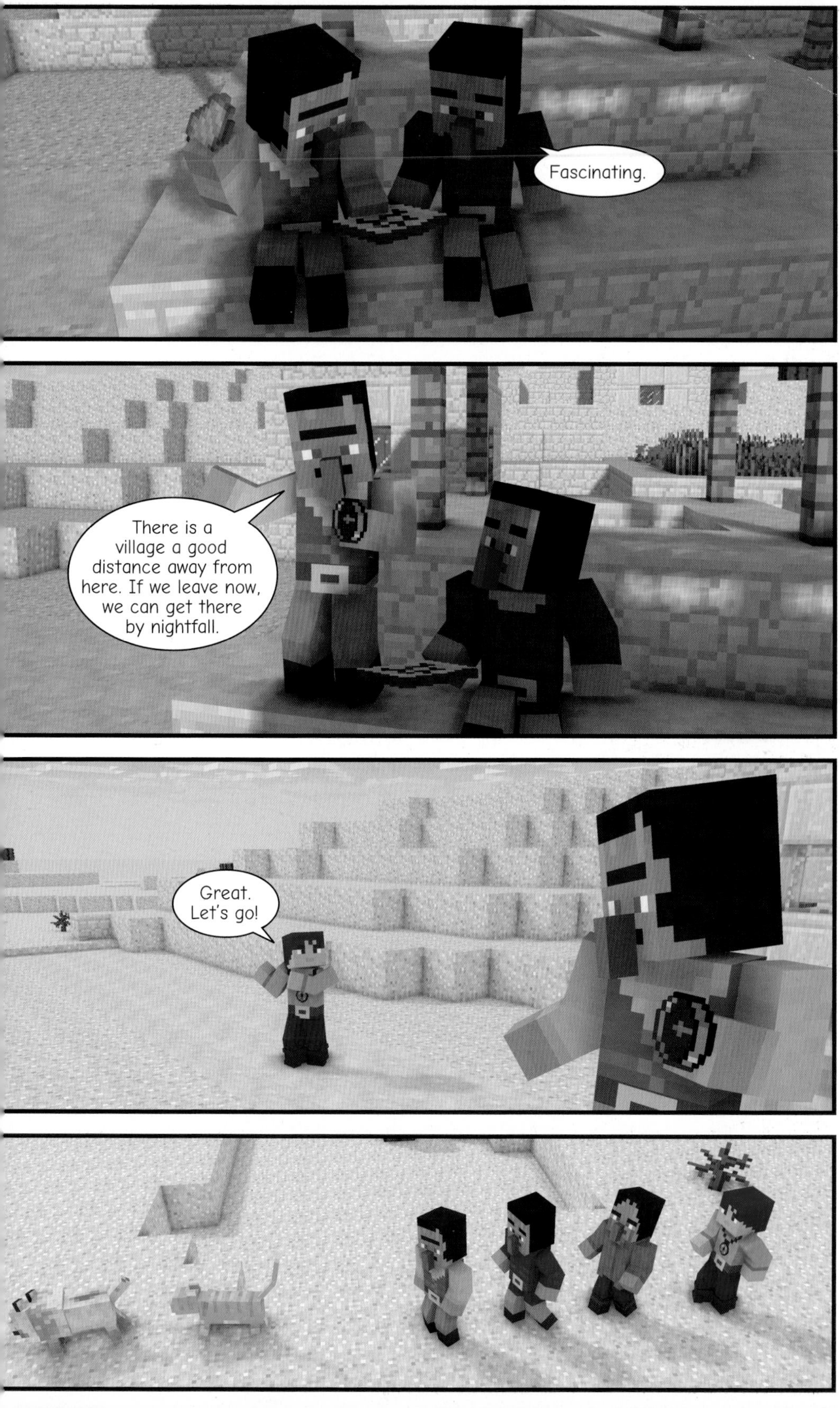
Fascinating.
There is a village a good distance away from here. If we leave now, we can get there by nightfall.
Great. Let's go!

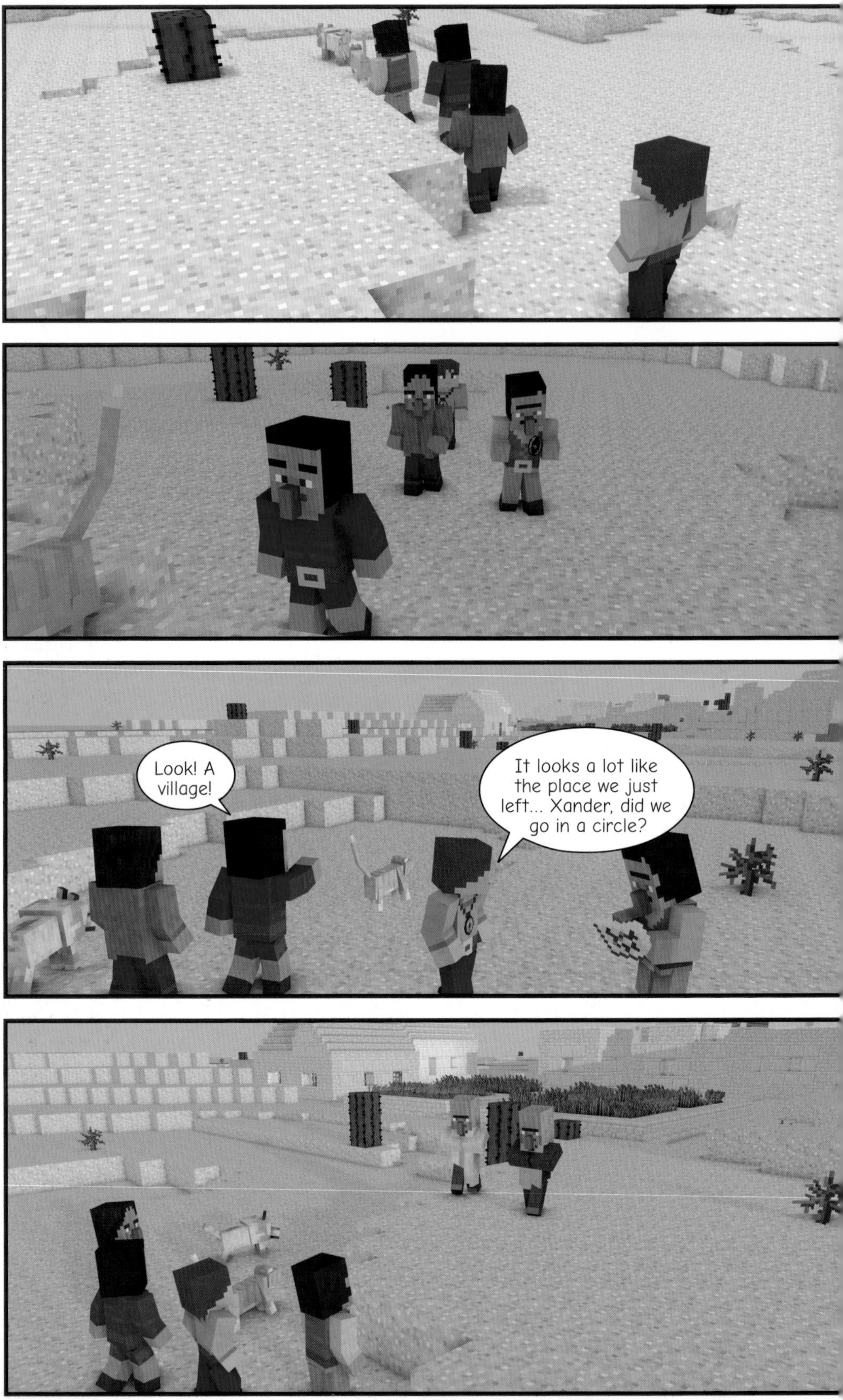
Look! A village!
It looks a lot like the place we just left... Xander, did we go in a circle?

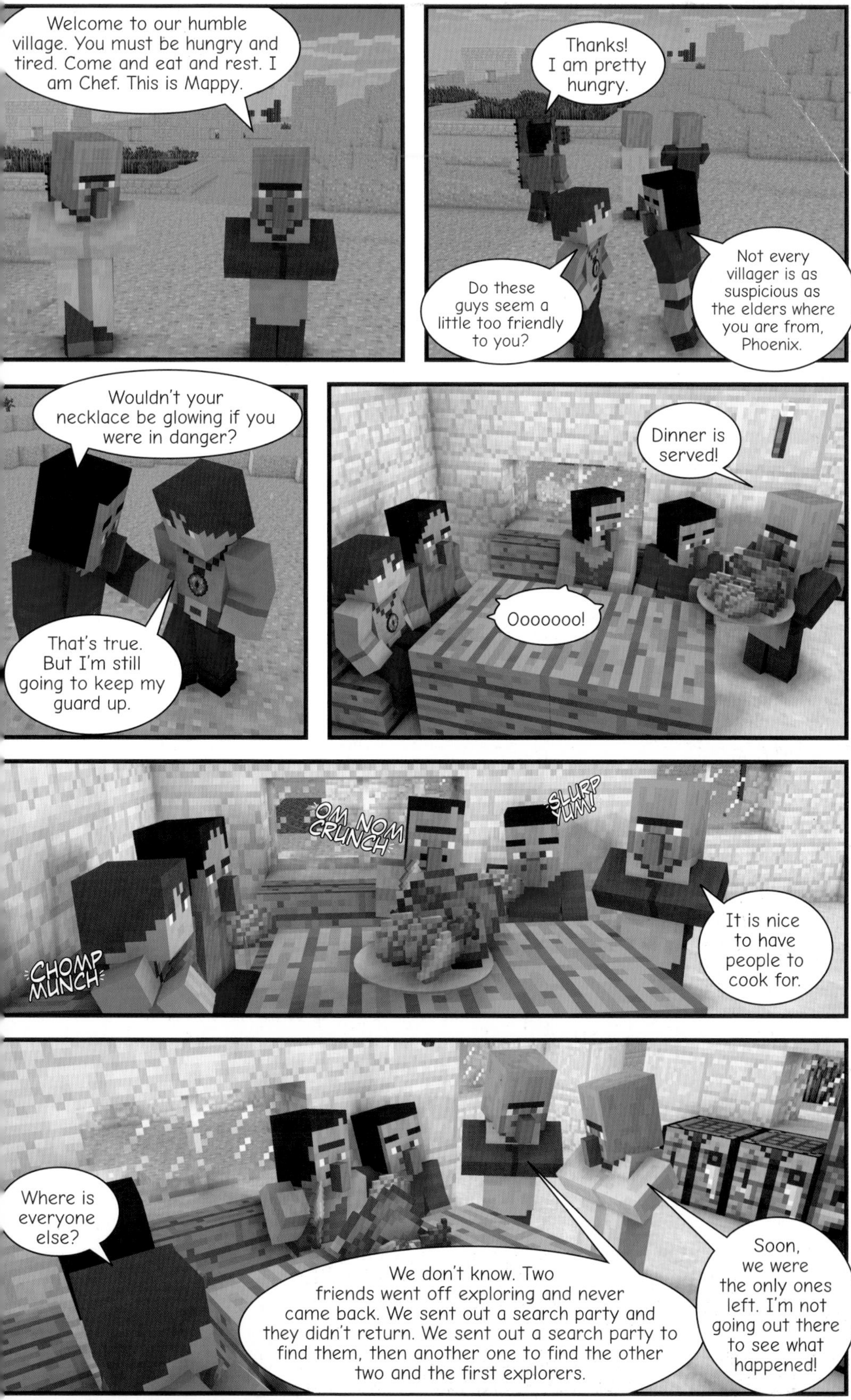
Welcome to our humble village. You must be hungry and tired. Come and eat and rest. I am Chef. This is Mappy.
Thanks! I am pretty hungry.
Do these guys seem a little too friendly to you?
Not every villager is as suspicious as the elders where you are from, Phoenix.
Wouldn't your necklace be glowing if you were in danger?
That's true. But I'm still going to keep my guard up.
Dinner is served!
Ooooooo!
OM NOM CRUNCH
SLURP YUM!
CHOMP MUNCH
It is nice to have people to cook for.
Where is everyone else?
We don't know. Two friends went off exploring and never came back. We sent out a search party and they didn't return. We sent out a search party to find them, then another one to find the other two and the first explorers.
Soon, we were the only ones left. I'm not going out there to see what happened!

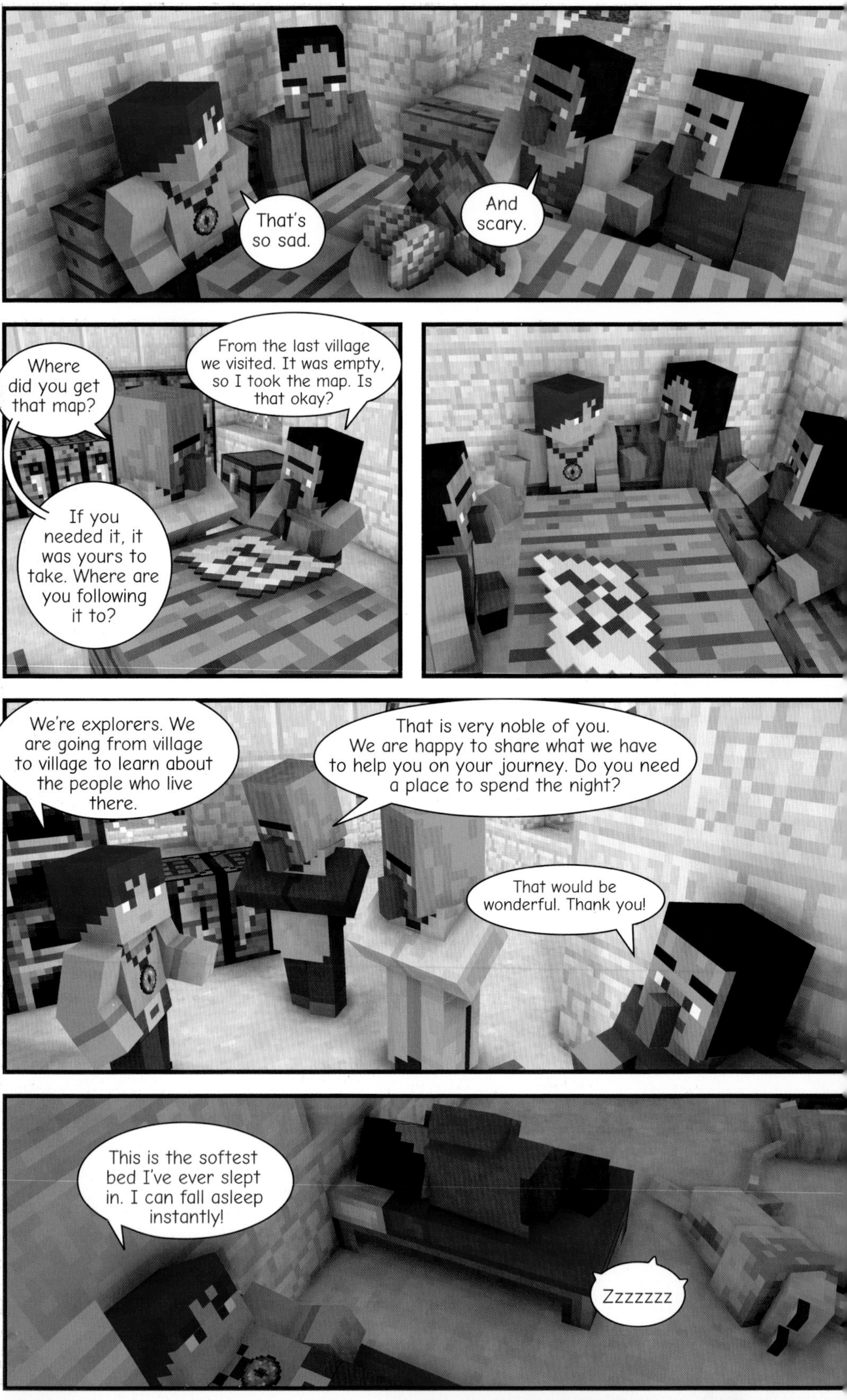
That's so sad.
And scary.
Where did you get that map?
From the last village we visited. It was empty, so I took the map. Is that okay?
If you needed it, it was yours to take. Where are you following it to?
We're explorers. We are going from village to village to learn about the people who live there.
That is very noble of you. We are happy to share what we have to help you on your journey. Do you need a place to spend the night?
That would be wonderful. Thank you!
This is the softest bed I've ever slept in. I can fall asleep instantly!
Zzzzzzz

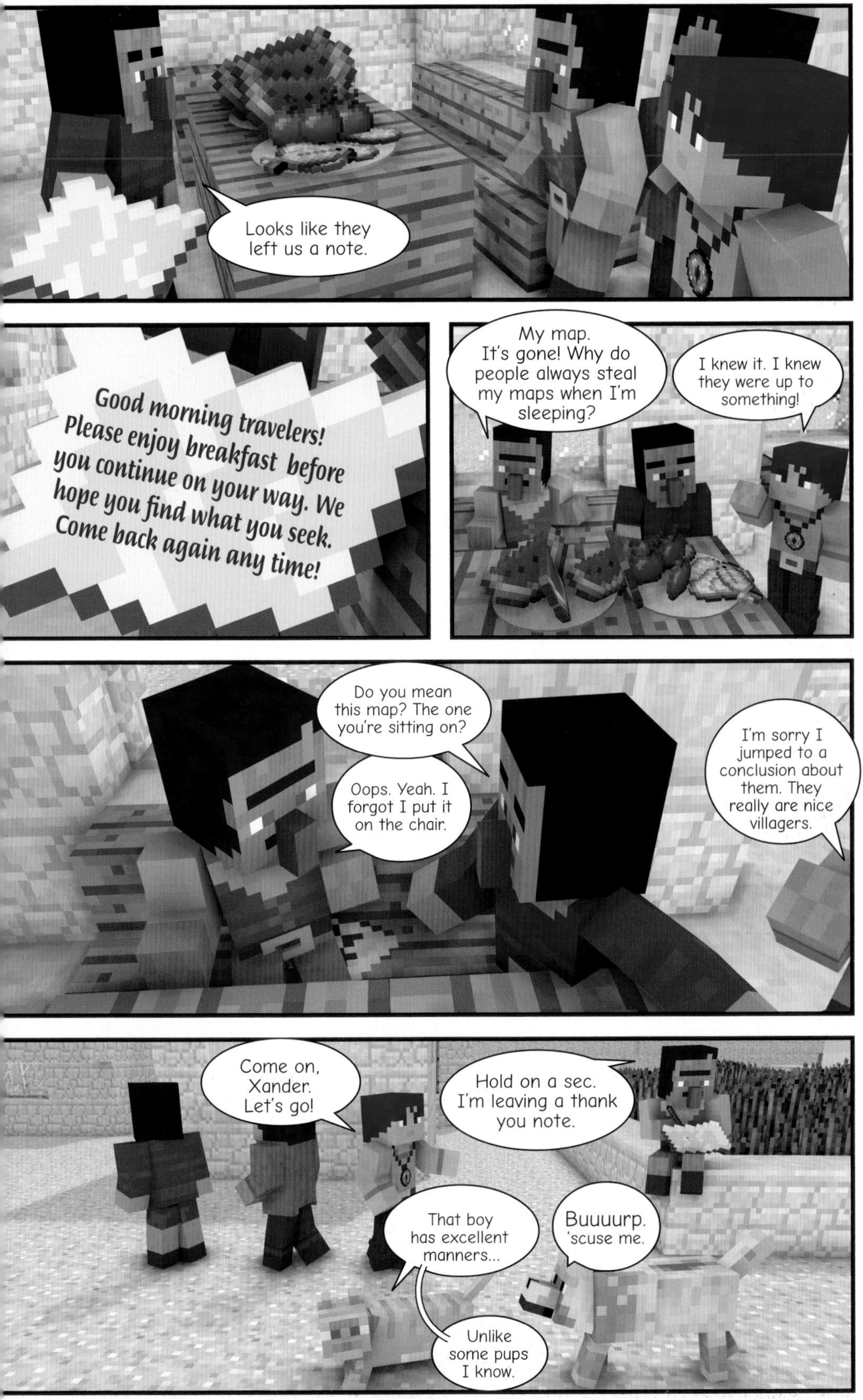
Looks like they left us a note.
Good morning travelers! Please enjoy breakfast before you continue on your way. We hope you find what you seek. Come back again any time!
My map. It's gone! Why do people always steal my maps when I'm sleeping?
I knew it. I knew they were up to something!
Do you mean this map? The one you're sitting on?
Oops. Yeah. I forgot I put it on the chair.
I'm sorry I jumped to a conclusion about them. They really are nice villagers.
Come on, Xander. Let's go!
Hold on a sec. I'm leaving a thank you note.
That boy has excellent manners...
Unlike some pups I know.
Buuuurp. 'scuse me.

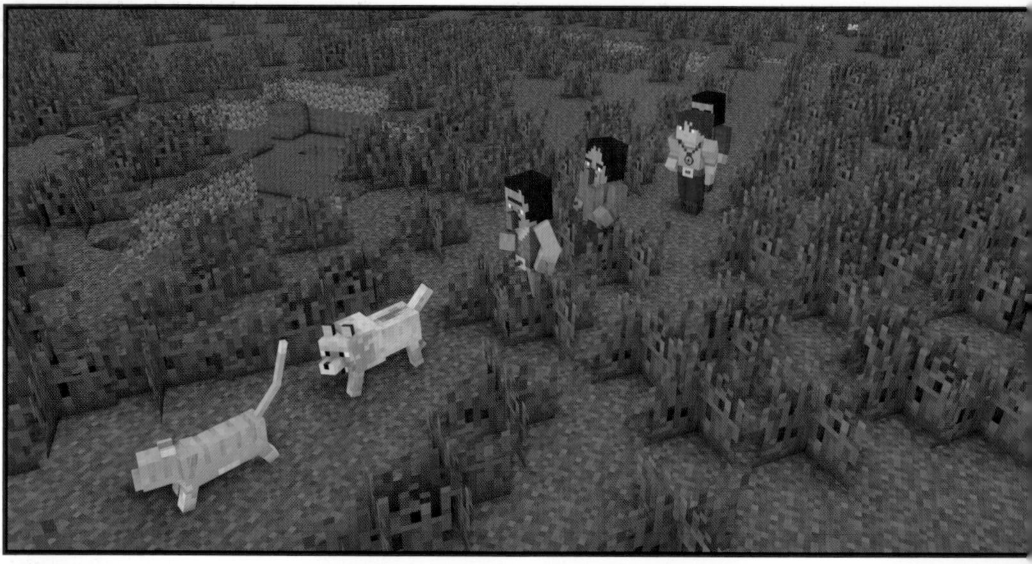

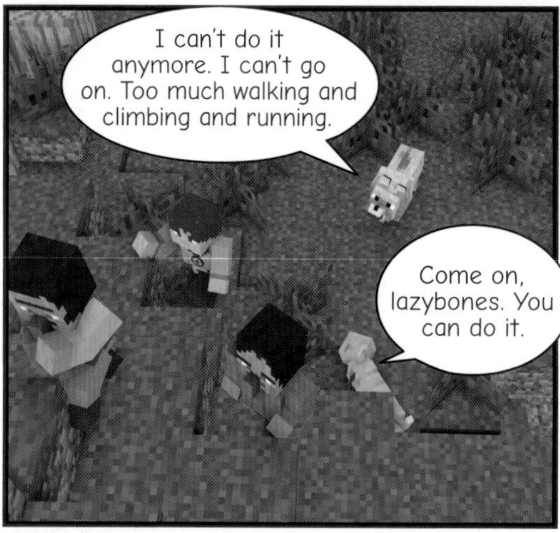
I can't do it anymore. I can't go on. Too much walking and climbing and running.
Come on, lazybones. You can do it.

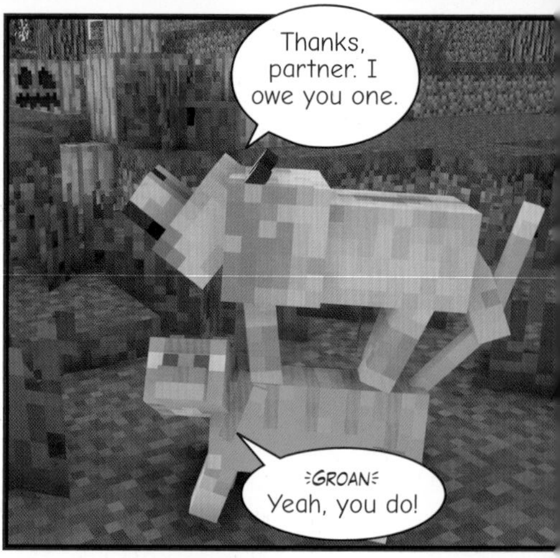
Thanks, partner. I owe you one.
GROAN
Yeah, you do!

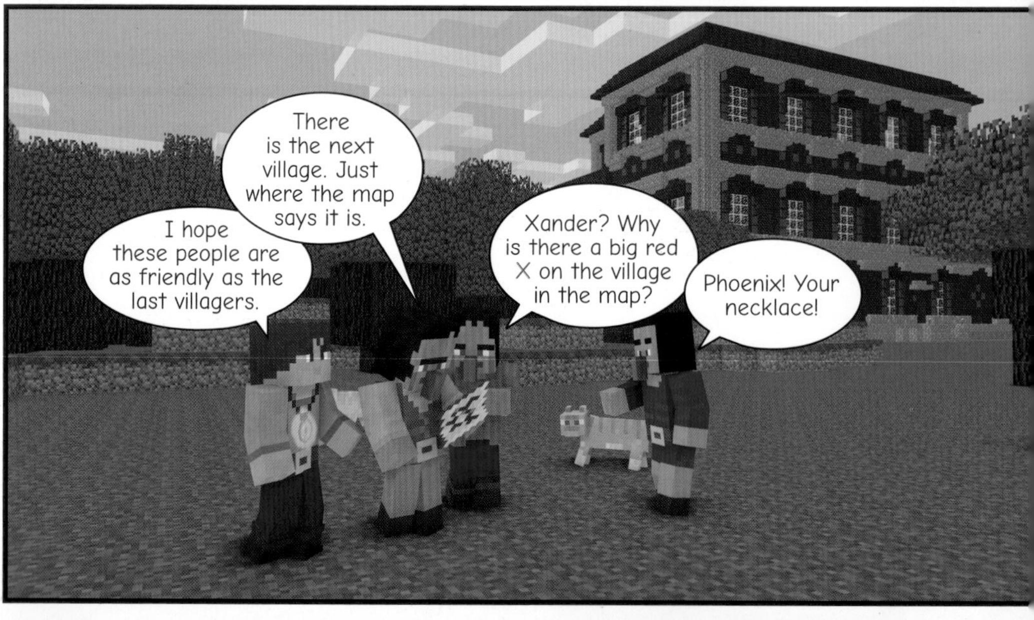
There is the next village. Just where the map says it is.
I hope these people are as friendly as the last villagers.
Xander? Why is there a big red X on the village in the map?
Phoenix! Your necklace!

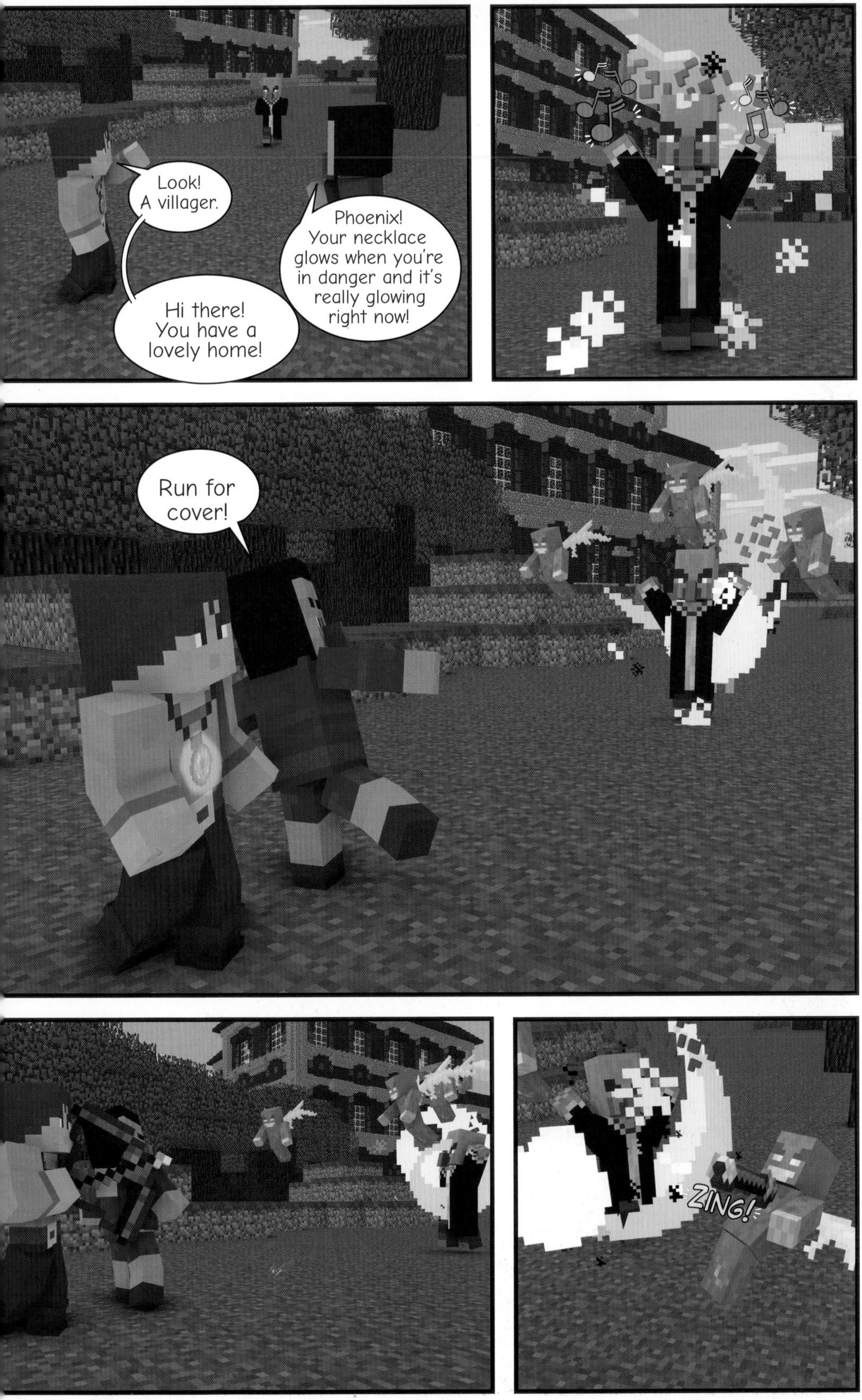
Look! A villager.
Hi there! You have a lovely home!
Phoenix! Your necklace glows when you're in danger and it's really glowing right now!
Run for cover!
ZING!

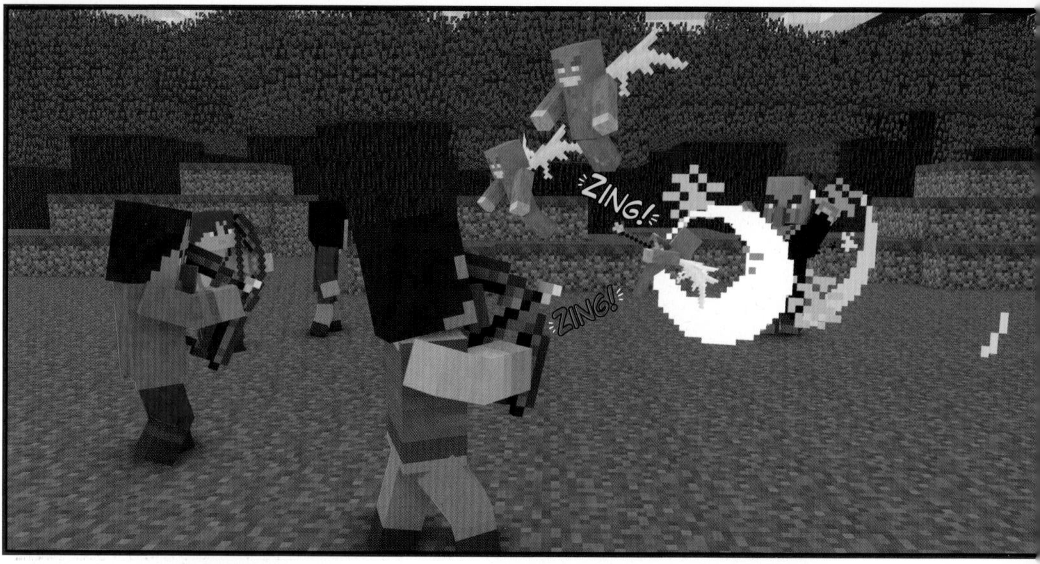
ZING!
ZING!

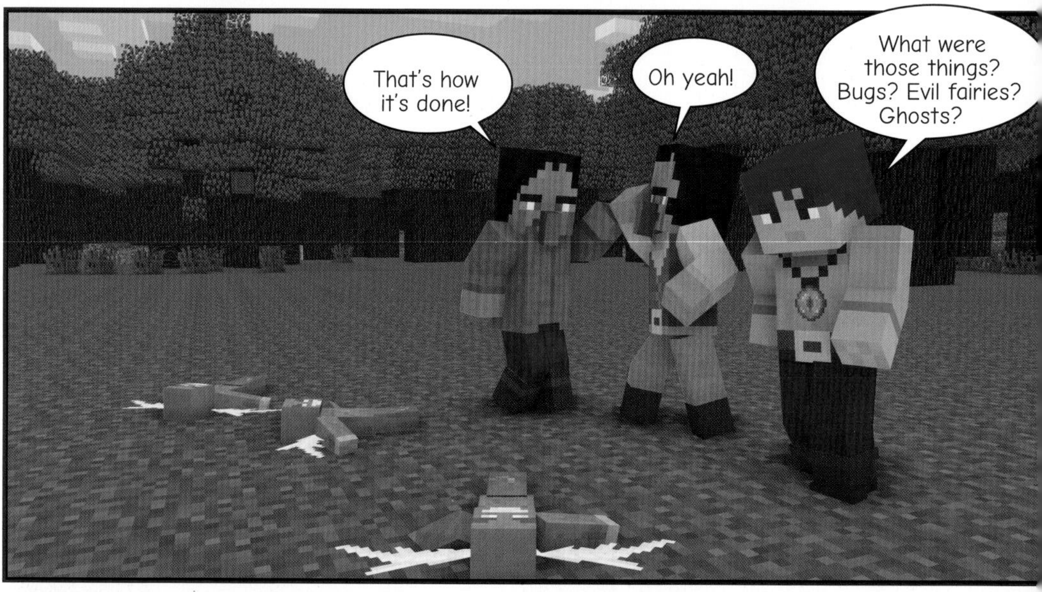
That's how it's done!
Oh yeah!
What were those things? Bugs? Evil fairies? Ghosts?

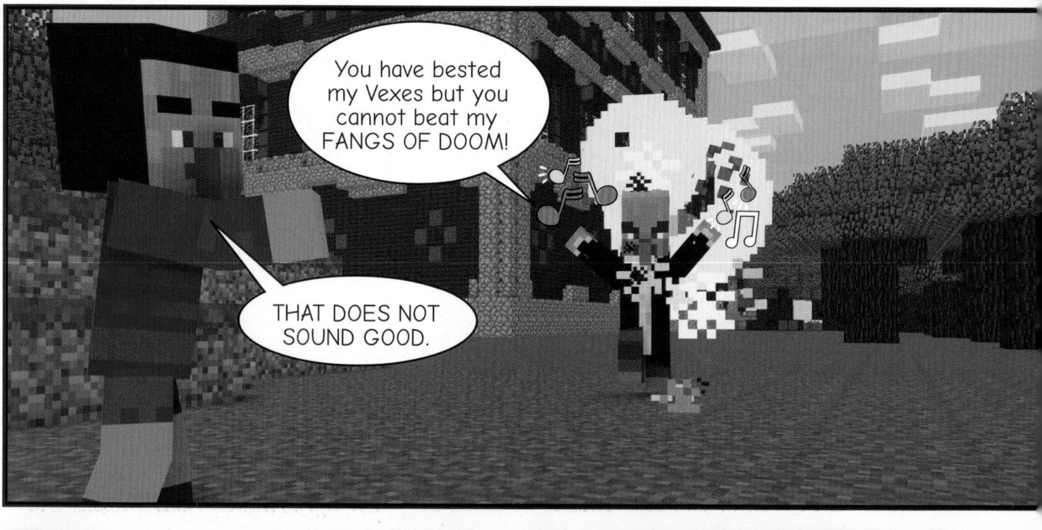
You have bested my Vexes but you cannot beat my FANGS OF DOOM!
THAT DOES NOT SOUND GOOD.

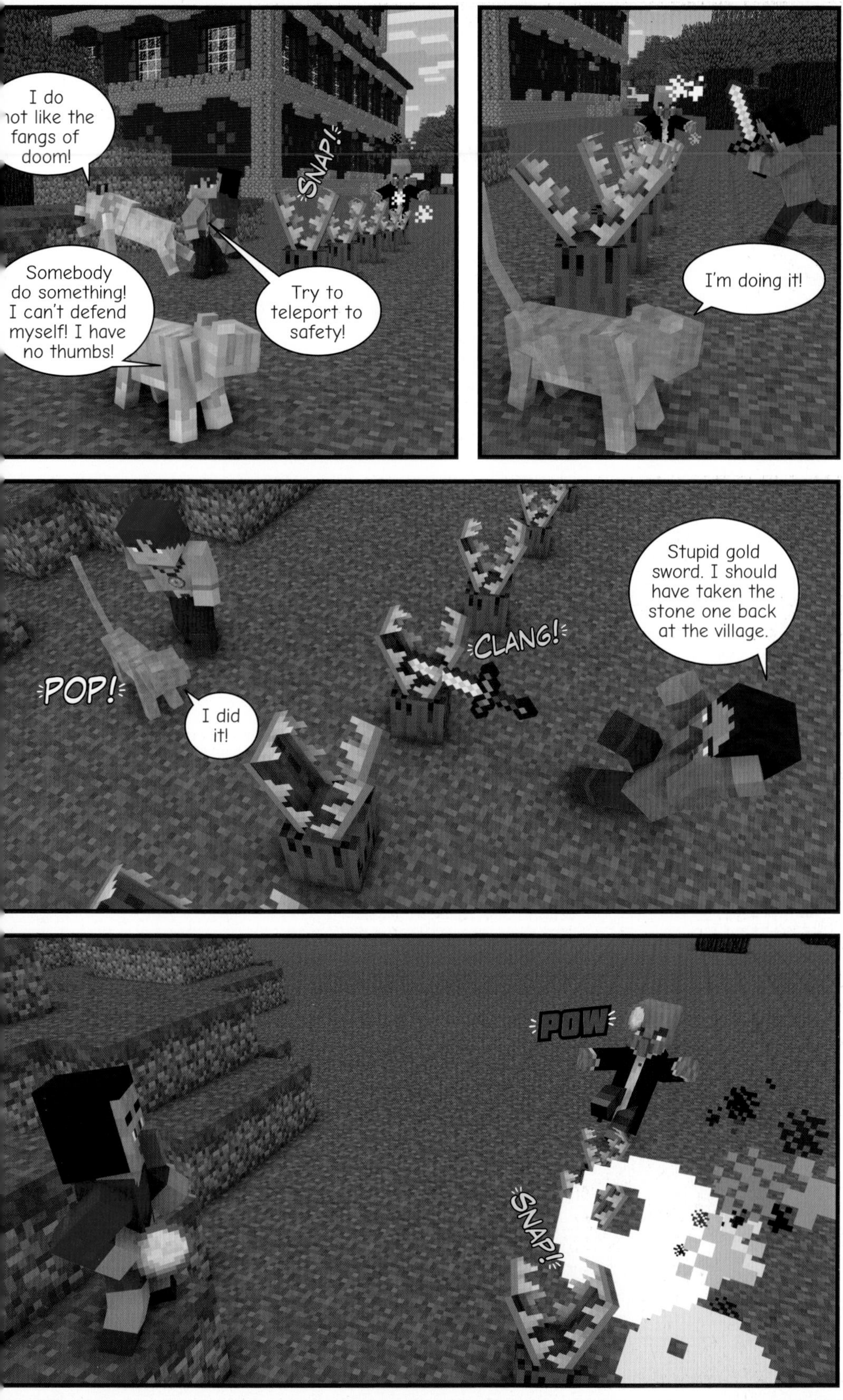
I do not like the fangs of doom!
SNAP!
Somebody do something! I can't defend myself! I have no thumbs!
Try to teleport to safety!
I'm doing it!
POP!
I did it!
CLANG!
Stupid gold sword. I should have taken the stone one back at the village.
POW
SNAP!

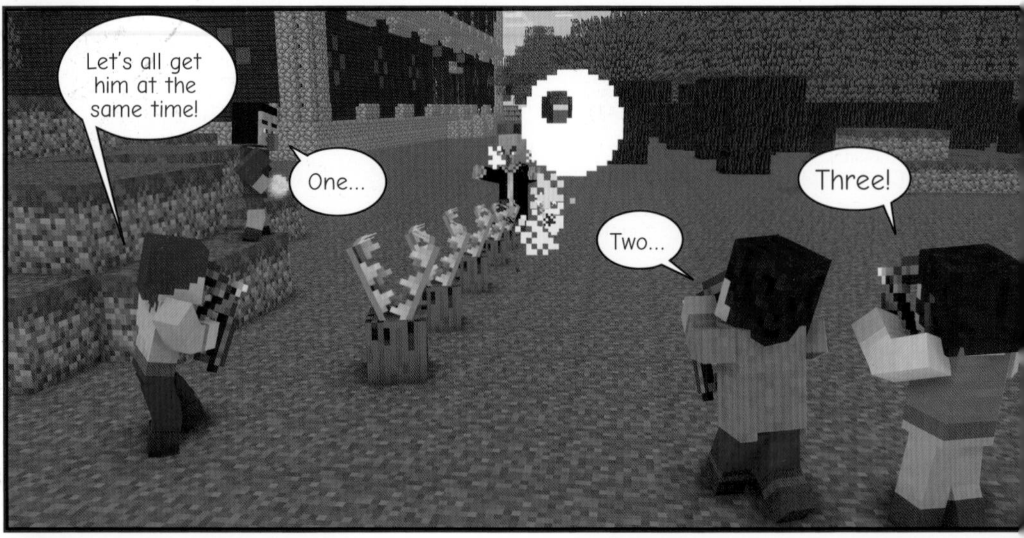
Let's all get him at the same time!
One...
Two...
Three!

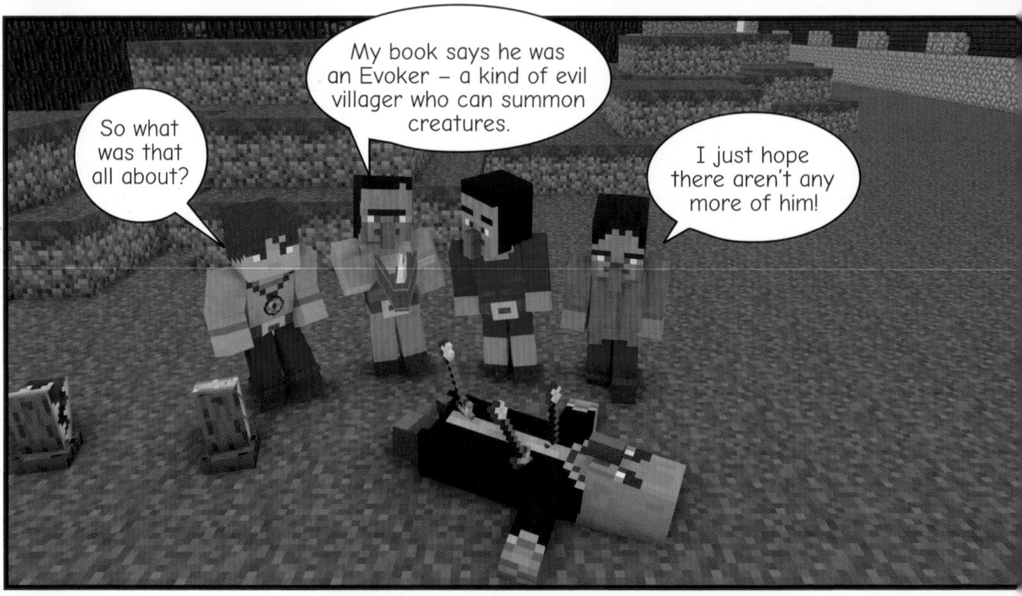
So what was that all about?
My book says he was an Evoker – a kind of evil villager who can summon creatures.
I just hope there aren't any more of him!

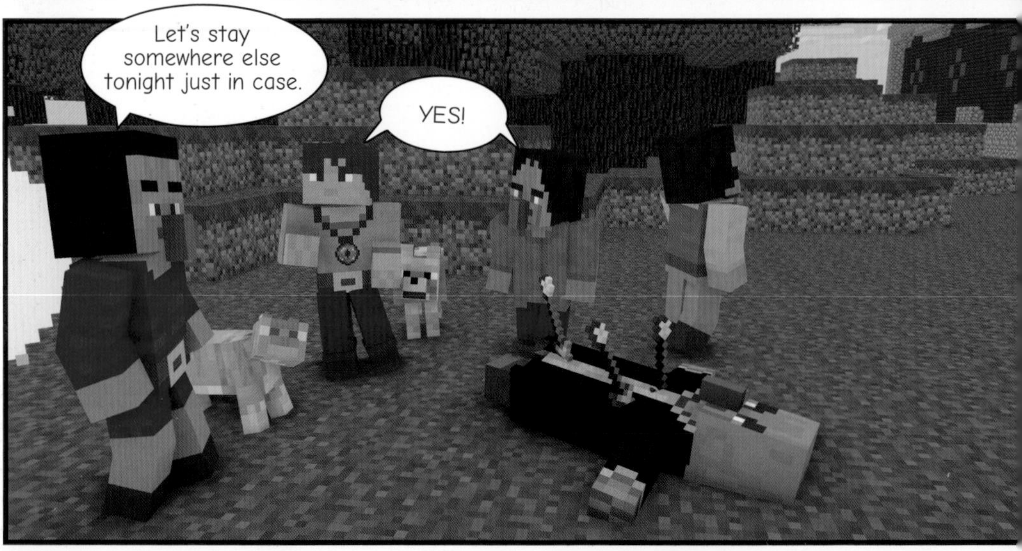
Let's stay somewhere else tonight just in case.
YES!

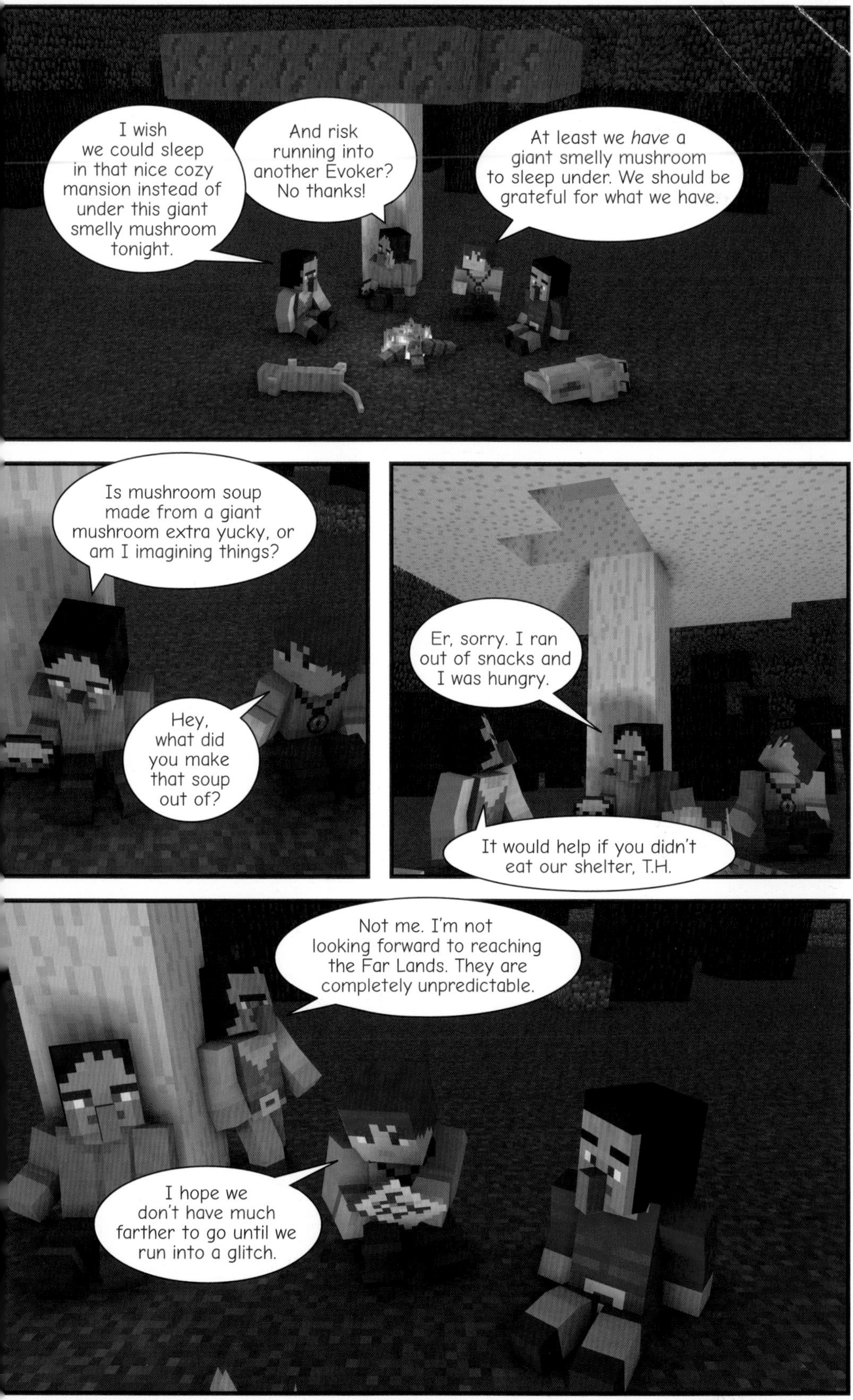
I wish we could sleep in that nice cozy mansion instead of under this giant smelly mushroom tonight.
And risk running into another Evoker? No thanks!
At least we *have* a giant smelly mushroom to sleep under. We should be grateful for what we have.
Is mushroom soup made from a giant mushroom extra yucky, or am I imagining things?
Hey, what did you make that soup out of?
Er, sorry. I ran out of snacks and I was hungry.
It would help if you didn't eat our shelter, T.H.
Not me. I'm not looking forward to reaching the Far Lands. They are completely unpredictable.
I hope we don't have much farther to go until we run into a glitch.

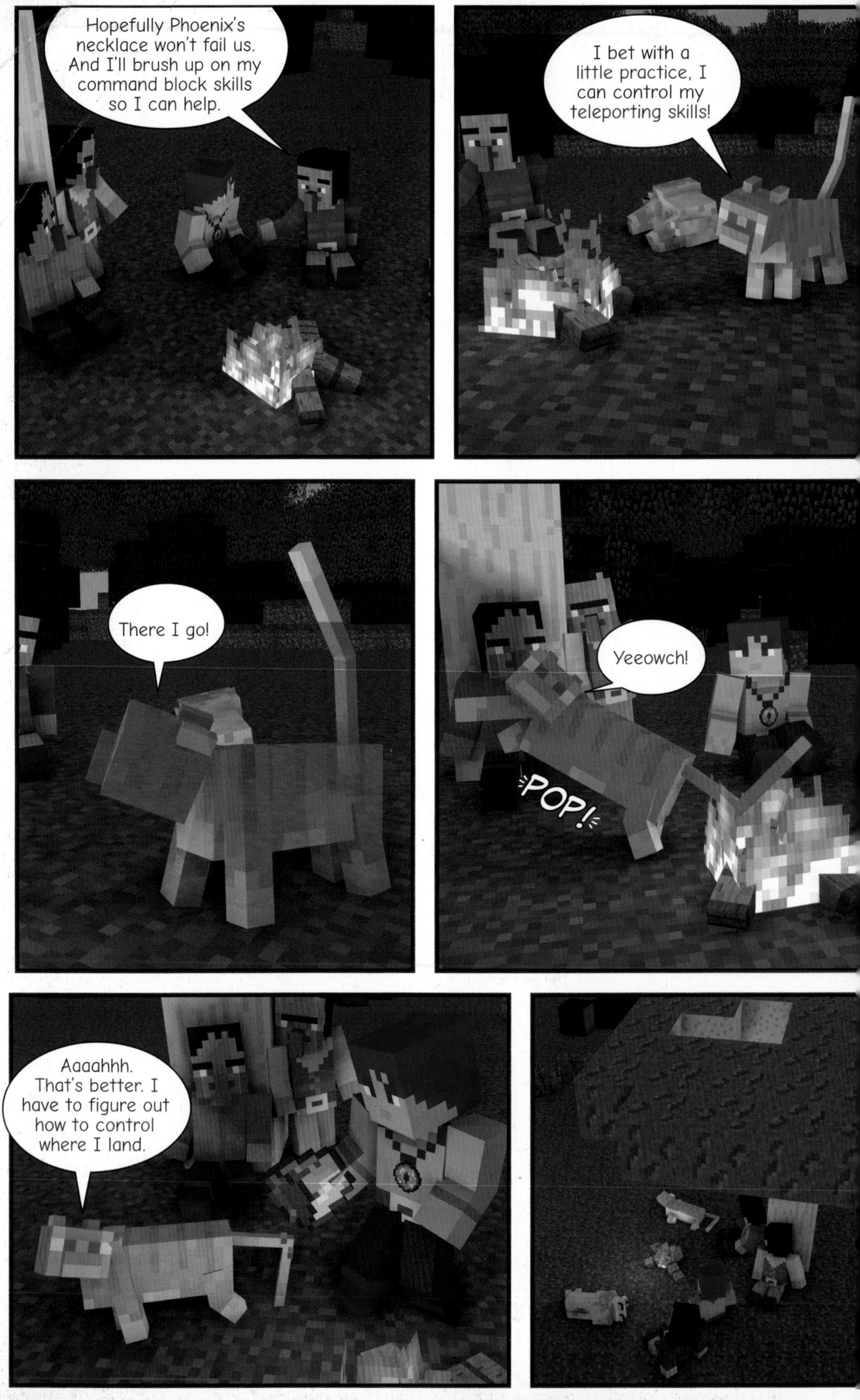
Hopefully Phoenix's necklace won't fail us. And I'll brush up on my command block skills so I can help.
I bet with a little practice, I can control my teleporting skills!
There I go!
Yeeowch!
POP!
Aaaahhh. That's better. I have to figure out how to control where I land.

CHAPTER 9

THE GLITCH

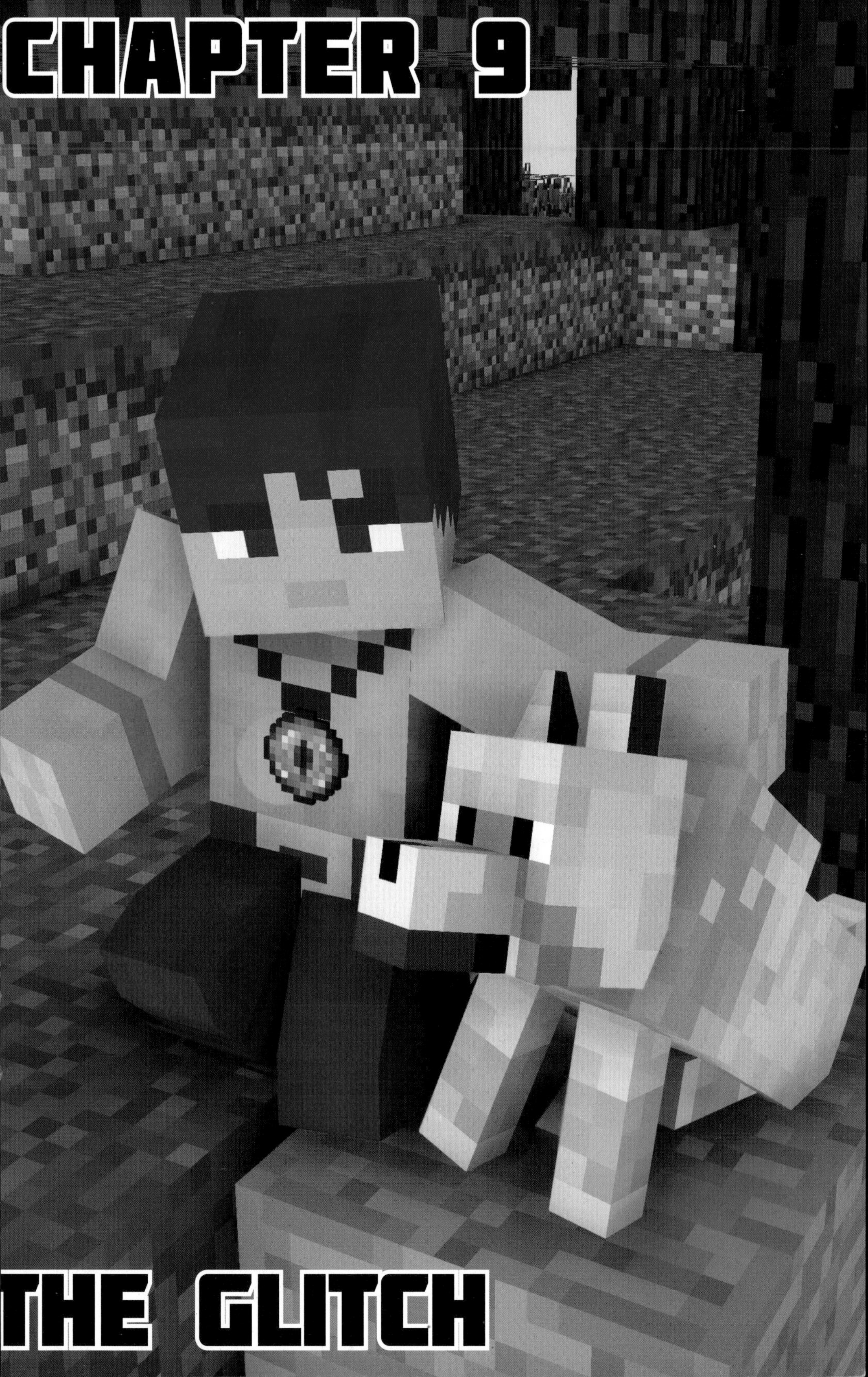

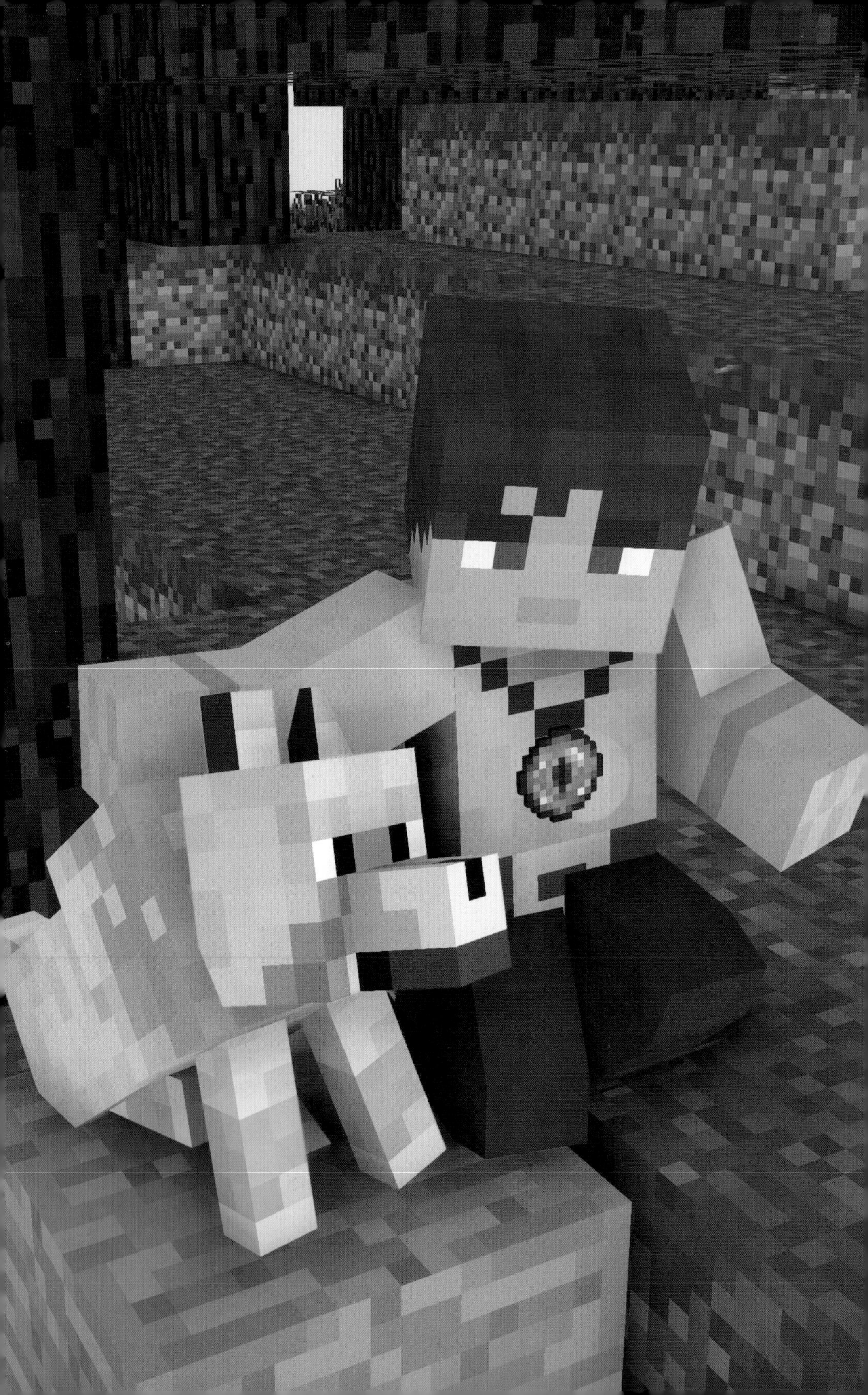

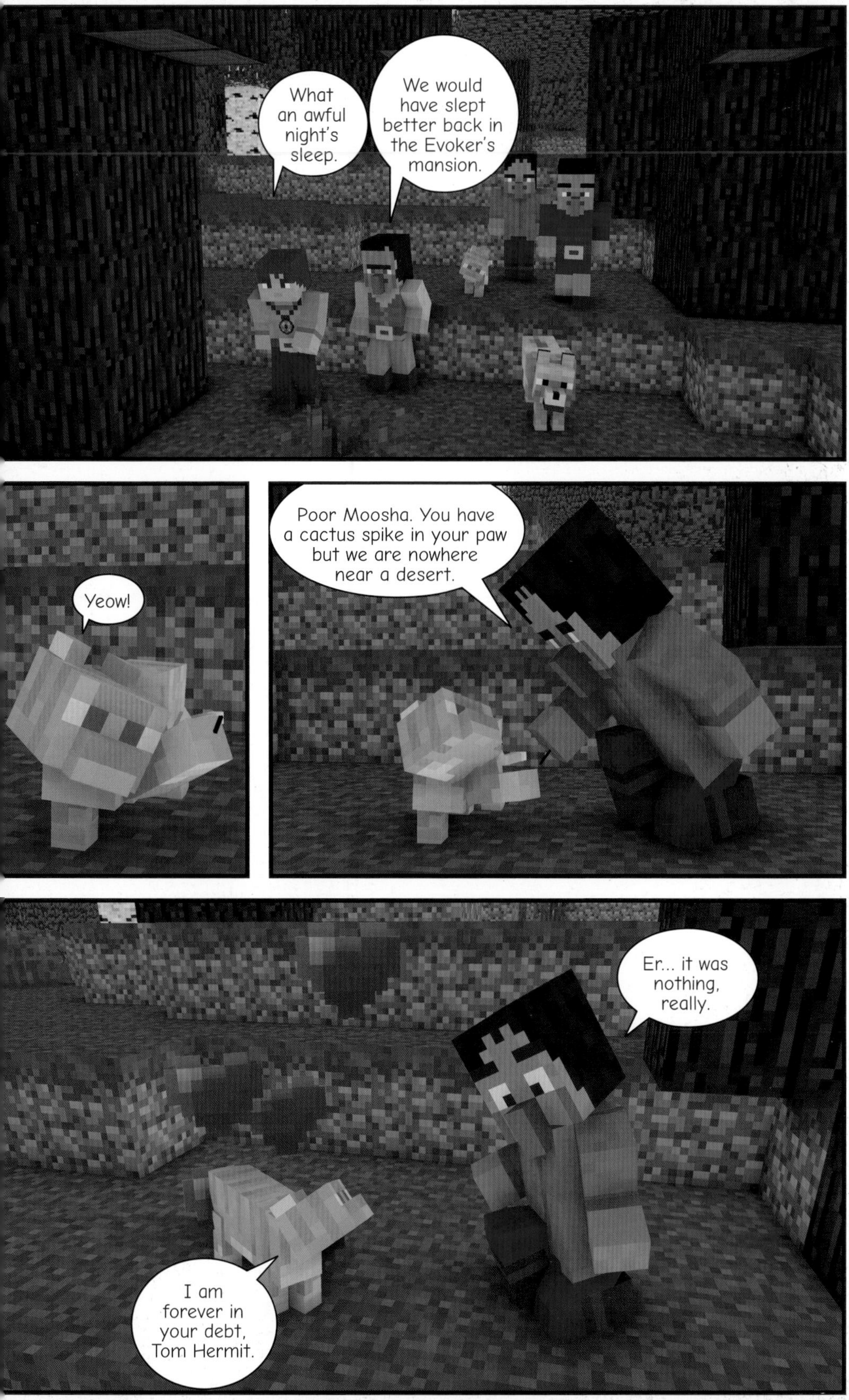
What an awful night's sleep.
We would have slept better back in the Evoker's mansion.
Yeow!
Poor Moosha. You have a cactus spike in your paw but we are nowhere near a desert.
Er... it was nothing, really.
I am forever in your debt, Tom Hermit.

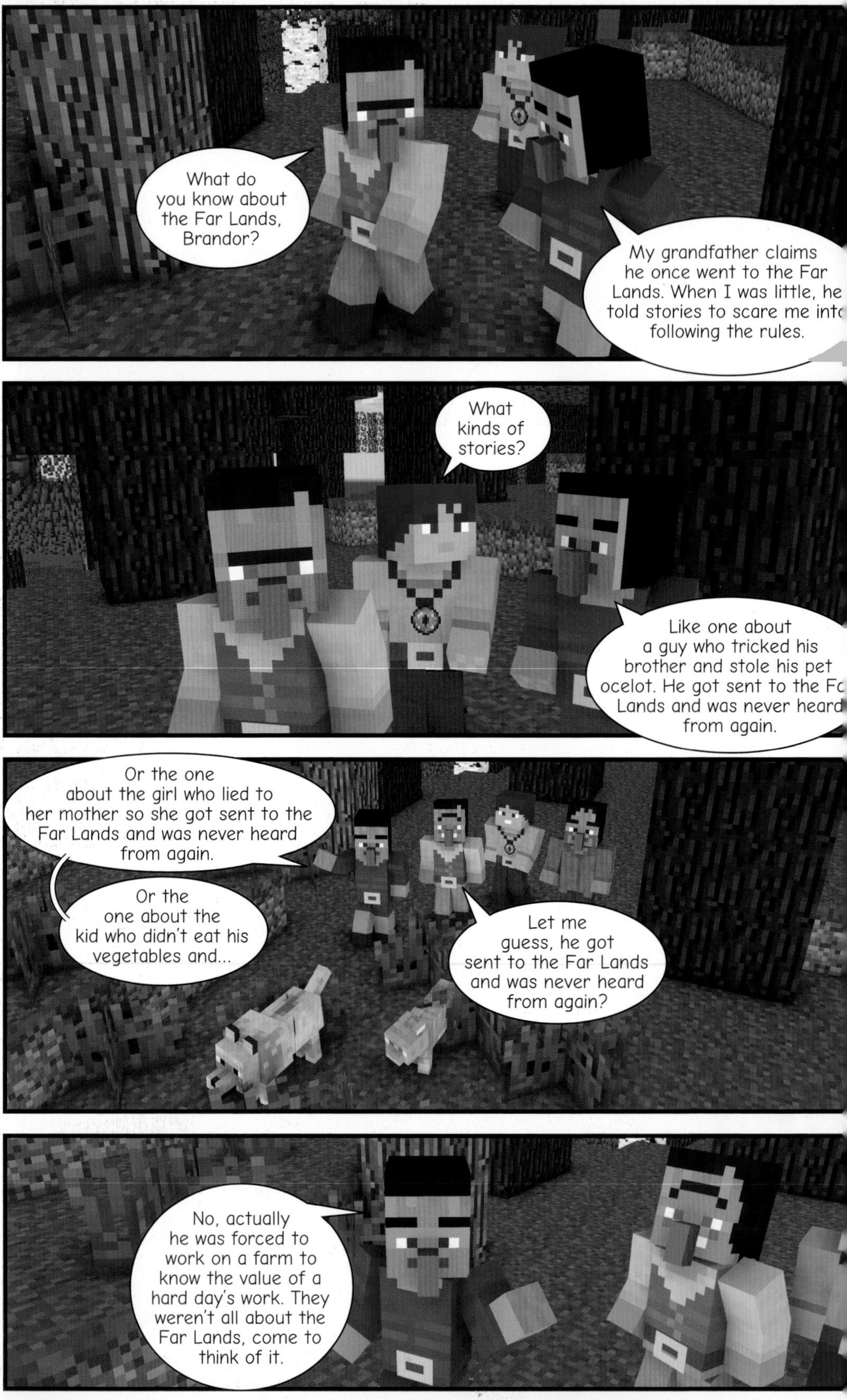
What do you know about the Far Lands, Brandor?
My grandfather claims he once went to the Far Lands. When I was little, he told stories to scare me
following the rules.
What kinds of stories?
Like one about a guy who tricked his brother and stole his pet ocelot. He got sent to the
Lands and was never heard from again.
Or the one about the girl who lied to her mother so she got sent to the Far Lands and was never heard from again.
Or the one about the kid who didn't eat his vegetables and...
Let me guess, he got sent to the Far Lands and was never heard from again?
No, actually he was forced to work on a farm to know the value of a hard day's work. They weren't all about the Far Lands, come to think of it.

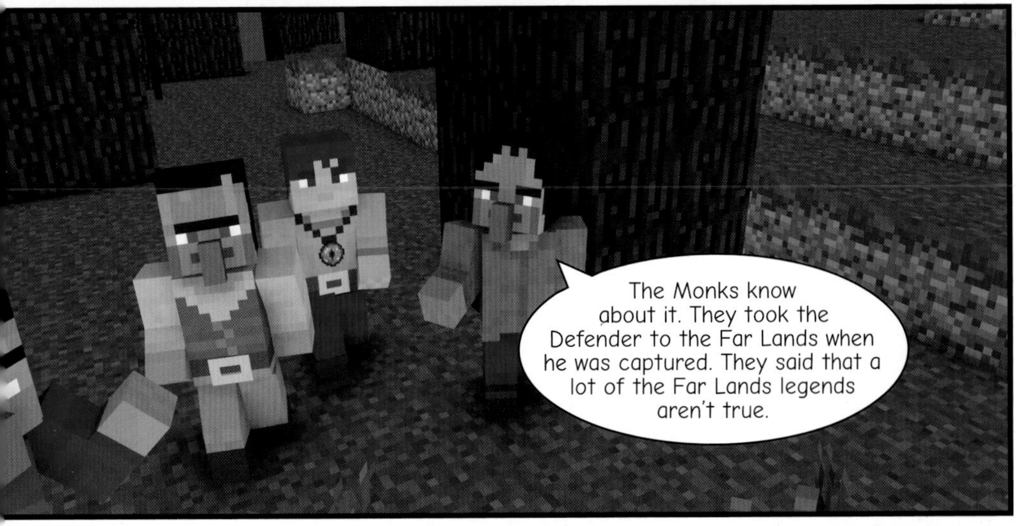
The Monks know about it. They took the Defender to the Far Lands when he was captured. They said that a lot of the Far Lands legends aren't true.

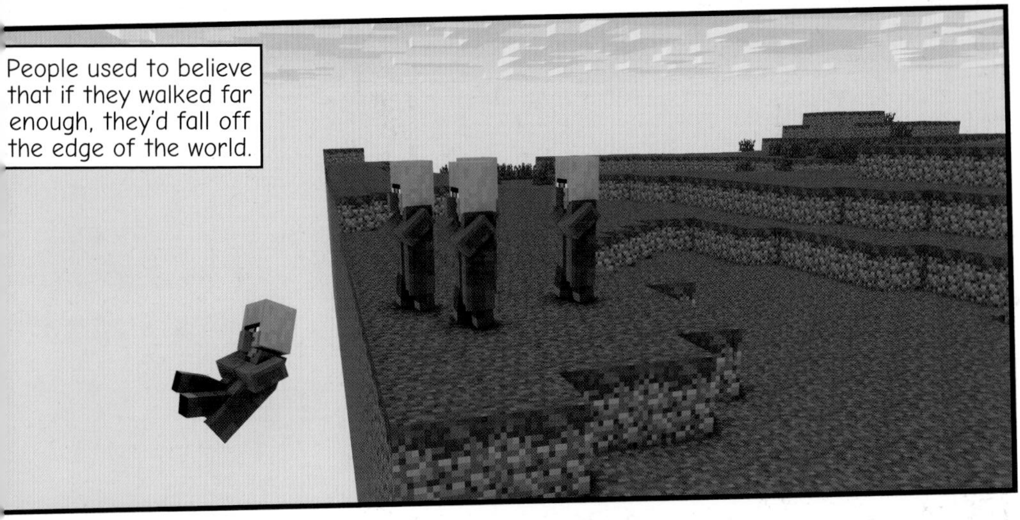
People used to believe that if they walked far enough, they'd fall off the edge of the world.

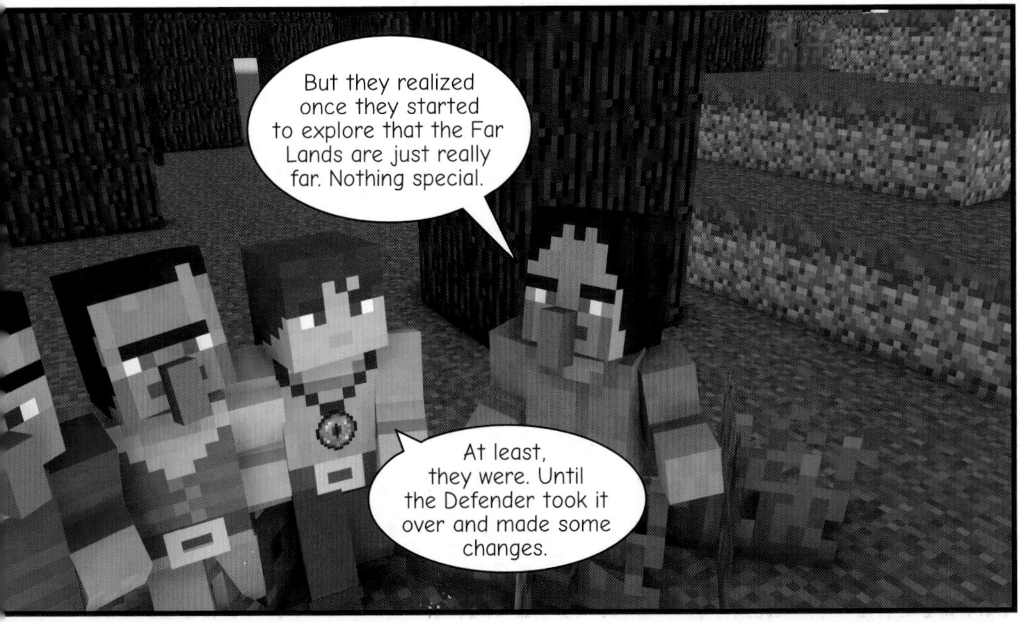
But they realized once they started to explore that the Far Lands are just really far. Nothing special.
At least, they were. Until the Defender took it over and made some changes.

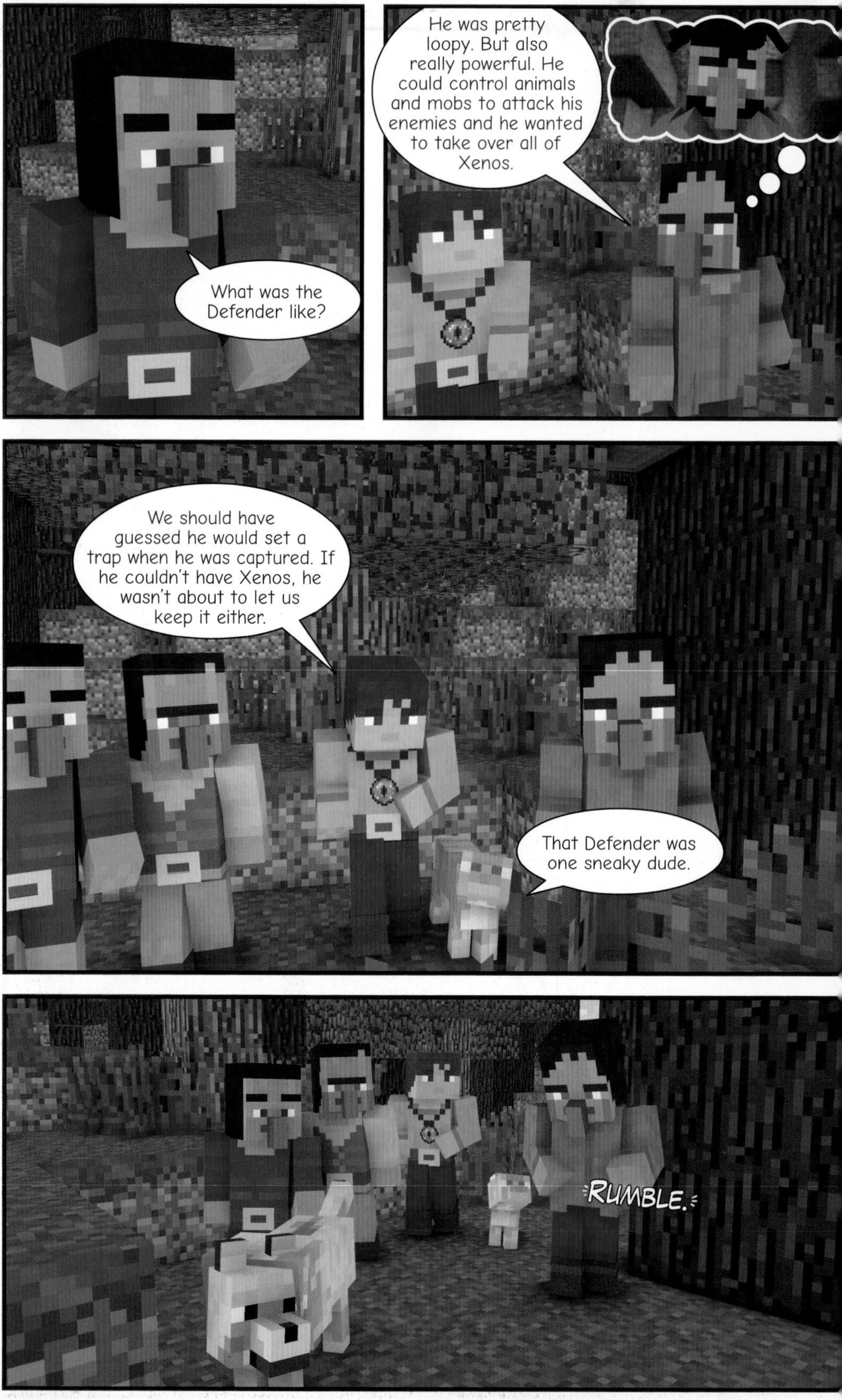
What was the Defender like?
He was pretty loopy. But also really powerful. He could control animals and mobs to attack his enemies and he wanted to take over all of Xenos.
We should have guessed he would set a trap when he was captured. If he couldn't have Xenos, he wasn't about to let us keep it either.
That Defender was one sneaky dude.
RUMBLE.

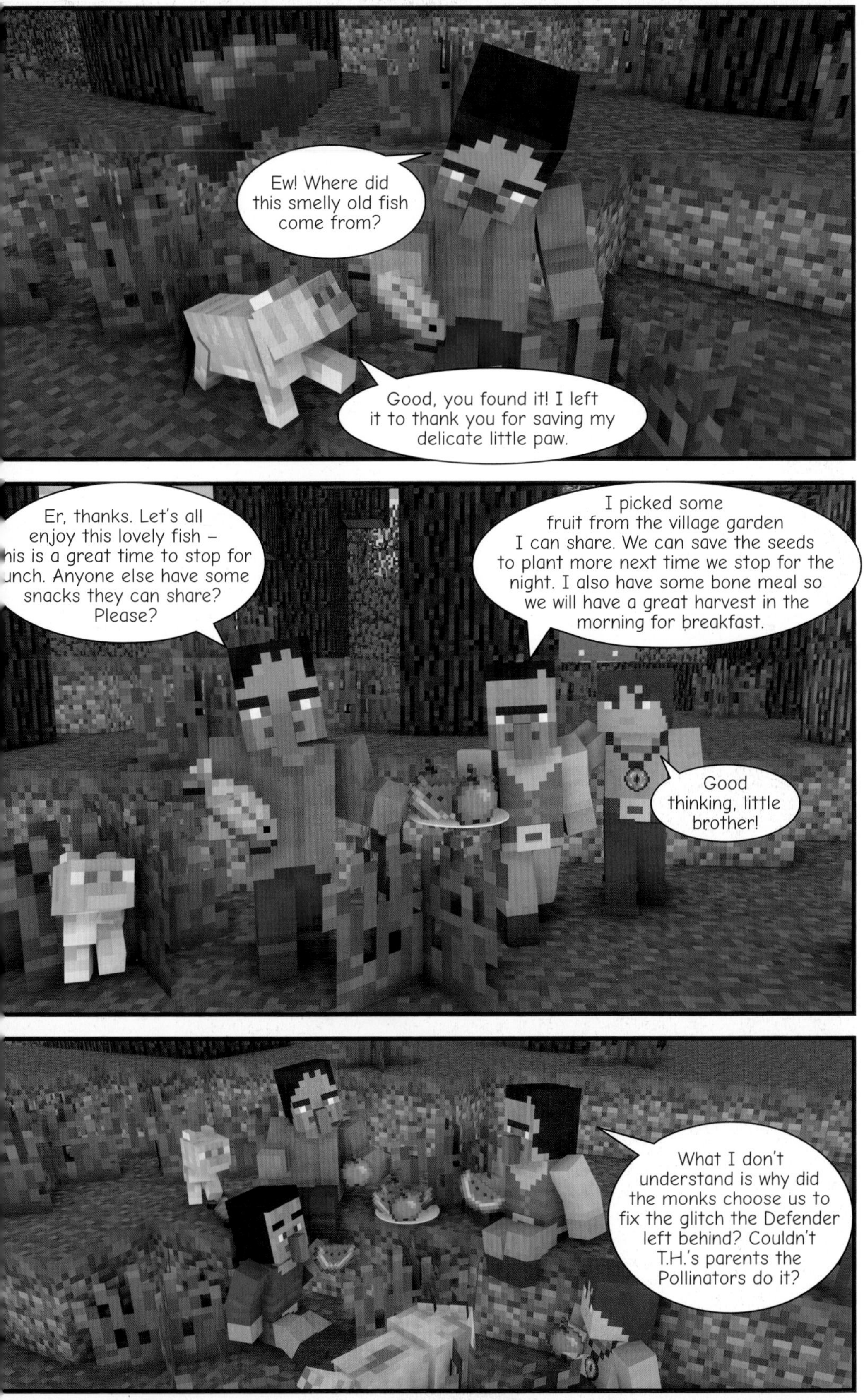
Ew! Where did this smelly old fish come from?
Good, you found it! I left it to thank you for saving my delicate little paw.
Er, thanks. Let's all enjoy this lovely fish – his is a great time to stop for unch. Anyone else have some snacks they can share? Please?
I picked some fruit from the village garden I can share. We can save the seeds to plant more next time we stop for the night. I also have some bone meal so we will have a great harvest in the morning for breakfast.
Good thinking, little brother!
What I don't understand is why did the monks choose us to fix the glitch the Defender left behind? Couldn't T.H.'s parents the Pollinators do it?

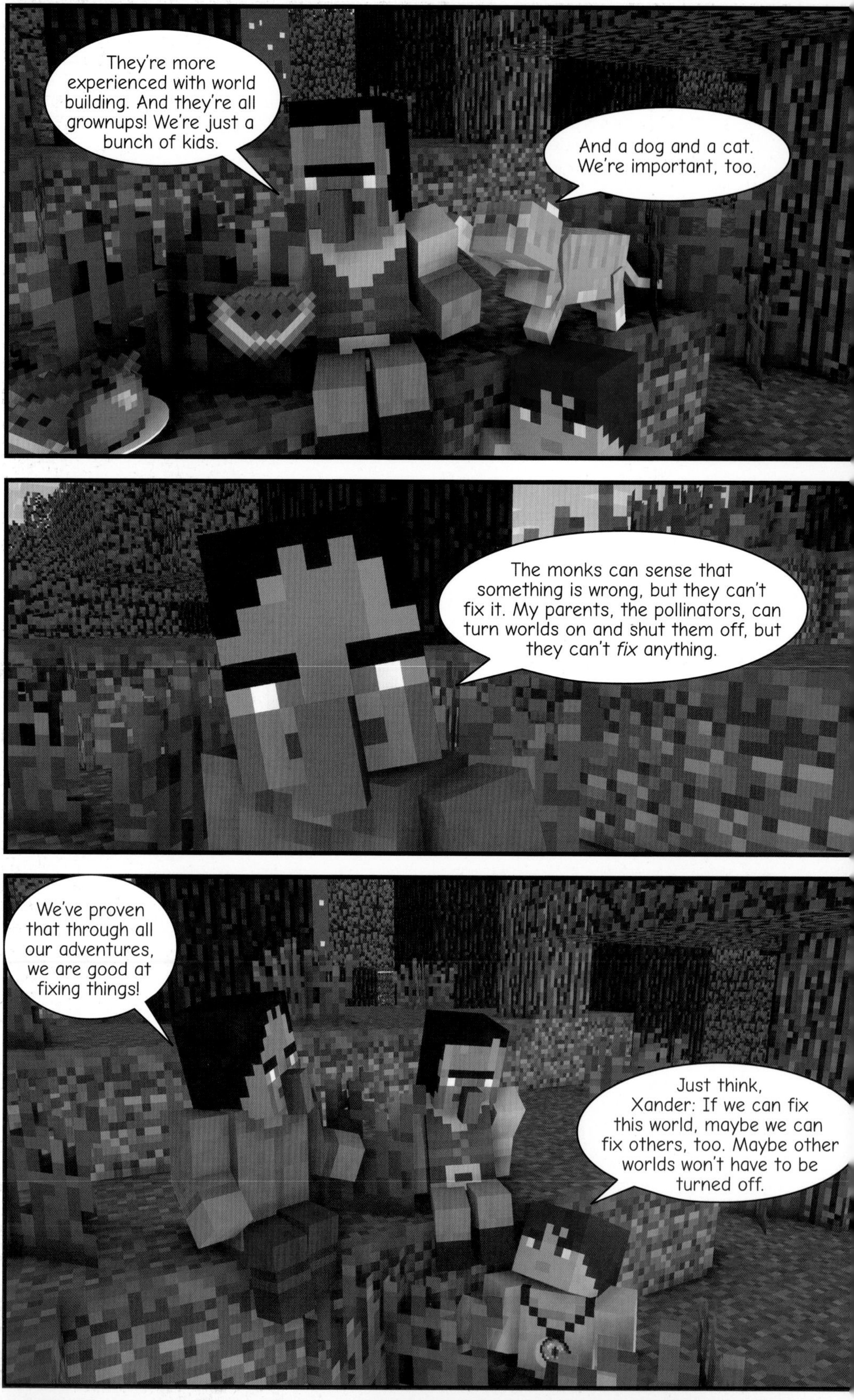
They're more experienced with world building. And they're all grownups! We're just a bunch of kids.
And a dog and a cat. We're important, too.
The monks can sense that something is wrong, but they can't fix it. My parents, the pollinators, can turn worlds on and shut them off, but they can't *fix* anything.
We've proven that through all our adventures, we are good at fixing things!
Just think, Xander: If we can fix this world, maybe we can fix others, too. Maybe other worlds won't have to be turned off.

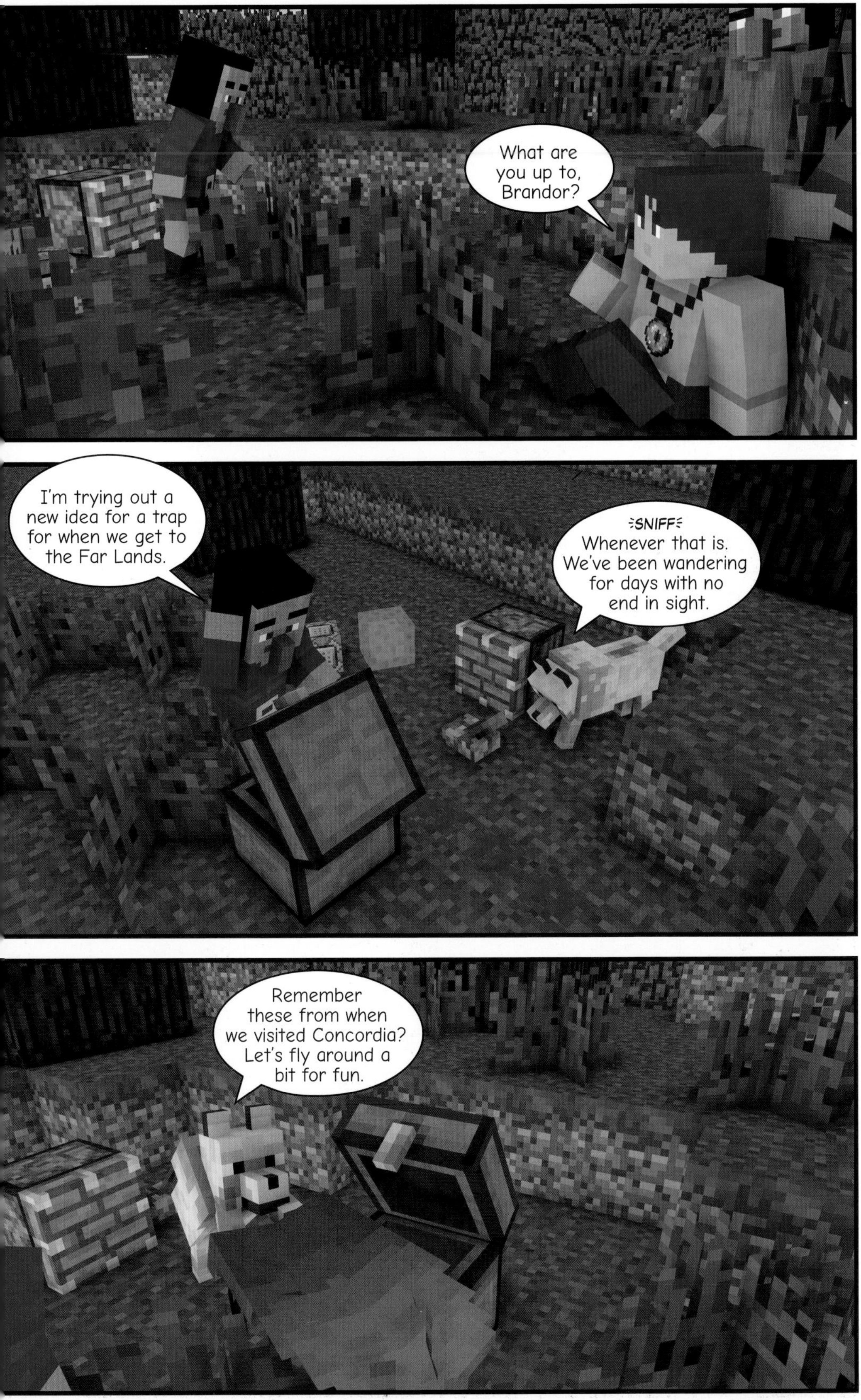
What are you up to, Brandor?
I'm trying out a new idea for a trap for when we get to the Far Lands.
SNIFF
Whenever that is. We've been wandering for days with no end in sight.
Remember these from when we visited Concordia? Let's fly around a bit for fun.

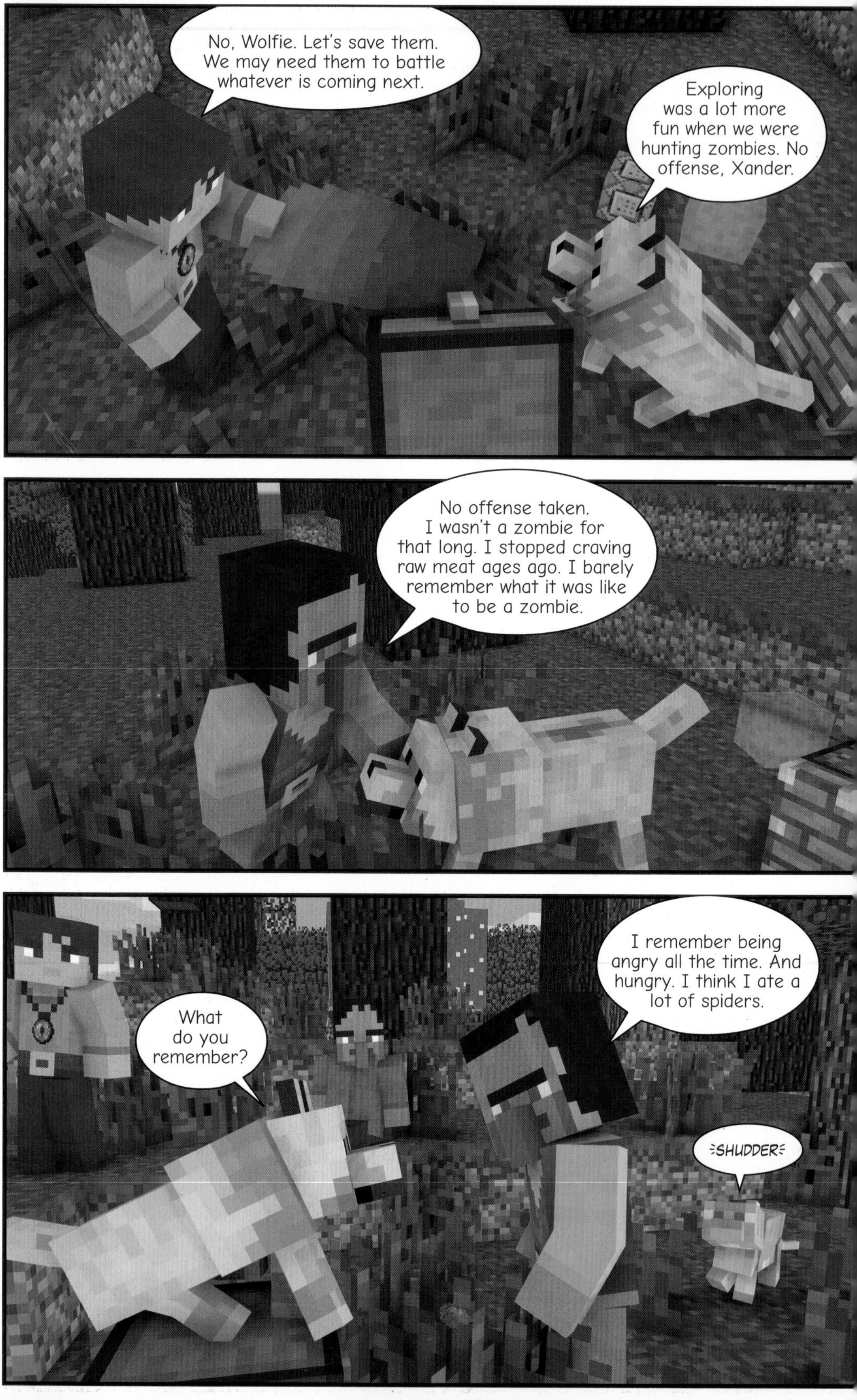
No, Wolfie. Let's save them. We may need them to battle whatever is coming next.
Exploring was a lot more fun when we were hunting zombies. No offense, Xander.
No offense taken. I wasn't a zombie for that long. I stopped craving raw meat ages ago. I barely remember what it was like to be a zombie.
What do you remember?
I remember being angry all the time. And hungry. I think I ate a lot of spiders.
SHUDDER

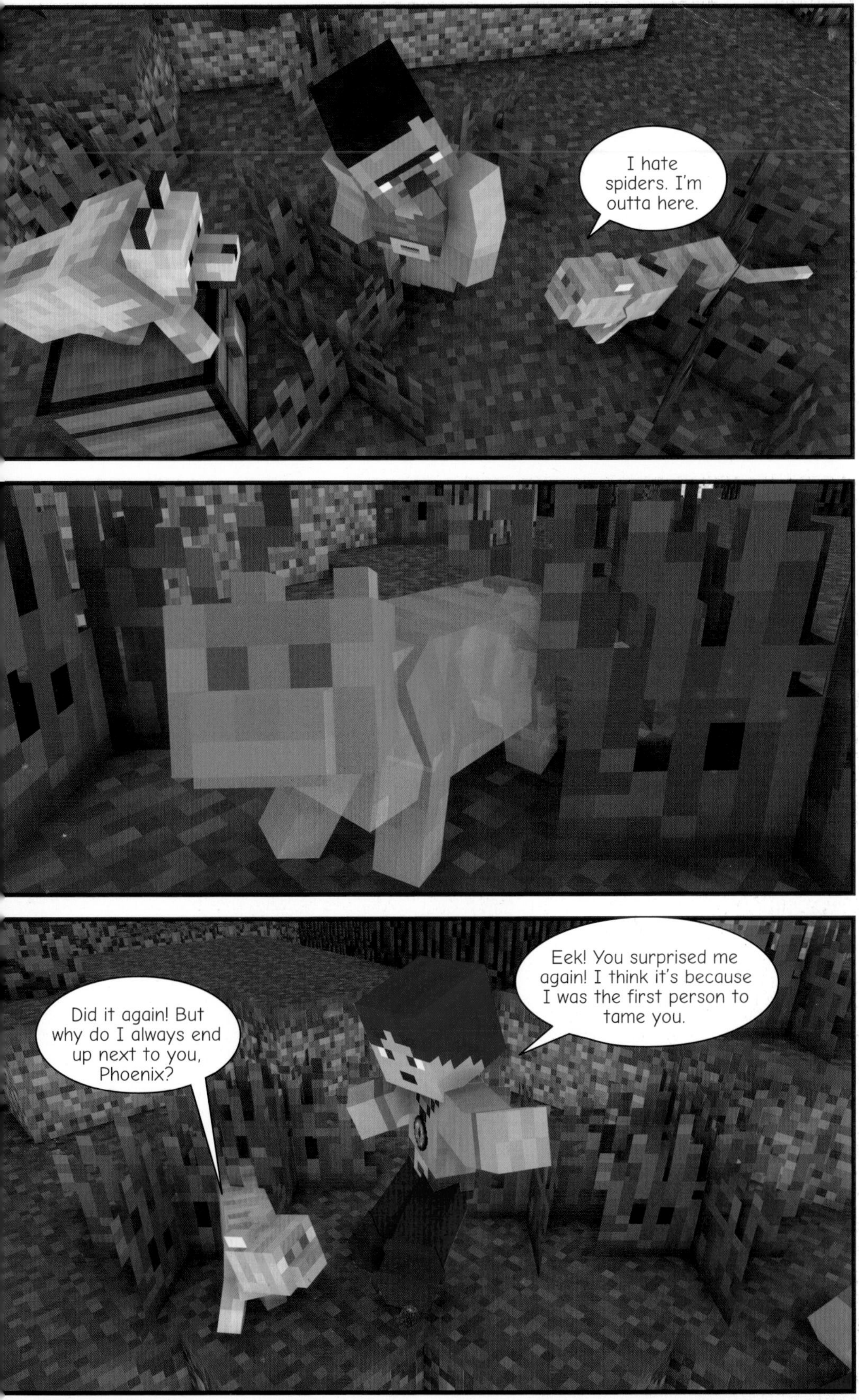
I hate spiders. I'm outta here.
Eek! You surprised me again! I think it's because I was the first person to tame you.
Did it again! But why do I always end up next to you, Phoenix?

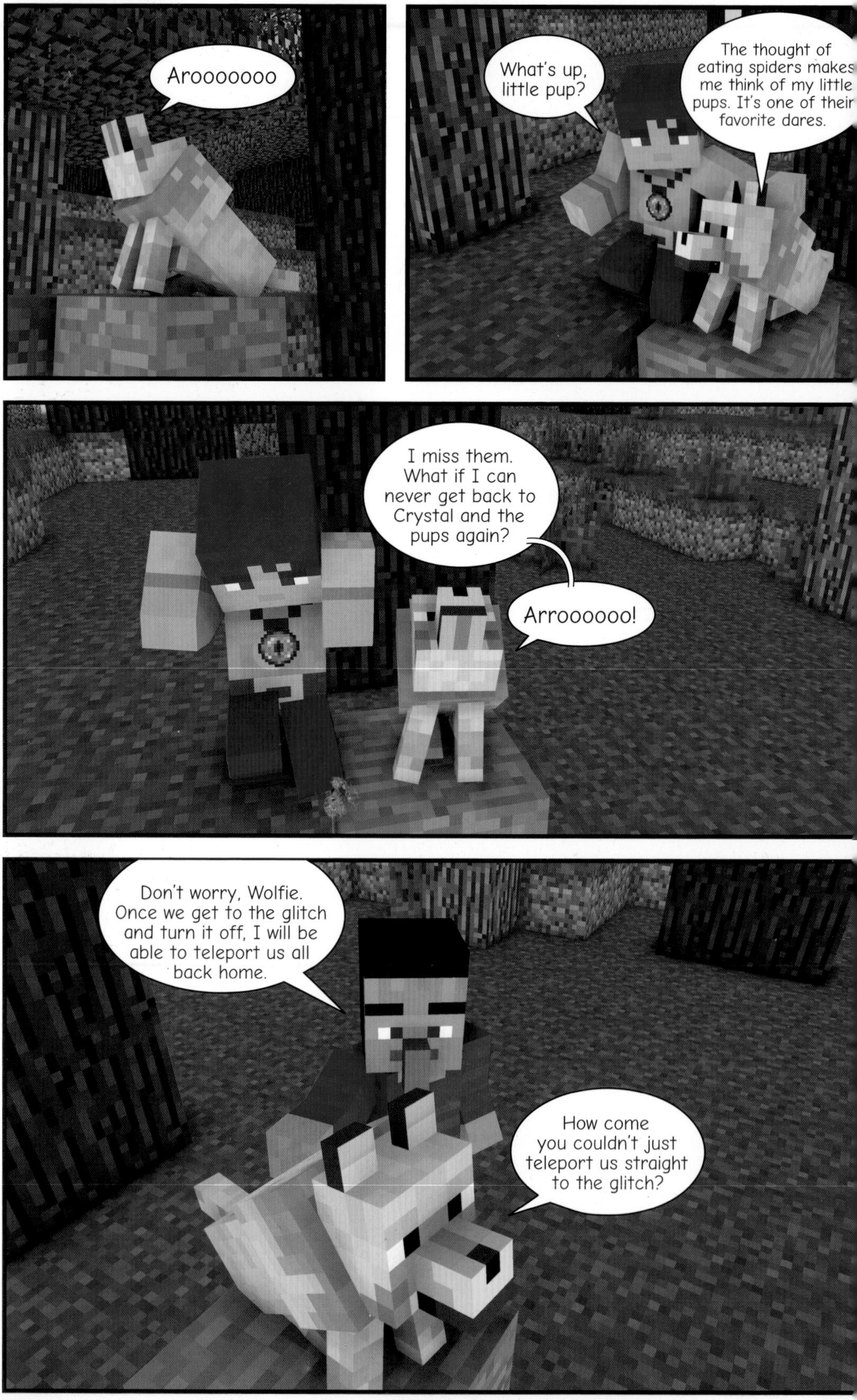
Arooooooo
What's up, little pup?
The thought of eating spiders makes me think of my little pups. It's one of their favorite dares.
I miss them. What if I can never get back to Crystal and the pups again?
Arroooooo!
Don't worry, Wolfie. Once we get to the glitch and turn it off, I will be able to teleport us all back home.
How come you couldn't just teleport us straight to the glitch?

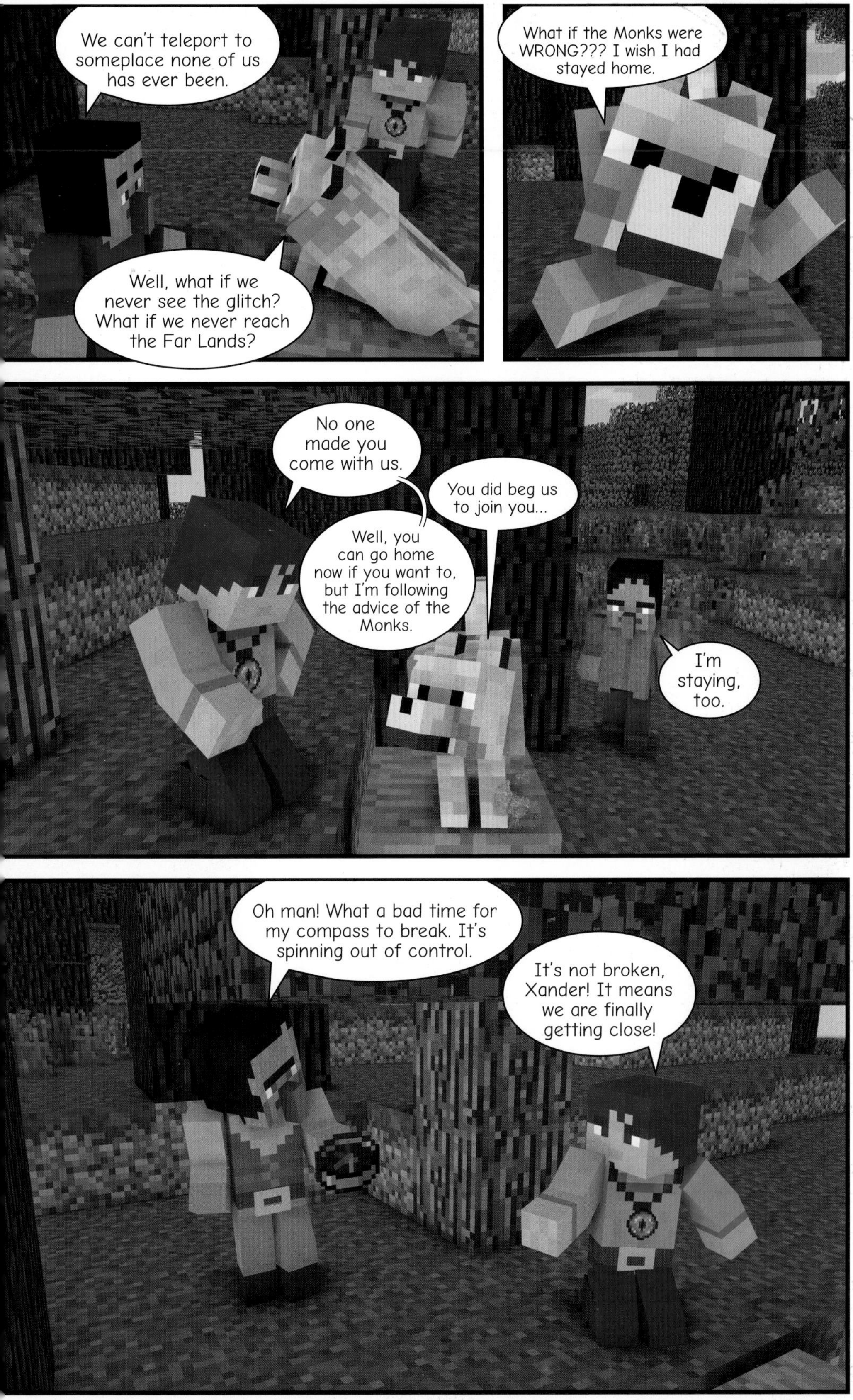

We can't teleport to someplace none of us has ever been.
Well, what if we never see the glitch? What if we never reach the Far Lands?
What if the Monks were WRONG??? I wish I had stayed home.
No one made you come with us.
You did beg us to join you...
Well, you can go home now if you want to, but I'm following the advice of the Monks.
I'm staying, too.
Oh man! What a bad time for my compass to break. It's spinning out of control.
It's not broken, Xander! It means we are finally getting close!

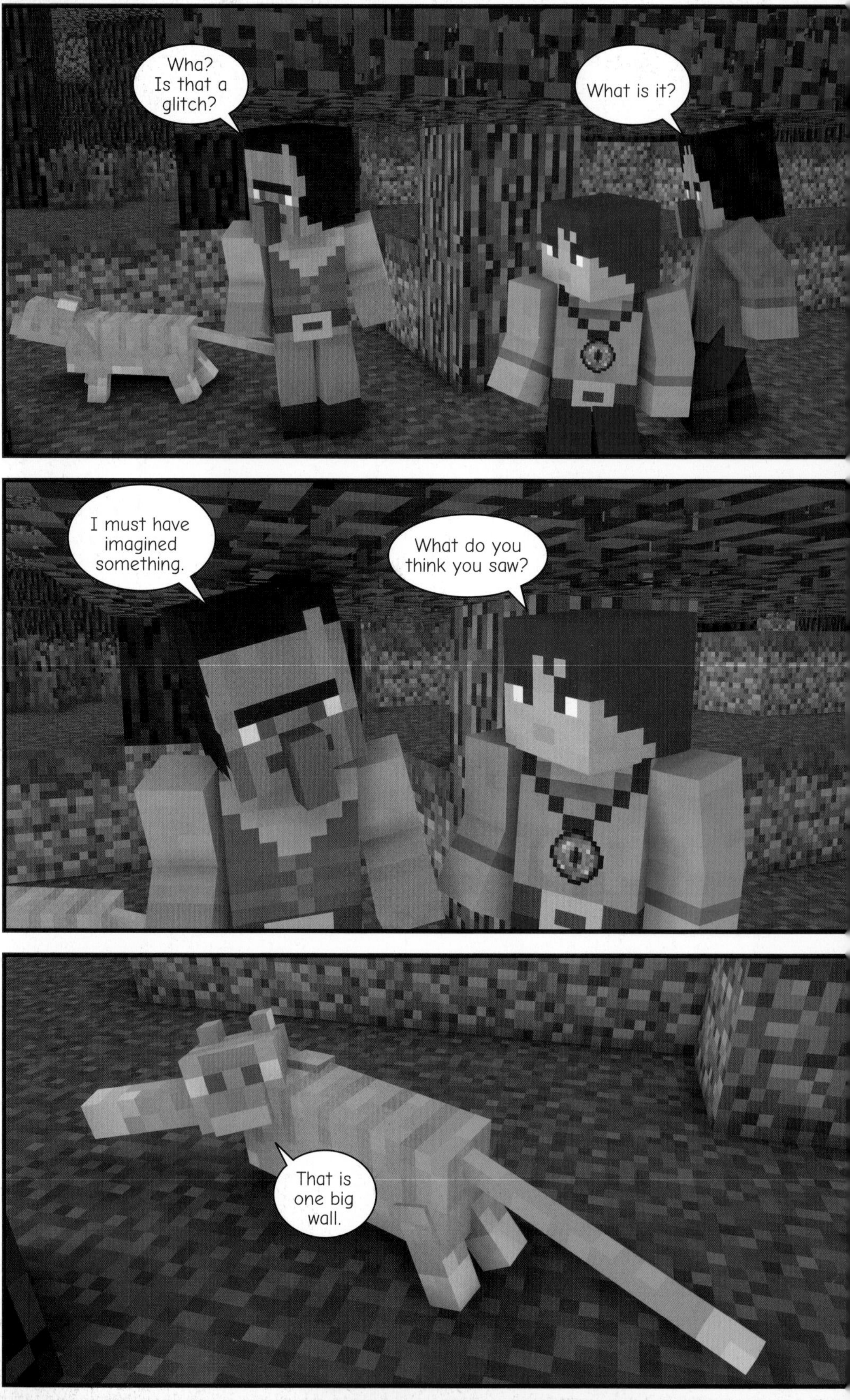
Wha? Is that a glitch?
What is it?
I must have imagined something.
What do you think you saw?
That is one big wall.

CHAPTER 10

ATTACK OF THE KILLER COOKIES

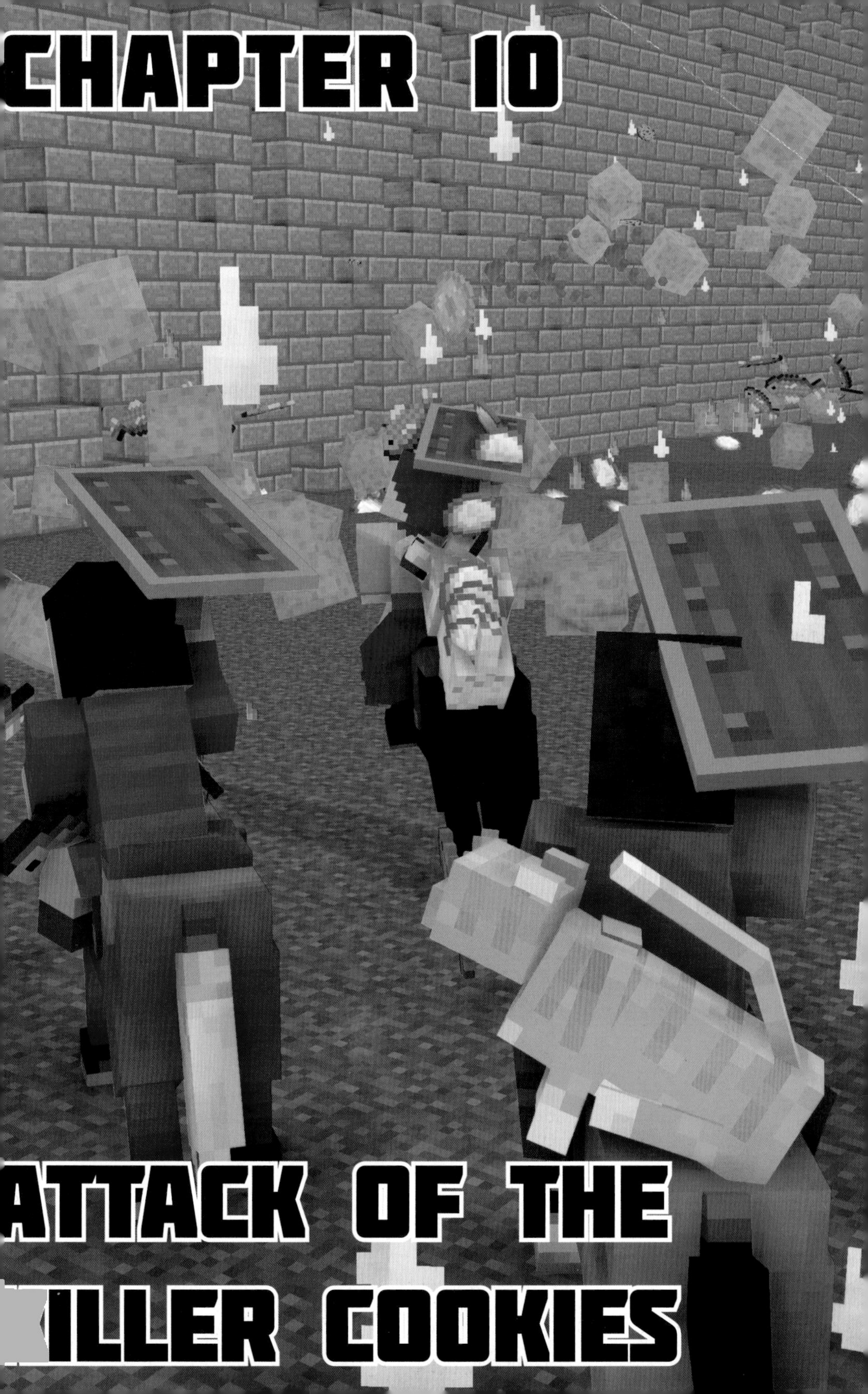

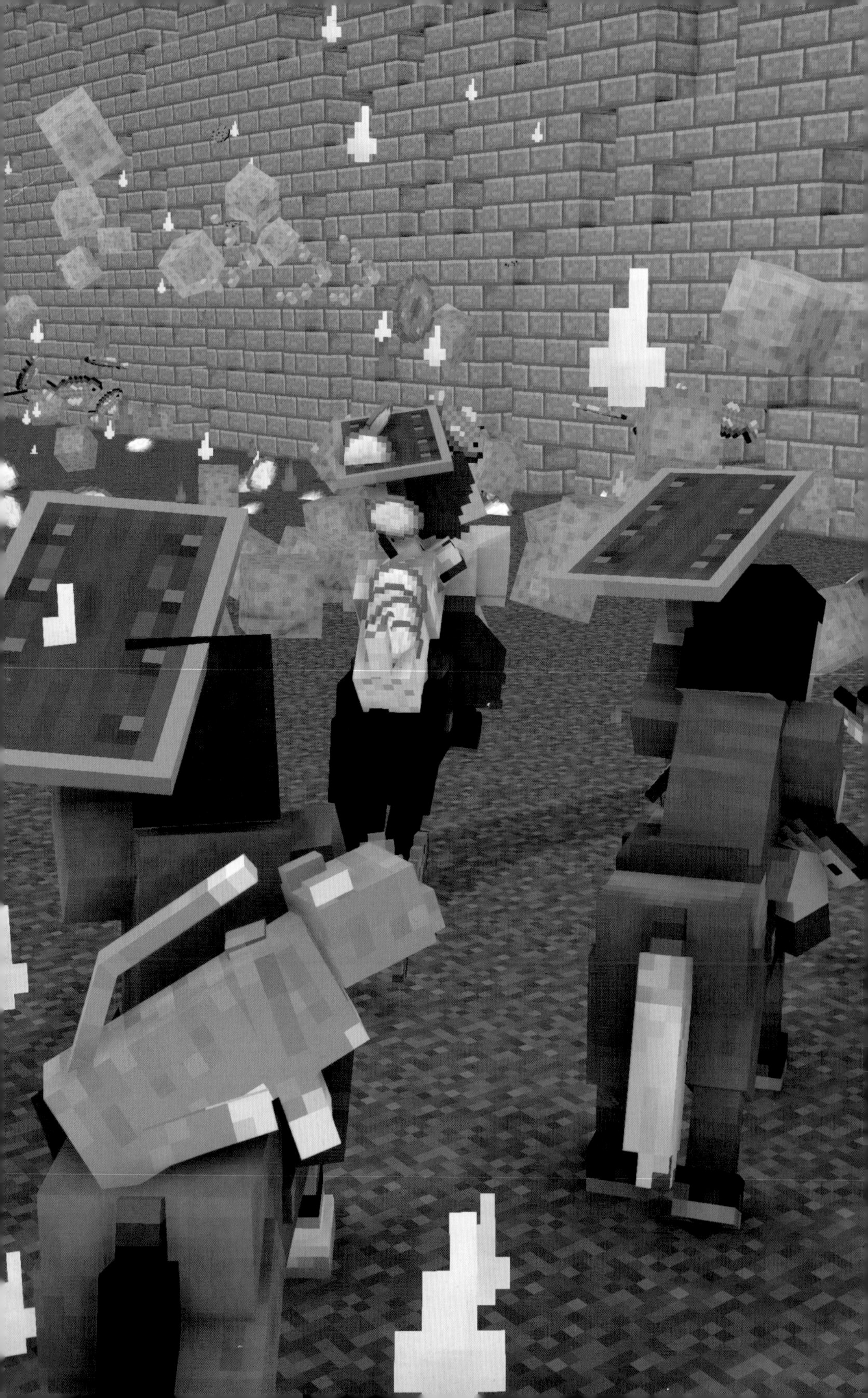

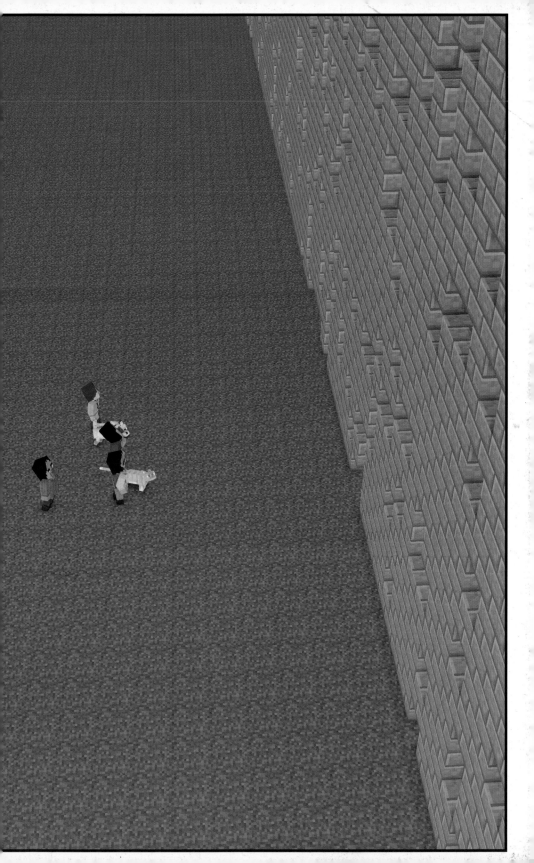

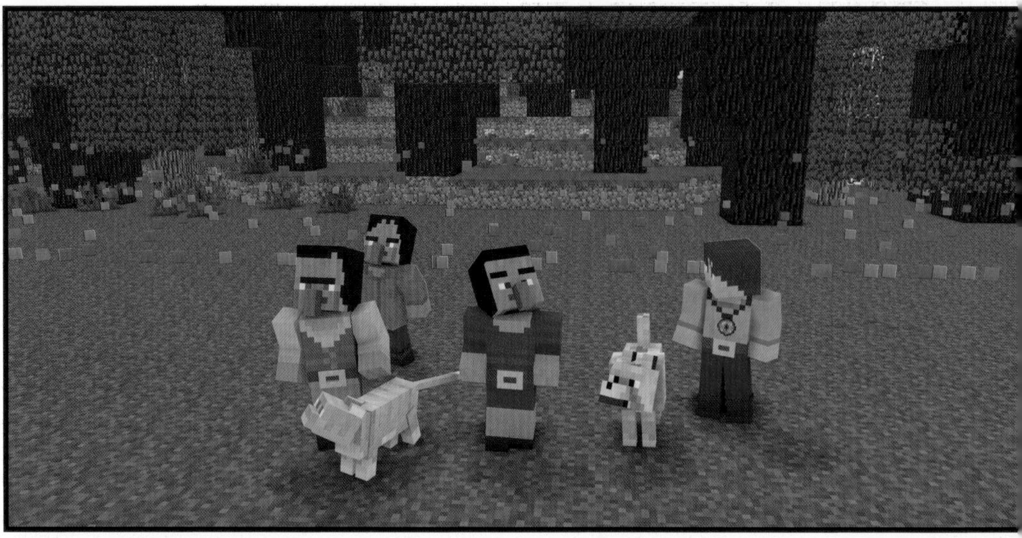

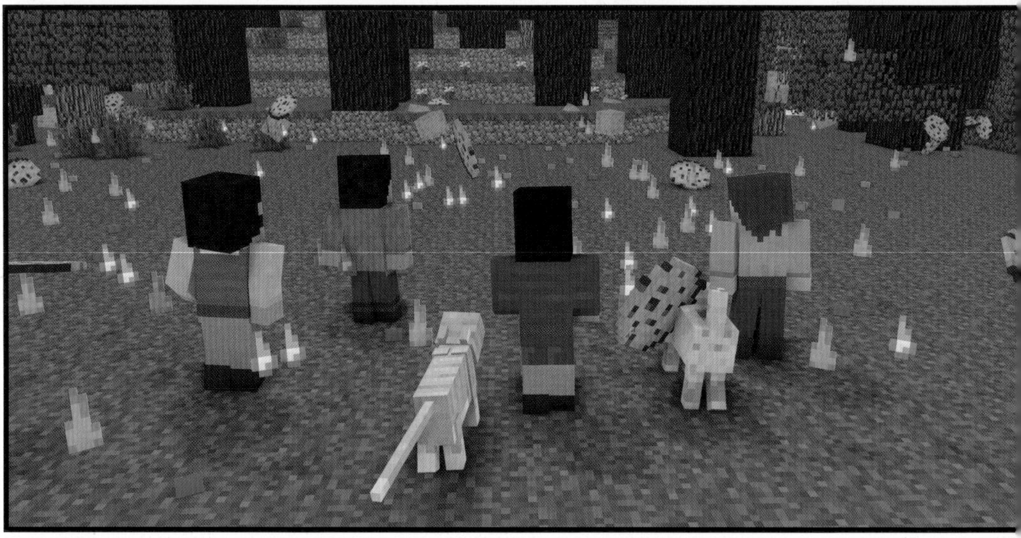

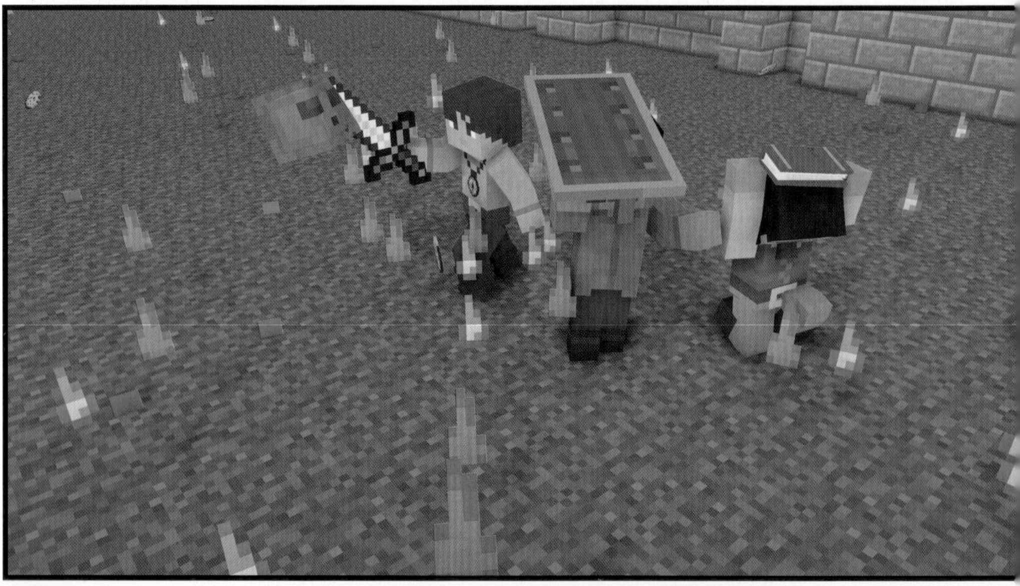

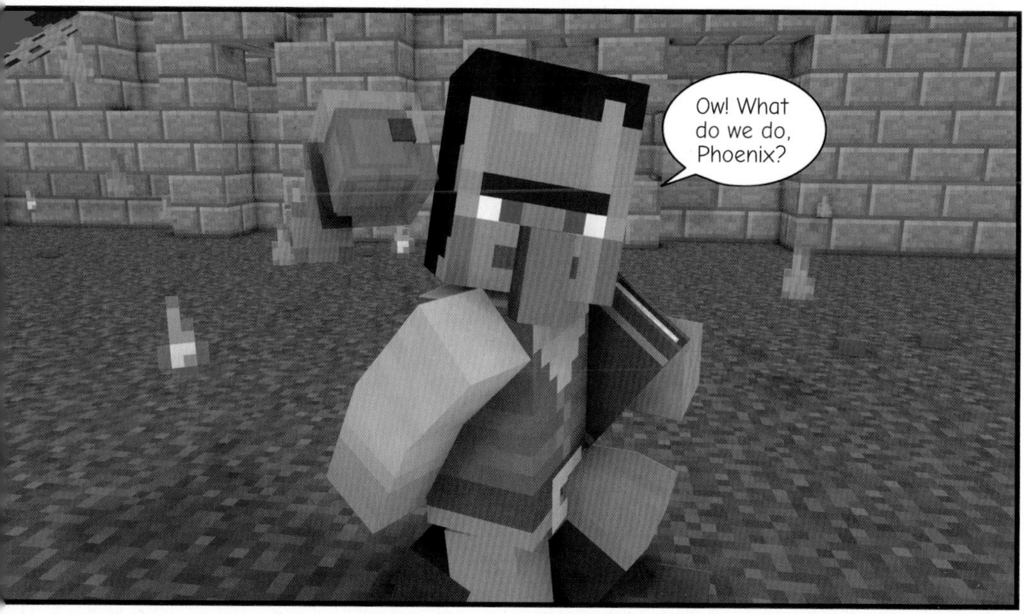
Ow! What do we do, Phoenix?

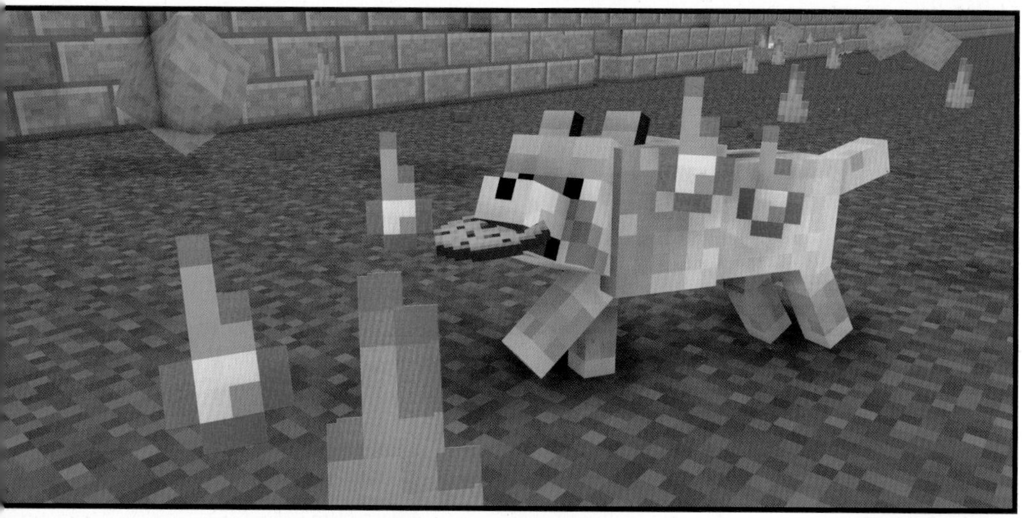

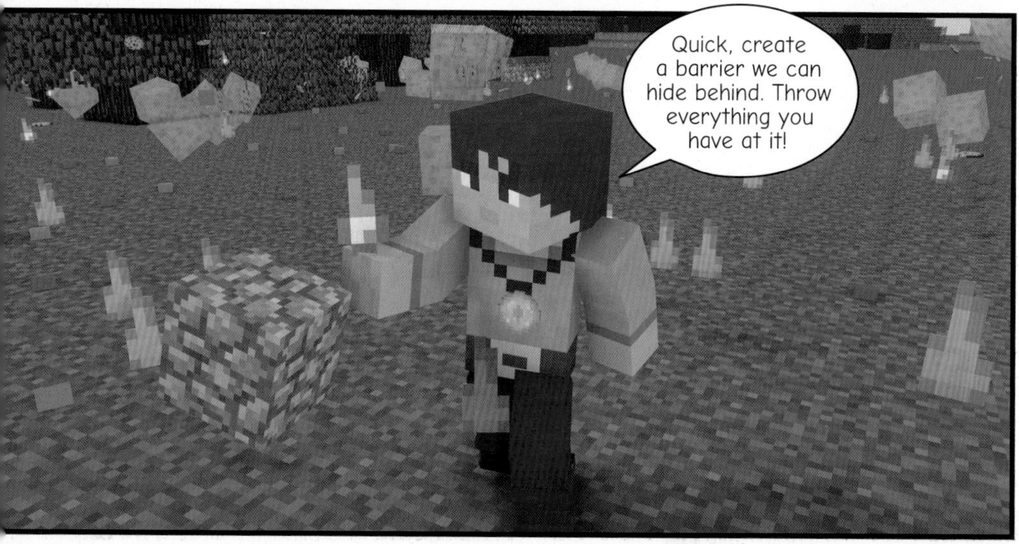
Quick, create a barrier we can hide behind. Throw everything you have at it!

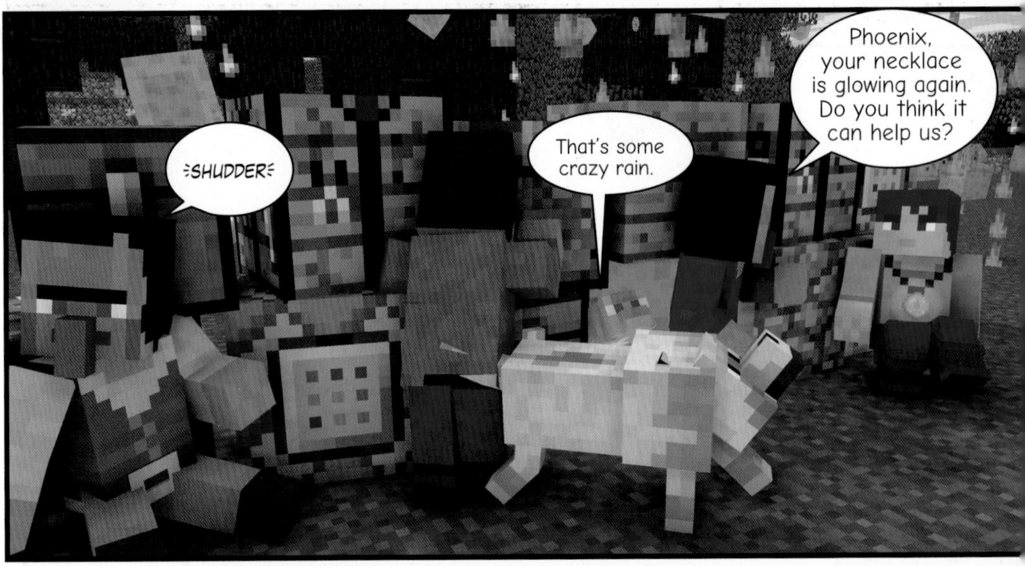
SHUDDER
That's some crazy rain.
Phoenix, your necklace is glowing again. Do you think it can help us?

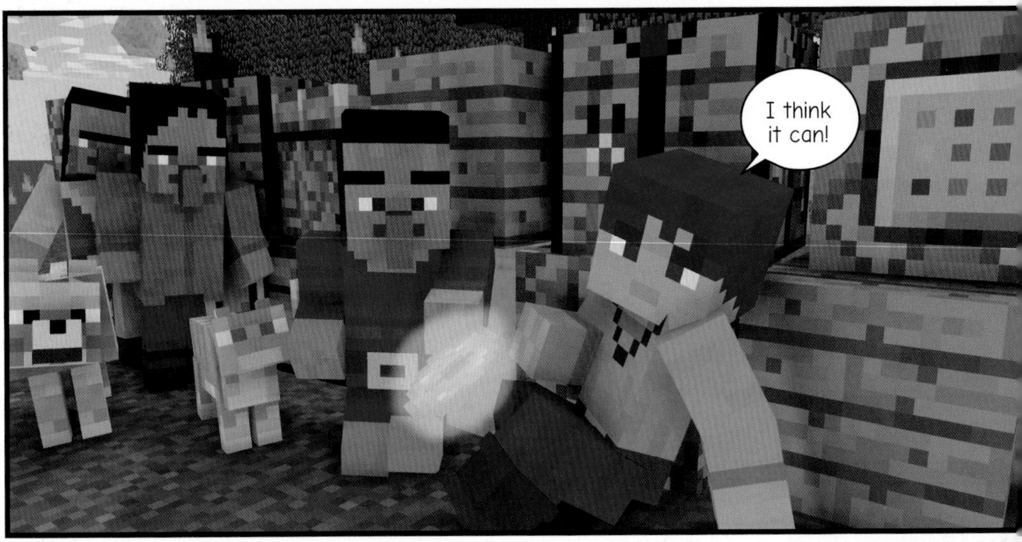
I think it can!

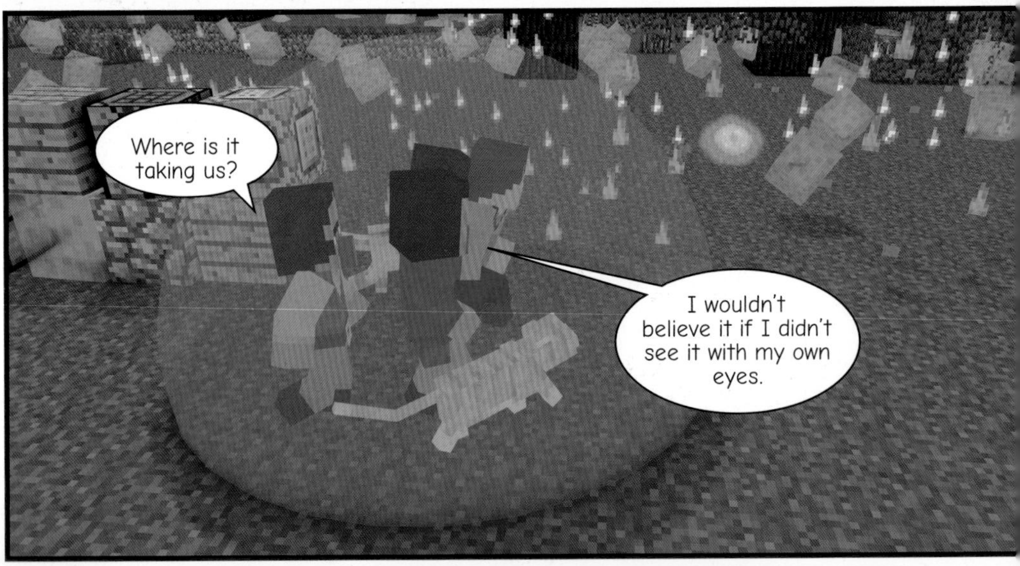
Where is it taking us?
I wouldn't believe it if I didn't see it with my own eyes.

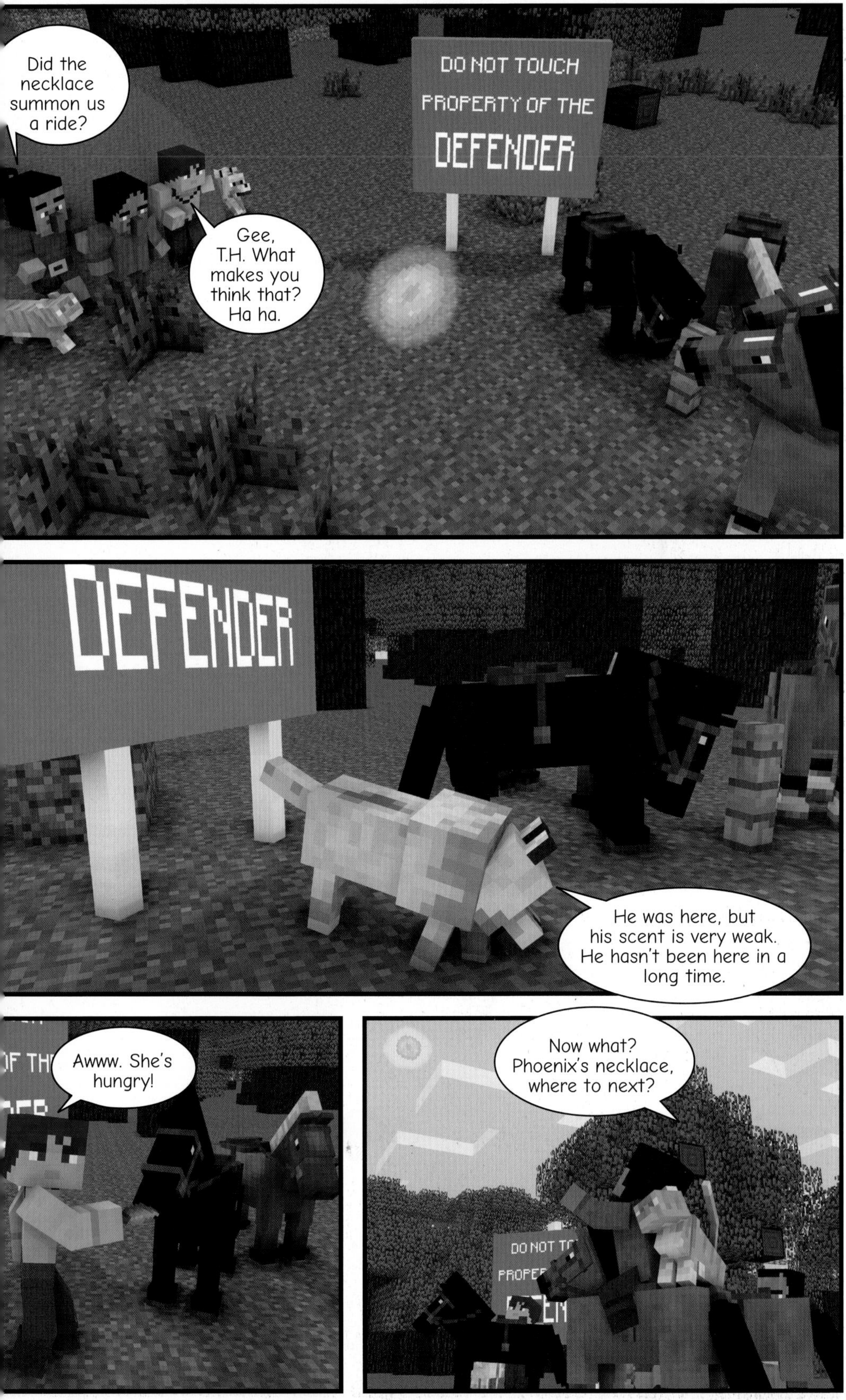
Did the necklace summon us a ride?
DO NOT TOUCH
PROPERTY OF THE
DEFENDER
Gee, T.H. What makes you think that? Ha ha.
DEFENDER
He was here, but his scent is very weak. He hasn't been here in a long time.
Awww. She's hungry!
Now what? Phoenix's necklace, where to next?

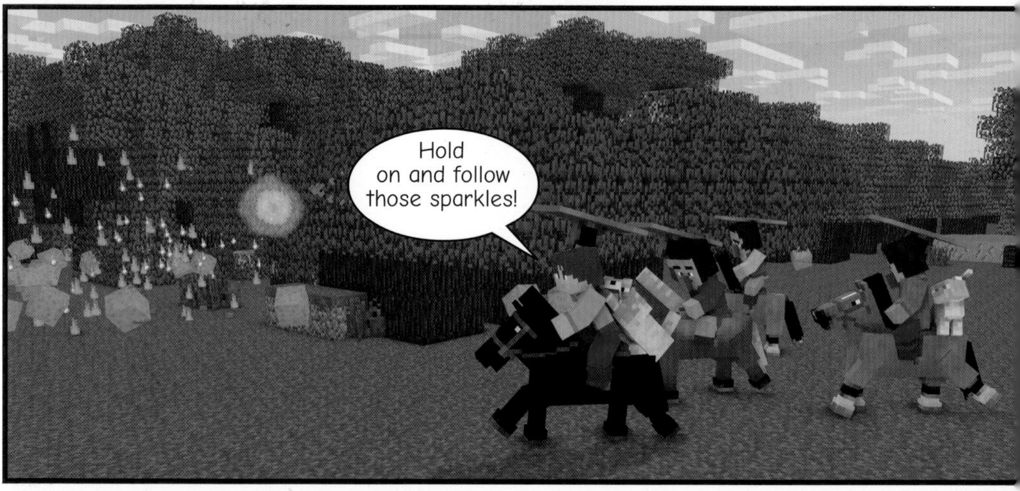
Hold on and follow those sparkles!

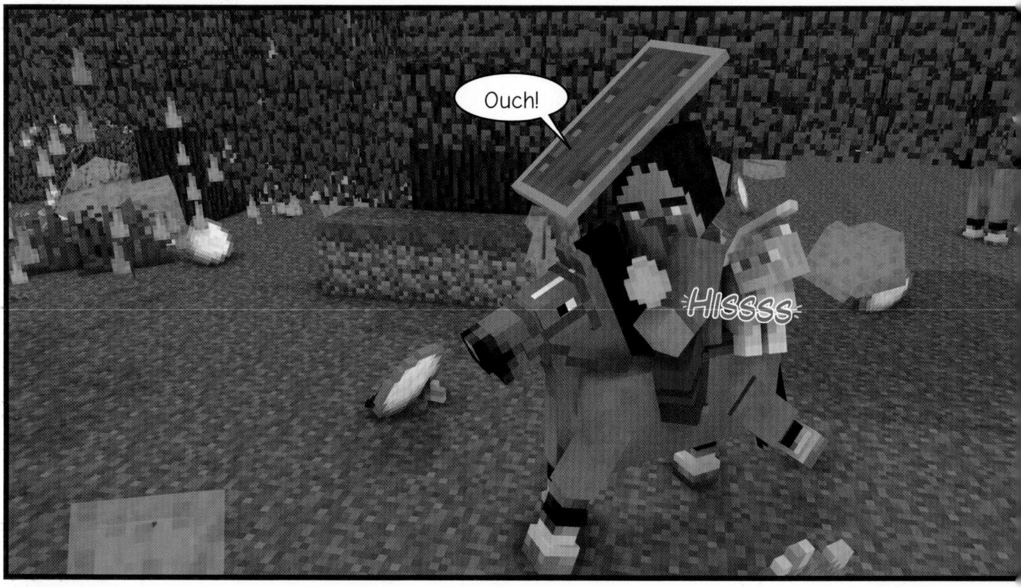
Ouch!
HISSSS

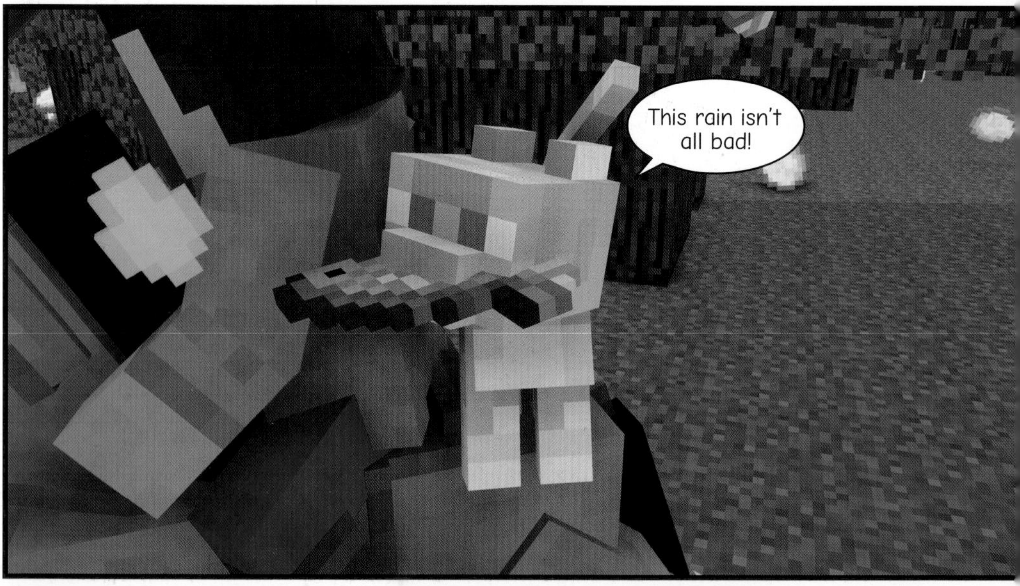
This rain isn't all bad!

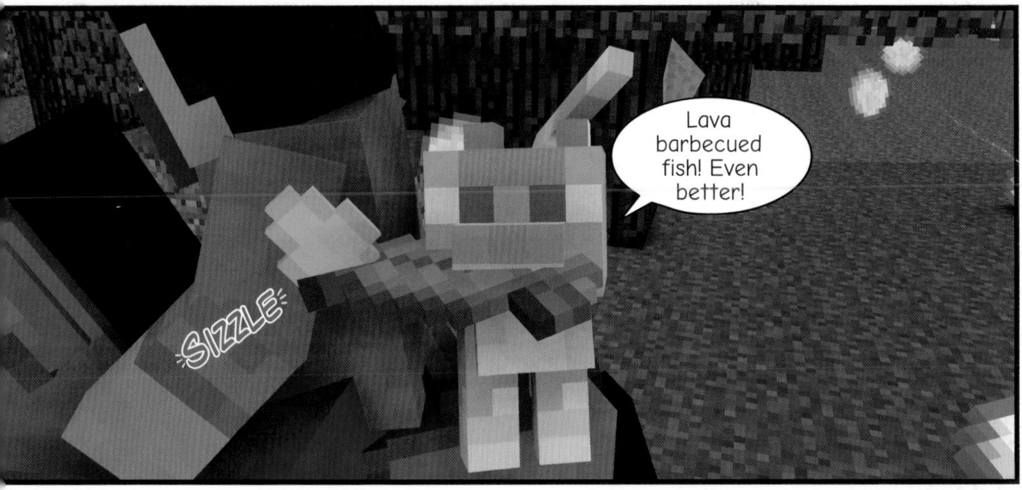
SIZZLE
Lava barbecued fish! Even better!

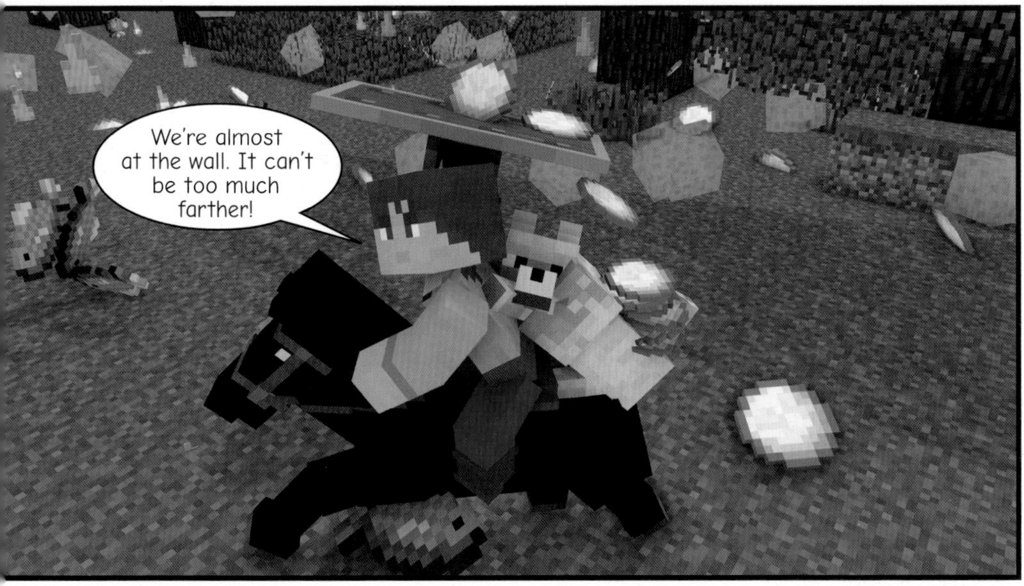
We're almost at the wall. It can't be too much farther!

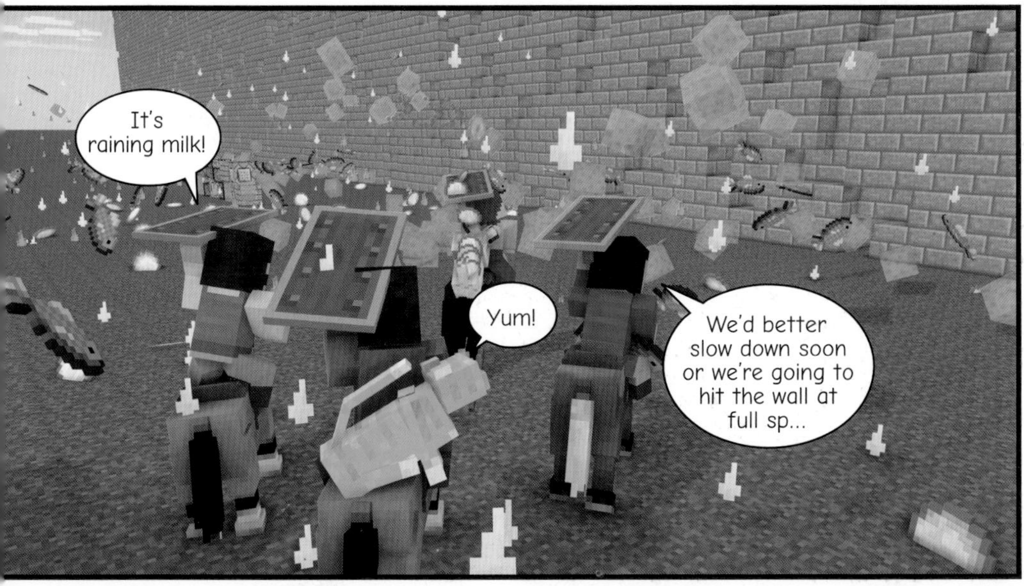
It's raining milk!
Yum!
We'd better slow down soon or we're going to hit the wall at full sp...

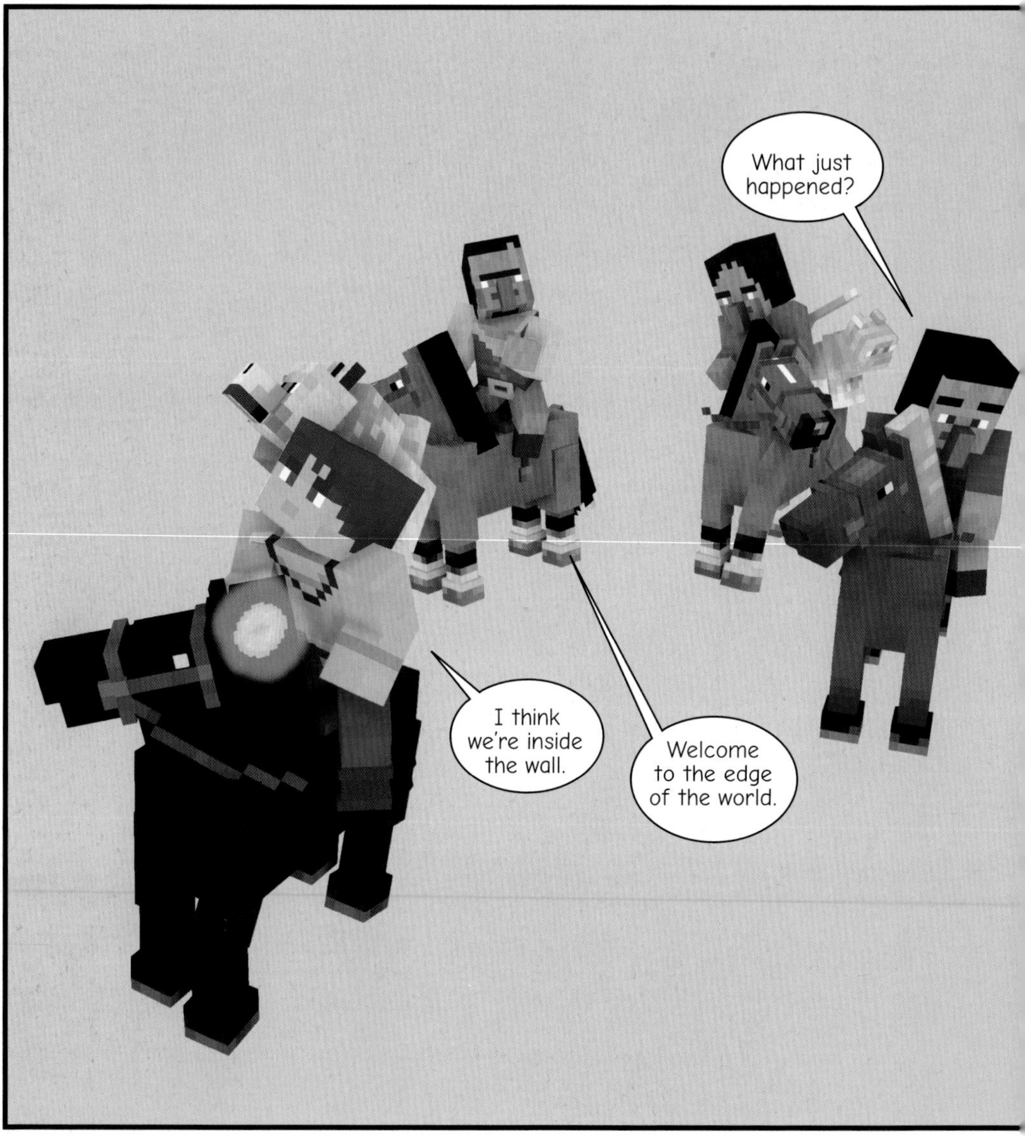
What just happened?
I think we're inside the wall.
Welcome to the edge of the world.

CHAPTER 11

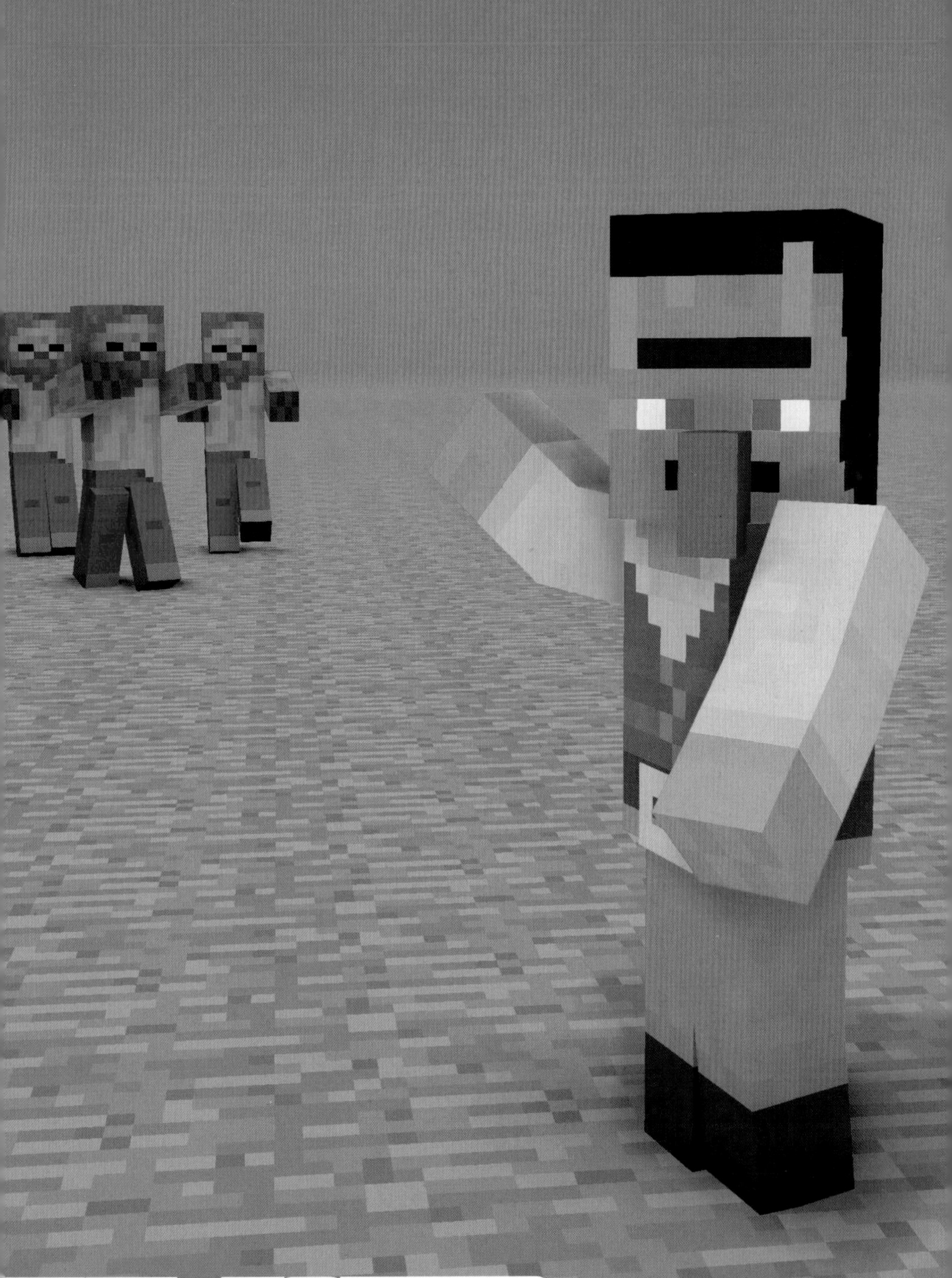

THE TOWER

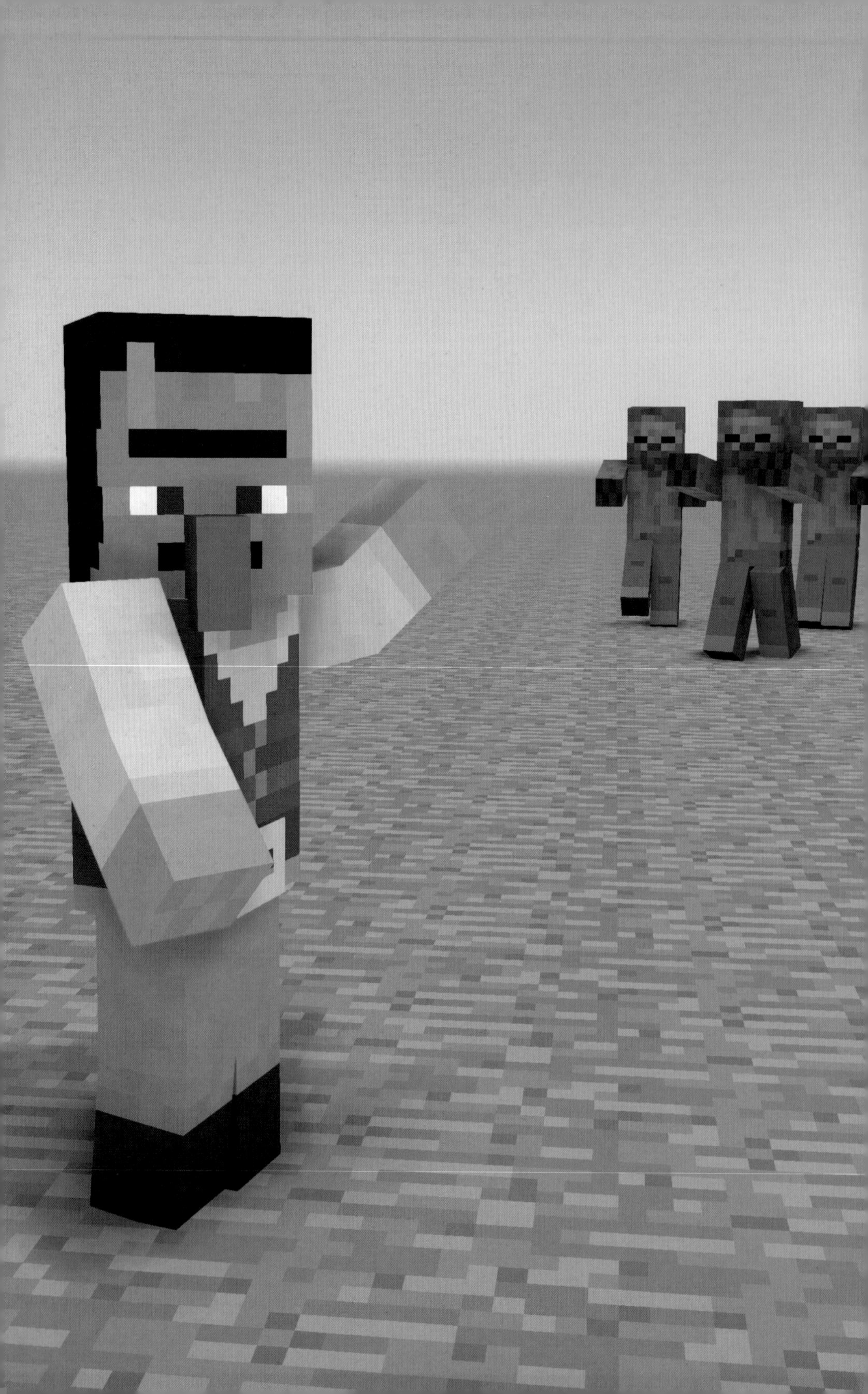

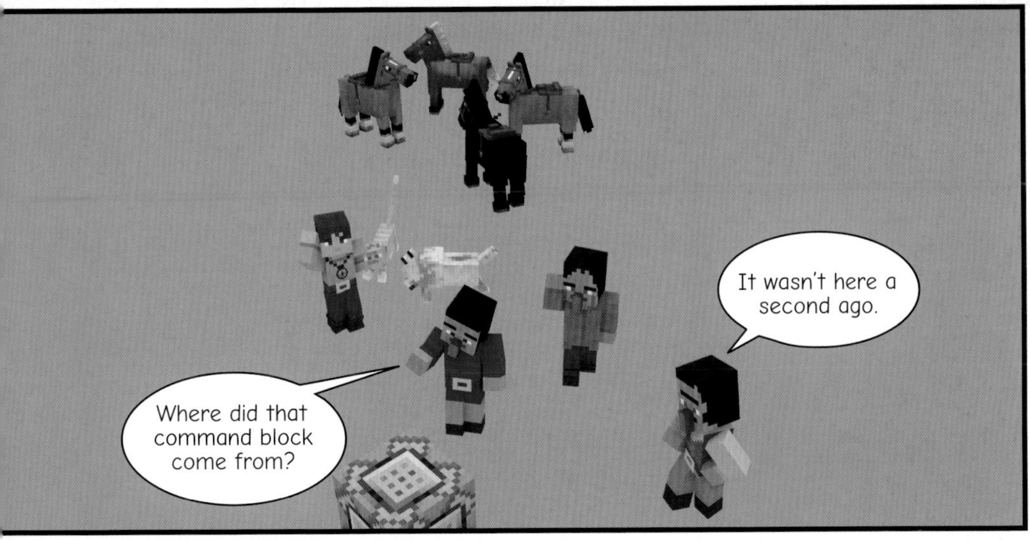
Where did that command block come from?
It wasn't here a second ago.

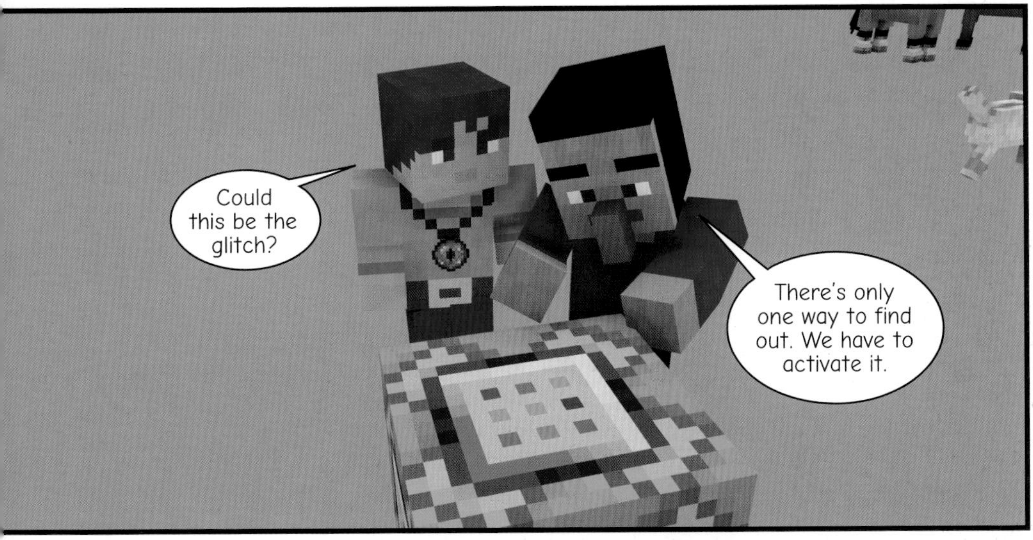
Could this be the glitch?
There's only one way to find out. We have to activate it.

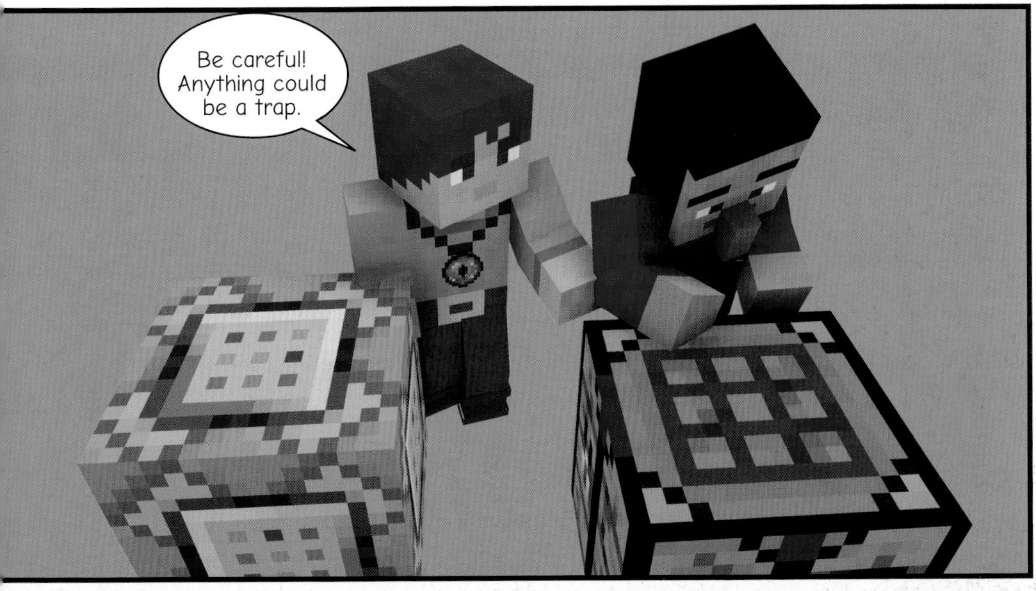
Be careful! Anything could be a trap.

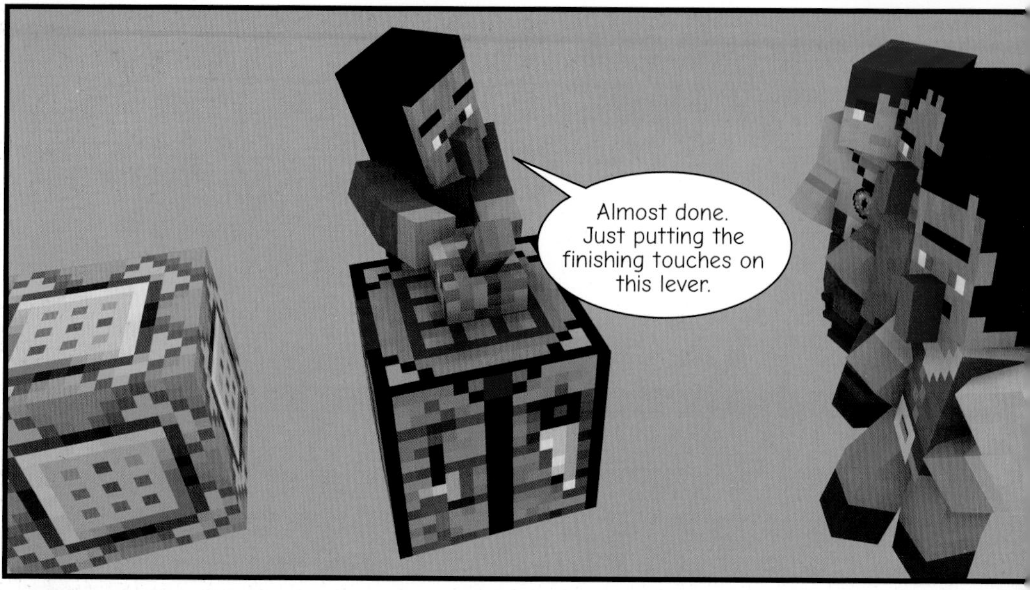
Almost done. Just putting the finishing touches on this lever.

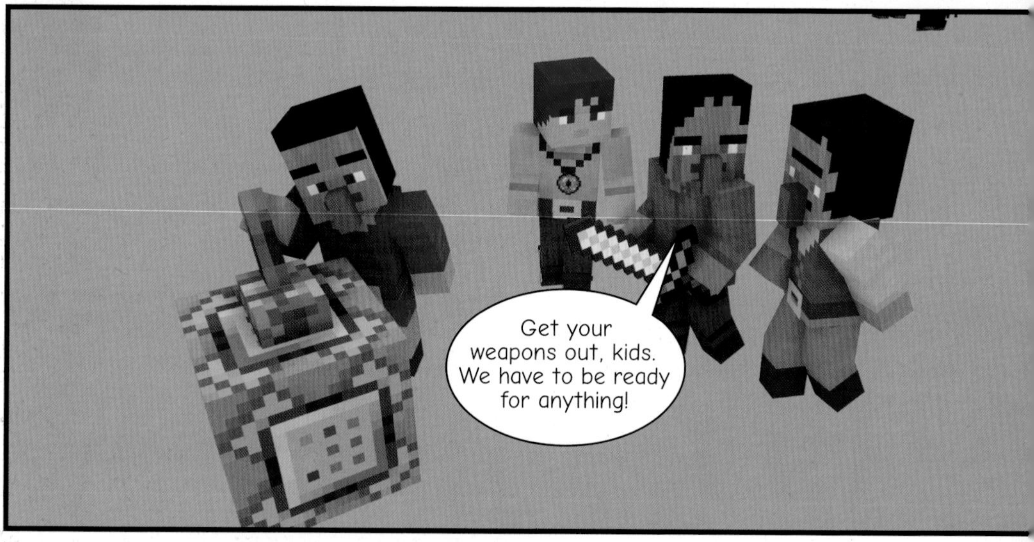
Get your weapons out, kids. We have to be ready for anything!

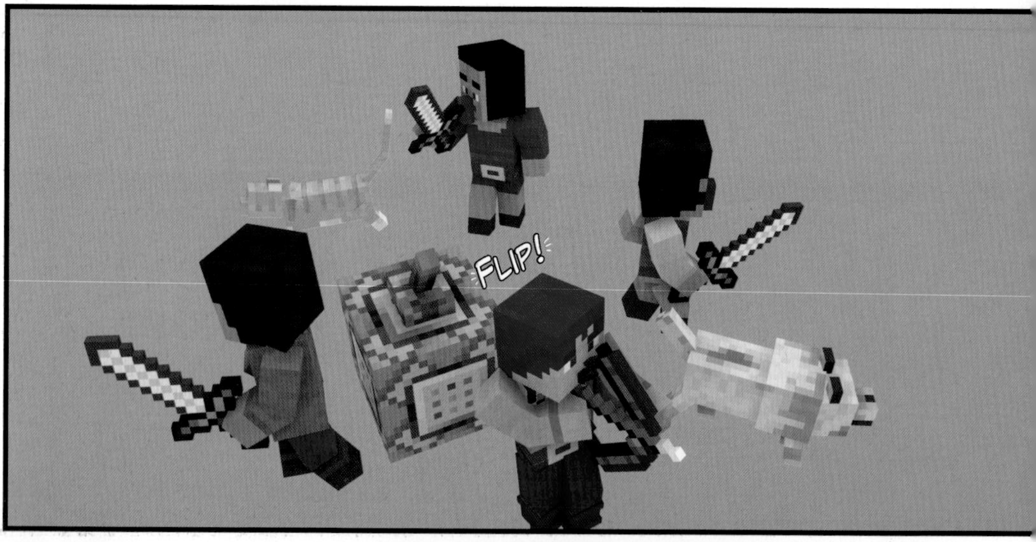
FLIP!

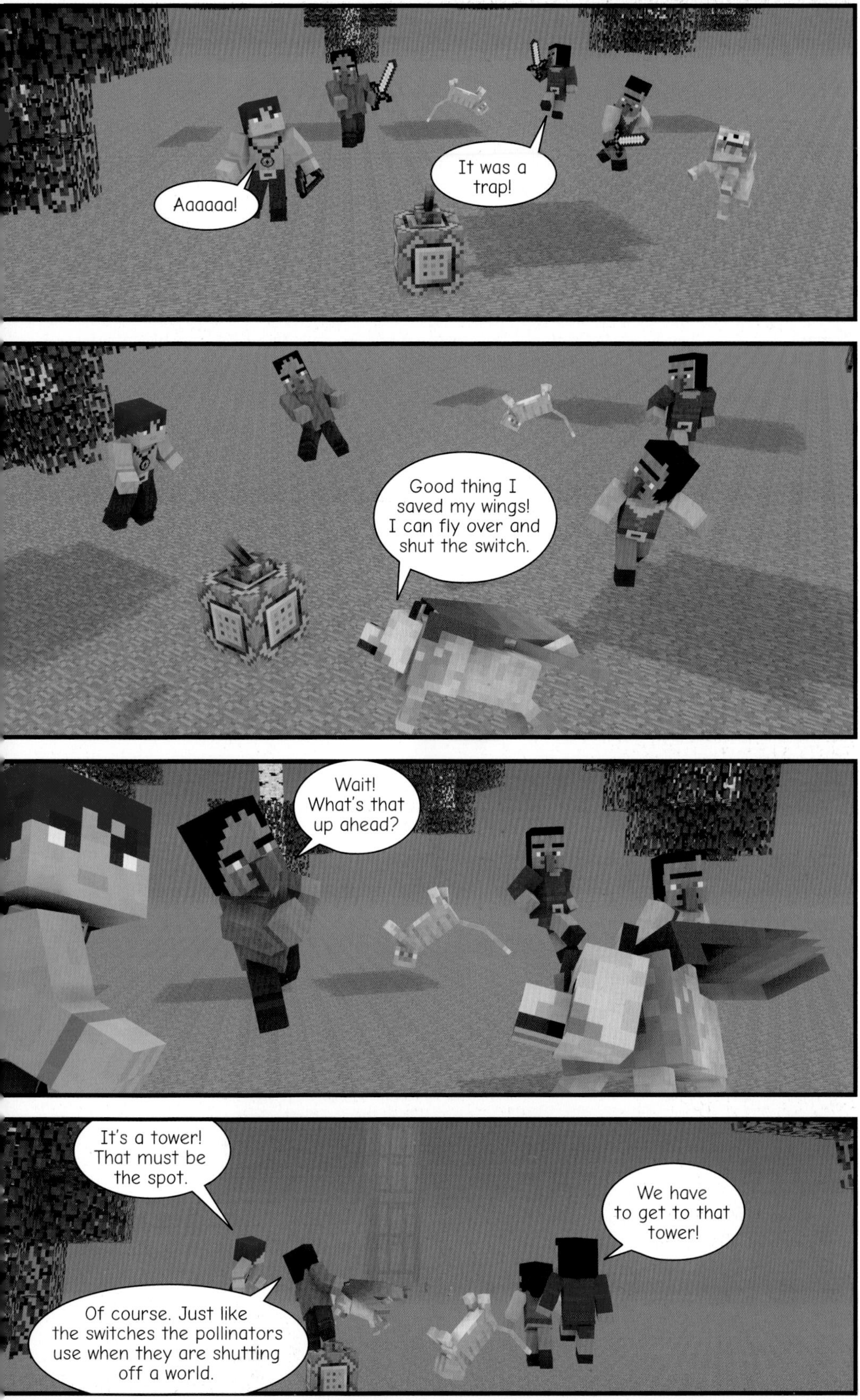
Aaaaaa!
It was a trap!
Good thing I saved my wings! I can fly over and shut the switch.
Wait! What's that up ahead?
It's a tower! That must be the spot.
We have to get to that tower!
Of course. Just like the switches the pollinators use when they are shutting off a world.

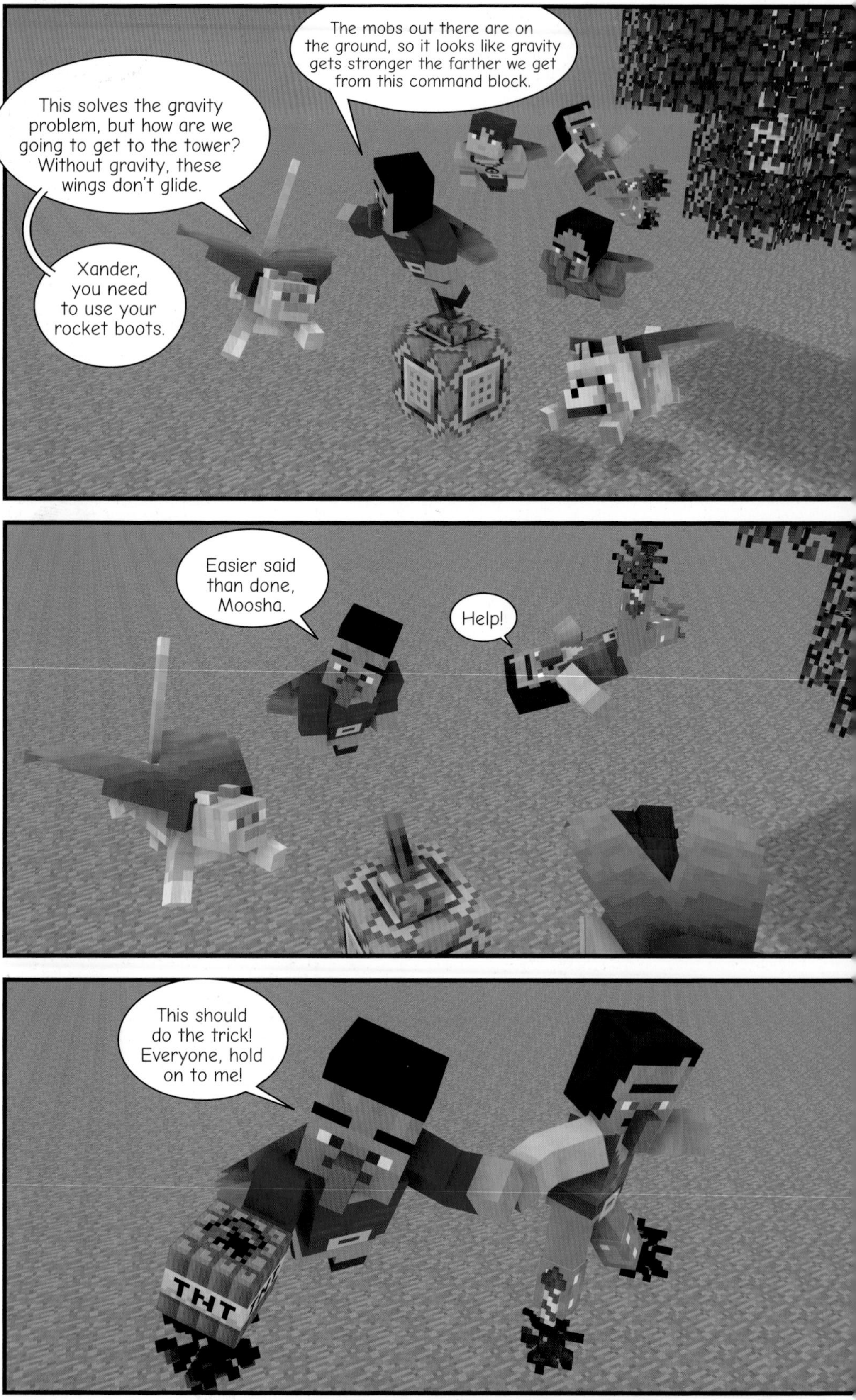
This solves the gravity problem, but how are we going to get to the tower? Without gravity, these wings don't glide.
The mobs out there are on the ground, so it looks like gravity gets stronger the farther we get from this command block.
Xander, you need to use your rocket boots.
Easier said than done, Moosha.
Help!
This should do the trick! Everyone, hold on to me!
TNT

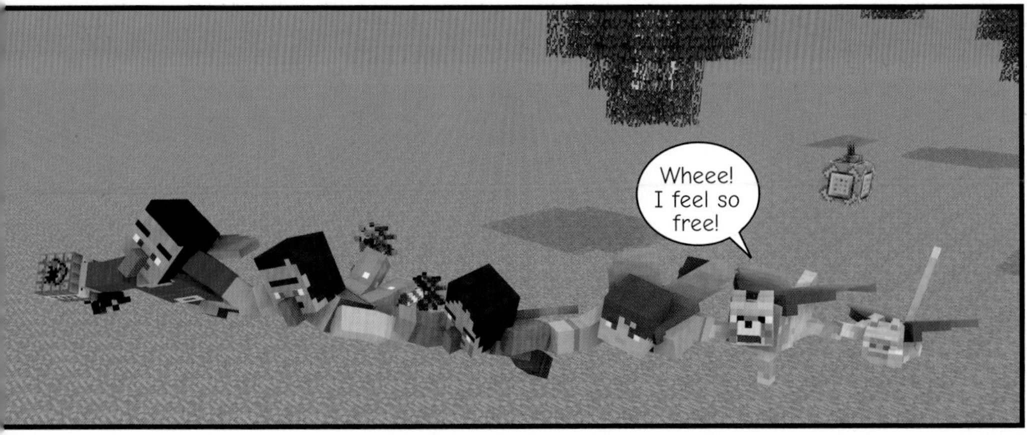
Wheee! I feel so free!

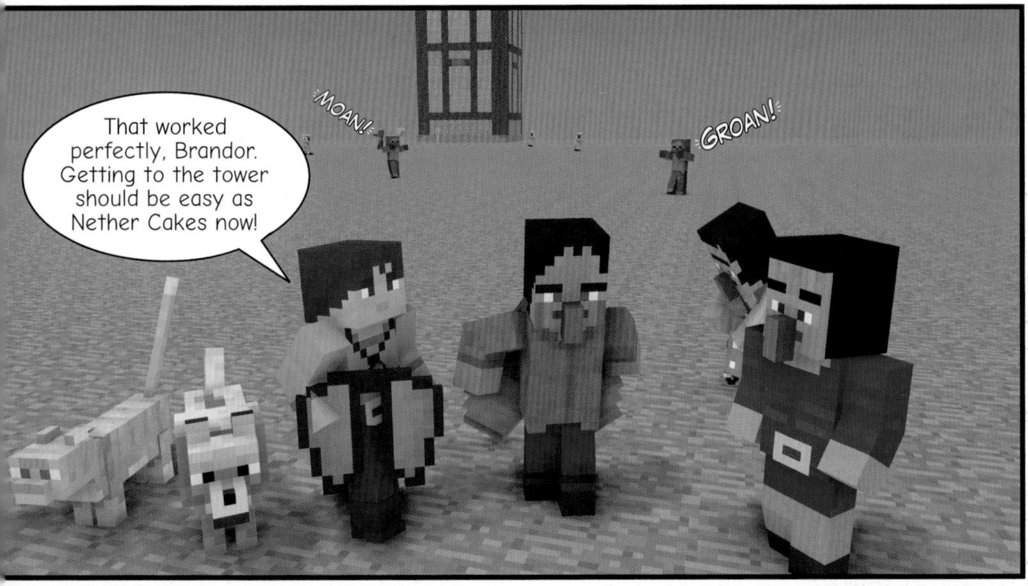
MOAN!
GROAN!
That worked perfectly, Brandor. Getting to the tower should be easy as Nether Cakes now!

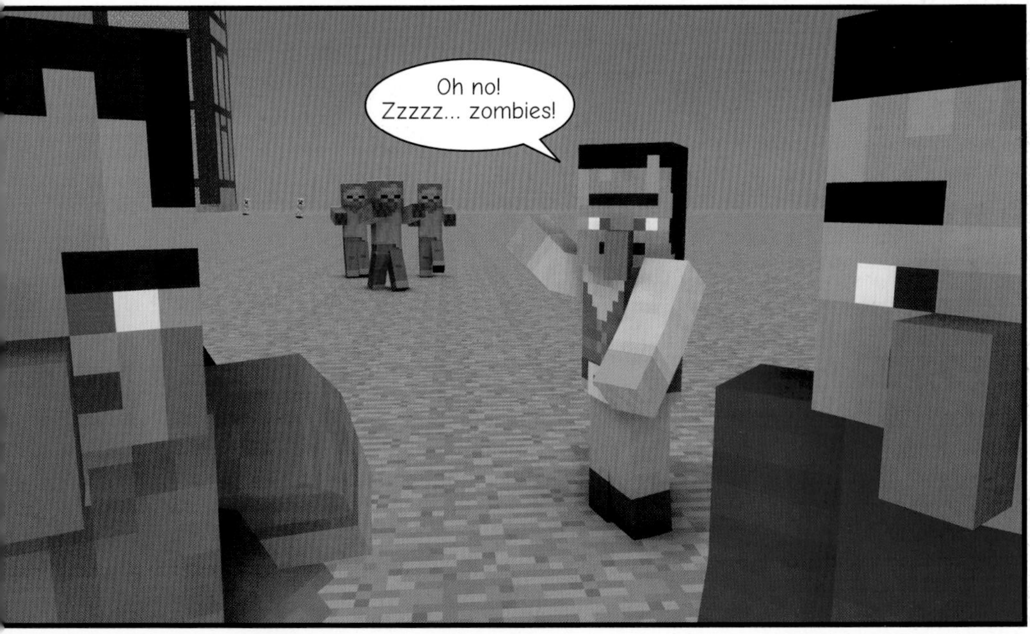
Oh no! Zzzzz... zombies!

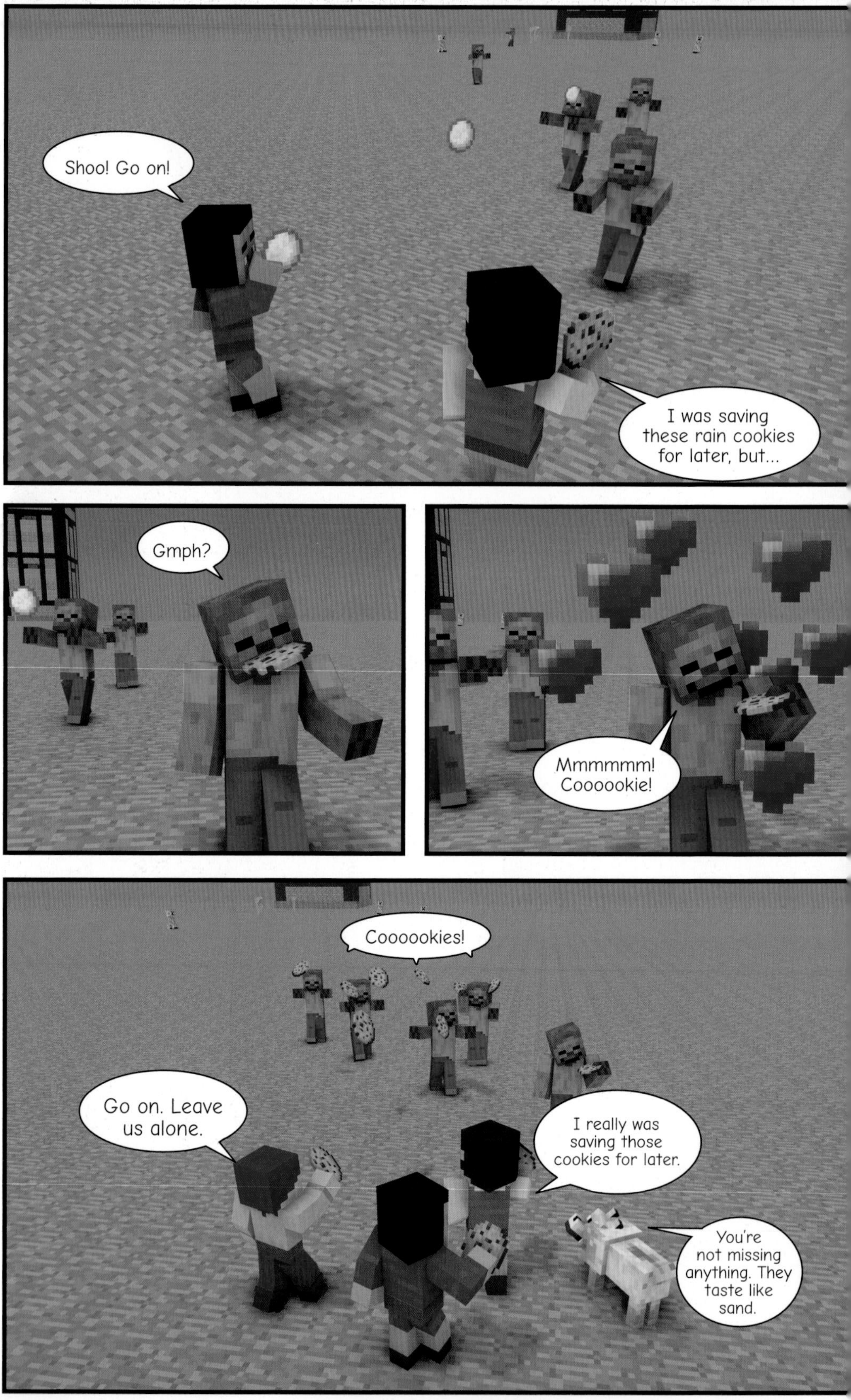
Shoo! Go on!
I was saving these rain cookies for later, but...
Gmph?
Mmmmmm! Cooooookie!
Coooookies!
Go on. Leave us alone.
I really was saving those cookies for later.
You're not missing anything. They taste like sand.

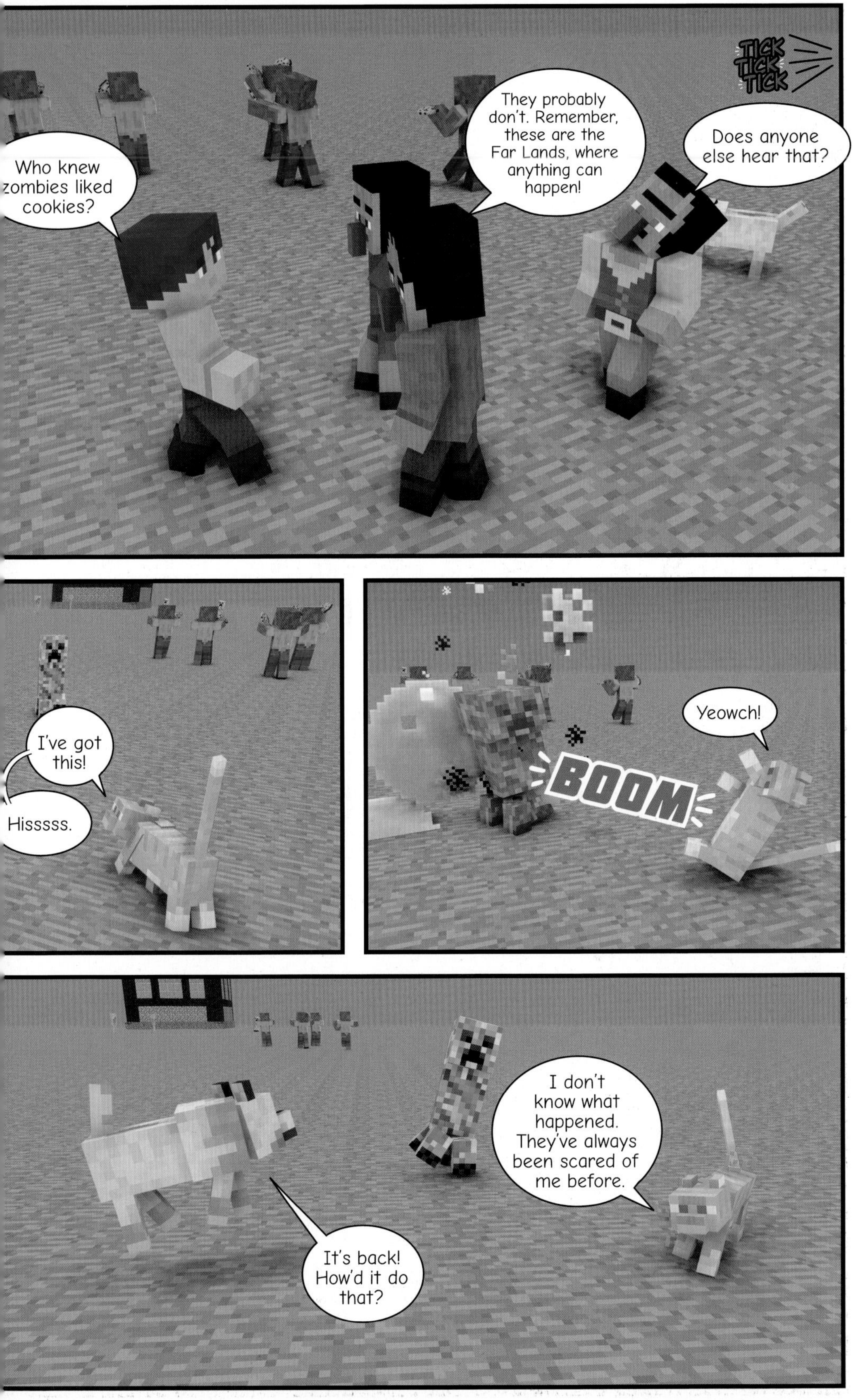
TICK TICK TICK
Who knew zombies liked cookies?
They probably don't. Remember, these are the Far Lands, where anything can happen!
Does anyone else hear that?
I've got this!
Hisssss.
BOOM
Yeowch!
It's back! How'd it do that?
I don't know what happened. They've always been scared of me before.

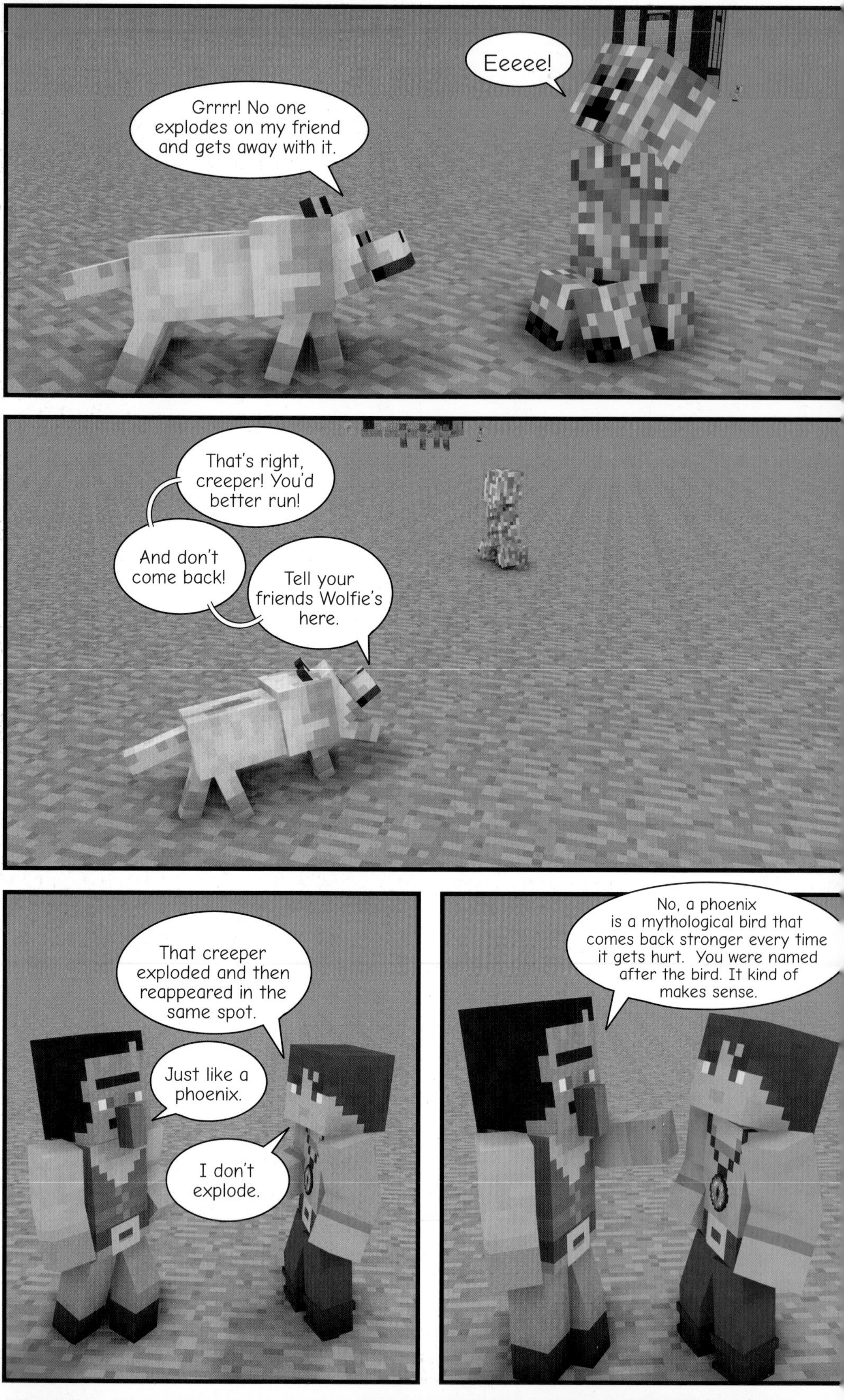
Grrrr! No one explodes on my friend and gets away with it.
Eeeee!
That's right, creeper! You'd better run!
And don't come back!
Tell your friends Wolfie's here.
That creeper exploded and then reappeared in the same spot.
Just like a phoenix.
I don't explode.
No, a phoenix is a mythological bird that comes back stronger every time it gets hurt. You were named after the bird. It kind of makes sense.

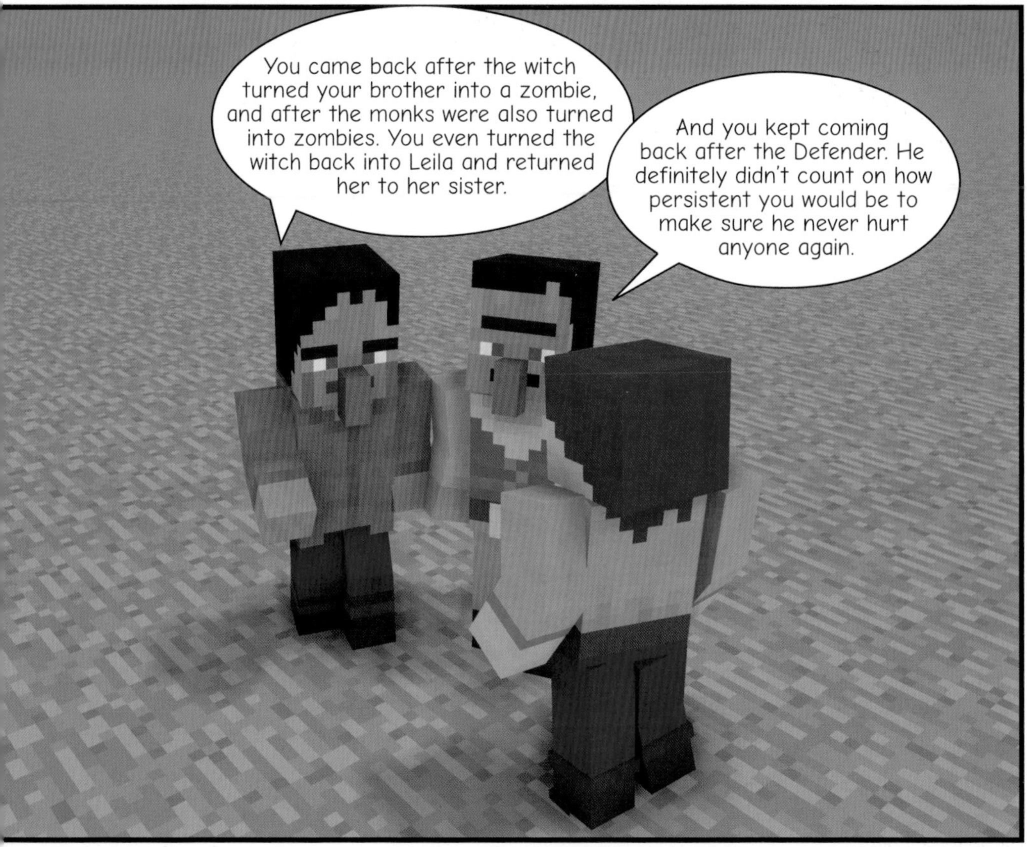
You came back after the witch turned your brother into a zombie, and after the monks were also turned into zombies. You even turned the witch back into Leila and returned her to her sister.
And you kept coming back after the Defender. He definitely didn't count on how persistent you would be to make sure he never hurt anyone again.

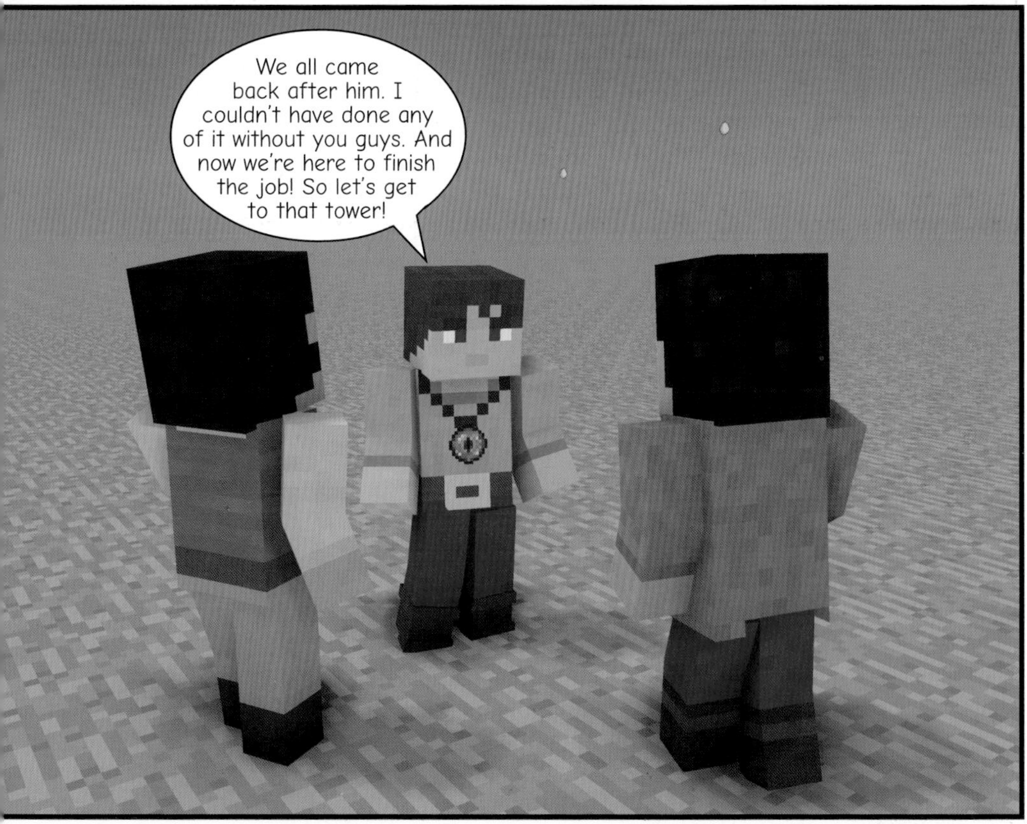
We all came back after him. I couldn't have done any of it without you guys. And now we're here to finish the job! So let's get to that tower!

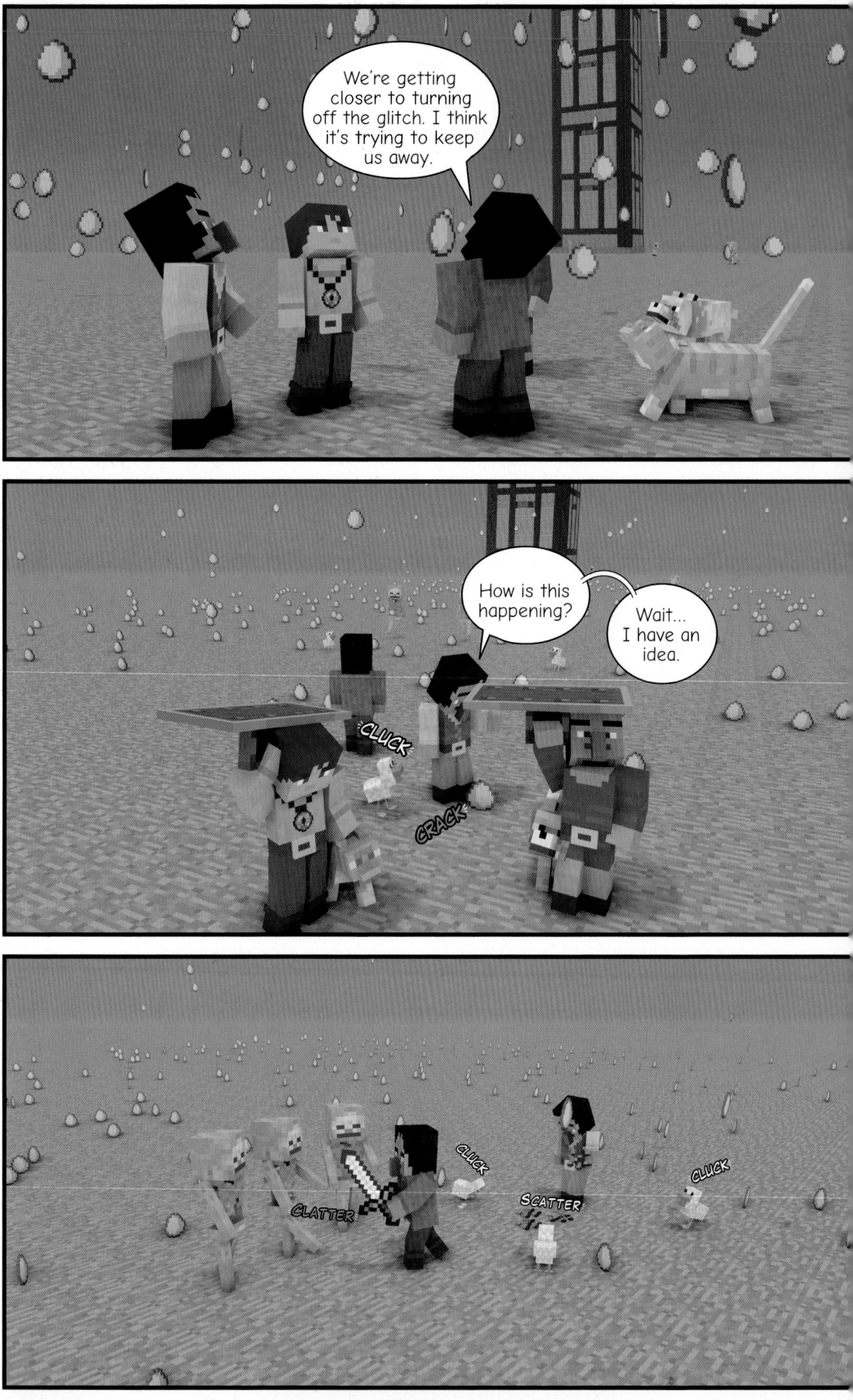
We're getting closer to turning off the glitch. I think it's trying to keep us away.
How is this happening?
Wait... I have an idea.
CLUCK
CRACK
CLUCK
CLATTER
SCATTER
CLUCK

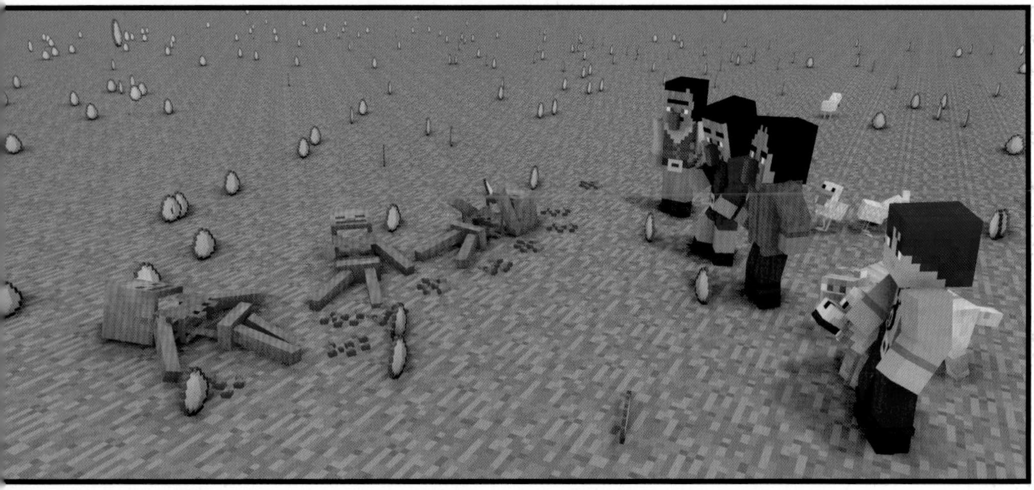

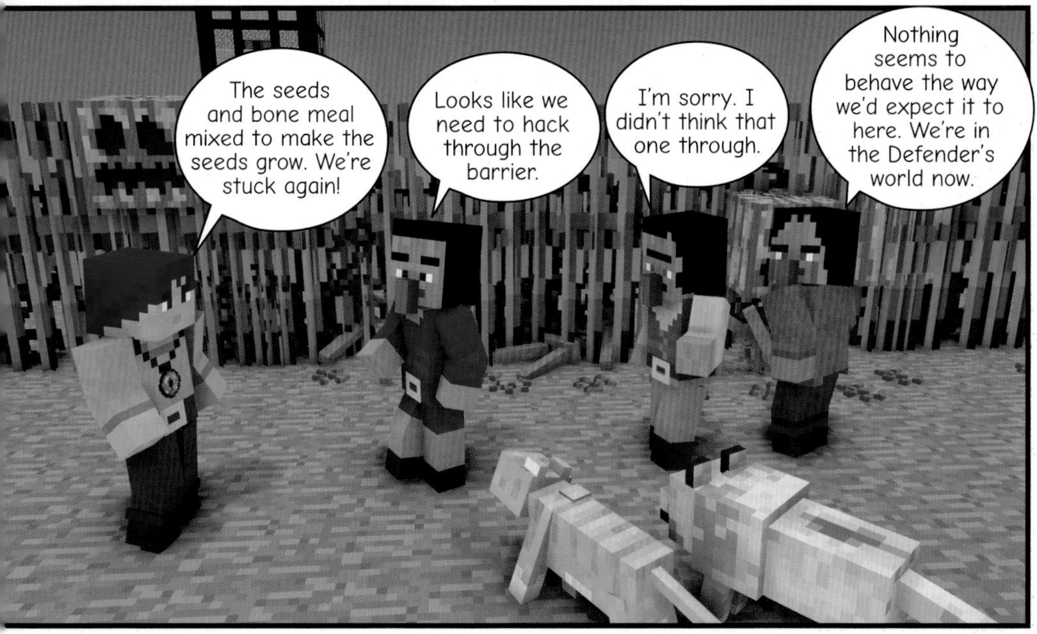
The seeds and bone meal mixed to make the seeds grow. We're stuck again!
Looks like we need to hack through the barrier.
I'm sorry. I didn't think that one through.
Nothing seems to behave the way we'd expect it to here. We're in the Defender's world now.

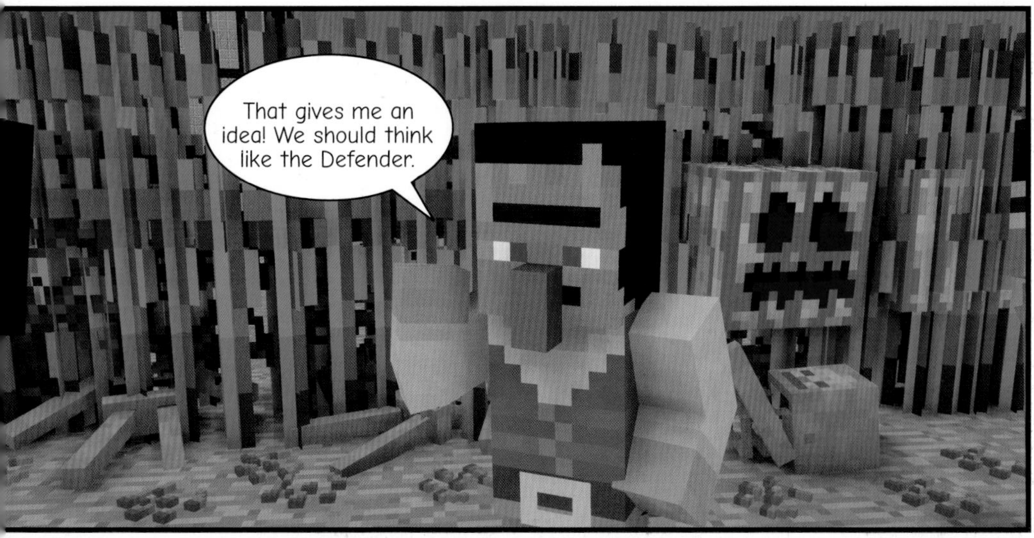
That gives me an idea! We should think like the Defender.

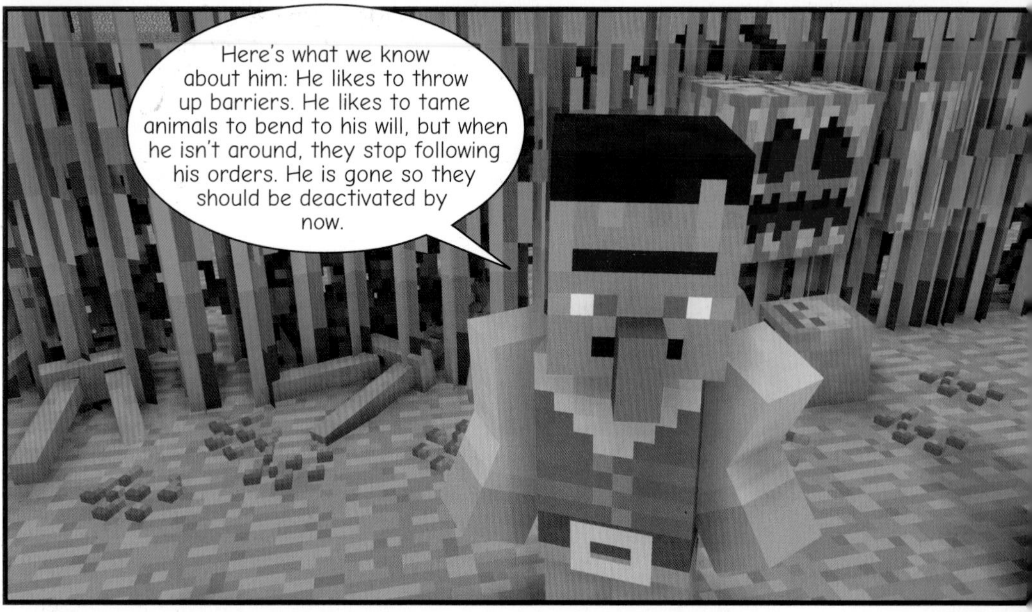
Here's what we know about him: He likes to throw up barriers. He likes to tame animals to bend to his will, but when he isn't around, they stop following his orders. He is gone so they should be deactivated by now.

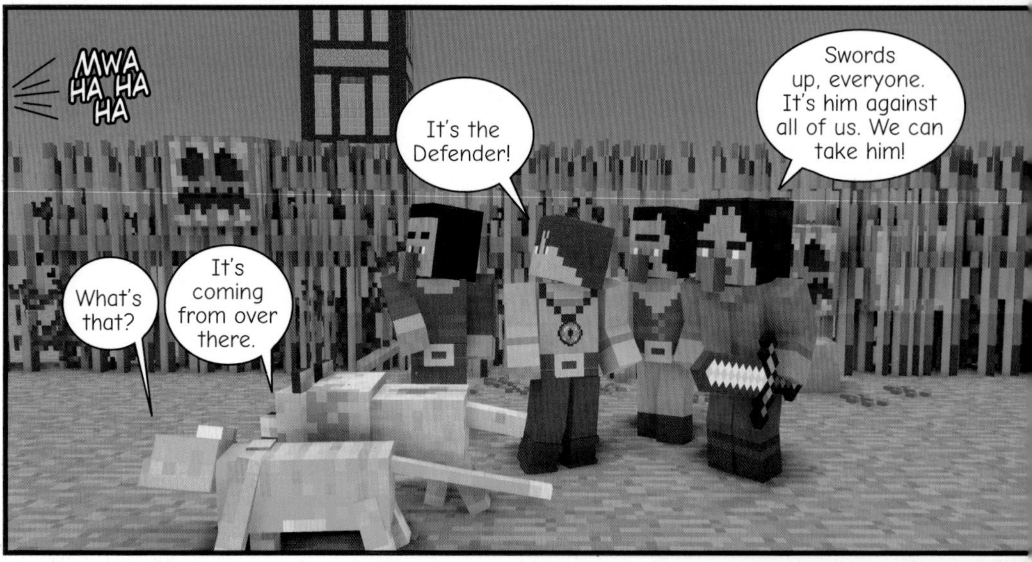
MWA HA HA HA
What's that?
It's coming from over there.
It's the Defender!
Swords up, everyone. It's him against all of us. We can take him!

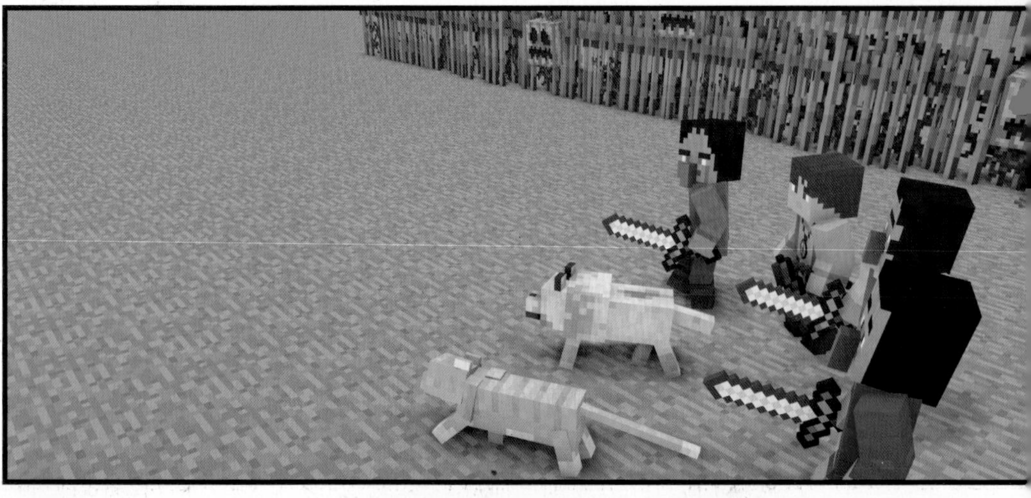

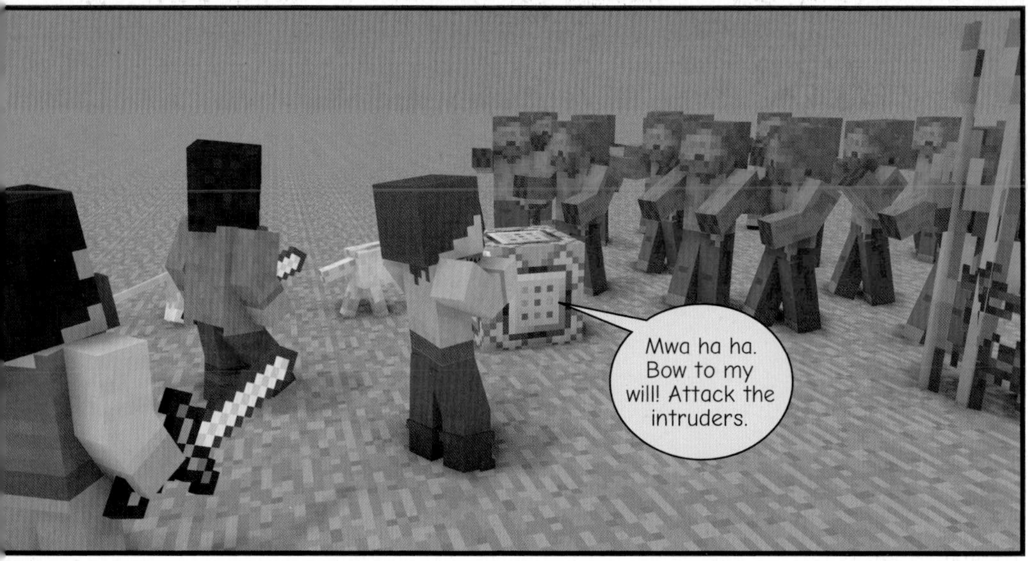
Mwa ha ha. Bow to my will! Attack the intruders.

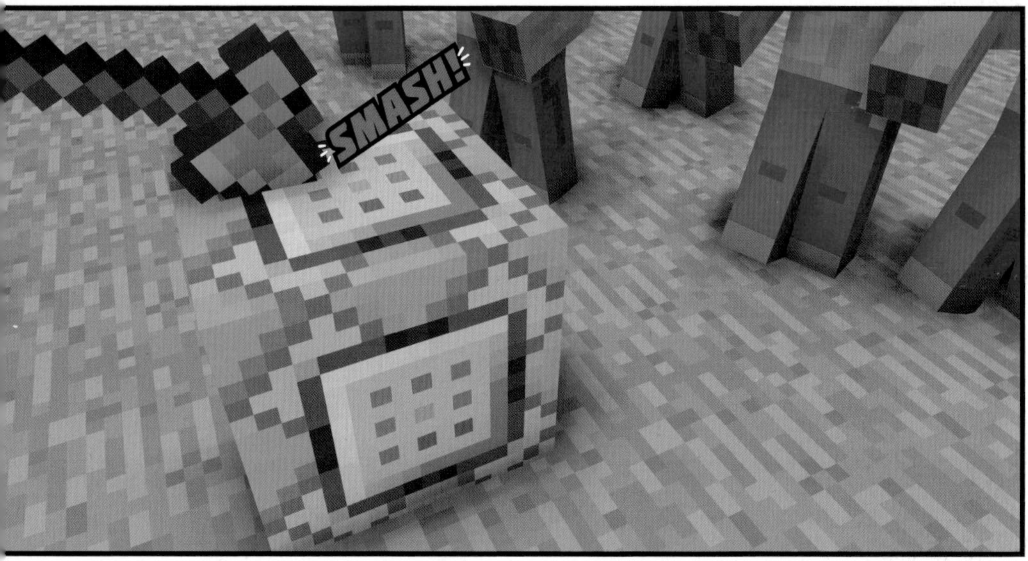
SMASH!

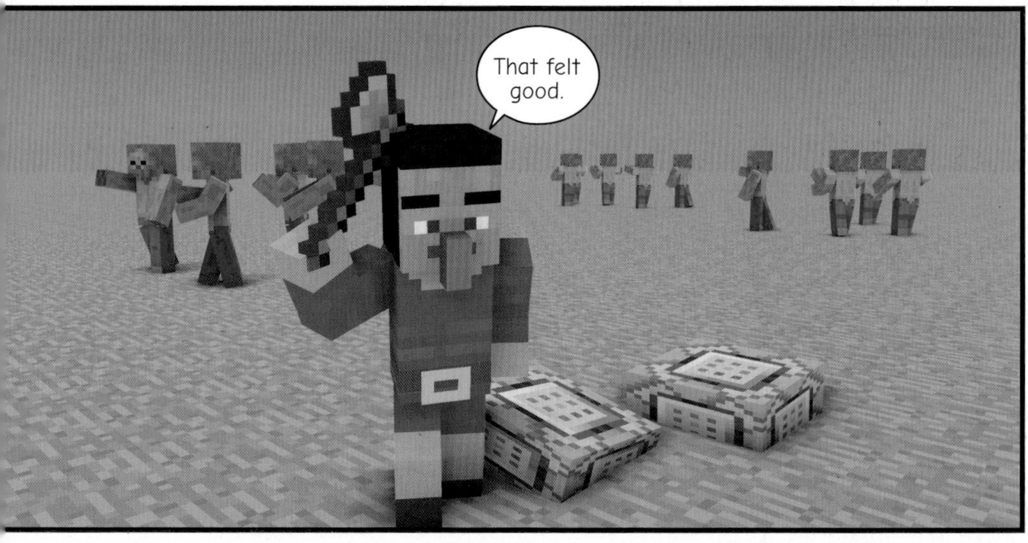
That felt good.

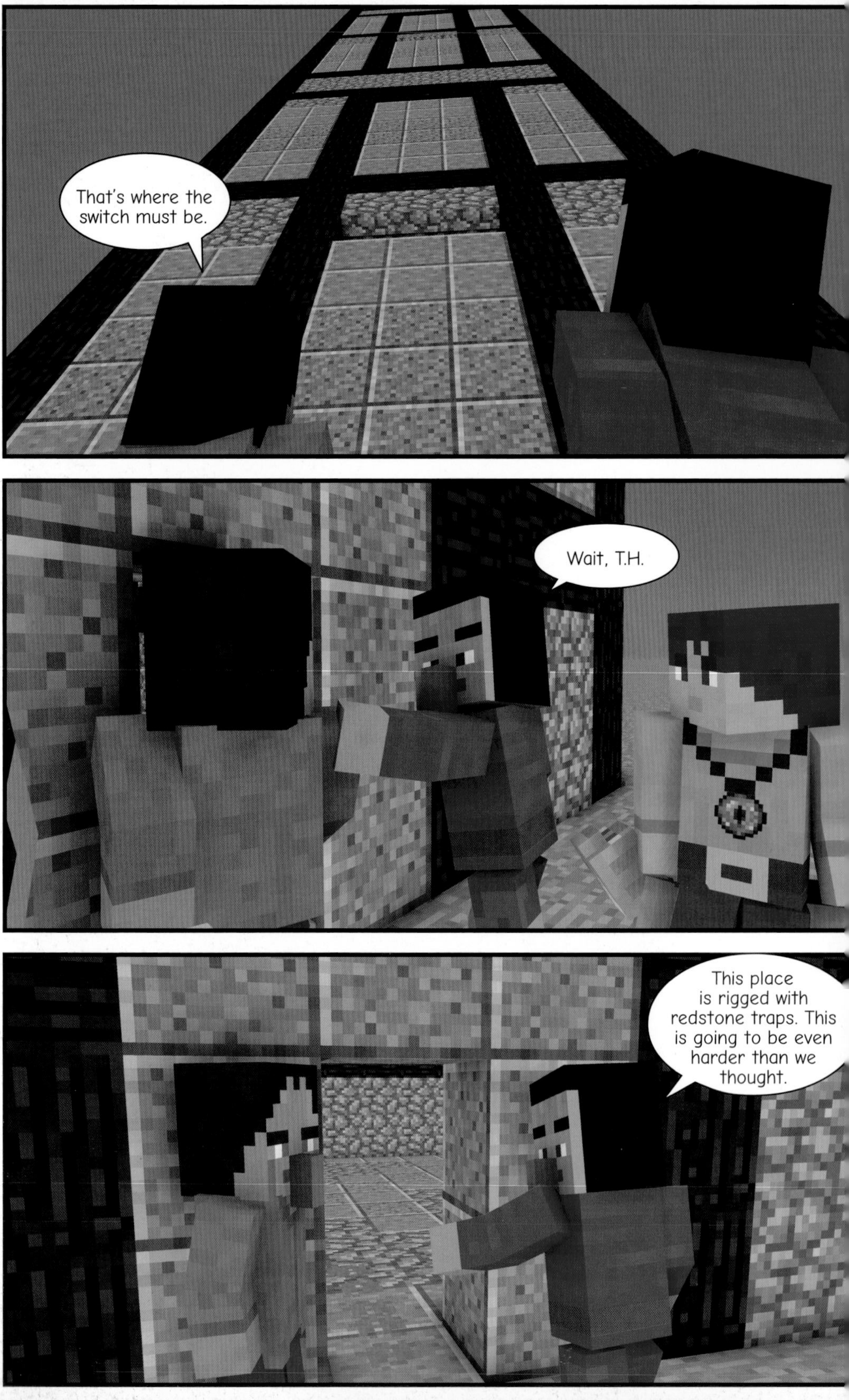
That's where the switch must be.
Wait, T.H.
This place is rigged with redstone traps. This is going to be even harder than we thought.

CHAPTER 12

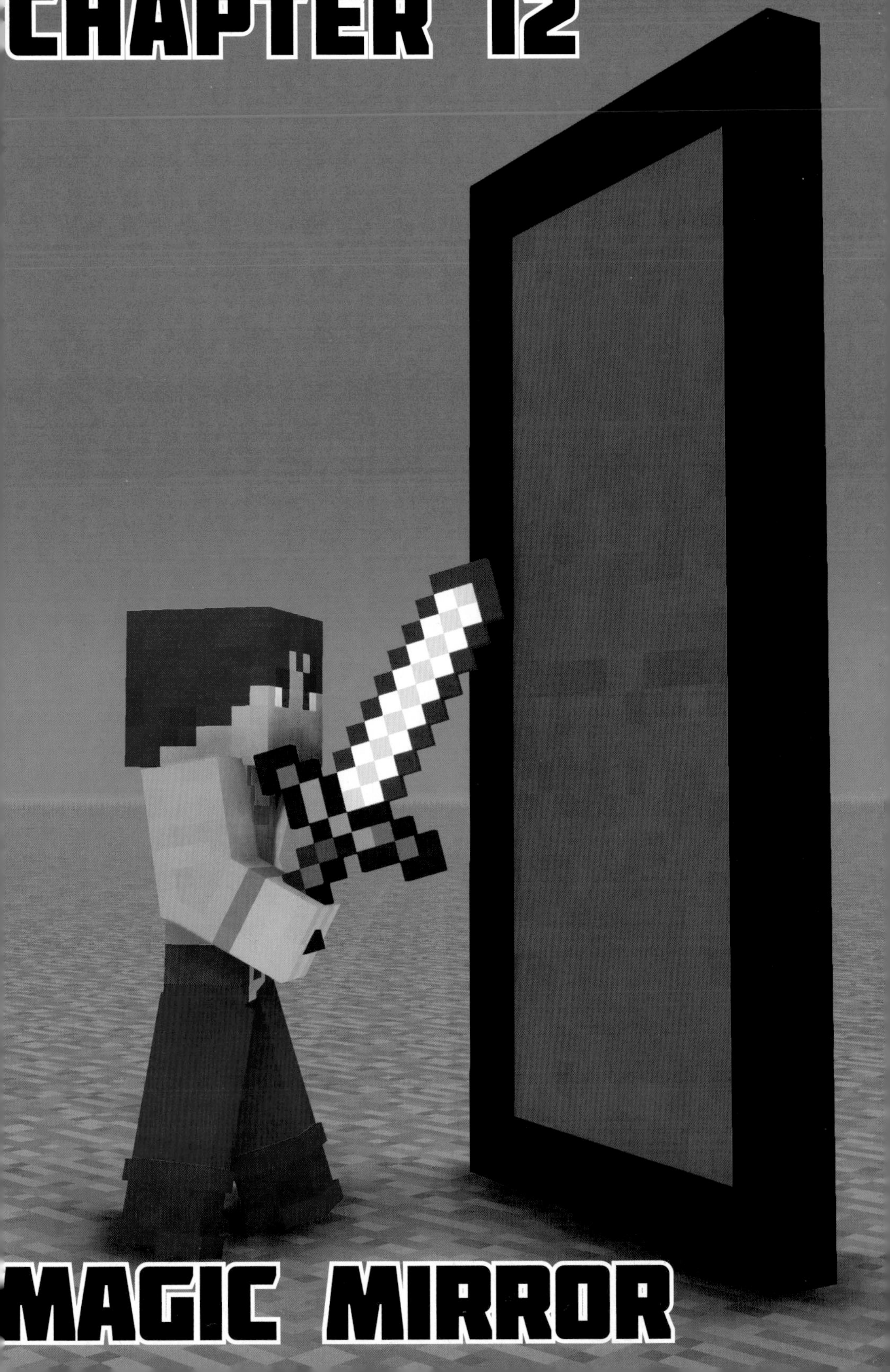

MAGIC MIRROR

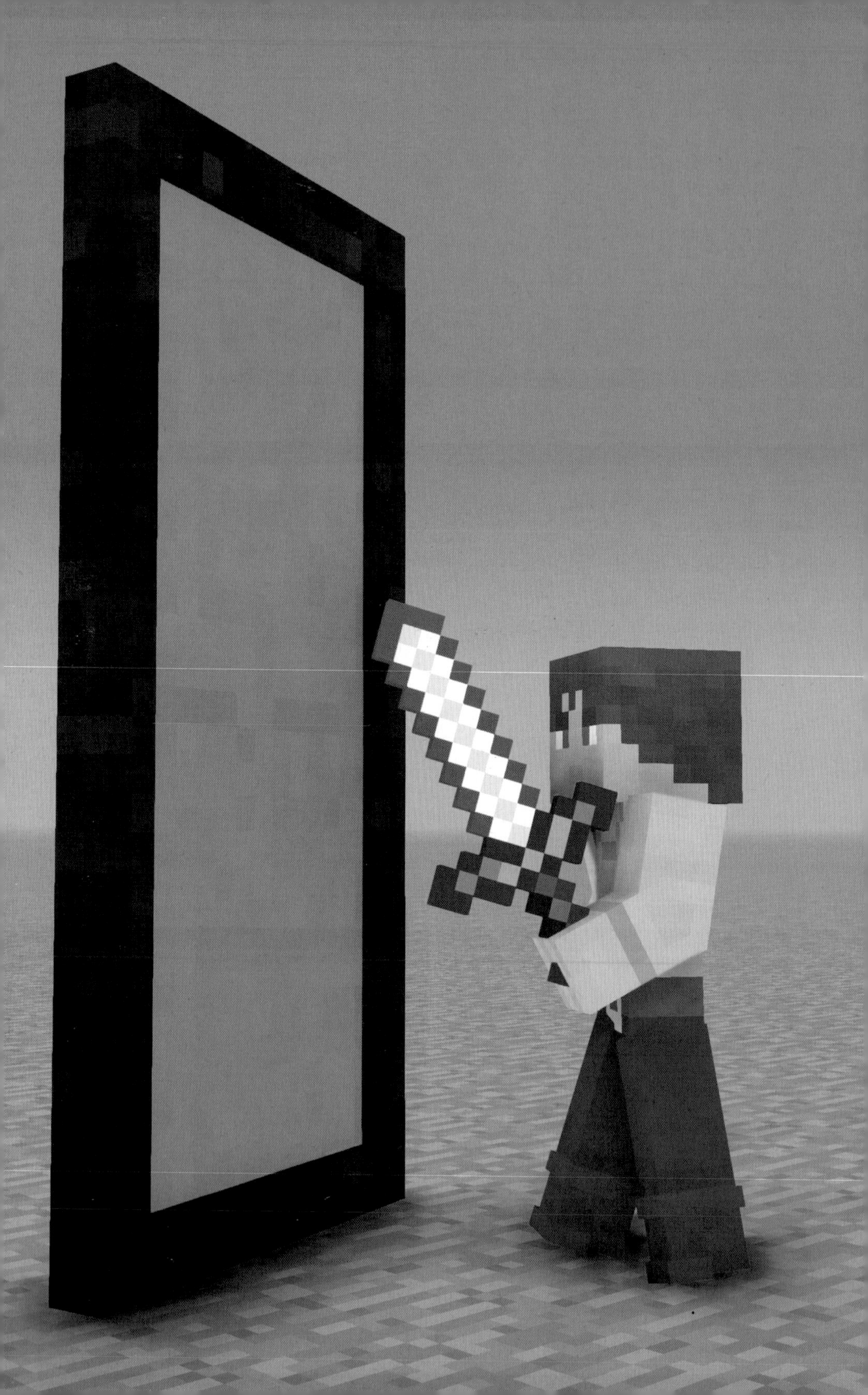

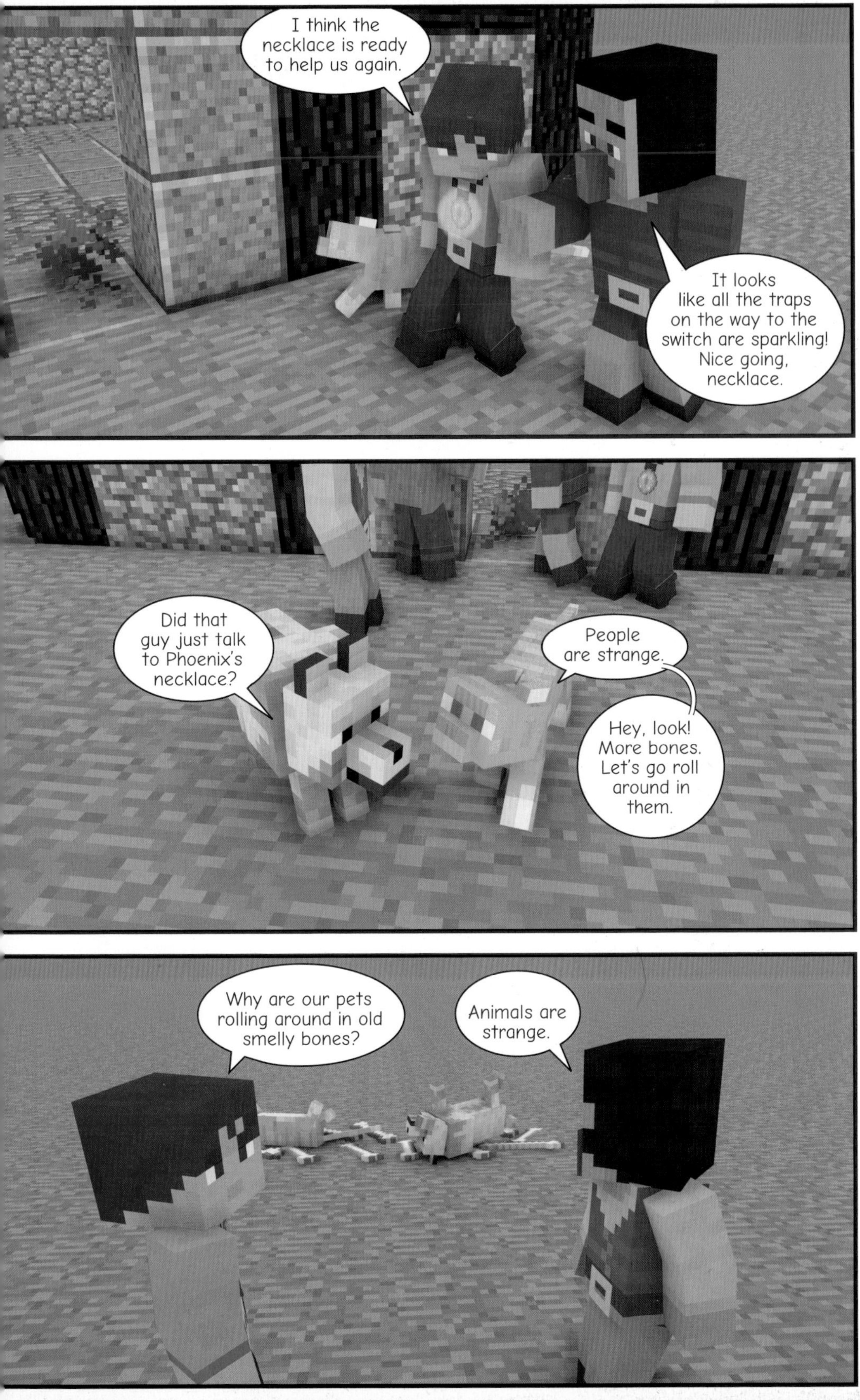
I think the necklace is ready to help us again.
It looks like all the traps on the way to the switch are sparkling! Nice going, necklace.
Did that guy just talk to Phoenix's necklace?
People are strange.
Hey, look! More bones. Let's go roll around in them.
Why are our pets rolling around in old smelly bones?
Animals are strange.

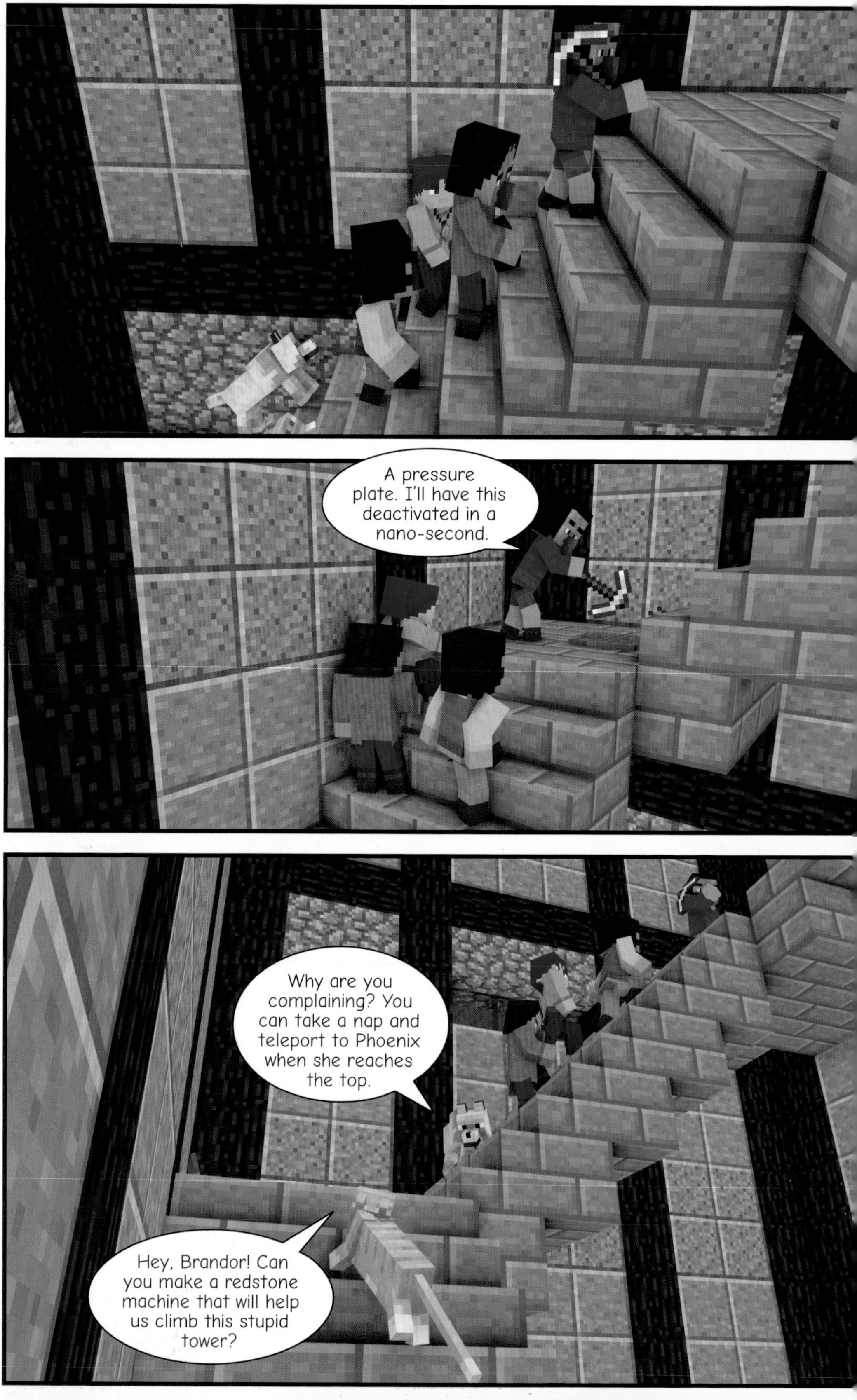
A pressure plate. I'll have this deactivated in a nano-second.
Why are you complaining? You can take a nap and teleport to Phoenix when she reaches the top.
Hey, Brandor! Can you make a redstone machine that will help us climb this stupid tower?

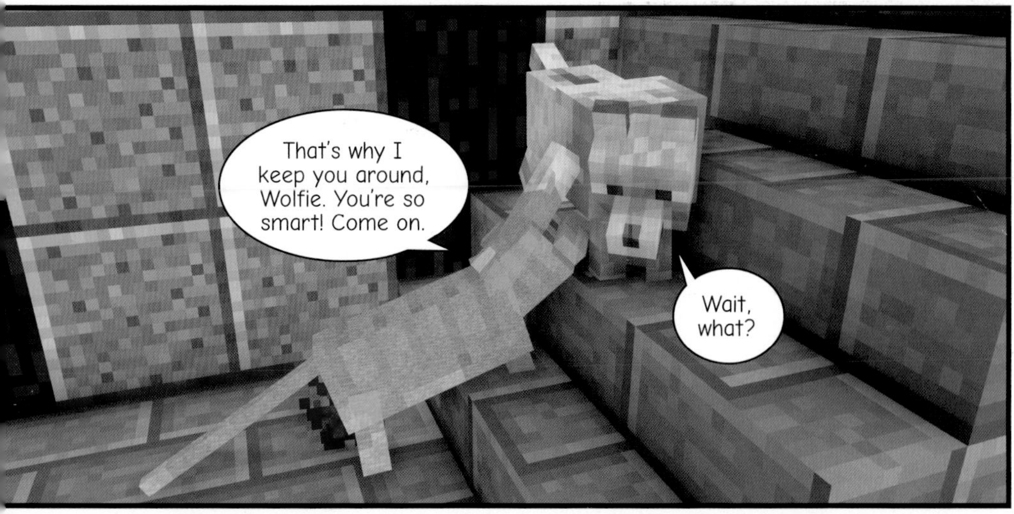
That's why I keep you around, Wolfie. You're so smart! Come on.
Wait, what?

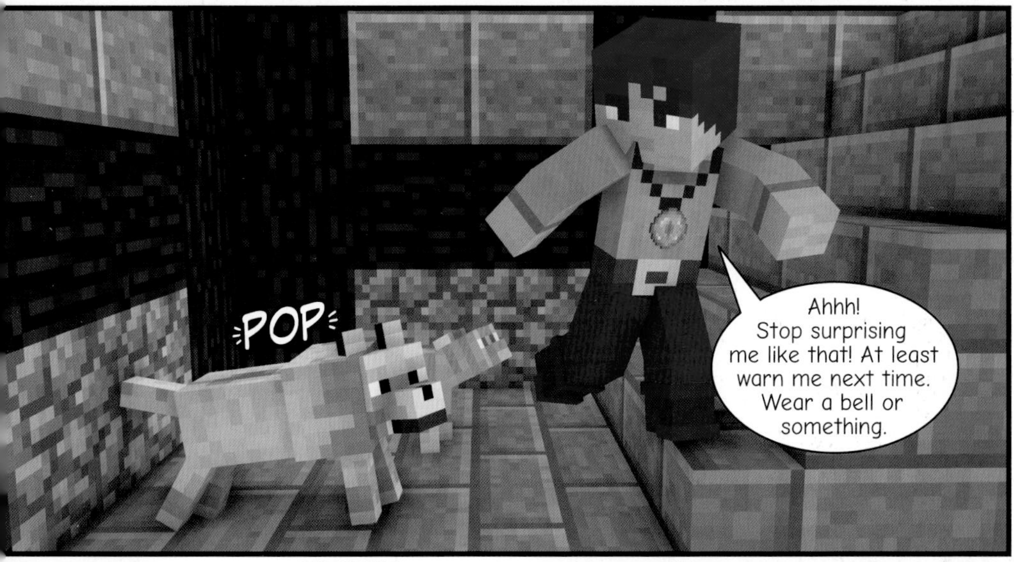
POP
Ahhh! Stop surprising me like that! At least warn me next time. Wear a bell or something.

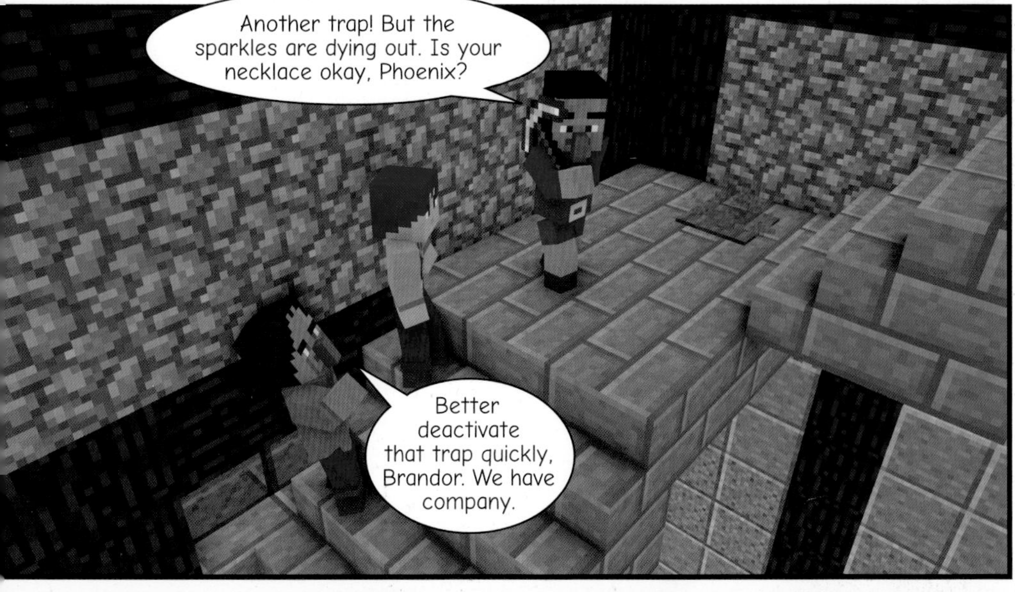
Another trap! But the sparkles are dying out. Is your necklace okay, Phoenix?
Better deactivate that trap quickly, Brandor. We have company.

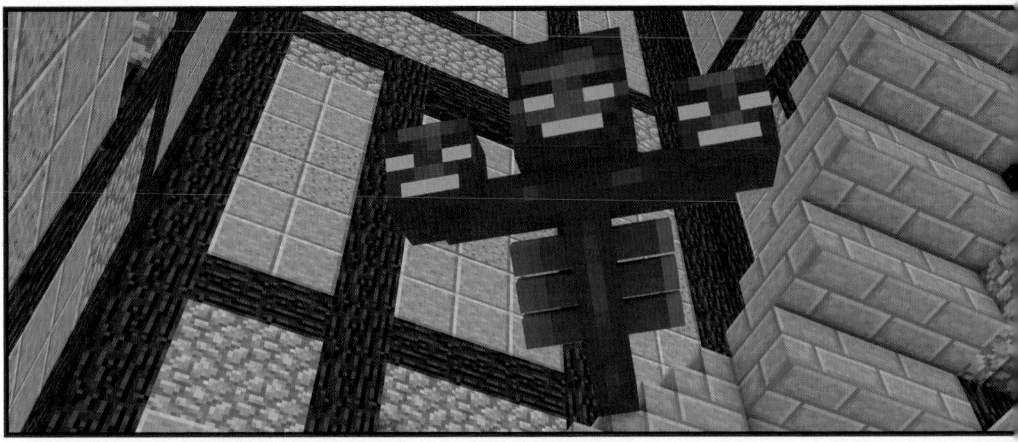

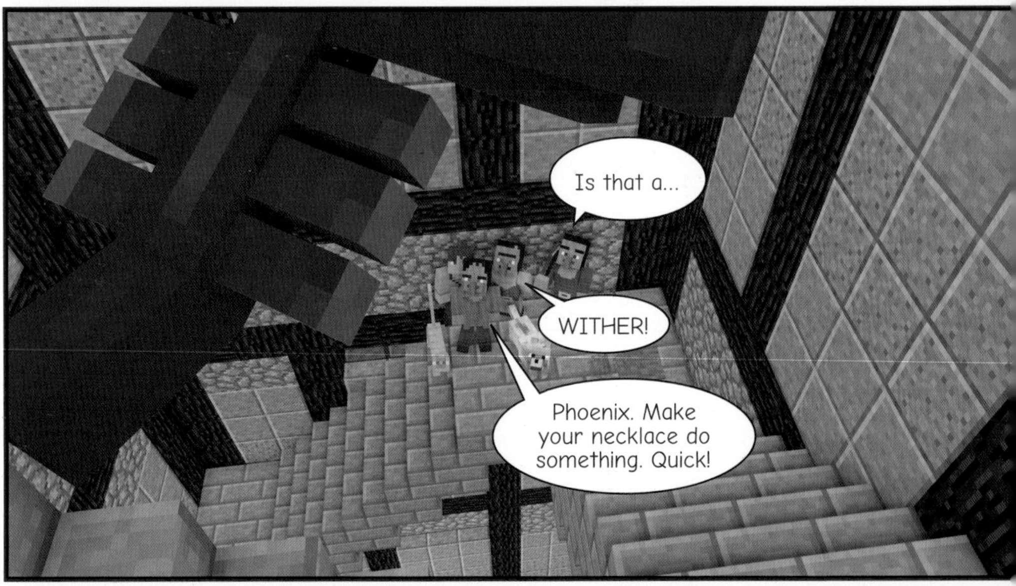
Is that a...
WITHER!
Phoenix. Make your necklace do something. Quick!

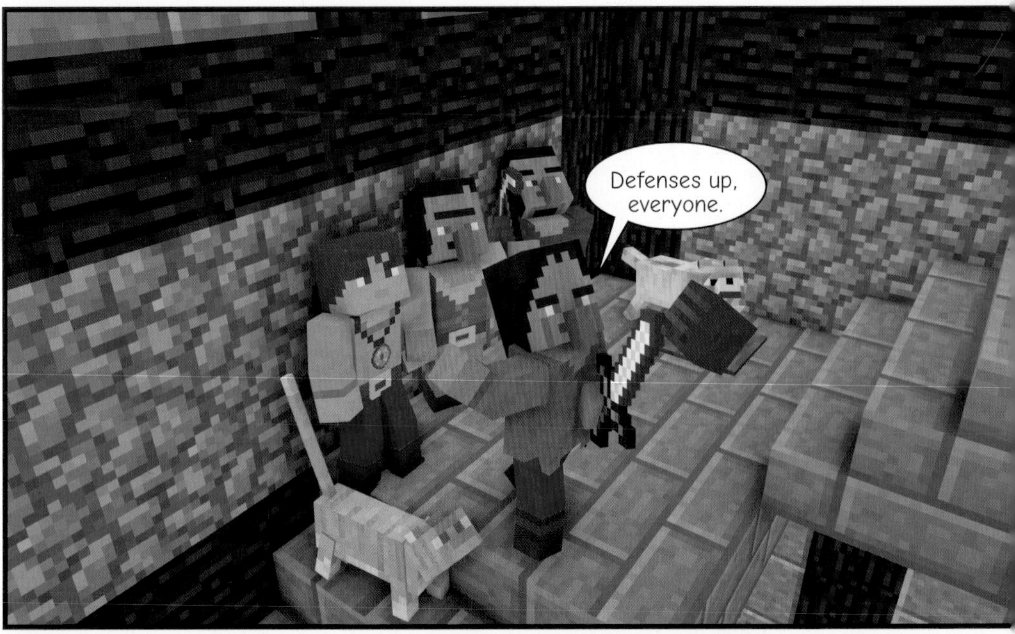
Defenses up, everyone.

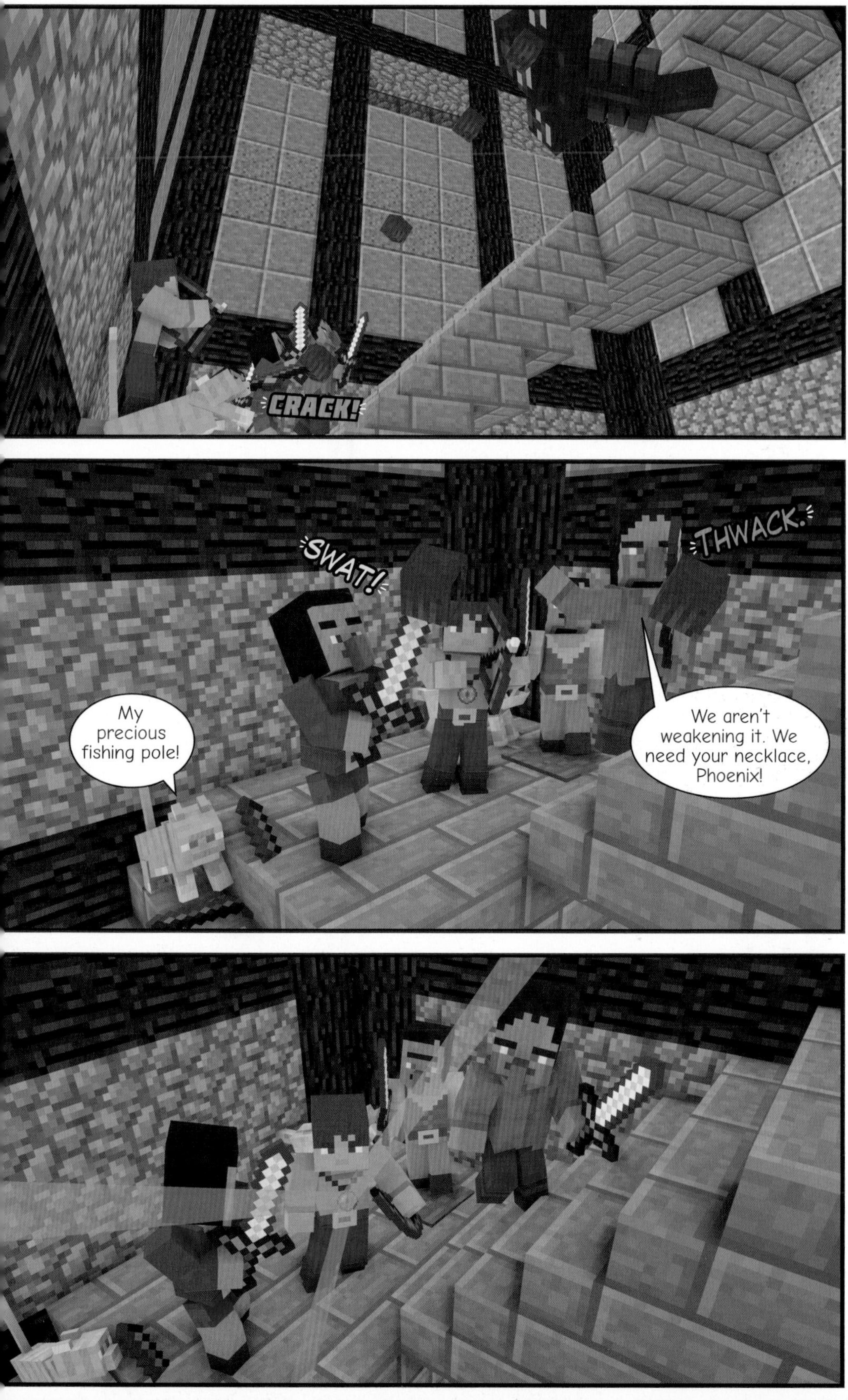
CRACK!
SWAT!
THWACK.
My precious fishing pole!
We aren't weakening it. We need your necklace, Phoenix!

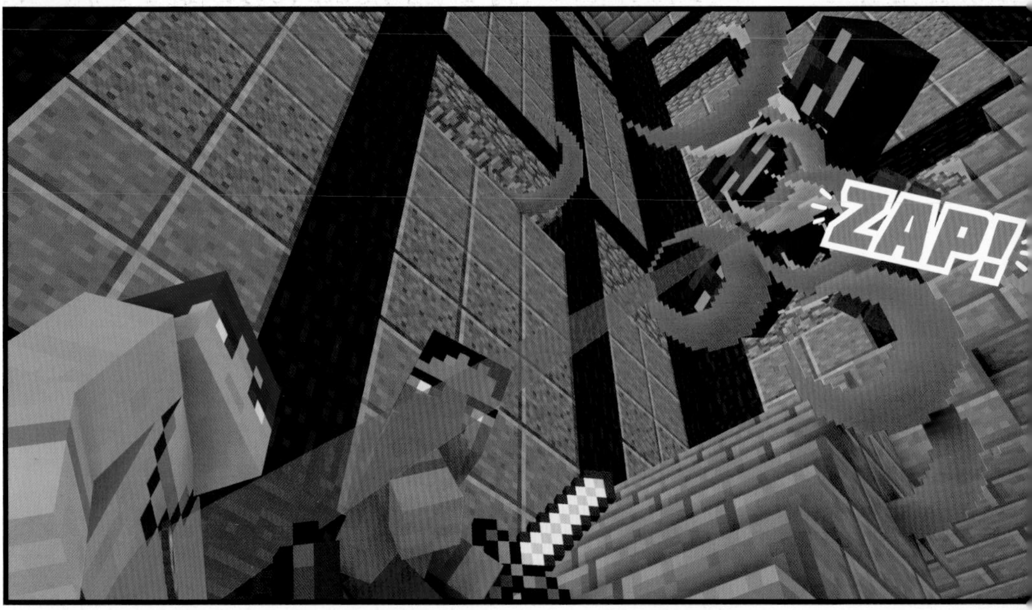
ZAP!

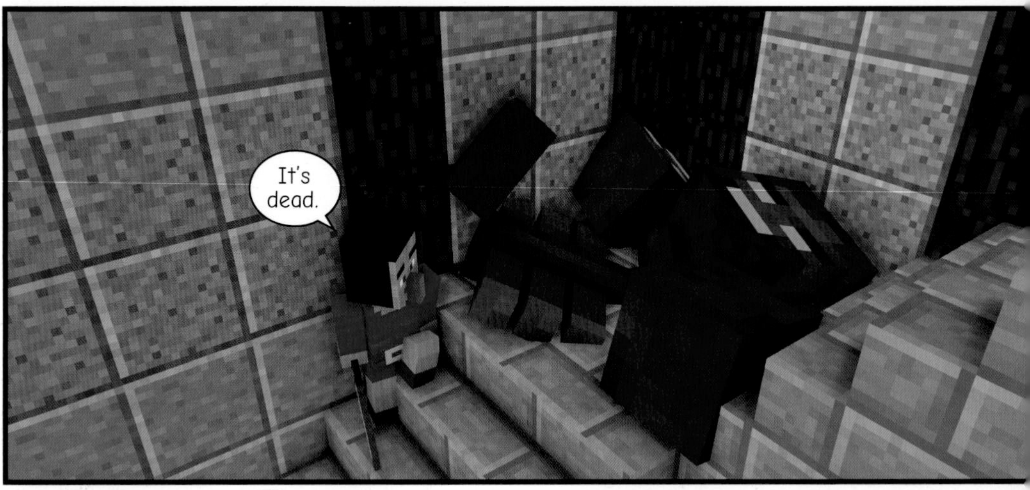
It's dead.

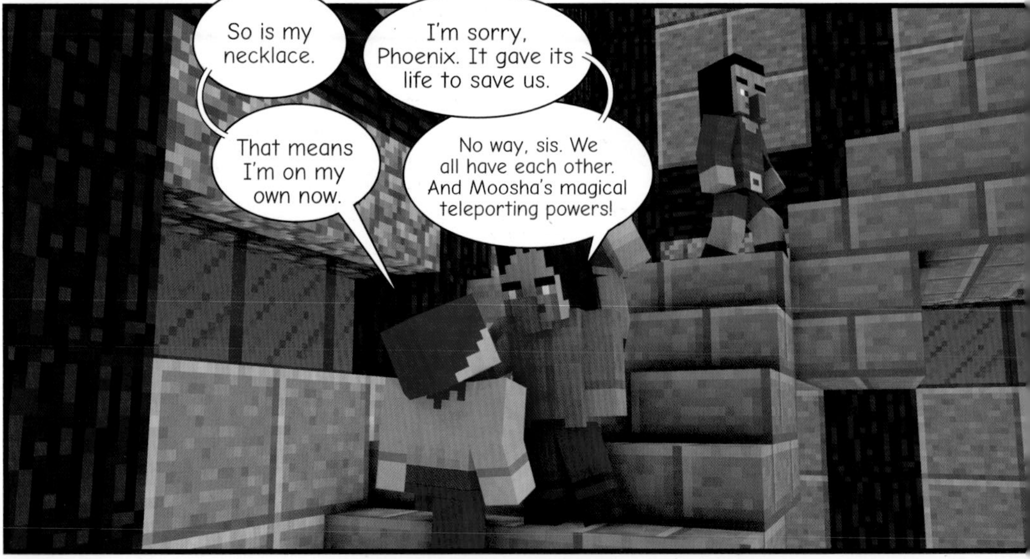
So is my necklace.
I'm sorry, Phoenix. It gave its life to save us.
That means I'm on my own now.
No way, sis. We all have each other. And Moosha's magical teleporting powers!

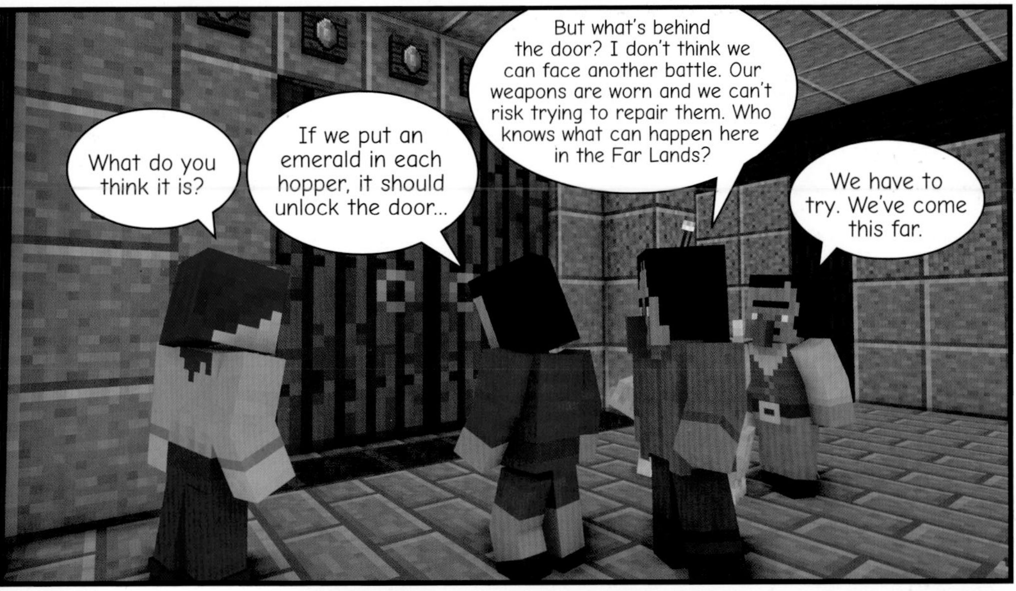
What do you think it is?
If we put an emerald in each hopper, it should unlock the door...
But what's behind the door? I don't think we can face another battle. Our weapons are worn and we can't risk trying to repair them. Who knows what can happen here in the Far Lands?
We have to try. We've come this far.

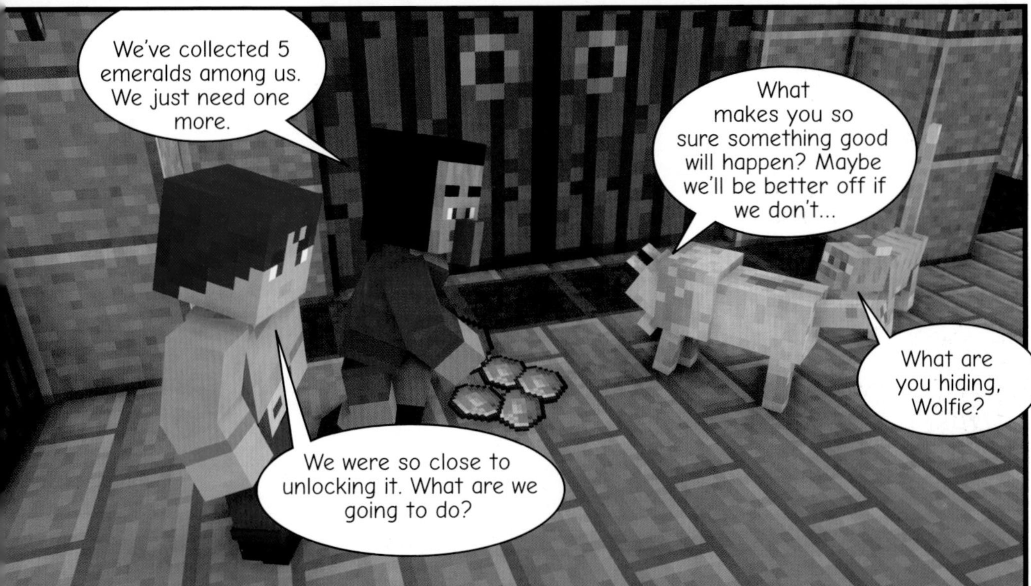
We've collected 5 emeralds among us. We just need one more.
What makes you so sure something good will happen? Maybe we'll be better off if we don't...
What are you hiding, Wolfie?
We were so close to unlocking it. What are we going to do?

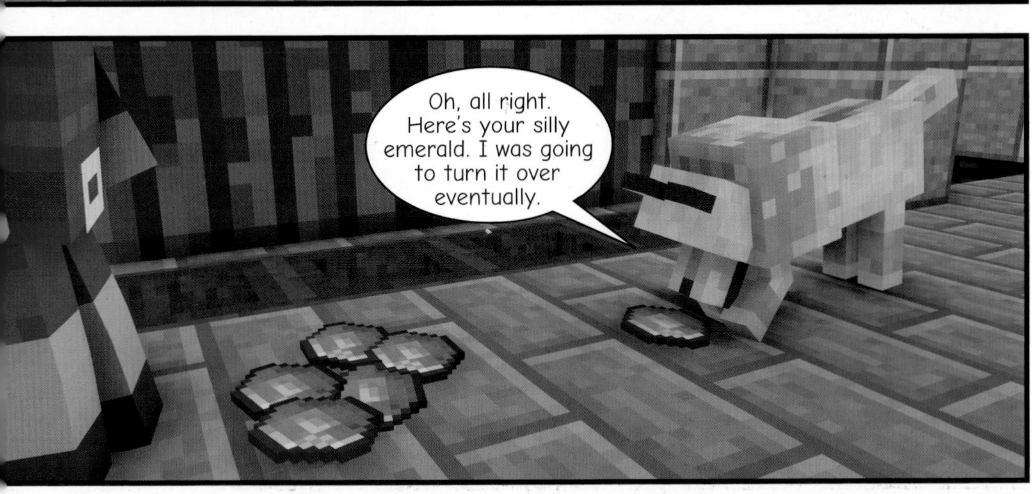
Oh, all right. Here's your silly emerald. I was going to turn it over eventually.

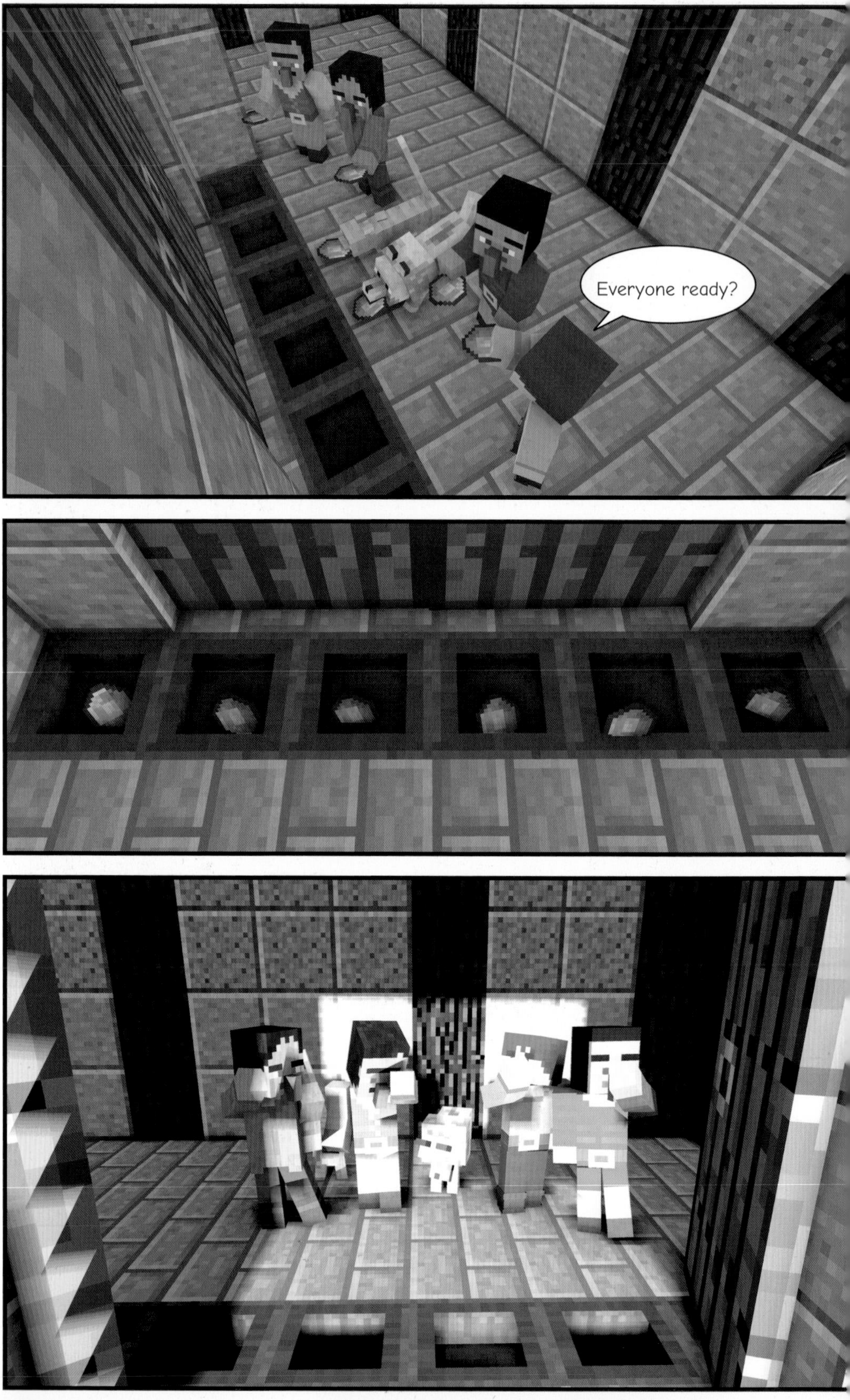
Everyone ready?

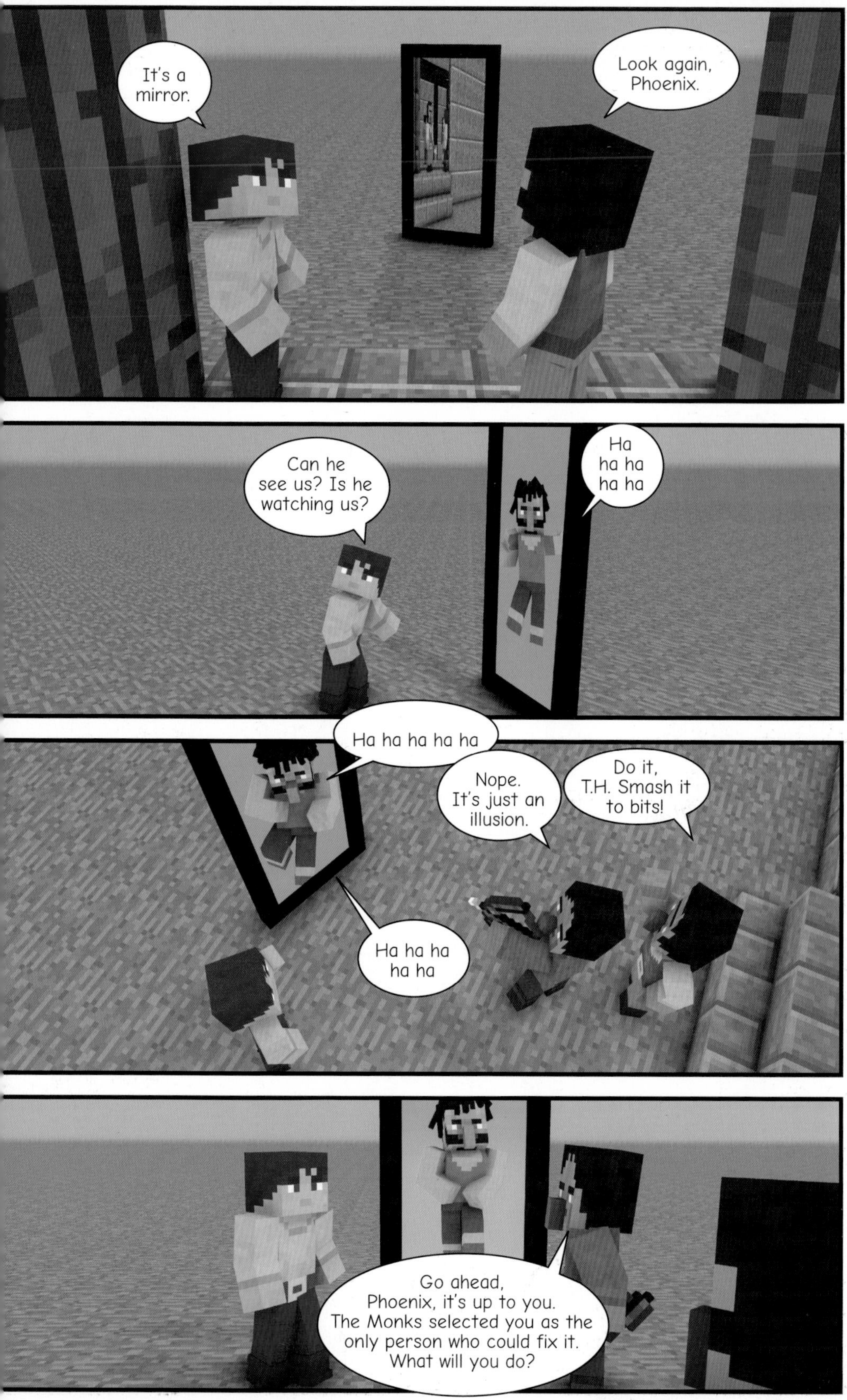
It's a mirror.
Look again, Phoenix.
Can he see us? Is he watching us?
Ha ha ha ha ha
Ha ha ha ha ha
Nope. It's just an illusion.
Do it, T.H. Smash it to bits!
Ha ha ha ha ha
Go ahead, Phoenix, it's up to you. The Monks selected you as the only person who could fix it. What will you do?

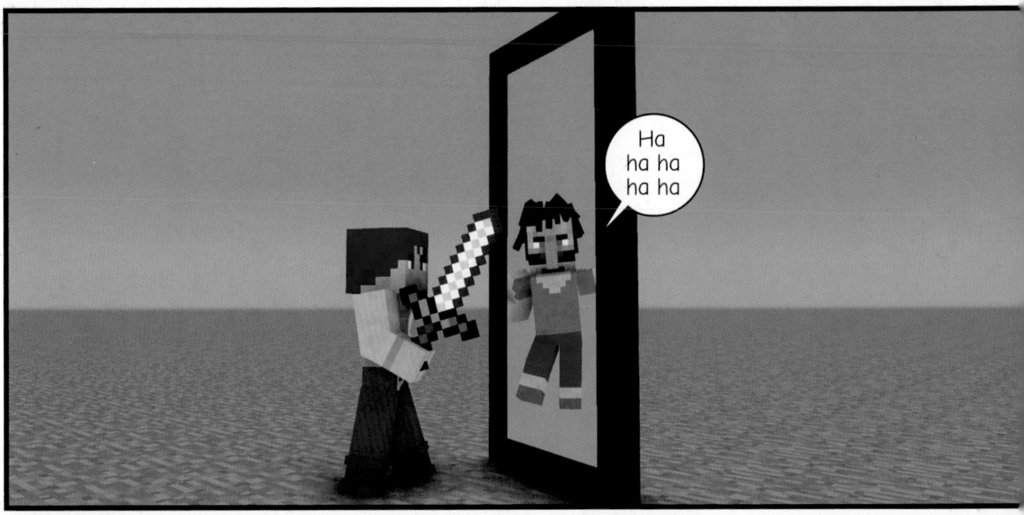
Ha ha ha ha ha

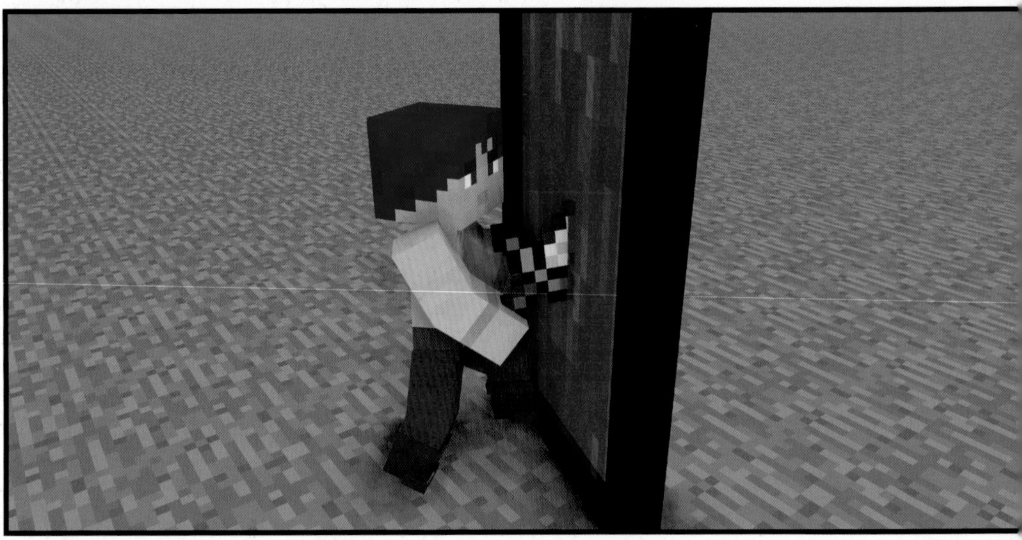

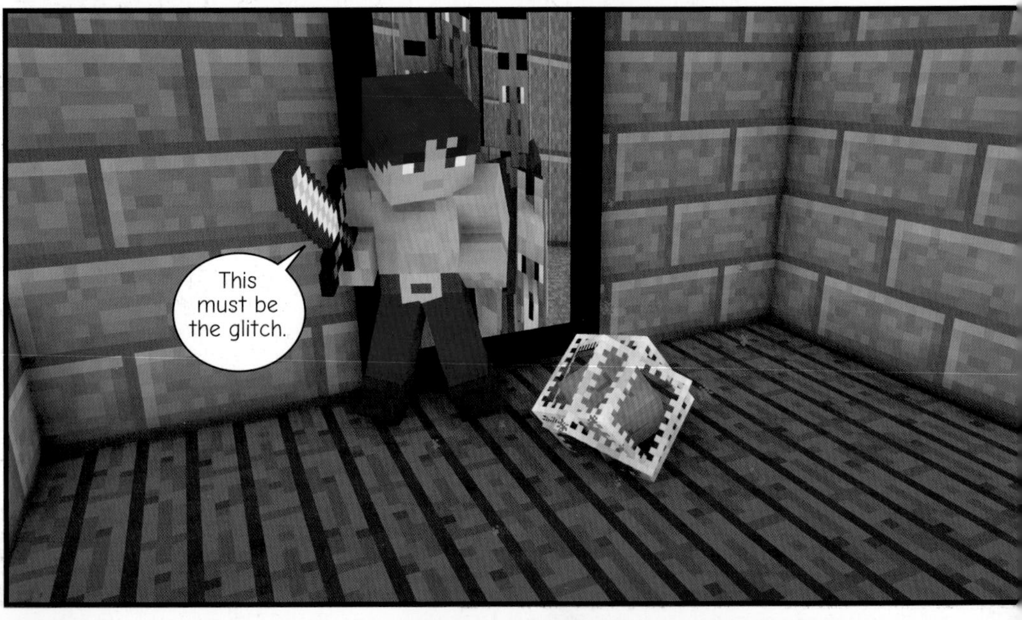
This must be the glitch.

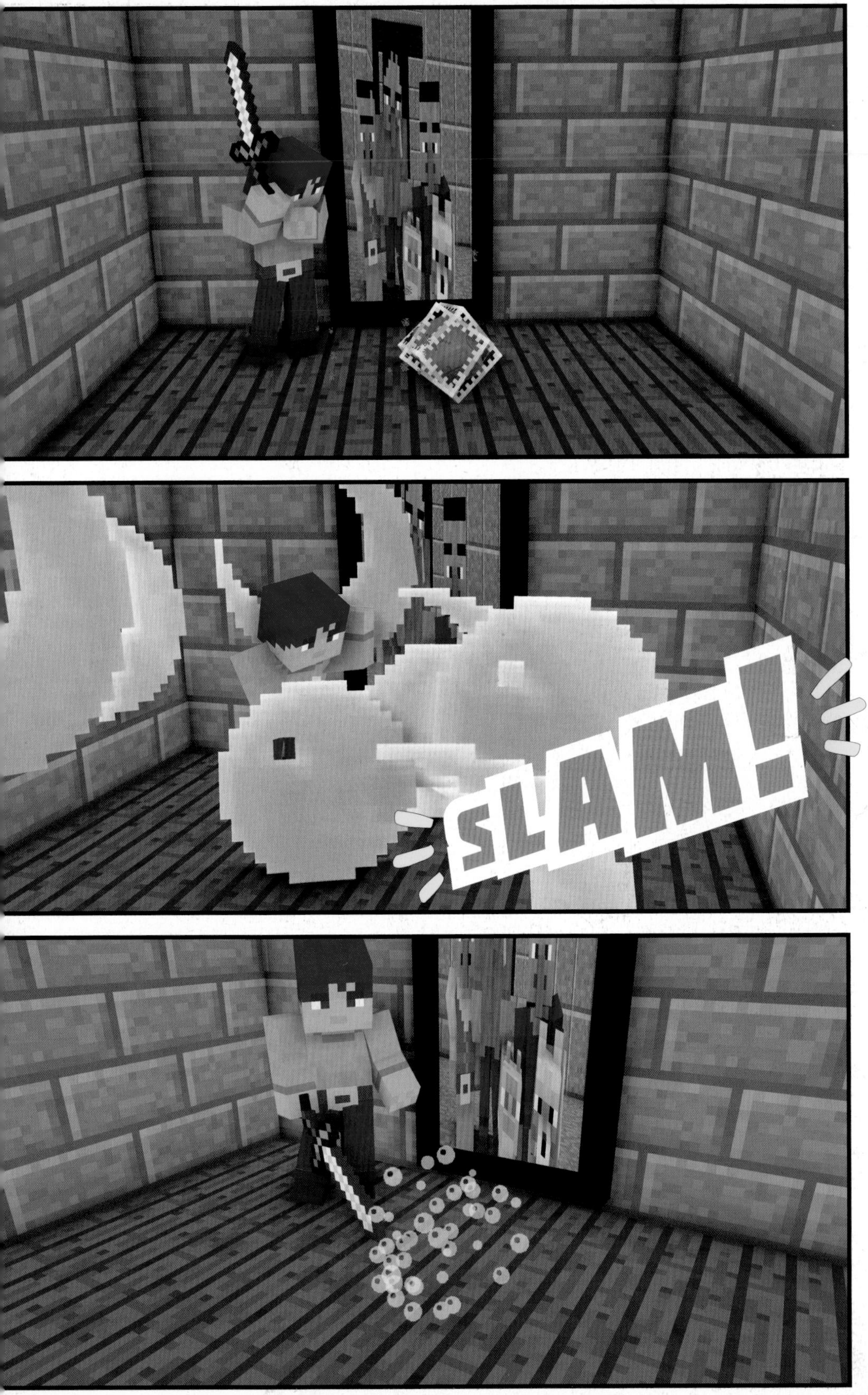
SLAM!

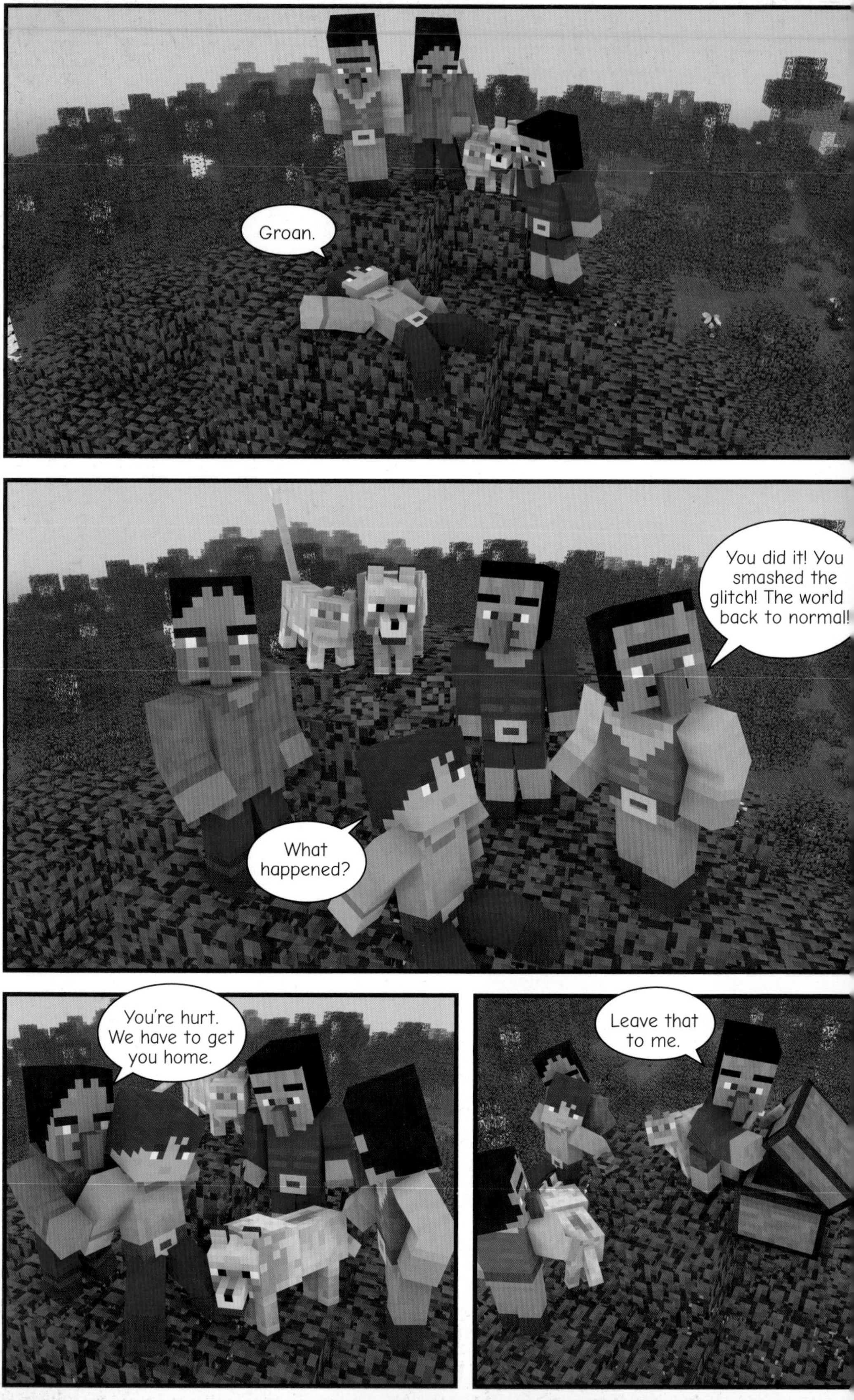

Groan.
You did it! You smashed the glitch! The world back to normal!
What happened?
You're hurt. We have to get you home.
Leave that to me.

CHAPTER 13

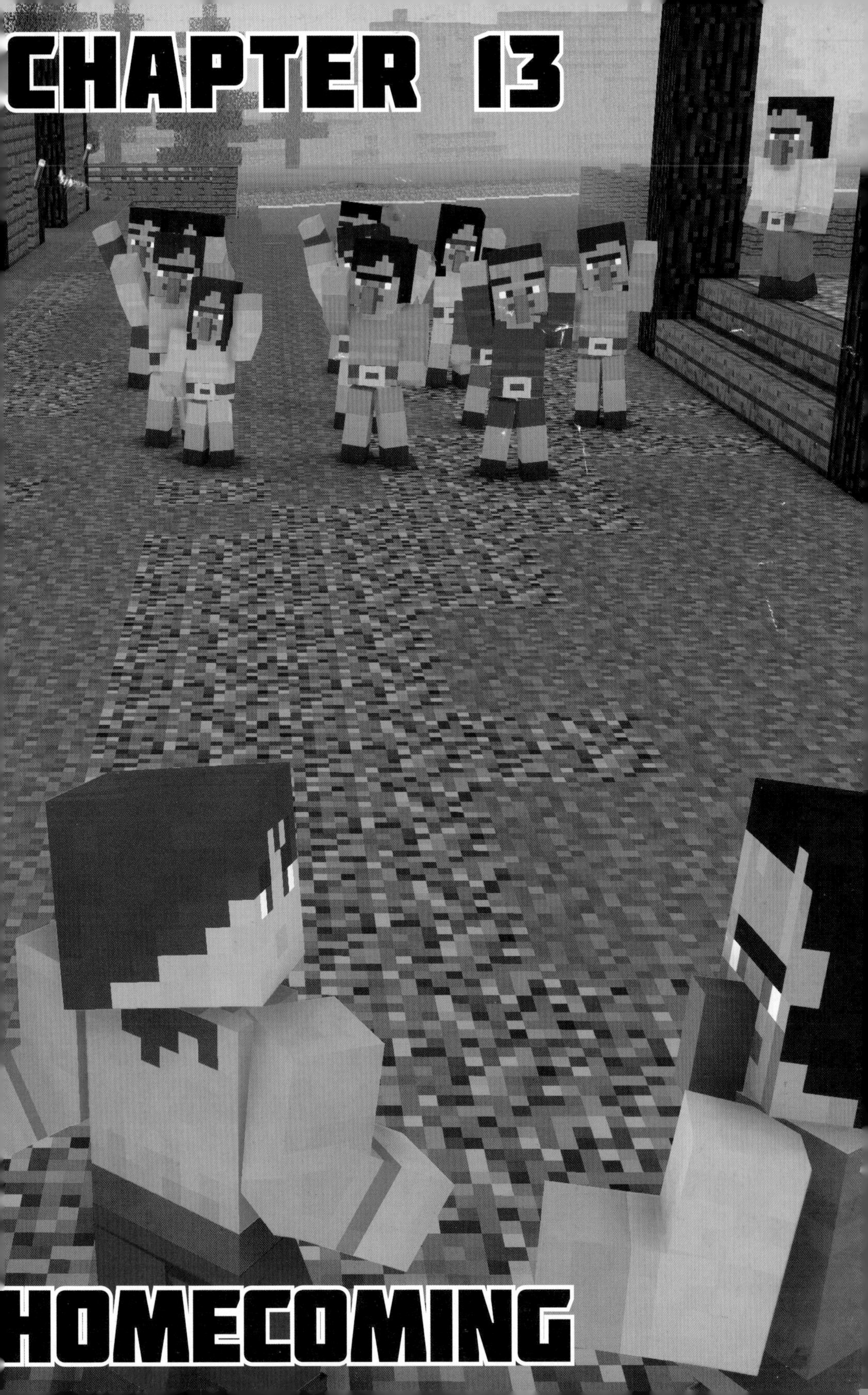

HOMECOMING

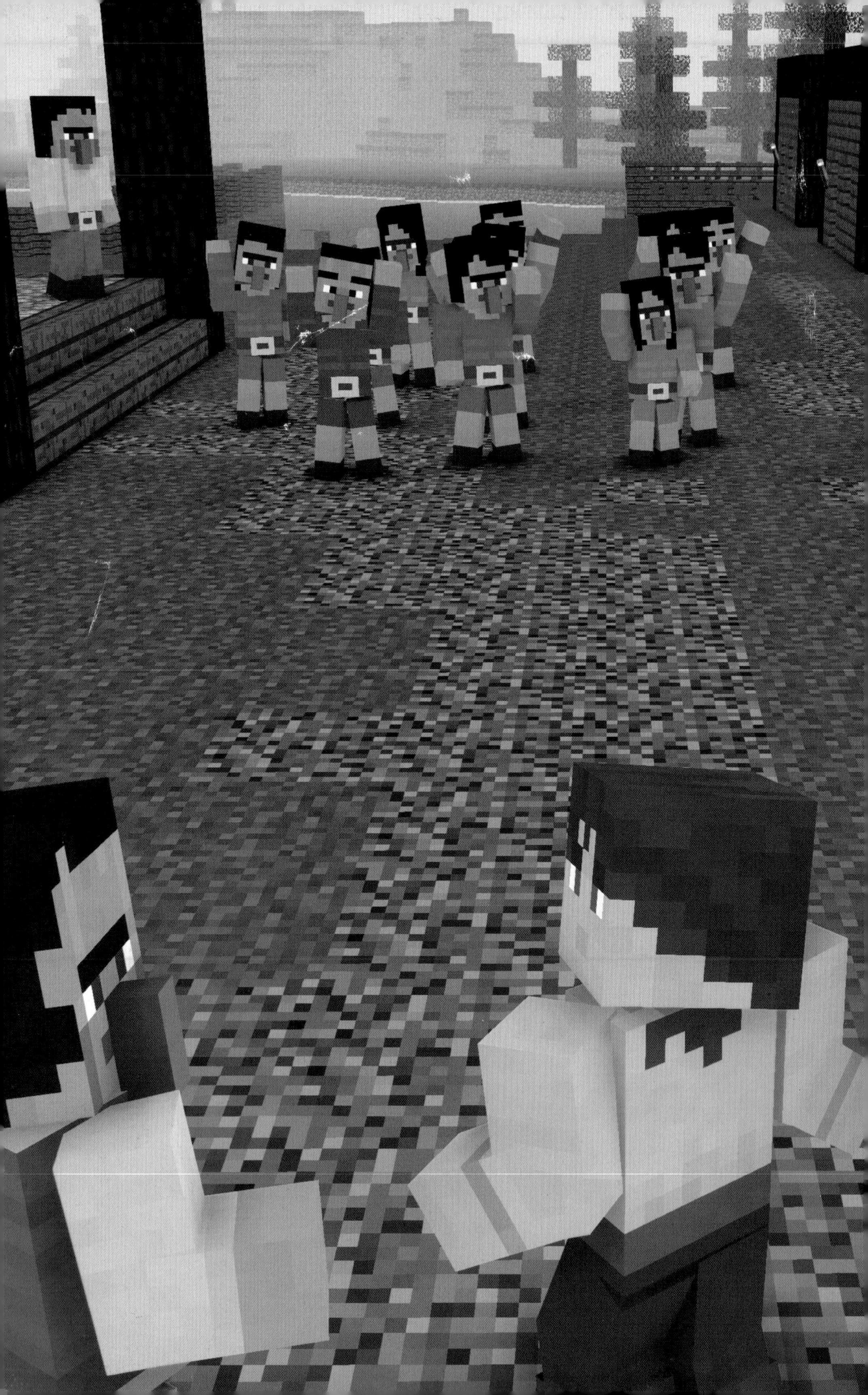

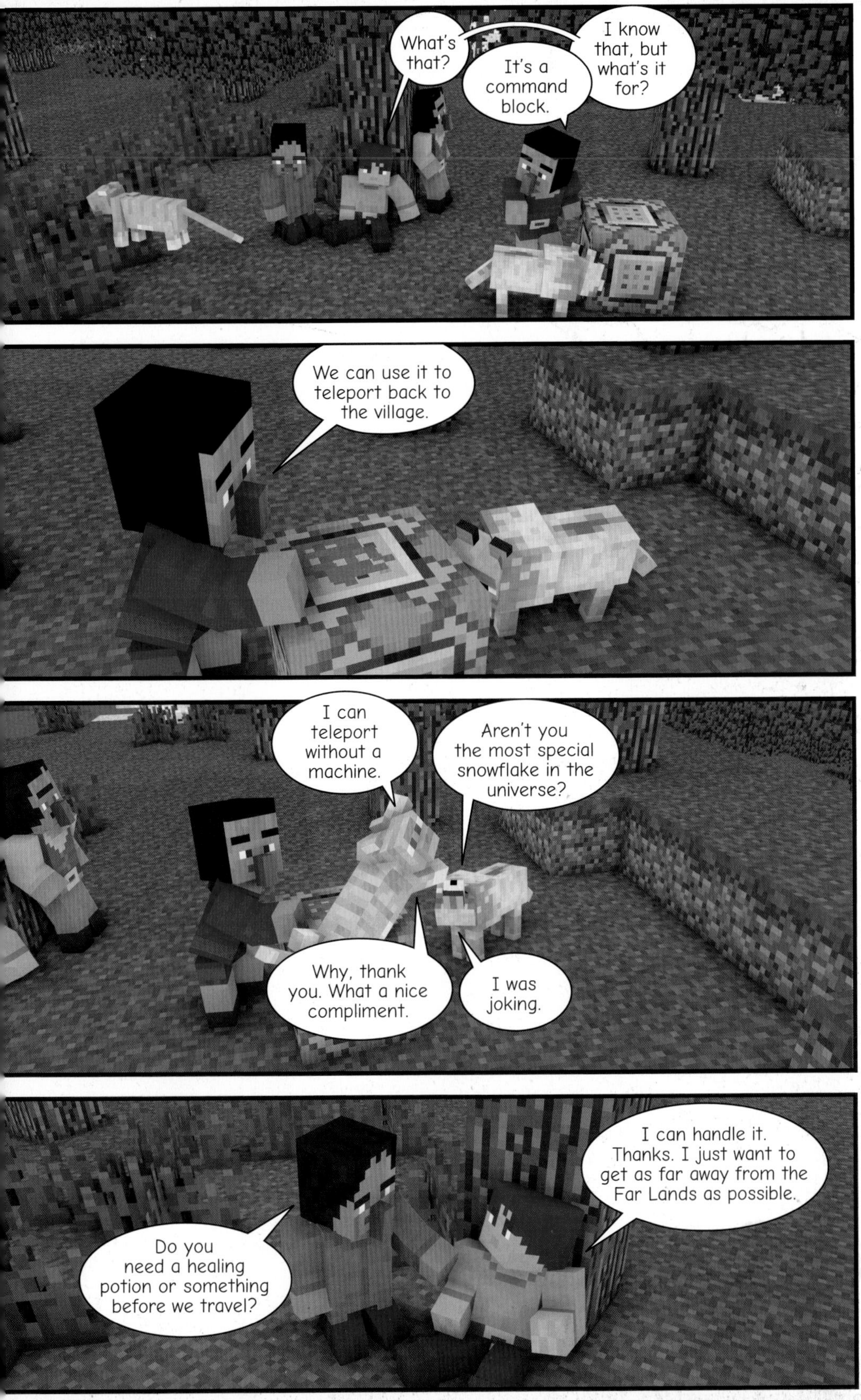
What's that?
It's a command block.
I know that, but what's it for?
We can use it to teleport back to the village.
I can teleport without a machine.
Aren't you the most special snowflake in the universe?
Why, thank you. What a nice compliment.
I was joking.
Do you need a healing potion or something before we travel?
I can handle it. Thanks. I just want to get as far away from the Far Lands as possible.

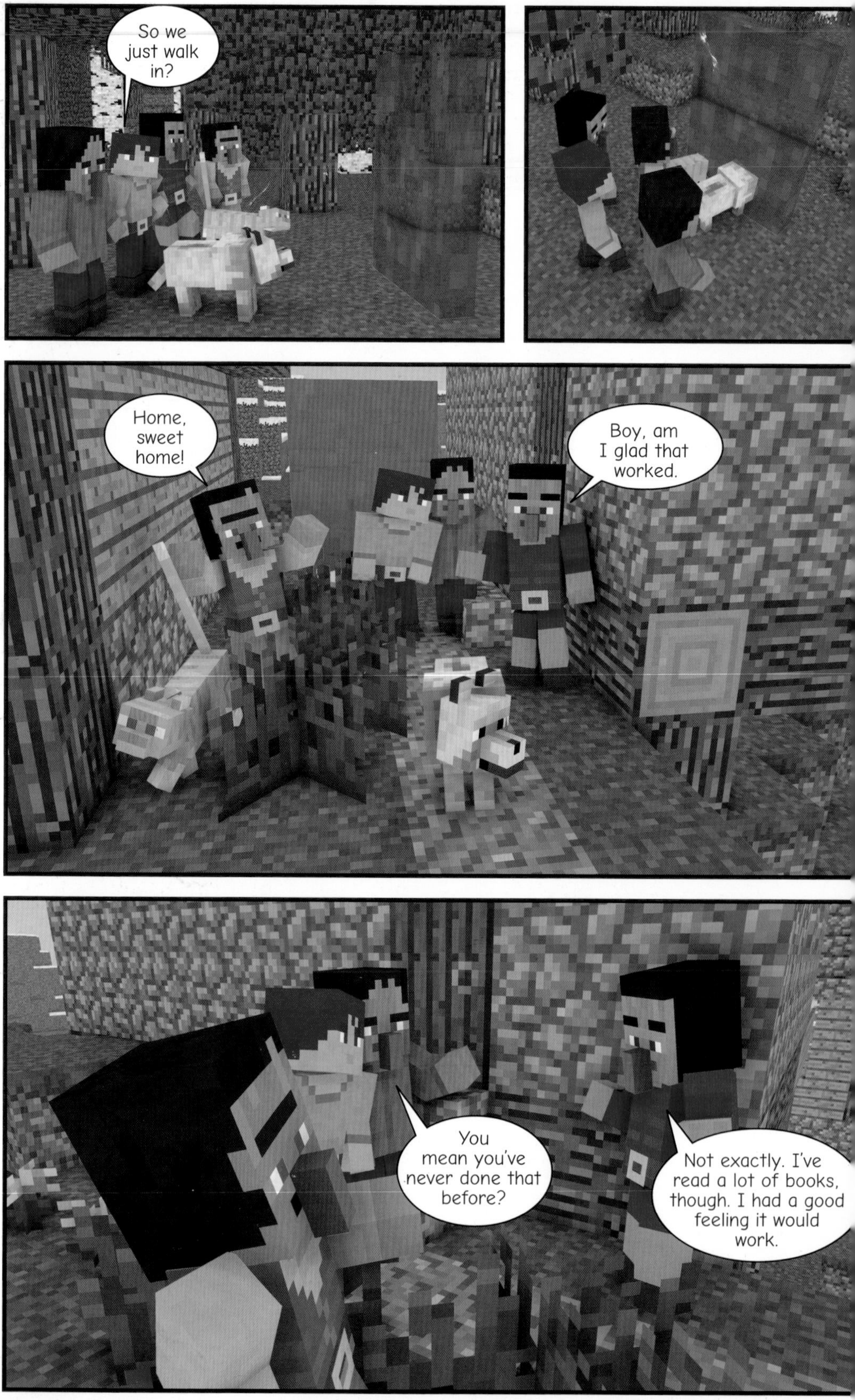
So we just walk in?
Home, sweet home!
Boy, am I glad that worked.
You mean you've never done that before?
Not exactly. I've read a lot of books, though. I had a good feeling it would work.

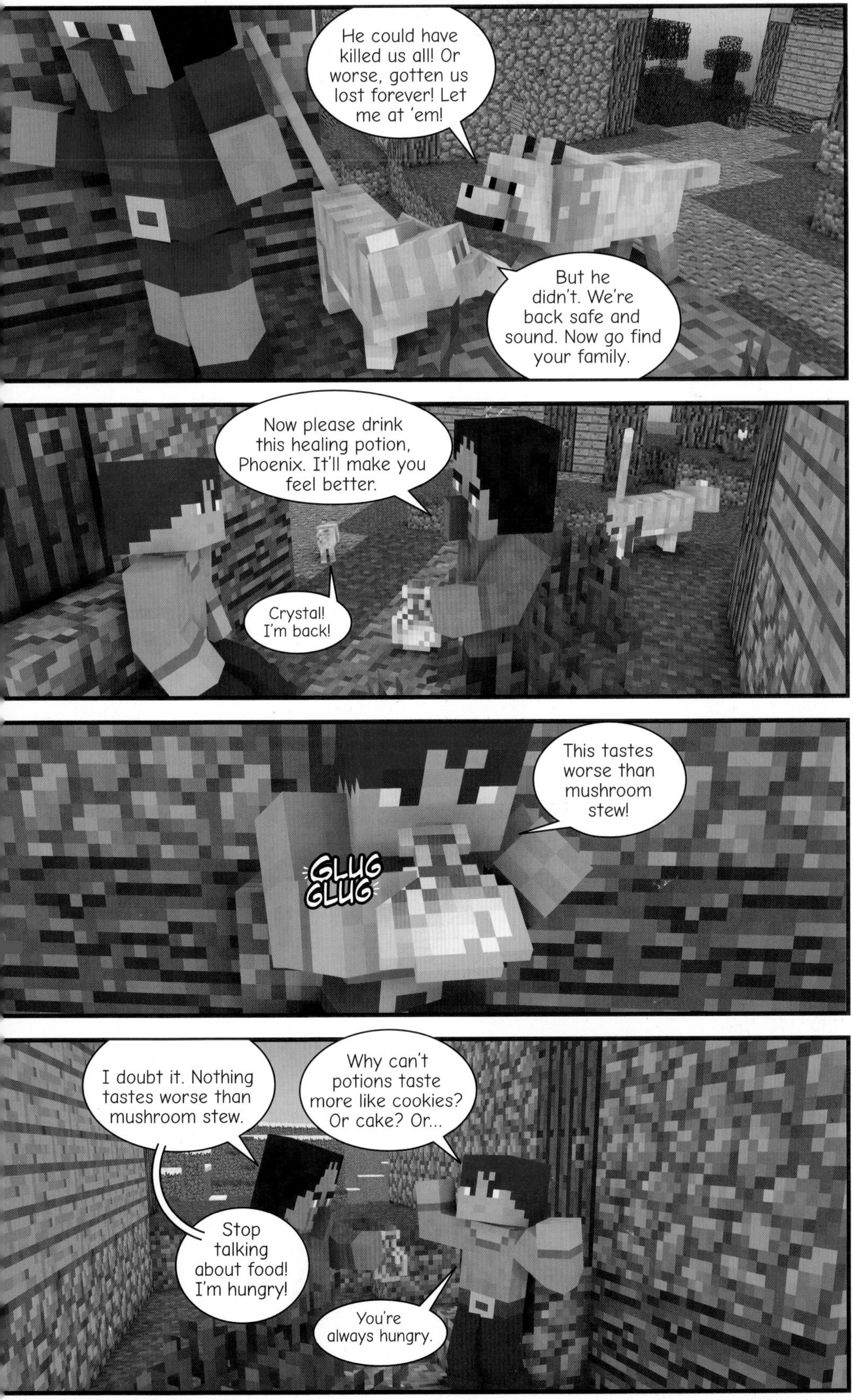

He could have killed us all! Or worse, gotten us lost forever! Let me at 'em!
But he didn't. We're back safe and sound. Now go find your family.
Now please drink this healing potion, Phoenix. It'll make you feel better.
Crystal! I'm back!
GLUG GLUG
This tastes worse than mushroom stew!
I doubt it. Nothing tastes worse than mushroom stew.
Why can't potions taste more like cookies? Or cake? Or...
Stop talking about food! I'm hungry!
You're always hungry.

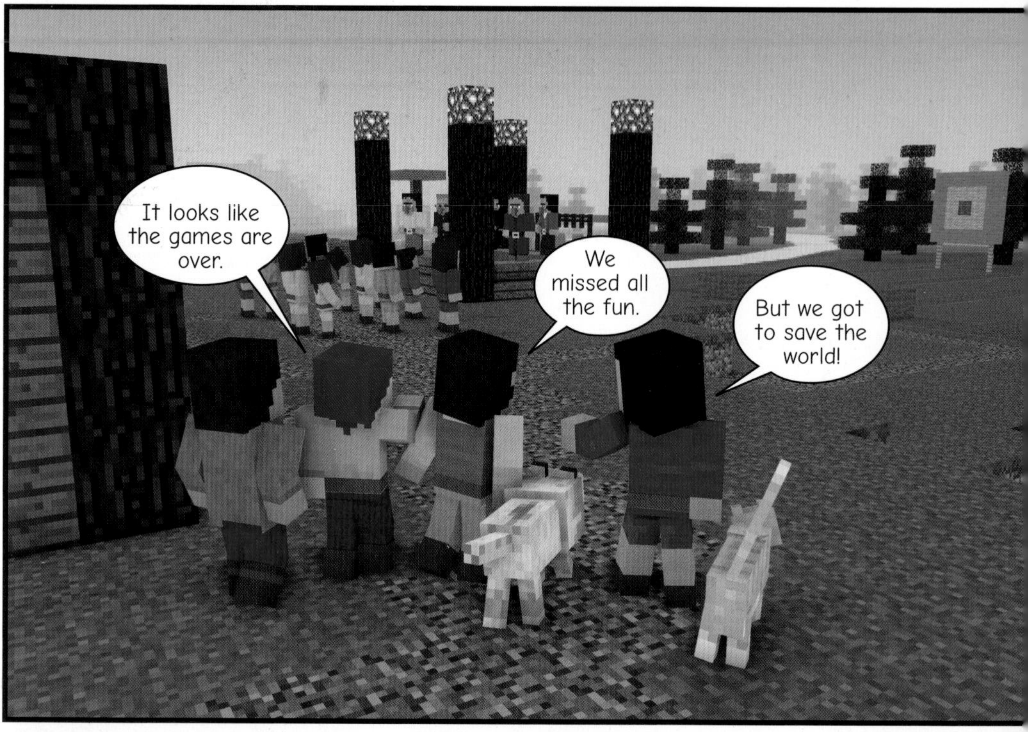
It looks like the games are over.
We missed all the fun.
But we got to save the world!

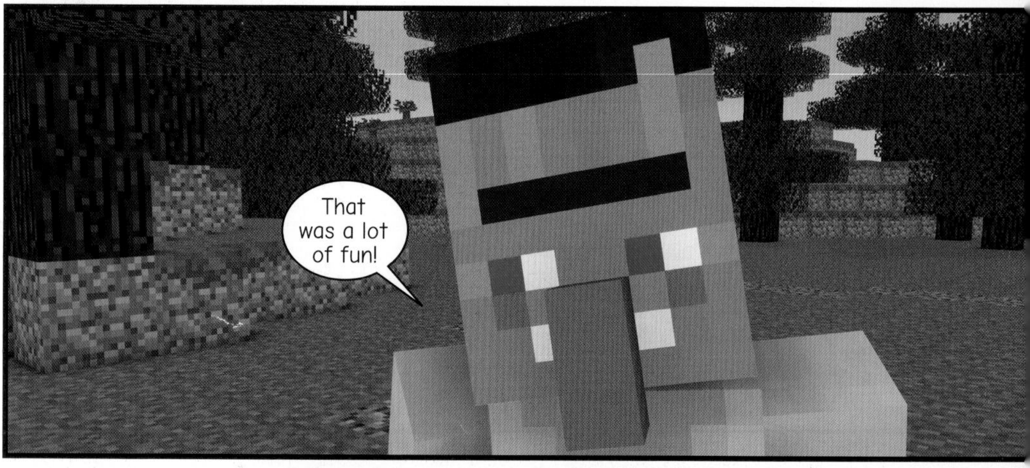
That was a lot of fun!

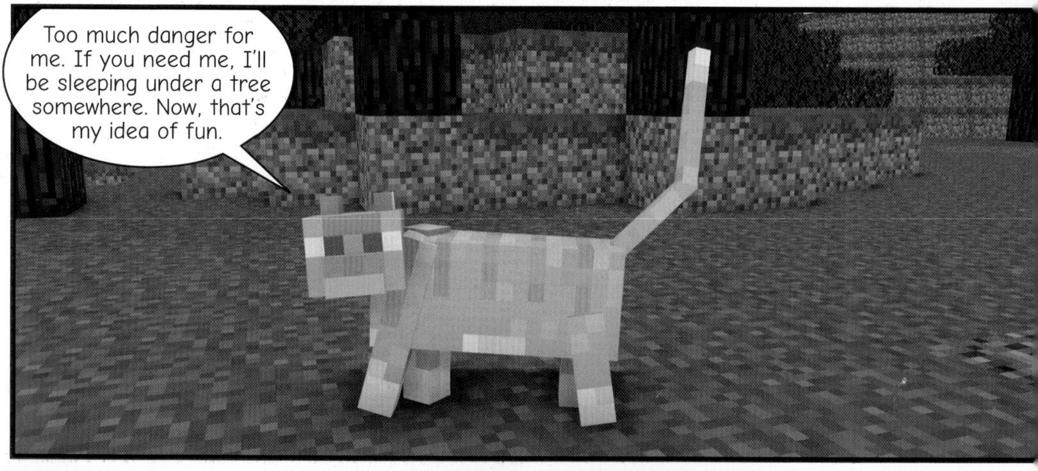
Too much danger for me. If you need me, I'll be sleeping under a tree somewhere. Now, that's my idea of fun.

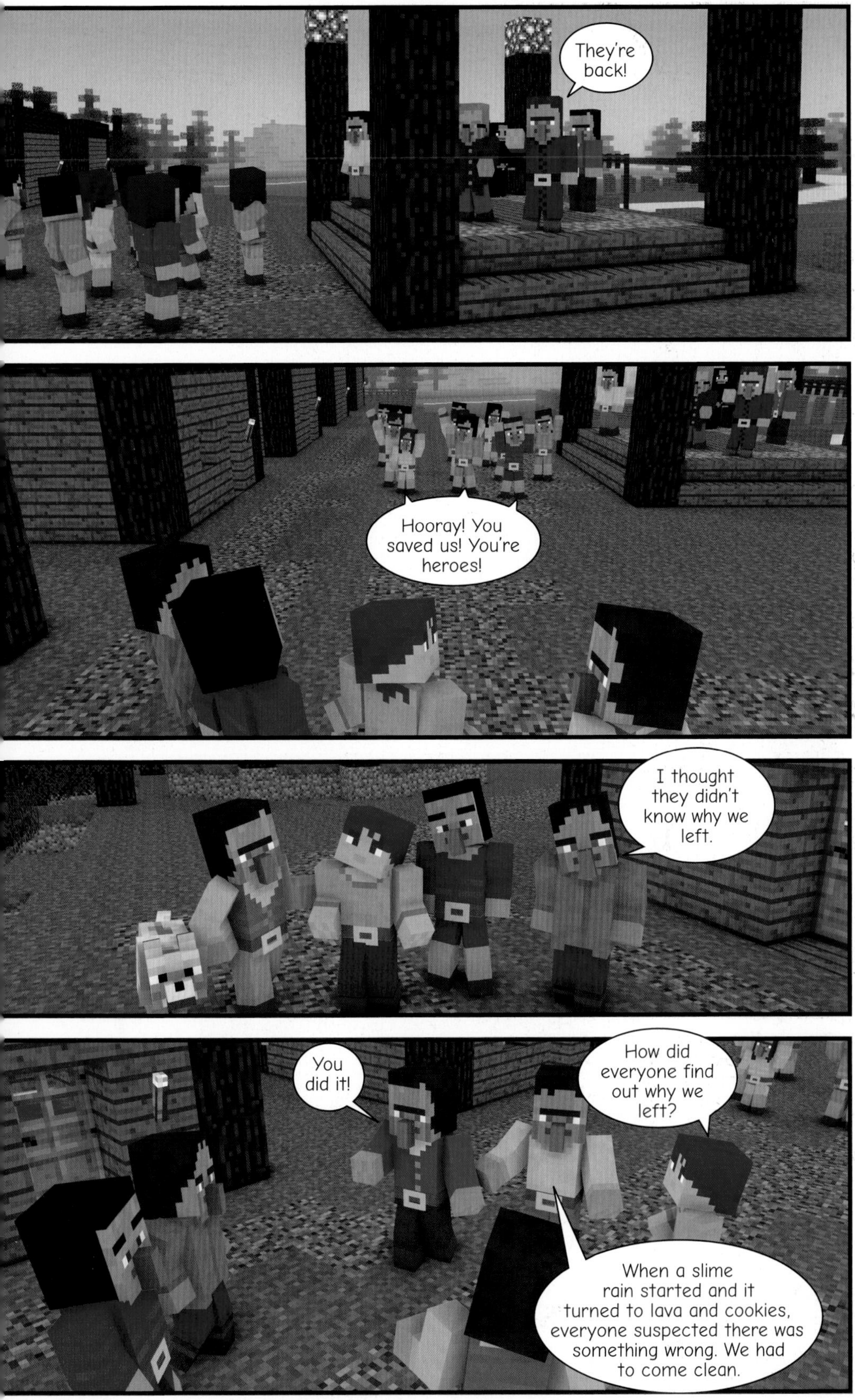
They're back!
Hooray! You saved us! You're heroes!
I thought they didn't know why we left.
You did it!
How did everyone find out why we left?
When a slime rain started and it turned to lava and cookies, everyone suspected there was something wrong. We had to come clean.

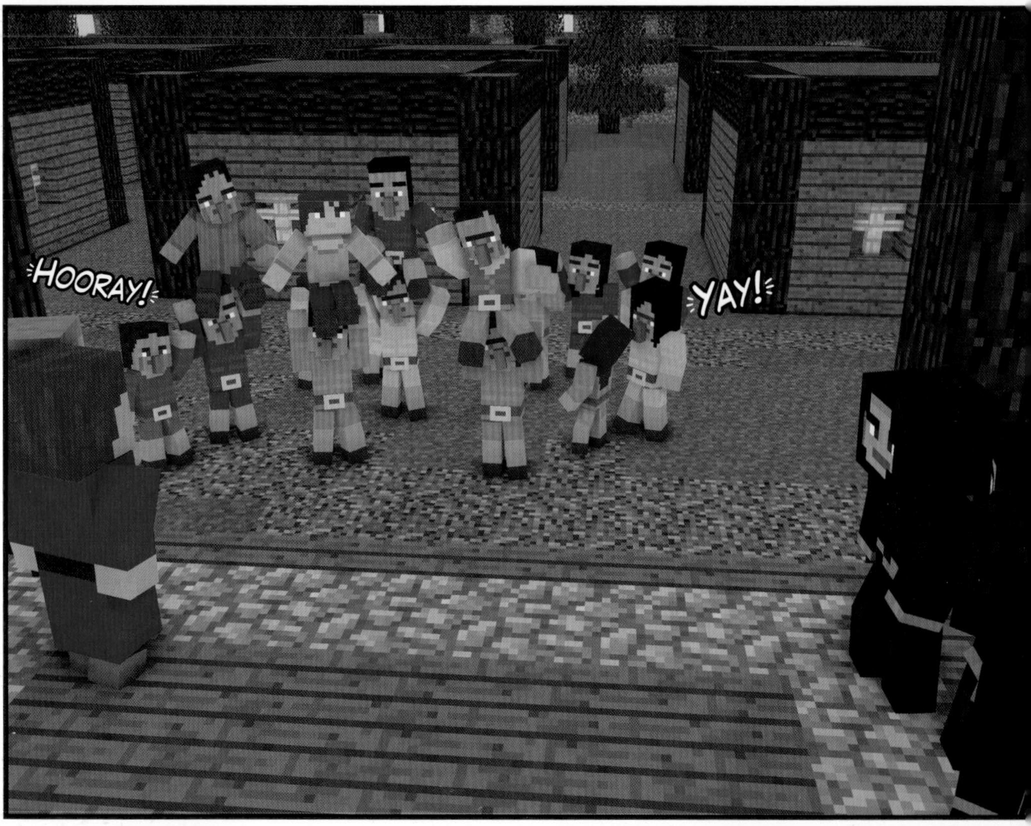
HOORAY!
YAY!

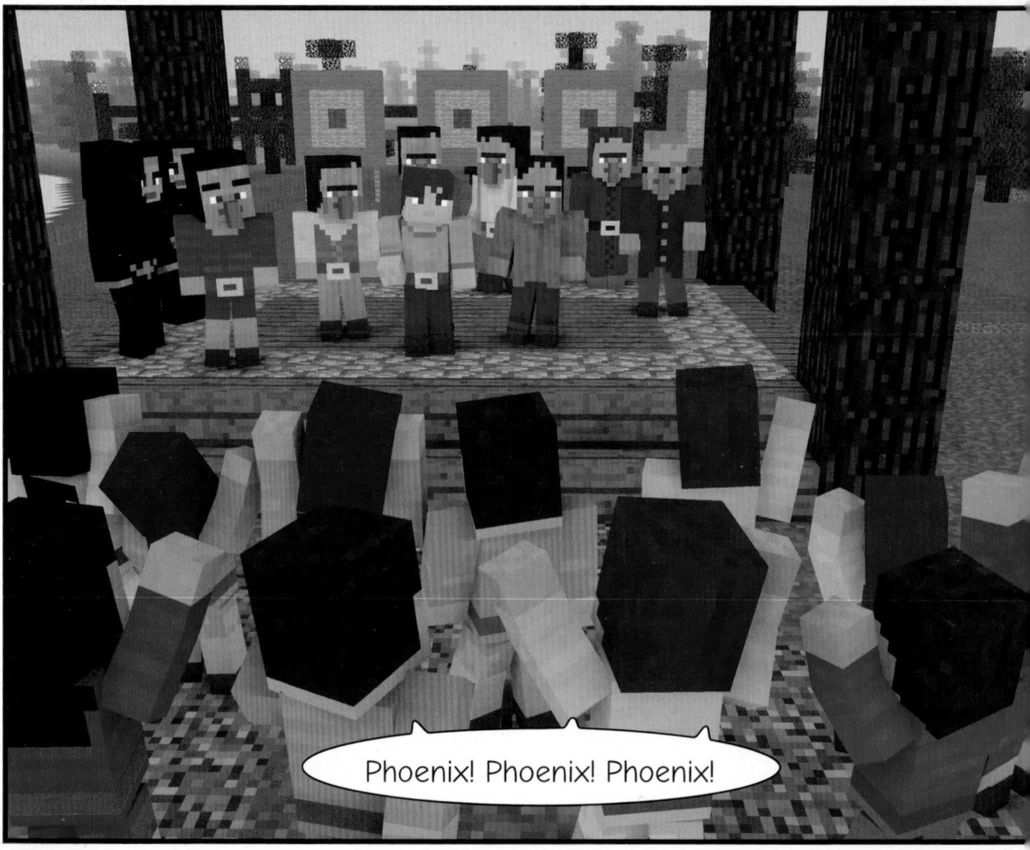
Phoenix! Phoenix! Phoenix!

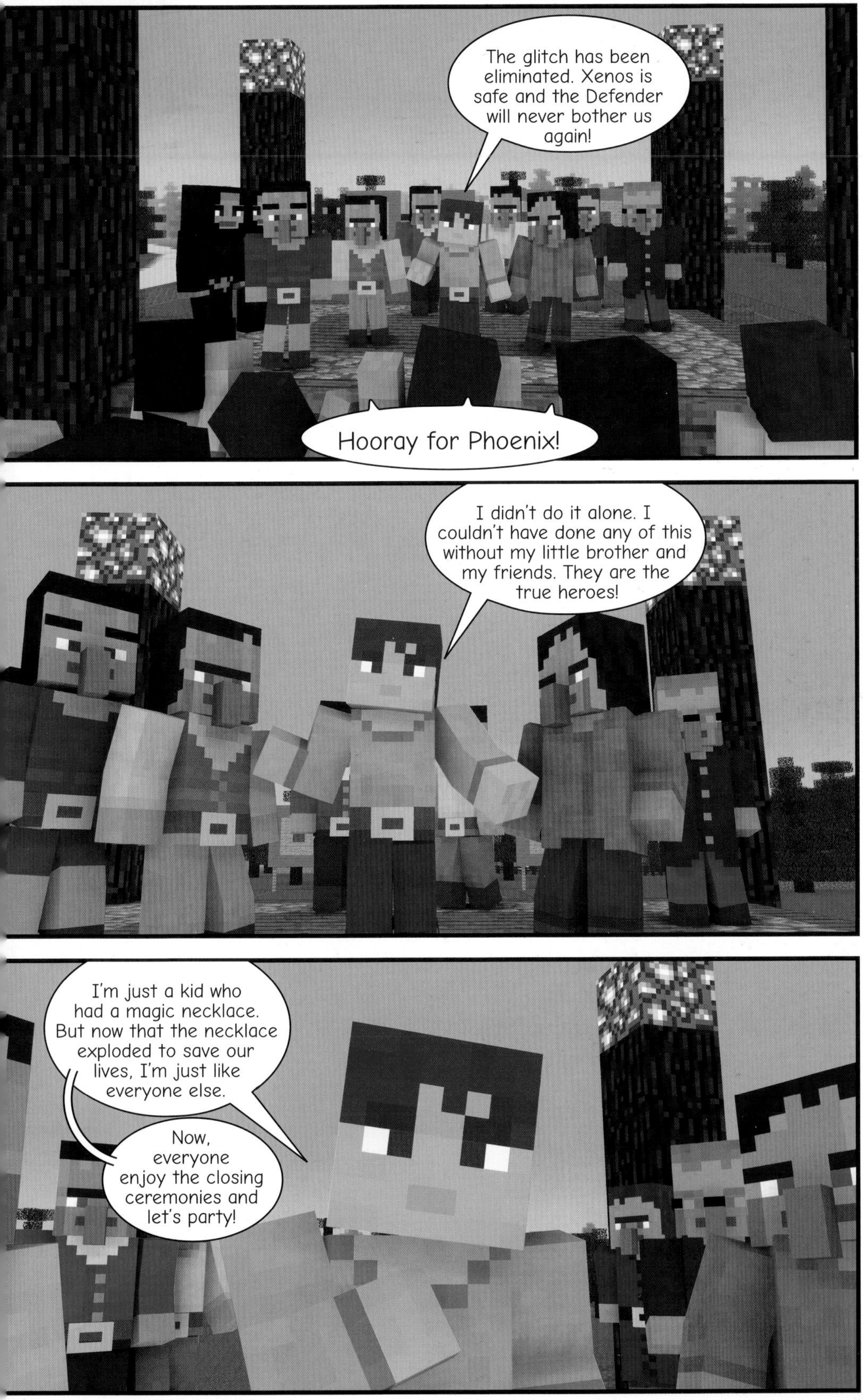
The glitch has been eliminated. Xenos is safe and the Defender will never bother us again!
Hooray for Phoenix!
I didn't do it alone. I couldn't have done any of this without my little brother and my friends. They are the true heroes!
I'm just a kid who had a magic necklace. But now that the necklace exploded to save our lives, I'm just like everyone else.
Now, everyone enjoy the closing ceremonies and let's party!

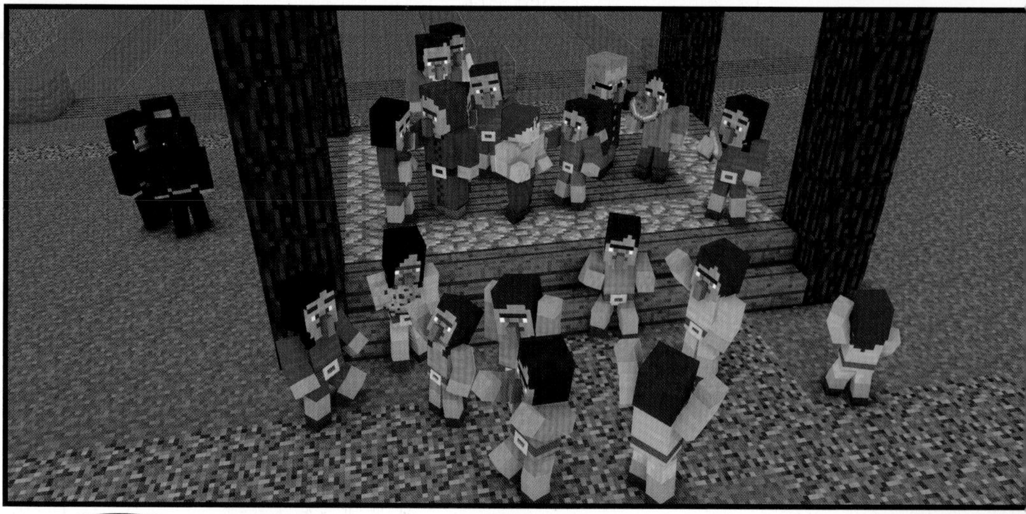

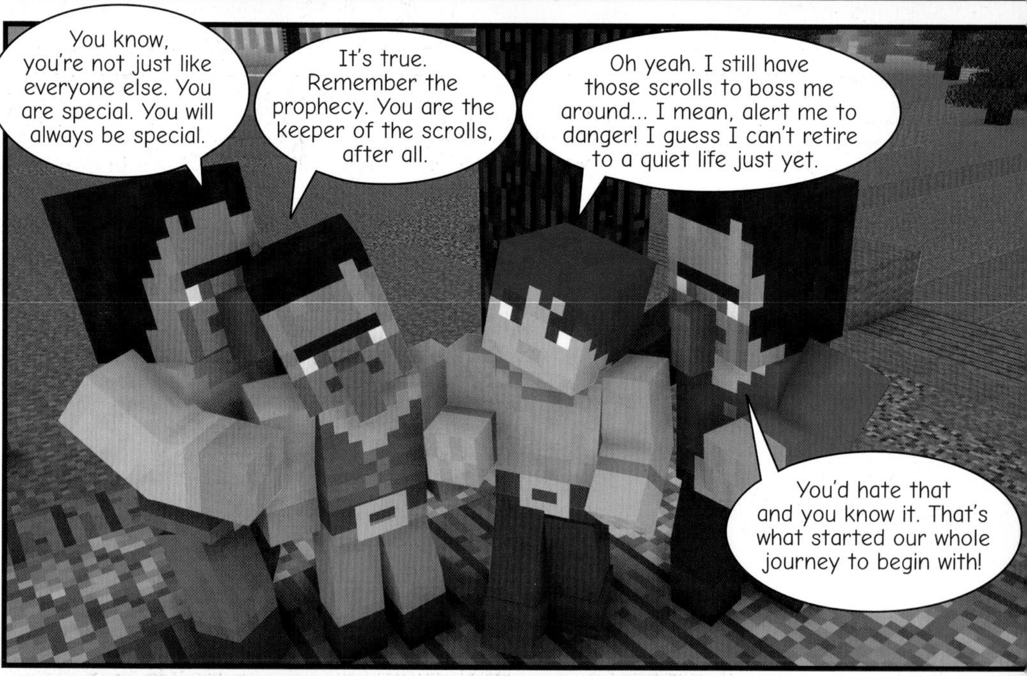
You know, you're not just like everyone else. You are special. You will always be special.
It's true. Remember the prophecy. You are the keeper of the scrolls, after all.
Oh yeah. I still have those scrolls to boss me around... I mean, alert me to danger! I guess I can't retire to a quiet life just yet.
You'd hate that and you know it. That's what started our whole journey to begin with!

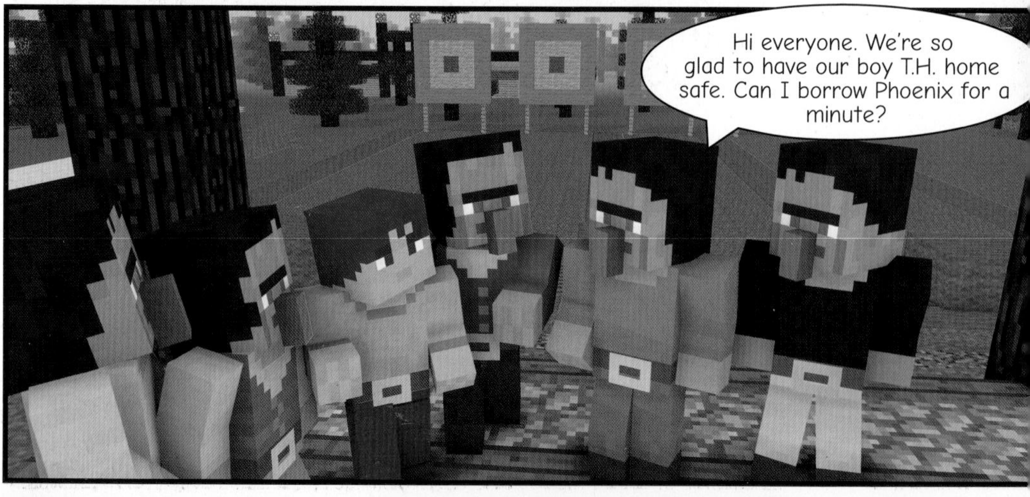
Hi everyone. We're so glad to have our boy T.H. home safe. Can I borrow Phoenix for a minute?

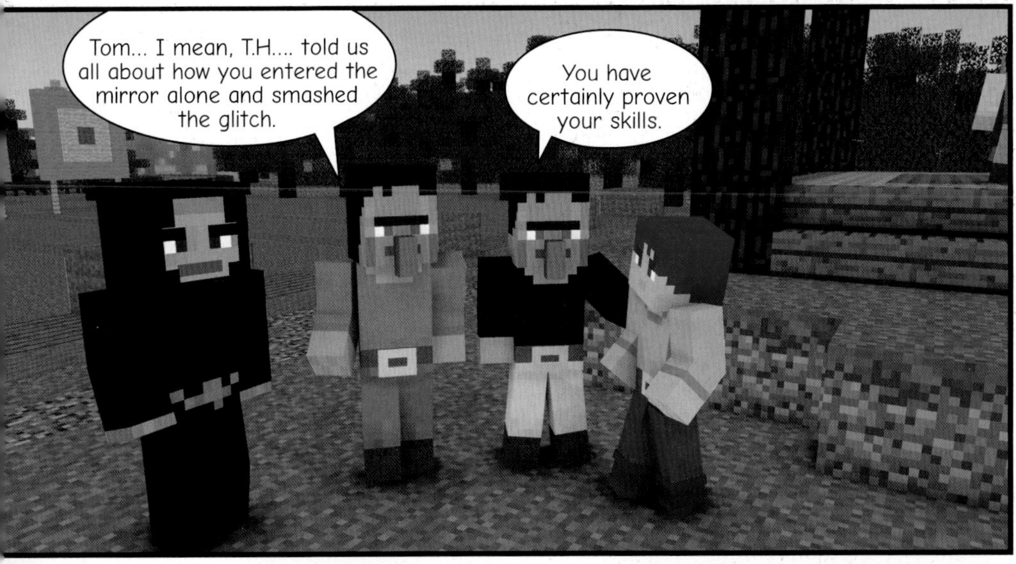
Tom... I mean, T.H.... told us all about how you entered the mirror alone and smashed the glitch.
You have certainly proven your skills.

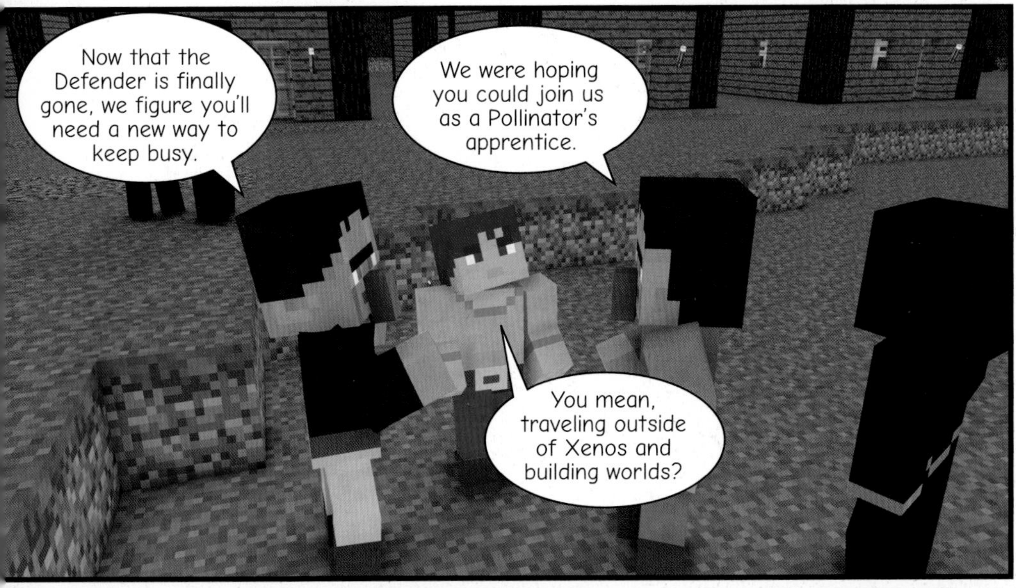
Now that the Defender is finally gone, we figure you'll need a new way to keep busy.
We were hoping you could join us as a Pollinator's apprentice.
You mean, traveling outside of Xenos and building worlds?

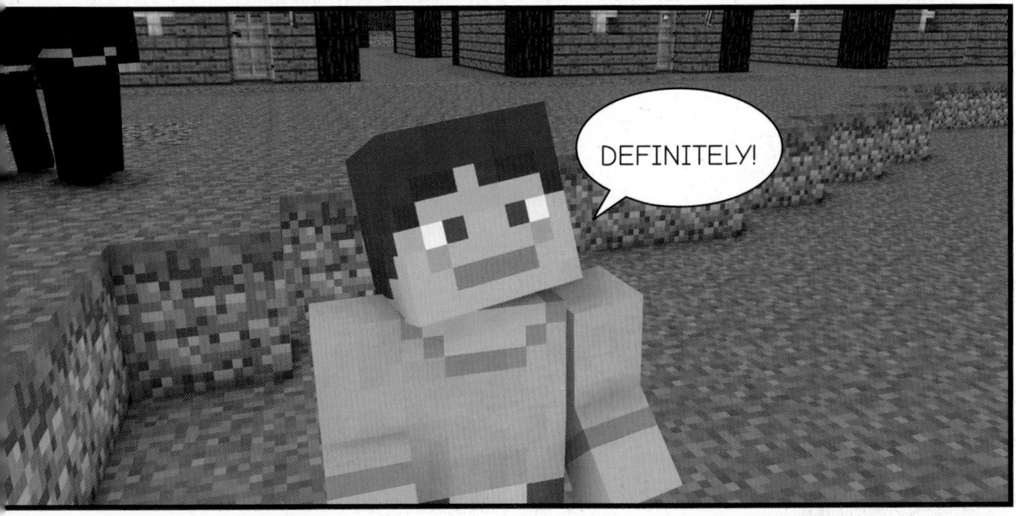
DEFINITELY!

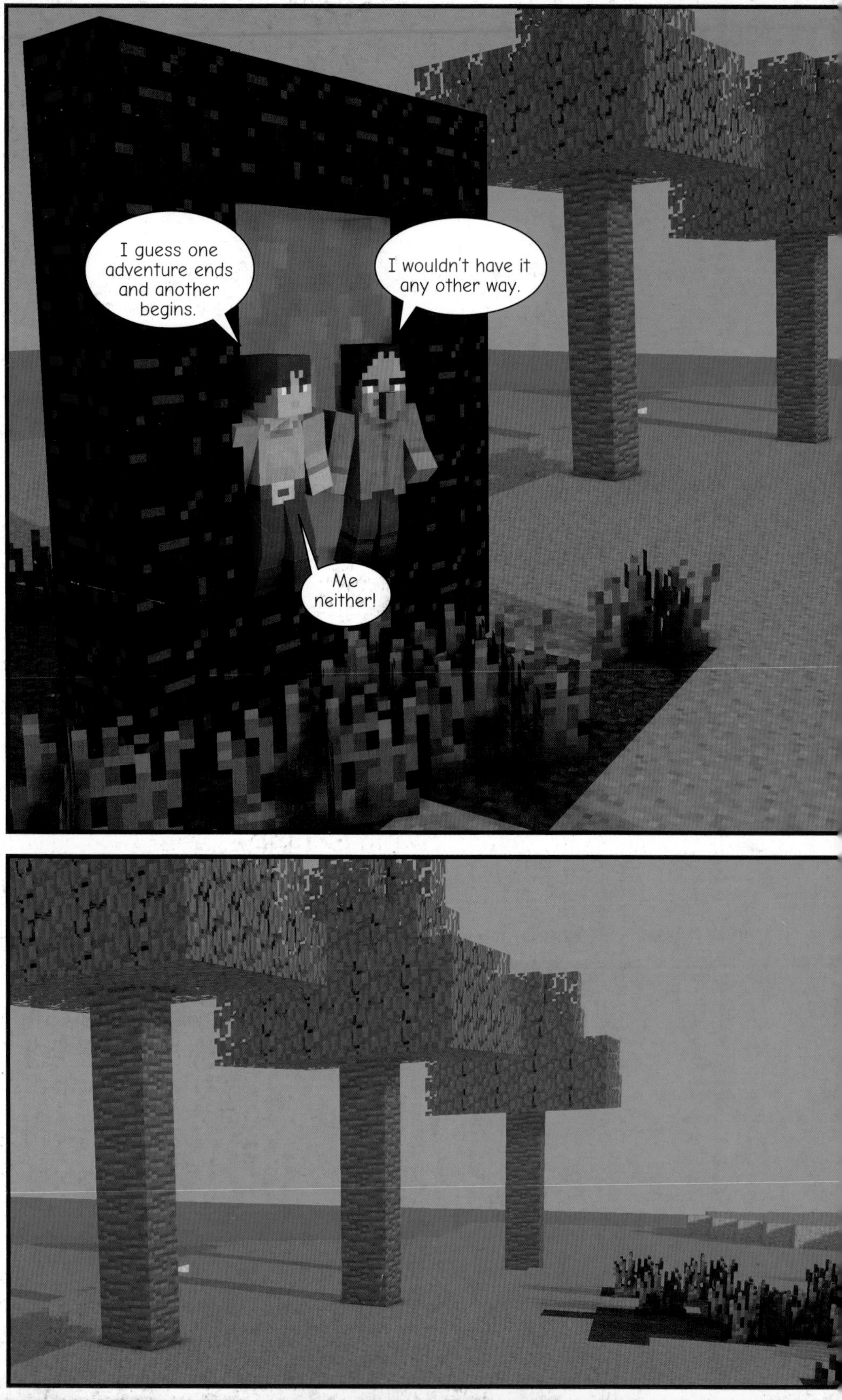
I guess one adventure ends and another begins.
I wouldn't have it any other way.
Me neither!